# THE REPLACEMENT SON

*A Novel*

*W.S. Culpepper*

Two Harbors Press
212 3rd Avenue North, Suite 290
Minneapolis, MN 55401
612.455.2293
www.TwoHarborsPress.com

ISBN-13: 978-1-62652-044-8
LCCN: 2013902790

Distributed by Itasca Books

Cover Design and Typeset by James Arneson

*Printed in the United States of America*

# THE REPLACEMENT SON

*A Novel*

*For my uncle,*
*George McLean*

## *Le Revenant*

MÈRES en deuil, vos cris là-haut sont entendus.
Dieu, qui tient dans sa main tous les oiseaux perdus,
Parfois au même nid rend la même colombe.

. . . . . . . . . . . . . . . . . .

Elle entendit, avec une voix bien connue,
Le nouveau-né parler dans l'ombre entre ses bras,
Et tout bas murmurer: C'est moi. Ne le dis pas.


## *The One Who Returned*

Mourning mothers, your cries are heard up above.
God, who holds all the lost birds in the palm of his hand,
Sometimes returns the same dove to the same nest.

. . . . . . . . . . . . . . . . .

Nestled in her arms, she heard
The newborn speak in a once-familiar voice,
And whisper softly: It is I. Tell no one.

*—Victor Hugo*

[English translation by the author]

# PART ONE

*Buddy*

# *One*

It was always about Buddy, way before Harry even knew about Buddy. Back then, Harry just knew things weren't right in his family. Maybe he had sensed a someone—more like a some*thing*, like a force, pulling at the family. Harry was confused, then sad and a little angry when he'd finally learned the force had a name. "Buddy" meant friend, but all that this Buddy had left behind seemed hurtful.

For someone who had died so young, Harry's brother left a lot of dashed hopes—unfinished business—along with painful scars on every remaining family member. Even before his uncle got involved, Harry had the most at stake and the most to gain by tackling that business. He'd often felt like his family was going to fly apart, just spin away from him if he didn't try to do something, anything, to hold them all together. But at age seven he wasn't feeling up to much of anything.

It was a Monday in early December when he'd first visited Buddy's grave. Harry knew this was no ordinary outing; his father had kept him out of school that morning to bring him to the cemetery. Harry had never talked with his father about his dead brother, and he really didn't know where to start. Two days before their visit little Harry hadn't known there ever was an older brother. He'd first learned of Buddy's existence from his grandmother, Maman, while his parents were out of town. He was overwhelmed by all the stories Maman had poured into his ear after his sister threw a hissy fit over something he'd innocently suggested.

Looking back, Harry remembered the eruptions were always like that: someone just popped. The someone was always Ma or sister Penny or both. Mostly, he ducked for cover when the big ones came along. Harry desperately wanted all the blowups and the hurting to stop.

Elmer, Harry's father, had decided to take their day together to apologize, ask forgiveness from his only surviving son. If he could finally start to offer up his own version of their family tragedy to the boy, all the better. But Elmer didn't know how much of those memories he could share just yet. It wasn't the first time since Buddy's death that he'd taken a day off for a family emergency, and he didn't hesitate to do so again after the events of the preceding weekend.

Elmer was a kind and deliberate soul. He was content to let their visit and their little care-taking chores lead his son into a discussion at the boy's own pace and choosing. Elmer's mother, Maman, had already told him about her long talk with Harry, and he had no intention of rehashing it all. Like his mother, Elmer felt that there was never any compelling reason to keep the story from Harry for this long. Even though Elmer had participated in the conspiracy of silence about the family's early loss, he'd done so mainly out of consideration for his wife and daughter's dark moods and tender feelings and not because of any distance from his beloved Harry. He was, in fact, relying on their strong bond of love to help repair this breach of faith.

Fortunately, throughout their lives together, that nurturing devotion had flowed both ways. As he and his father walked along the grassy divide between the rows of massive monuments and raised plots, little Harry was thinking back on an earlier time that reassured him: whatever was about to happen, he could always trust in his dad.

◆　◆　◆

From as long ago as he could remember, Harry had loved to wait outside for his pa to return from work every evening. Sometimes he would slip out to look for him when he started to miss him a lot and just couldn't wait any longer. When he finally saw that slim figure with the jaunty stride and big fedora coming past the hackberry trees on the corner, he felt a part of himself filling back up. He felt safe and happy again. He ran down the sidewalk into the arms of the person whom he loved the most in all the world. Those strong, welcoming arms and the familiar scent of hair tonic brought reassurance and a measure of comfort. But Harry needed a daily catechism to complete the ritual magic of their reunion. His mind as well as his heart needed to know that his dad had not just disappeared from existence when out of his sight but that his dad was always in the world, out doing all the wonderful things that dads had to do when away from their families. Before he could put Harry down to mount the front steps, Elmer had to recite his quotidian adventures on the city transit system.

"Well, son, I get up every morning before you have even blinked, and I walk down our street, South Johnson, to the Napoleon

Avenue line. Mr. Farrell usually takes the same streetcar with me down toward the river. At St. Charles Avenue, we hop out and transfer to the St. Charles car heading downtown. Mr. Farrell gets off at Lee Circle, and I go around the circle and get off at Girod Street. I walk over to Magazine where Mr. William Boatner Reily himself says, 'Top of the morning to you, Mr. McChesney! We have some wonderful coffee beans to roast and taste this morning. See you upstairs!'

"When we have the best-tasting coffees in the Deep South all sorted out and packaged up for the stores and loaded into the big railroad cars, Mr. William Boatner Reily blows the evening whistle, gives me a smile and a firm handshake, and escorts me to the door. I pick up my evening paper from the boy on the corner and board the streetcar for the uptown run. As I get close to our house, I always see my best friend, Harry Emerson McChesney, who runs to me with his best hug, puts on my hat, and lets me carry him the rest of the way home where I keep him safe and sound."

"How come you don't get lost going all that way every day, Pa?"

"I am lucky. They don't move the streetcar tracks very often. Otherwise, Mr. Farrell and I might be in big trouble." He paused a moment for dramatic effect. "That's not nearly as much trouble as you *shall* be in if I find out Mrs. Farrell has had to bring you home from over on Claiborne Avenue again."

"No, sir. I won't do that anymore. I just couldn't wait for you to get home from work that day."

"Son, it was eight o'clock in the morning. You are only four years old, and it is too dangerous for you to be wandering about busy streets like Claiborne and Napoleon by yourself. Stay right out here on our corner where I can be sure to find you every evening. Also, eight in the morning is *way* too early for us to start looking for each other. We are clear and straight on all that, aren't we?"

"Very clear, Pa. You're not going to show me your strap again, are you?"

"No, I don't think I will ever have to use that on you. But, I wanted you to know what it sounded like when my father used it on me. What happened behind the bedroom door is just between us men. It's all right if your mother thinks you got a licking for running off. You're not likely to do anything foolish like that again."

"Boy, I hope not. Thanks, Pa."

# Two

Young Harry had worn a light jacket the day he and his father first went to visit Buddy at Metairie Cemetery. A swirling breeze made the early December air chilly in the morning shadows. The elegant granite and marble tombs were a dazzling array of brilliant whites, pinks, and grays in the stark winter light. Harry thought the whole place looked like a strange toy village with heavy stone houses, baby churches, and lots of statues. He held his pa's hand tightly as they walked to the McChesney family plot.

"This day was Buddy's birthday, and yesterday was the anniversary of his death. We're going to bring some fresh flowers as a remembrance and see if anything needs sprucing up around the tomb."

"How come Ma didn't ride with us?"

"Your mother is still grieving for her other little boy something terrible, son. Your sister's had a bad time of it too. They both saw him suffer a lot and somehow blamed themselves a lot for whatever happened to him."

"I don't get it; they never did anything to him. Did they?"

"No, of course not."

"And I don't really understand what you mean by grieving, Pa, but I'm real sorry Buddy died. I'd love to have a big brother—you know, one who's still around, I mean."

"I wish Buddy were still here. God knows, we all do, but that wasn't His plan."

Elmer wanted to keep things pretty simple for now. Healing the family was still a long way off. They arrived at a raised double-burial plot surrounded by heavy granite coping with "McChesney" carved in relief at the end footed by a broad granite step. A large bronze urn sat atop a wide marble headstone at the opposite end.

"Here, I'm going to toss these old flowers in that trash bin, and you refill the vase from the faucet over there."

Harry peered into the moldy bits of stems and dark water that remained in the old flower urn. Some sort of buggy things squiggled just under the scummy surface.

"Ick! That green water smells icky. Do dead people smell, Pa?"

"What a question, Harry. Who have you been talking to?"

"Nobody, but I remember that dog that got hit by the car down the street last summer when the garbage men were on strike."

"Well, you certainly have an inquiring mind, lad. The answer is, yes. If we didn't attend to the dead promptly, they could end up like that poor dog. But that never happened to our Buddy. Now, take some of these new flowers, and let's put them in the vase together."

"Pretty blue flowers. What are they called?"

"Forget-me-nots."

"Good name. Blue flowers for a blue brother."

"Hmm. That's one way to put it, I suppose."

"That's what Maman said was wrong with him, on account of a bad heart or something. Kinda wish I'd known him, but you won't forget him, will you, Pa?"

"No, I shall always love little Buddy. But you must remember, Harry, you are the son of the family now—*here and now*. We all love you very, very much and always will. And I'm very sorry we did not tell you about your brother sooner. You deserved to know."

Harry was quiet for some time. He gazed at the headstone and then turned and looked directly at his father's face. His pa's eyes were moist and bloodshot; his nostrils flared with emotion and concern. Harry felt his father's concern—for him, for all of them—in the pit of his stomach.

"I'm not upset about that, the not-telling-me-until-now part. I *am* sorry that Ma feels so sick, especially around this time of year."

"She still wants Buddy back, and I guess part of that sickness is worrying sick about you, too. She knows all about boys' desires for adventure and daring behavior. She had a brother, growing up. But it's not the same for her when *you* do wild things. She lost Buddy, and she is frozen with fear of losing you, even now."

"Boy! I don't know what I can do about all that, but I'll try to make it up to her somehow, if I can. Someday. I promise. As for Penny, well, she's my sister, and sometimes it seems like she loves me and sometimes she can't stand me around. Jack—you know Jack Pitre—he says he and his sister fight and then make up all the time too."

"I suppose, but . . . ."

"Well, I'll try to do whatever you say; I want to be good like you, Dad. And I want to make you proud of me when I grow up. I will try very hard; I promise"

"I am already so very proud of you, my dear Harry."

Father and son embraced as they sat facing one another. As tender as the moment was for them both, Elmer felt a sudden surge of anxiety and fear of losing this wonderful boy and gave an involuntary shudder. Harry pulled back and looked again at his suddenly pale-faced father.

"What's wrong, Pa?"

"Nothing, nothing, I'm OK."

Elmer quickly stood up and busied himself with a pair of grass shears.

"I was afraid you'd seen a ghost, something scary."

Elmer felt drained and exhausted, a little light-headed.

"No, no such thing." He gathered his son to him again for a big hug and kissed him on the top of his head. "Put the paper and foil from the florist in the trash while I trim some of the grass growing up around the headstone. Then we'll go for a nice seafood lunch out at West End, over the lake. We can watch the shrimp boats coming back to Bucktown while we eat."

"Bucktown! Fun!" Harry jumped up and down a couple of times but stopped. The spirits hovering over the morning weren't quite ready to let go. "Pa, what's all that mean, up there?" Harry pointed to the two brief inscriptions on the stone. Whoever had carved the monument had also left a little trademark, an odd cross or something, and his tiny initials below it, way down in the corner where his dad had just clipped away some of the taller grass.

"Well, you're an exceptionally good reader for the second grade, son. You tell me."

"OK—over on that side it says, 'At Rest,' and over by you it says, 'Serve and love them, in My name.' Two different things, I think. What side is Buddy on?"

"He's over here, on this side where I'm standing."

"Well, what does it mean?"

"Your great-grandfather put these up when they first bought the plot and wrote a whole lot of instructions down and passed them on to your namesake, Uncle Harry. He will tell you all about that and a lot more besides when you get older."

Harry's thoughts had already run on to boiled shrimp and root beer. The sun was getting a lot warmer, and he'd heard enough about his ancestors over the past several days for a boy twice his age.

## *Three*

It was just two days before that trip to the cemetery when the latest round of troubles had started for Harry, and that time it was his sister who had tipped over his universe.

"Don't play with those lights, Harry. You're going to break them, and I'll get in trouble. We're not supposed to put them on until Maman gets up from her nap."

Penny didn't look up from the magazine she was reading at the dining room table. She could hear the clinking of the strings of colored Christmas tree lights out in the front room.

"I'm not playing with them; I'm checking to make sure that they're all OK."

"Oh, no! You're going to electrocute yourself. Unplug them, and put them back in the box, now. I am *not* kidding. You're not going to be allowed to put on the garlands *or* hang the ornaments *or* do the lights if you don't behave."

"I know more about electricity than you do, and you know it, big sister. You don't even know how an electromagnet works."

Harry concluded his sweeping self-defense with a facial expression of high ridicule that he'd learned in second grade, just this week. He was comfortable with its effectiveness, having practiced in the mirror, and equally comfortable knowing that his bossy sister was still absorbed in her magazine, paying him little heed.

"I'm excited about the lights too. Just be patient—that's another thing you're an expert on, isn't it? Patience, ha-ha!"

"C'mon, Penny. I couldn't wait to look at them and plug them in. Mom bought them right after last Christmas and put them away with all of our other decorations. All I saw were the boxes going in the attic. I'll bet we're the only family in New Orleans who takes down their wreath and tree on the morning of the day after Christmas."

"At least our family has decided to join the twentieth century this year. There aren't going to be any more candles on our Christmas tree, not after poor Mrs. Schexnaydre burned down the tree along with half her house last year."

"I think the main reason we have them is that Ma really liked the idea of getting the lights on sale after Christmas last year. That's when she buys all of her greeting cards too."

Penny knew what Harry did not: they were lucky to have a Christmas this year. Since the stock market crashed right after Harry's birthday two years ago, things had gotten much worse. New Orleans was not spared the unemployment and bank failures that swept the country. Mr. Reily had been able to keep all of his top people at work in the coffee business, but he had reduced their salaries in order to do so. She had heard her parents talking about hard times after dinner again the other evening. All of her father's fears and worst memories of the Panic of '07 were returning. He had little confidence that the government was going to help them, whoever was running the show. With the money crisis coming together at the same time of year that her mother suffered terribly with her depression about Buddy's death, this was going to be a doubly difficult holiday.

"I *don't* want to talk about it," was what Mom had whispered to silence Dad's suggestion last Sunday as they filed out of services. "I am not going to go over it all again with Reverend Hunter. I don't think much of his sermons, and I detest his clammy hands around mine, leading me in prayer." And later in the car on the way home, "I am certainly not ready to discuss the topic with Harry. When I think of the time that Penny had to suffer along with the rest of us, I want to scream. I don't want to have to explain to my only living son that the Heavenly Father has sorely tested this mother's faith and likely finds her wanting."

Penny had invented all sorts of reasons why she had to spend more time than ever this year with friends during the Christmas break. Unfortunately, that plan hadn't worked this weekend. Her parents had driven to the Gulf Coast for a much-needed getaway with the Boylans. Grandmother Elvige—the grandkids called her Maman, short for *La Bonne Maman*—had come over from Aunt May's to look after Penny and Harry. Penny was stuck at home with her brother waiting for Maman to wake up from her afternoon rest.

"When are Ma and Pa getting back from Waveland? I don't think Maman is ever going to get up, and I have a great idea that I want to show everybody."

"Well, Tom Swift, I guess the whole world is going to have to wait to see your next great idea. Is it another death ray machine that will blow all the fuses or another chemistry demonstration that will stink up the kitchen all evening?"

In fact, Harry had already put his new plan in motion while waiting for the tree decorating to start. He was pleased that he'd thought of it and wondered why others had not seen the obvious before he had. Ever since he could remember, their modest-sized Christmas tree had been in a corner of the front parlor farthest from the front door. It was in the same corner as the built-in bookshelves. His dad's big easy chair and reading lamp and brass standing ashtray were in the opposite corner at that end of the room. When the tree was set up every year, it was hard to get to the bookshelves. It was clear to Harry that the tree was crammed into the wrong corner; there was nothing in the front corner to the right of the door. The wall space in the room was decorated with a few paintings, a large Audubon print given to them by Uncle Harry, and some old silhouettes of his Emerson relatives. But the walls forming the empty front corner had no adornment other than a small crucifix.

That cross gave Harry the final encouragement that he needed. This was obviously the perfect place for the Christmas tree. It would be out of the way; it would have its own place of honor. The Baby Jesus in the crèche under the tree would be right at home in the corner with the crucified big Lord Jesus who'd died for our sins.

Harry had already finished sliding the bare tree and stand across the heart-pine floor to its proud, new location when Penny came in to see why he had fallen quiet for the last quarter of an hour.

"Help! Oh. My. God. Oh, Harry, what?—"

Either Grandma Elvige had bolted out of bed upon hearing Penny's screams, or she was already on her way toward the front of the house. She arrived in the parlor almost simultaneously with her granddaughter and understood immediately what had provoked her alarm. She knew what had to be done. She took charge.

"Penelope, my dear, you may be excused. I'll handle this."

"But, Maman! Harry doesn't—"

"It's high time that he *does* know, and I am just the person to tell him. Do not make me ask you again. *Laissais nous. Tout de suite.*"

Harry stood, thunderstruck and dumbfounded, looking from his sister to his grandmother. As Penny marched out, his Maman embraced him and sat him down next to her on the sofa. She gently turned his head with both hands so that their eyes were gazing directly into one another's, no more than a foot apart. She smiled reassuringly and reached for his trembling hands. She rested them in her lap as she began to speak softly.

"Dear Harry, do not be frightened. You have done nothing wrong, my love. You have just been trying to do something clever and nice, and for reasons you don't yet understand, you have managed to alarm your sister. Your Maman will try to explain what is going on."

Elvige hesitated and took a deep breath. She wanted badly to help heal her son's family. Might this be a beginning to that healing? She wanted to make sure little Harry loved and understood his family. Best to start with someone the boy already knew and trusted. She would start with herself.

"I am going to tell you a family story that begins with me and ends with someone you've never met. But, first things first. You know your Maman was born here in New Orleans. Ah, and what a splendid place it was, way back then."

# *Four*

Late nineteenth-century New Orleans was a wealthy, cosmopolitan city, surpassing any other in the South. The New Orleans Cotton Exposition of 1884 was considered a fitting celebration of its national and international prominence. French Catholic Creoles like Julian and Francoise Simon were proud, active members of one of several dominant cultural groups within the city. Julian Simon represented the family's agricultural interests as a broker at the Cotton Exchange and played a supporting role in organizing the world exposition.

Many of the more affluent families in the city were hidebound and insular; the Simons were more avant-garde and freethinking. More spiritual than fervently religious, they made a conscious decision to provide all of their children with a nonsectarian education. The boys were sent to board at Deerfield Academy in Massachusetts, and Elvige was enrolled at the Newcomb School rather than the Academy of the Sacred Heart. She was more than happy to elude the nuns' attention.

Elvige was the only daughter of Julian and Francoise. A diminutive, vivacious beauty with lush brown curls and a flawless complexion, she was also exceptionally bright. None of the young men felt very comfortable around her; she did not suffer fools gladly. More at ease with her parents' friends than her contemporaries, she had reluctantly consented to be presented with her year's class of debutantes and even participated in a few of the season's carnival balls. She had known who Arthur McChesney was before she allowed him to sign her dance card at the winter cotillion.

Her betrothal to Arthur was a true test of her parents' inclusive philosophy. He was a Presbyterian, about as far from the Holy Roman Church as one could find in New Orleans. They loved one another, and Arthur had more in common with his French Creole in-laws than with his biological family. With the help of some generous donations to sacred building funds, they took their vows in two fine churches on two different Sundays and swore to both priest and minister that their children would only be raised in The One True Faith. They did not elaborate further and left it to each cleric to interpret that vow according to his wont. Ultimate truth be told, the children had a taste of both Protestant and Catholic upbringing, depending on the exigencies of the liturgy, travel plans, and secular calendar.

The McChesney side of the family regarded Arthur and Elvige as unrepentant fallen souls. The young couple's young friends either couldn't care less about their religious bicameralism or found it titillating to be on a first-name basis with such a handsome, controversial pair. Arthur went to work in Julian's cotton trading business, and he and Elvige were equally industrious in their efforts to grow a large family. Elvige gave birth to five children early in the marriage. Unfortunately, only two survived beyond the age of four years. Harry was the older of the two, and Elmer survived the smallpox outbreak in the summer of 1895 to grow up under the shadow of his spectacularly attractive, intelligent, and successful big brother.

Harry Stuart McChesney had the world wrapped up with a bow and delivered to him at birth. He excelled in his class work and on the athletic field. Young women adored him. Early in life he was aware of his ability to charm anyone, yet he took advantage of no one. Everyone felt as though they were the most important friend whom Harry had ever had the good fortune to encounter.

While an undergraduate at Yale, he witnessed all manner of youthful excess and indulged in more than one. After he had written home to request that considerable extra allowance be sent along before the end of his second term, his father decided that Harry needed some schooling outside of school. He got him a job during his first summer home from college on the docks at the Port of New Orleans. He hoped exposure to a community vastly different from Harry's privileged chums in New Haven would be instructive.

Harry grunted, sweated, and strained to move bananas alongside massively muscular Negro and Irish stevedores. They handled cargo for the Lykes Brothers, United Fruit Company, and other big shippers. As the men labored up and down the gangplanks with huge stalks of fruit on their shoulders, he noticed one portly fellow comfortably seated with a clipboard and a pencil, keeping a chit-mark tally of the number of stalks passing by. The workers all referred to this lucky man as the banana checker.

"That's the job for me, Elijah. Hey, man! How can I apply for your post? My friends and I want to swap these loads for your clipboard."

"Keep moving, McChesney. Ya see, I not only got your number, but I got your name."

Harry had no intention of taking retribution on an ignorant man. However, he did not hesitate to draw up a plan to improve upon the stevedore company's income statement and his own as well. He knew that if every ship at every port that dealt with cargo handled by individual workers had to have a counter of something, then replacing this man with a mechanized, wage-free alternative would yield an instant, incremental improvement in cash flow. Harry and his fortune soon met. Shortly after graduating from Yale, Harry's patented "Mechanical Cargo Counter" went into production. A reliable turnstile with a gear-driven counting display, this invention assured that he would never have to tote freight for anyone again.

Harry married Sidonie May Villerie in the Holy Name cathedral in 1910, and a lavish reception followed at the well-appointed home he had built for his bride on Louisiana Avenue Parkway. He had wisely sidestepped the financial misfortunes that had befallen his father and much of the city in 1907. He and his beloved May lived a comfortable and fashionable life while becoming major donors to every worthy charity and philanthropic effort in New Orleans in addition to helping support his father and mother and brother Elmer until the cotton business recovered.

They enjoyed a bountiful life together, but the good Lord in his wisdom withheld a singular blessing from this loving couple. They were never to have children of their own. Too many rooms in their splendid home remained vacant throughout their long marriage. Years later, when his father died in a packet boat explosion on the Mississippi, they were happy to welcome Elvige into their home on a permanent basis. By that time Harry had matured and taken his role as head of the McChesney clan very seriously, both within the community and the family.

# Five

Harry's younger brother, Elmer McChesney, was not what anyone considered handsome, charming, or exceptionally brilliant. But his parents, having lost so many, treasured him and Harry equally. Others in the family and across the city were prone to making comparisons between the brothers. Elmer was not often favored in these odious metrics. His only refuge was the fact that he and Harry were separated in age by seven years.

Amateur boxing was a sport that Harry had never taken an interest in. Elmer was not only interested but soon quite proficient. Arthur thought it was a healthy activity and a way for Elmer to take a poke at his critics. His younger son was, in fact, quite proficient at many things. He simply did not soar into the firmament alongside his sibling.

Elmer also "worked in the shipping business," as he described it, for several summers as a stevedore. After the 1907 bank crash and steep decline in the family cotton business when he was sixteen, Elmer started working in earnest to help keep a roof over their heads. He held two part-time jobs for more than one year while he also struggled to complete high school. Finances began to improve slowly. However, there was not yet enough money for Arthur to put a portion toward a college education for his younger son.

"Son, your brother has offered to help out with continuing your studies. He wanted you to be able to go to Yale or someplace up East, but I don't think you have the grades to get accepted into an Ivy League school. I don't blame you for not having a better academic performance. You have been working hard to help the family. It's taken a toll on you."

"If it's all the same, I really don't want to continue in classes right now. I am sick of teachers and grades and cramming useless facts into my brain. Most importantly, I don't want to be beholden to Harry for this. He's done enough for me. I appreciate what he's done for all of us. I love my brother, but I don't want to grow up to be like my brother—not that anyone in Orleans Parish believes that I could. Hell, I might even move to look for work in another city if things don't work out for me here."

"No swearing, boy. Don't let your mother hear you say that, for goodness' sake. Any of it. She will insist that you continue on to university. What will you say to her?"

Elmer had wanted to have this conversation and had anticipated this question in particular. He gave his carefully rehearsed response.

"I will say that she has been an excellent example to her sons. I will say that even though she does have a college education, her devotion to learning did not begin or end there. A prime rule for life that she has instilled in us is that our education is primarily our own responsibility and that obligation continues throughout our lives. You and she have taught us how to read and think and research important issues for ourselves, how to stand up for our ideas and learn from experience. I will never abandon these good habits, but for now, I want to learn some practical skills to support myself and maybe someday, a family."

"I think you make a plausible case, Elmer, but don't expect your mother to cede the field easily. She will reason, rebut, then cry and use her best feminine wiles to convince you otherwise. I will support whatever decision you and she come to an accord upon. Do you have a profession or line of work that you're keen on? Without a formal education you will need to apprentice yourself in something where there are successful men willing to take you on."

"Mr. Aron said that he would be willing to teach me all about coffee, Dad. I really think coffee is the future. The tonnage of green coffee coming into the port of New Orleans is growing more than any other commodity. I want it to be my future."

"I'm impressed. You haven't spoken to me about this topic before. I didn't know that you'd given this serious thought. Jacob Aron is a good man; I've known him and his family for years. He will not take advantage of you. He certainly has done well for himself in the coffee trade. What part do you see yourself preparing for?"

"I want to learn everything I can, of course. I don't know what I don't know yet. Mr. Aron told me that there are big advances coming in roasting and blending technology that will elevate a man with these skills, one who can bring the right beans together to make the best-selling coffee for the American markets. A man with these talents may never grow as wealthy and powerful as the growers and importers, but he will be an increasingly valuable member to the industry."

"Sounds like you'll need to be part engineer, part chemist, and part magician to fill that kind of job."

"It's just the kind of challenge that whets my appetite, if you get my joke, Dad."

"Yes, but I'm quite sure your dear mother will not be laughing. You're right, however; she's taught you well. You're damned convincing."

Elmer won over Elvige and started with J. Aron and Company the following month. His first post was out on the Poydras Street Wharf in the company warehouse space. All the importers had their inspection men stationed under company flags so that the largely illiterate stevedores would know where to drop their huge burlap sacks. He recognized some of his old co-workers from his toting days and noted the toll that the day-laboring life had taken on those men in the space of a few years.

He loved the crosscurrents of commerce found on the wharves, the excitement and energy that international shipping and the movement of diverse goods provided. Men shouted orders across the riverfront in a dozen different languages. Scents of aromatic spices, coffee, and hundreds of agricultural products mixed with the wood and coal smoke from the paddle wheelers and steamers. The mighty river exuded a pungent, animal odor all its own. Diesel tows with their rafts of barges and luggers under sail moved deftly out in the main current along with a half-dozen passenger ferries. Ox wagons and mule carts fought for right-of-way with the larger motorized vehicles making their way to and from loading platforms. Vegetable refuse and manure blended under their busy wheels.

Like a baptism in the river, Elmer found new life along the river. Reborn in body, mind, and spirit, he felt equal to any man and at peace with himself. Coffee was his mistress and his inspiration. He plunged his hands and all of his senses into every shipment. He quickly learned to recognize different green beans from all the major growers and markets. He knew the advantages and the drawbacks of wet versus dry processing. He confidently identified and rejected damaged goods and saved his company considerable sums.

After about seven months he moved from the wharf into the brokerage offices, but this part of his education only confirmed what he had suspected earlier: arbitrage and trading of coffee or any other commodity held no allure. He craved an intensely physical, sensual relationship with this mistress. He wanted to spend his days roasting, grinding, and blending the best coffees in the city. He stayed with the firm a full year and then convinced Mr. Burkenroad, the managing partner, that his skills would be better utilized at one of the roasting companies than with the importers.

"Elmer, you have a love and a real talent for the nuances of the beans. I think I know just the man who would value what you bring to our industry. Boatner Reily has done one hell of a job and built a young coffee company that is giving all his competitors a run for their money. Mr. Aron and I have found him to be an honorable gentleman and a knowledgeable customer for our product. I am going to have lunch with him at the Bon-Ton this week. I will put in a good word for you if you're certain that you don't want to continue here with us."

William B. Reily & Company hired the genetically gifted young talent who could discern over eight hundred different flavor characteristics found in the world's coffees. His formidable assets and dedication to his work were accordingly valued and rewarded. After his third year with the firm, Elmer was promoted to vice president of testing and production. His nose and palate were insured for $250,000. He was in charge of tasting every shipment of beans after roasting and grinding.

Within a very short time, Boatner Reily entrusted the final decisions on which beans were chosen for blending in daily production runs, new coffee blends, and product viability to only one man. Elmer would continue with the firm for over fifty years.

# Six

Elmer married Julia Ayers Emerson shortly after his early promotion within Reily & Co. They had met a year earlier during a charity raffle and social at the First Presbyterian Church on Lafayette Square. Elmer wasn't a regular at any of the church's activities; he was there representing his company. Mr. Reily had made a substantial donation of merchandise and vouchers for the raffle and personally requested Elmer's presence at the drawings and awards. Julia was on the raffle prize committee. Julia liked volunteer work; Julia liked committees. Julia loved chairing committees. Unfortunately, Julia was more of a bully than a good boss.

She was a sober, earnest young woman, a product of the sturdy New England Emersons and the hard-driving, Scotch-Irish McLeans. Both families commanded respect for God, money, and their elders—precisely in that order. Neither family valued women's contributions to society outside the traditional roles of wife, mother, and homemaker. Julia suffered accordingly. Her education got short shrift, and her forays outside the home were limited to religious and charity work. She felt most comfortable in situations where she controlled most of the variables, or at least when she had assessed them as controllable. However, her commanding, hearty exterior hid a deep hollow of self-doubt and insecurity.

Julia's main goal at the time of her work at the church, on the board of the Poydras Boys' Home, and around town was to find a suitable man to wed. Romantic love, emotional compatibility, and physical attraction were rather down her list when it came to fleshing out the individual who might be deemed suitable. In her view, a husband's primary function was to ensure stability and provide sufficient capital for the marriage to prosper. The couple's commitment to raising a family in the Presbyterian faith would be a given. Reasonably compatible intellectual and social interests were optional but vaguely desirable outcomes for Julia.

Elmer had never entertained any exalted notions about finding the perfect mate. As a holdover from the days when he was a living testament to the world's version of his presumed shortcomings, he tended toward self-deprecating humor. With his new career he began to live each day more confidently and secure within himself, but his view of the world remained heavily tinged with irony.

"Mother, you know I am likely to find just the right woman to wed in this town about the same time an honest man stands for governor."

"Diogenes never found an honest man *and* never married, Elmer. You might wish to put aside your Cynic's lantern and begin a fresh look for an intelligent, considerate young woman to share your life."

Julia had innate good sense and cunning and could be sweet and considerate when it suited her, and it suited her during her quest for a suitor. She was charmed by Elmer's courtesy and genuine kindness toward everyone regardless of their social standing. She was gratified to find that he truly loved children and could listen to and communicate with people of all ages. She thought his humor tragicomic and wry. She certainly never felt his empathy with the world. Elmer was keenly aware of how the world could wound and disappoint. He had the soul of a poet; she had the soul of a pragmatist.

Julia's family considered Elmer a trifle frail but wholly decent-looking, "proper and respectable, flawed but acceptable," in her father's words. He was happy that his daughter's prospects were moving along. Elmer's recent success in the coffee business won the day. After the wedding, Julia did her best to warm up to her in-laws, but she found Elvige too high-strung, too emotional, too French, too Catholic. Julia resented the warm and loving bond between Elmer and his mother, Elvige, but she ultimately resolved just to live with that, content not to have to supply too much of the same. She found it almost impossible, however, to abide a woman whose intellect and modest self-assurance intimidated her so.

In the second year of their marriage, the poet and the pragmatist were blessed with their first child. Penelope Ayers McChesney was a red-haired beauty with hazel-green eyes like her grandmother Elvige. She'd hung the moon as far as her father was concerned. Julia surprised herself at how much maternal affection this bundle of demand and dependency extracted from her in spite of the fact that she had her mother-in-law's eyes. Happily, Bertha, the wet nurse, proved skillful in providing most of the unpleasant aspects of care for the infant. Bertha became so indispensable that Julia hired her as their full-time housekeeper and wet nurse-in-waiting for any more blessings that might come along.

# *Seven*

After a seemly interval of two years and two months, the Heavenly Father brought them Elmer Wilson McChesney, Jr. At first sight, his earthly father was transported to heavenly heights. With tears of delight and a frog in his throat, he named him "my precious boy, my Buddy." From Elmer Senior's perspective, Buddy was the most joyous surprise from a union that, thus far, had held few, if any, surprises. Julia, to no one's surprise, didn't relish surprises.

"He has your head, Elmer, and your feet."

"Let's hope he grows your lovely hair, my dear. He could use some before the cold weather arrives."

"Hush, silly man, the midwife said that babies born with little hair were the ones who were blessed with a full, rich growth throughout later life."

"That's good, but right now he looks like he's working on a tonsure for an early start in the priesthood."

"Stop it! You know he's going to be baptized and raised in John Knox's church. You could use this opportunity to get reacquainted with that church, *our* church, at the same time."

"Well, he's a beautiful son, hair or no hair. But, I would rather spend my Sundays teaching him how to fish and play baseball and chess and poker and—"

"I am sure you will find time for all of that, too. Just don't oppose me on the importance of proper religious upbringing. We don't have that laissez-faire attitude about faith in my family that has crept into yours."

Like Penny, Buddy was delivered at home with a midwife in attendance. Dr. Archinaud came by a few hours later and pronounced the boy to be present and accounted for, ready for service.

Elmer left Julia and the baby and Penny in Bertha's care and went to deliver the good tidings in person to Julia's father, then to Brother Harry, May, and Elvige. Two grandparents would never hear the news. Elmer's dad, Arthur McChesney, was killed in a riverboat explosion in 1919, and Julia's mother, Abigail Emerson, had died later the same year.

Julia's father, Harrison Emerson, lived two blocks away, just between Elmer's home and his brother's, so he decided to walk the joyous news to all of his immediate family. His arrival was not unexpected. Greeted with hearty backslapping and huzzahs, he handed out cigars to his father-in-law and a distant cousin who was visiting from Panama. Each hoisted a short cordial and toasted the newest member of the family. After a decent interval, Elmer excused himself.

"Of course! Be off, my dear boy. God bless your new heir and my welcome grandson."

Elmer ran the short distance to Harry and May's home. His mother, still in mourning for Arthur, had just moved in with them. They exchanged warm hugs and kisses of congratulations all around. In the high spirits of the moment, he lit a cigar for Harry and offered them to his mother and sister-in-law. Elvige accepted a cigar, handed it to her older son to light, then puffed at it briefly. It was a good excuse to remain silent for a while. She felt pensive and a little out of step with the general gaiety.

May spoke to the future, "Harry and I expect to be named godparents for this one, dear Elmer. You know we hold credentials in the Protestant church as well as being on a first-name basis with His Holiness."

May took Elmer's arm as they walked out into the cool December air of the side garden. Elvige followed with Harry and gave him a meaningful look before speaking.

"Yes, yes, May, that dual citizenship might get you and Harry by with Julia, but what can I do to gain her affection? I do so want to be close to her and the children."

"Mother, you are the only *grand-mère* now for both our children, and you shall be received as such. I think you might be mistaken about Julia's feelings for you."

"Elmer, you are a kind and loyal son, but you dissemble poorly. Remember to whom you are speaking. You're fooling none of us. Nevertheless, in the interest of religious tolerance and proper upbringing, I am bringing a christening outfit and blanket for the new McChesney at a suitable hour tomorrow morning."

"I can assure you that the balance of family power has shifted back, at least, to neutral with Buddy's arrival. We shall all welcome you warmly and happily after breakfast."

# Eight

The following morning Elvige arrived at South Johnson Street with gifts for her new grandson but few illusions about a spirit of détente having blossomed within. Big Bertha responded to her knock and swung the door open with a smile.

"Hello, ma'am, how you doing this fine morning? I expects you here to check up on the new master. He been pretty quiet most of the morning since he fed a little round daybreak. Mrs. Mac woke up and took a little hot broth, took herself another pain pill what Doc Arshy-no left for her, and is back in the land a dreamy dreams. Miss Penny back in the kitchen with me, having some cinnamon toast and café au lait."

"Bertha, you are clearly in charge and most appreciated, I'm sure. I will leave these gifts in the parlor for now and say hello to Penny before I visit with our blessed new arrival."

"Don't know bout preciation; I gets lotsa complaints and orders mostly. Didn't want me round the birthing room; folks acted like I never seen the head nor tail of no squalling infant, no afterbirth, no bilical cord, no caul, no nothing."

"Midwives are very jealous of their calling these days, Bertha. I am sure you could have been most helpful if the situation arose. I would not take things too personally. After all, you are the member of our family entrusted with most of Elmer Junior's care. That is quite a responsibility."

"I do loves the young man of the house; that's for sure. He ain't no more trouble than any of the grown-ups round here. Less, in my book."

"Hello, Penny! How are you, and how are you and Mr. Buddy getting along?"

"Maman, come have some toast and jelly with me. I have a new doll and a new baby brother."

"Yes, I can't wait to see both of your new playmates. I'll just go peek in at little Buddy first and then come breakfast with you, sweetie. Bertha, put some milk on to heat for me, please. I shall be back shortly."

Elvige planted a big kiss on jelly-sweet lips and then walked softly down the hall to the nursery. She did not want to wake Julia before she'd had an uninterrupted survey of her new grandson. The mid-morning light filtered dimly through the lace curtains on the north windows of the baby's room. Bertha's cot was freshly made and neat as a pin. The scents of rose water, lanolin, and talcum on the changing table commingled with a whiff of disinfectant in the diaper pail. She parted the netting around the bassinet and took a deep breath. She gazed down upon the infant without focusing on any particular feature, simply adoring his presence. She closed her eyes and said a brief prayer.

"Amen." Opening her eyes, the light in the room seemed brighter. Perhaps a cloud had moved from the sun. Buddy lay on his back and was clothed in a long silk gown trimmed in blue ribbon and a matching blue and white cap. His feet were hidden under the bottom of the gown, and his clenched hands were bare. A crocheted baby blanket was off to one side. Had he moved it? As she edged closer, the infant briefly opened his eyes and startled when she touched his forehead.

Just then, without any signs of choking or outward distress, the baby's lips and hands turned a faint, dusky blue-purple color. Everything else that happened in the room that day seemed to Elvige to take place in an underwater dream. Her thoughts raced, but her movements seemed to slow to a snail's pace. A span of, perhaps, ninety seconds felt like dreadful hours.

Elvige first looked over at the window to see if the light level from outside had changed again. If anything, it was getting brighter, easier to see colors accurately. She felt Buddy's cheek and reached under his gown to feel if his belly was cold. No. She now began to examine the child in earnest and with the eyes of a mother who had seen too many ill and dying children.

He was breathing fast and regular but not laboring or grunting. She pulled back his gown and put her ear to his chest, back and front. She could hear air moving and his little heart tapping. Fast? Slow? Not sure. She also heard something else, a swishing sound—among his heartbeats?—a foreign noise that terrified her. His belly was flat and soft; he was kicking both legs and flexing both arms. Not knowing why, she flicked her finger against his little toes to see if he would cry. He responded with a weak little protest, but his lips and skin turned a more-alarming color, like a bloody slice of raw calf's liver. She snatched up his blanket and ran with him in her arms to the kitchen.

# Nine

"**B**ertha! *Mon Dieu*, something is very, very wrong with Buddy. Hurry, get Dr. Archinaud's office on the telephone right away. We need him here immediately; I think—" Elvige abruptly stopped talking and tried to hold back her thoughts.

*No, he is not dying. Do not always think the worst. You are scaring little Penny. No, merciful God, do not take this beautiful boy from us. Three of my sweet children already dead. Enough offerings from our family. No!*

After roughly swaddling him in the blanket, she supported him upright, clutched to her bosom, while rubbing his back furiously. She could not fight the instinct that told her he was merely chilled. What more to do? He did not appear to be any worse, but that was not reassuring. He was not strong enough to cry. He was breathing but did not seem to be getting any air. How could that be?

"Ma'am, you better come talk to this lady. She say Doc ain't there."

Elvige refused to stop massaging and could not make herself relinquish the little thing, even to Bertha. She yelled into the standing mouthpiece while Bertha held the receiver to her free ear.

"This is Mrs. Elvige McChesney, Elmer's mother. We have an emergency here: the little newborn . . . . Yes, we need Dr. Archinaud as soon as possible— Oh? *Oui!* I understand. Well, how long ago did he leave the office? Very well, we shall be looking for him. Pray for us. Good-bye."

Penny had been crying softly, holding her doll while sucking her thumb since the commotion began. She was fixed to her chair, staring at the limp bundle that was her baby brother.

"Bertha, the nurse told me the doctor was making house calls. He told her that he planned to stop by here first. Take Penny with you and go to the front porch and get him in here as fast as you can. Penny, my dearest, little Buddy is not well, but the doctor will make things right very soon. Now, be very brave and go with Bertha to watch for Dr. Archinaud. I love you very much, but I must stay with your brother right now. Go."

Elvige walked over to the cold stove where the heated milk had gone to room temperature again. She moistened her little finger in the pot and offered it at one corner of Buddy's mouth. He rooted around clumsily but found the tip and sucked. He seemed to swallow without difficulty, and she repeated the maneuver. This time he latched on more readily and seemed a little stronger. Slowly, his color began to lighten. Even though his lips remained dusky, his cheeks began to show some blotchy patches of pink among the darker hues. His breathing slowed over several minutes, and he started to squirm a little. He no longer felt like a rag doll. An infant slowly returned under the blanket. Elvige kept wetting her finger, feeding him dribbles of milk, and praying to all the saints in heaven.

"Well, well, Mrs. McChesney." Dr. Archinaud entered the kitchen briskly with hat in one hand and medical bag in the other. He bowed perfunctorily and gestured. "Let's get the child over on the kitchen counter where we have some good light for a closer look."

"Oh, thank God you're here, Doctor. I pray you can help him. This all happened so suddenly . . . ."

Elvige continued a brief account of the morning while the examination proceeded beside the empty coffee cups. She stopped talking when Dr. Archinaud put his stethoscope to the child's chest. Her breathing ceased involuntarily; the room began to spin and her vision faded.

"Lordy, ma'am, sit yourself down right this minute. You's fixing to drop. We don't wants to have two mergencies for the doc today."

Bertha quickly fetched a chair and some smelling salts and revived Elvige, who began again at trying to discern the doctor's thoughts while ignoring a buzzing in her ears.

"His color is much improved from when I first rushed in here from the nursery. I apologize for that distraction; I have just been so worried about our little one."

"I certainly understand the shock you've had. And, I agree; he does seem to be out of any immediate danger. Give me just a moment more to finish my exam."

Elvige's strength and clarity of thought returned quickly. She opened her arms to invite Penny to come sit in her lap, but her granddaughter stayed motionless, hunkered down against Bertha's ample bosom, clutching her doll and nursing her thumb.

Dr. Archinaud swaddled the baby with his legs and hips fully flexed so that his knees rested snug against his abdomen, then handed him over to Elvige. He sighed deeply and rubbed his eyes, perhaps concealing a world-weary frown.

"I'm afraid this is quite serious. His condition has only manifest since I first examined him yesterday, just after delivery. These things happen. But before I go into this further, I think we'd better see what condition Julia is in. She must be advised."

"Of course, of course. Things happened so fast this morning. I have not yet seen my daughter-in-law. Perhaps a blessing that she has slept through this alarm, not even a full day since giving birth." Elvige stopped babbling; she felt a flush of guilt and embarrassment in her cheeks. She hadn't thought of Julia since walking down the hall to the baby's room.

"You folks stay here while I go gets Mrs. Mac presentable." Bertha rose from her chair. "She been sleeping like a log with them pills you give her, Doc. I'll take Penny with me and put her in bed with her momma. She still struck dumb by all of this. Gimme five minutes; then come on to the front bedroom."

With one eye still on the McChesney baby, Dr. Archinaud used the time to call into his office to have his nurse notify the rest of his house calls that he would not be around until evening. He had a full afternoon clinic to get back to shortly. No lunch again. No matter, this family needed to understand what they were facing. He was not going to rush through it.

# *Ten*

"Elvige, Dr. Archinaud, please come in. I have rested as well as can be expected; thank you for the laudanum, Doctor. But, please, I am so eager to hold my boy, my little Elmer. Do give him to me, Elvige."

"I am glad you're feeling rested and stronger, Julia. I am glad your mother-in-law was here this morning, too. You see, the baby has had—"

"Why are his little legs wrapped so tightly against his tummy? Bertha, did you do this? Bertha, why are you crying, you silly goose? You've seen plenty of beautiful newborns in your day. I—"

"Mrs. McChesney—Julia—I was trying to tell you. We've, well that is, Elmer Jr. has had some serious problems earlier this morning. Your mother-in-law found your boy in quite a lot of trouble and rendered some valuable assistance while alerting my office. Luckily I was on my way over to check on you both, but she snatched the baby up once she saw what was happening and—I think—helped to stabilize him for the moment."

"Oh, good Lord, this sounds so serious. Now you're crying too, Elvige. So, Doctor, what is the matter? I do not know if I am ready to hear what you have to say, but you must. Oh, sweet Jesus! Proceed."

"Madam, your child has a serious heart condition, a birth defect; it's not formed properly. Today was the first time after being born that it showed itself. This happens. Big changes in the way his little heart and blood vessels move the blood around the body take place in the first twenty-four hours. I could not detect any problem when I saw him right after birth. I think I know the general category of problem that he has, but I am not an expert, a specialist, in these matters. Because his heart did not develop properly, he is not able to get a normal amount of blood to his lungs. The blockage to the lung blood flow reduces the amount of oxygen that is circulating in his body. That is why his lips and skin have a dusky, bluish hue—cyanosis. He is what people call 'a blue baby.'"

"Can you be mistaken? He doesn't look blue to me. You didn't see this at first. Can't it be something that will just go away or get better? God! What are you telling me?"

Julia wept profusely and angrily. In fact, she was in a seething rage: at Elvige for finding this problem, at the doctor for not finding it and then confirming that this woman who had three children die on her had found a problem in her precious son, at the pathetic McChesney family in general for having brought this upon her, and finally, at the Father, *His* Son, and the Holy Ghost.

"I am very sorry to say that I am sure that little Elmer has a serious problem. It seems to me similar to a case that I saw about eight years ago where the level of oxygen in the body fluctuates quite a bit. You are correct. His color is almost normal right now, but the profound spell he had earlier this morning is a grave portent, a signal feature of his underlying heart defect. I think the way I have him swaddled may be helping him force more blood into his lungs. When I examined him today, I heard a telltale sound, a murmur, coming from his heart. I believe this is another hallmark of his type of malformation."

"Quite right, sir. As you said, you are not a specialist in these matters. I believe my husband and I will want to consult an expert in this field as soon as possible so that we can find a means to correct this, this whatever you think is wrong. There must be help for him!"

"Our community is blessed with *the* most gifted and knowledgeable man on diseases of the heart and blood vessels alive today. His name is Rudolph Matas. Dr. Matas is the president of the American Association for Thoracic Surgery, a distinguished professor on the medical faculty of Tulane University, and editor of our city's premiere medical and surgical journal. I will arrange for an urgent consultation for your little boy. If anyone can sort this out, it is he. I must caution you, however, do not—"

"Enough, Dr. Archinaud, please. I ask you to arrange an appointment with your esteemed professor tomorrow, if possible. I shall be able to move about and travel across town quite well enough. Also, I shall communicate what information I have taken away from our meeting today with my husband when he arrives home this evening. I do not wish you to upset him as terribly as you have me already with your surmises."

"Julia, you may believe as you wish, but I think my son deserves to speak with whomever he may need to speak. I hope the doctor remains and gives us some guidance on what we might do to try to prevent any more bad spells like the one he had earlier. Beheading the messenger is not the best way through this crisis."

"Thank you, ma'am. You were quite remarkable today, if I may say so. I know we are all glad that you were here."

"Yes—oh, Elvige—you are quite correct, Doctor. Please forgive me. I am not right in the head with all of this. I am deeply thankful for you both. Thank you for helping my little Elmer. I feel so lost right now and very, very afraid. God help us all!"

Bertha sat on the bed and rocked Julia in her arms. Penny, largely invisible throughout the storm and flood of tears, had crawled under her mother's bed and remained there, lying on her side, clutching her doll and sucking her thumb. She'd heard everything but was certain now of only one thing: God might come any day and take her and her baby brother away.

# *Eleven*

Elvige met Harry and May at the door; they had come together, only a few minutes after Dr. Archinaud exited for his office. She provided them with a capsule version of the terrible events of the morning and the gist of the doctor's diagnosis. May was devastated by the news, but Harry held out hope for a more encouraging verdict from the august Dr. Matas. They insisted on a brief word of commiseration with Julia, who had morphed between angry victim and distraught mother several more times over the past hour. Finally exhausted, she welcomed her brother-in-law and his wife into her bedroom and encouraged them to hold the baby.

"Don't be shy. You can't break him any more than he already is, I suppose. Oh, what did I just say? I am such a terrible mother."

"He is absolutely precious, my dear Julia. Harry says that he has heard wonderful things about Dr. Matas. He's a famous surgeon, you know. Dr. Archinaud would not be sending you to him if he didn't think there was something, an operation or something, that he might be able to offer the poor child."

"Yes, Julia, try to stay positive. God may answer all our prayers."

"I'm afraid of what tonight and tomorrow morning might bring, much less what we will learn from Dr. Matas. Elvige has kindly offered to stay, but I think I will be much better when Elmer gets home. She's looking after Penny now. My Lord, such terrible things that daughter of mine has had to suffer today. Elvige has been a saint, first saving my son's life, now breathing some love back into my daughter. I am incapable of such. I feel like an empty, worthless vessel."

"Do you want me to stay with you while you speak with Elmer this evening?"

"I think that your mother and I will be able to tell him what he needs to know for now. He loves you both very much. Oh, do whatever you think is best, Harry. I am just not in control right now. It's terrible."

"May and I will be at home all afternoon and this evening. You have Bertha call us if you want us or need us for absolutely anything. We are at your command."

Elvige had taken the opportunity provided by Harry and May's visit to take Penny for a walk outside. It was a refreshingly mild December afternoon, and the bright sunshine felt good on her back and shoulders. Her granddaughter did not ask too many questions about the events of the day. Elvige knew there would be plenty of time for that. She sang Penny's favorite French nursery rhymes; the child joined in on *"Frere Jacques."* They held hands and made another round of the block in silence.

"I'm getting hungry, Maman. Can we go in now?"

Elvige smiled and happily answered, *"Mais oui, ma Cherie. Mais oui."*

Bertha managed to lift everyone's spirits by preparing a hot meal, the first solid thing that Julia had eaten in almost two days. Soon after, Harry and May left Elvige rocking the baby. Across the room, Julia and Penny were cuddling in bed together.

A couple of hours later, Julia and Elmer embraced warmly as he sat down on her side of the bed. She was weeping silently from the time she heard his footsteps in the front parlor. Two bedside lamps illuminated the room. His mother was sitting in the rocker with little Buddy. She had dark circles of stress around her eyes, but her face gave away little else. She seemed to be waiting for Julia to begin speaking. Before he asked either woman what was wrong—who had died—he walked over to the other side of the bed and gently welcomed Penny into his arms. He carried her back to Julia's side where she made room for him to sit with Penny in his lap. He stared, unblinking, at his wife.

"Oh, El, it's our little baby. He's not well. He had a terrible spell, turned blue . . . out of the blue . . . there's a murmur, a heart blockage is what Dr. A. thinks. I'm not telling this right. Elvige, please, you were here from the beginning. She saved our baby's life. Please tell him; I am too . . . I can't get it all straight myself right now. Oh, El!"

Elmer held Penny close as a terrible sword cut through his heart. His mother spoke evenly and sweetly, trying to distance him from the trauma and terror that she had just lived through. Pointless. It was immediately clear to him how sick his boy was and how horrible her ordeal had been. Without knowing any more details of Buddy's ailment, a serious birth defect was how Elvige said the doctor referred to it, he knew that he would see his son die.

"Thank you, Mother, for everything you've done here today. Penny, I love you very, very, very much. Now, give me a big kiss and go climb back under the covers with your mommy." He remained sitting and held his wife for several minutes and then rose from the bed. "I want to hold little Buddy now."

He walked with his son and rocked with his son and patted his son and fed his son and changed his son and sang to his son and mourned his son, all on a winter's day. Bertha found them asleep together in Mr. Mac's favorite chair when she went to fetch the milk off the front porch the next morning.

## Twelve

Dr. Archinaud's office called around eight o'clock to say that Dr. Matas would be in surgery at Charity Hospital all morning but that he expected to complete his last case shortly after noon. He asked that the family report to the surgery clinic in the hospital at quarter-past twelve.

At precisely 12:20 p.m., Elmer, Julia, Buddy, and Elvige were ushered into an examination room in the surgery wing of the hospital overlooking Camp Street. Julia appeared very worn and pale, more like the patient than her son. She had always been extremely uncomfortable upon entering any hospital. The gravity of today's occasion made her turmoil almost unbearable. Elmer had hardly slept, but he sensed the overwhelming inevitability of this encounter. He was resigned to hearing a bleak report. He had exhausted his fear and rage during his vigil with his son the preceding night. Elvige was determined to be a source of strength and solace for the entire clan. Buddy was sleeping. The off color of his lips and eyelids was easily noticeable in the bright light that coursed through the tall west windows.

The door to the room was left slightly ajar. Muffled noises from the hall filled the silence within. The space between the family members seemed filled with emotionally charged cotton wool. Into this dense atmosphere of dread glided an erect, imposing figure, impeccably dressed in a four-button wool suit and vest, modern-collared shirt, and modest necktie. He was of medium height, on the plump side, and wore metal-rimmed spectacles. His light-olive complexion spoke to his Spanish heritage. A Vandyke beard and mustache and slightly receding hairline were tinged with a liberal amount of gray. Elvige guessed him to be a well-preserved gentleman in his late fifties. He moved with deliberate assurance and spoke in a deep baritone with a trace of foreign accent, giving rising inflections to his statements and questions. His hands were large in proportion to his body, with exceptionally long and delicate fingers. He moved easily over to the McChesneys and greeted each one of them with a warm smile and firm handshake. He held each of them intently with a penetrating gaze and seemed to be able to focus his attention on each one of them simultaneously as he spoke.

"I have had a preliminary conversation with Dr. Archinaud a few minutes ago, so I will dispense with most of our history gathering and take some time to examine your little fellow. Please, nurse . . . ."

Matas moved expertly through the evaluation. Elmer happily noted that the doctor rubbed his hands together to warm them each time before touching, gently prodding, and palpating his son with those gifted fingers. He also warmed his stethoscope and spent considerable time listening over chest, head, and tummy. He then glanced briefly at his attendant; she immediately redressed and swaddled the infant. He took the opportunity to gather his thoughts while moving a chair so that he sat directly facing all of the family members. Once again, his eyes engaged and held all of theirs at once.

"I wish I could contradict my good friend and esteemed colleague, Dr. Archinaud. I regret that I can only amplify somewhat on his diagnosis and present the situation to you in my own words. Your little boy has a birth defect of the heart. It is, I am sorry to report, a bad one. Knowing how his problem has presented since birth and what I have observed for myself, I firmly believe that he has a cluster of malformations within his heart called the tetralogy of Fallot."

Elmer, Julia, and Elvige received this dire message in stunned silence, punctuated only by the reflex sighs and sniffles that accompany weeping into handkerchiefs. Dr. Matas drew a few simple diagrams to help explain the details of the heart as it should have been and how he understood Buddy's case to be.

"The natural history of a child who presents with blue spells in the first days or weeks of life is uniformly poor. This presentation is consistent with more severe forms of the problem. This is not only my experience but accords with information published only recently by Dr. Maude Abbott in Canada. She is at the forefront of this field, a brilliant woman, to be sure. As a surgeon, my focus is on understanding the details of these problems in order to find some way to try to palliate or repair them. I only wish I could offer you and your precious son such an option. We have made many advances since the Great War, but alas, this is beyond us at the moment."

"How long do you think he can live with this, Dr. Matas? What will his life be like without a normal amount of oxygen? Will he suffer? Is he suffering now?" Elmer stopped. He realized that he had rapidly asked four questions, the answers to which he could likely provide himself. But Julia and Elvige needed to hear the surgeon's verdict.

"I cannot be precise; his lifespan could be a matter of months or several years. He is unlikely to be with us very long, however. His growth and development will be impaired. Suffering? Pain? Possibly during those acute episodes of very low oxygen. But, the good Lord has ways of dulling the brain's perceptions in states of oxygen deprivation so that it might not be nearly as difficult for the little one as for those who must observe and endure along with him.

"There is a New Orleans company that is now supplying our hospital with cylinders of pure oxygen. We can try to arrange for you to get this at home to help him through, possibly shorten, some of the worst spells. It's not something that can be used continuously, and it won't do anything to alter nature's course: inexorably progressive, inevitably worse with time. I am so very sorry that I am unable to offer more than this. I speak for all of my colleagues around the world. We just haven't progressed to this level in our struggles with man's suffering. We have much to learn. I fear we shall lose him before the Lord blesses us with that knowledge and skill."

"I do not know what the Lord has to say about these matters, Dr. Matas. As a mother, I can tell you it seems that He has left our family, left my heart, left our little child to the devil's hands. Perhaps this is a test or a punishment for my sins. After all, he formed within my womb. It must be an unholy place for this to have happened."

"My dear lady, if you've heard or understood nothing of what I have said to now, please, please listen most carefully to me on this point. You have no guilt, no blame, no part in this whatsoever. I cannot answer for the problems of evil and suffering in this world. These questions test my faith daily, but I am a man of science first and foremost. I can assure you: your son's illness is not your fault."

# Thirteen

Julia found little solace in the good doctor's closing message. All of them left the clinic with a slightly different interpretation of the facts. As time passed, individual interpretations mattered little. Buddy had cyanotic spells of increasing severity and duration. The oxygen from the cylinder, delivered through a tubing and paper mask (really just a paper cup with a hole cut in the end), was clumsy and difficult for the distraught family members to administer effectively. Julia blamed Bertha for leaving the cylinder valve open after one late-night episode. Julia blamed herself for mostly everything else, mostly everything that was really out of her control to begin with. This only made her more angry and withdrawn and depressed.

Buddy fed poorly, and whatever he took in did not seem to help much anyway. He only weighed thirteen pounds at one year of age. His birthday was a miserably sad affair. Julia refused to have any celebration whatsoever. Penny had drawn a picture of an angel for his birthday card. She put it on Buddy's pillow. He still slept in the infant bassinet. She did not understand why he hadn't progressed to her old baby bed. Aunt May brought over an outfit that was way too big even though she had instructed her seamstress that he was small for his age. Julia somehow managed to take the poor woman's mistake personally.

Elmer spent as much time with his boy, his Buddy, as he could after work and on weekends. On fair-weather evenings the neighbors always saw him out walking with "the blue baby" on his shoulder. He kept up a running monologue, even supplied Buddy's parts when a dialogue was essential, on their strolls. He told him all about the world that he knew the boy would never get to see, all the wonders that any boy would want to visit, many of the great thoughts and problems that wise men have pondered, all of the love and kindness that his own mother and father had shown him growing up, all of the great and wonderful things his brother, Uncle Harry, had accomplished. He hoped that upon this vast canvas—an outpouring of oral tradition, family myth, and fascinating gewgaws of man's world—Buddy would somehow grasp the immensity of an entire lifetime within the small crucible of time allotted to them, distilled into the magic elixir of a father's love, this father's love, for his son.

On the eve of his second birthday, Buddy had his final cyanotic episode. Penny, who was now four and one-half years old, had come to deliver another hand-colored card for his pillow. She saw her father holding him in his arms, rocking back and forth as he sat on the cot in the nursery. Bertha was standing up to put away the oxygen tubing and little paper cup. Penny knew that was a good sign; another one of her brother's bad spells was over. She ran over to give him and her daddy a big hug. Elmer did not turn away but held Buddy closer to him and leaned toward her at the same time. Penny kissed him on the cheek. When she looked at Buddy, she thought he was sleeping. When she also noticed that his color was very dark, her father told her that Buddy no longer had to struggle or suffer. Elmer used all the metaphors he could think of to tell his daughter what had happened.

She swallowed hard as she stroked Buddy's head and said what her father could not, "He's not gone away; he's just dead."

"Yes, my precious child, you have cut to the truth. Give our little Buddy a kiss because he *is* going away. We shall have a good-bye ceremony for him. All of his family, those who love him dearly, will come to the house to say their good-byes. You have a chance before everyone else comes to tell him anything you think you've forgotten up until now. Is there anything you'd like to say?"

Without much pause Penny leaned down close to her brother and spoke her benediction, "Buddy, please tell God that I like it here with Mommy and Daddy. I am not ready to be an angel. Ask Him, please, to just leave me alone."

The visitation was at their home on South Johnson. Buddy's tiny coffin sat in the front right corner of the parlor on a small stand provided by the funeral home. A tall, slender candle stood at each side of the coffin, and a small crucifix hung above it on the wall. The candles and the crucifix were Elvige's suggestion. Elmer had to intercede with Julia, who thought them too Catholic, but she was too depressed to engage in any power struggles. She managed to appear, seated, at the gravesite and endured the interment. After the services, she retired to her room and did not reemerge for two weeks. She had no idea what day it was when she bathed and dressed and came out to the kitchen to ask Bertha for some breakfast. Christmas was only a week away.

# *Fourteen*

"And so, you can understand, Harry, how sad and mournful your mother was. She had lost a little boy, her first son, who was as special then as you are to her now."

"What did she do when Pa told her that Buddy had died when she wasn't home?"

"She had been to church that morning. I think she knew that he was not doing well, that he only had a little time left. I think she went to pray and ask God to take good care of Buddy whenever He decided it was time for him to go up to heaven. These are just things that mothers know. Take my word. Besides, whenever she saw Buddy have his bad blue spells, she had to let your father or Bertha look after him. She just couldn't stand to see him like that. I think she was very relieved that she did not have to see him in those last moments."

"They put him over there in the corner, right? The one with the cross?"

"Yes, Harry, that's where he rested in his coffin for a short while before he was buried. When Christmas came your mother decided that nothing else was ever going to go in that corner, especially not the Christmas tree. She had a lot of trouble with the whole idea of God's love and mercy and fallen sparrows and the like for quite some time—still does, I fear. When God sent you to them, your parents began to see the world a little differently. I pray that things in this family will be much better again someday."

"Well, she still doesn't allow the Christmas tree to stand where it belongs. Or did I get the wrong message from Penny a little while ago?"

"It depends, my sweet child. With grown-ups some things take longer than others. Perhaps if you were to tell your mother that moving the tree was your idea, it would be quite all right again."

"I have a better idea, Maman. How about if *you* tell her it moved, and I can take credit if she says OK?"

# PART TWO

*Gathering Storms*

# Fifteen

It wasn't only for the exercise or the solitude; Harry did some of his best thinking while walking in Metairie Cemetery. As he'd grown older, he'd found the place attractive. All that terrible stuff from his early years was still around in the shadows, but the cemetery was part of a greater community of lives as well as deaths. His warm feelings arose from abundant memories of family and friends, dear ones who were linked to his life—not just the buried ones. By now there were lots of the buried ones too.

This morning he had driven over to the cemetery from his neighborhood of Lakewood South. Even with an early start, more than a couple of hours in the August heat and humidity were too debilitating for a man about to turn eighty-one. In cooler weather he liked to take the back way in and walk the whole route from home: along the top of the levee of the 17th Street Canal just behind his house and across the Southern Railroad tracks, entering the cemetery through a back service gate. He loved his morning walks, but this was *not* cooler weather. It seemed like the summer of 2005 had started way back before Easter. Hurricane season was already in full swing, and it wasn't even September yet. Those poor folks over in Florida had gotten smacked again yesterday with one called Katrina, and nobody knew if that storm was done yet.

He stayed in the shade of the live oaks as he did a few turns around one of the shorter oval avenues close to the central lagoon. While ambling along, Harry was trying to decide what to tell his daughters about his coming birthday. Last year Mary Lee and Libby had made a really big deal about his "big eight-oh." He certainly did not want a repeat of all that. Mostly, he didn't see the point, especially since his beloved wife, Lorna, had died. Each year the occasion seemed less joyous, and the celebrations seemed more elaborate and overdone. Enough already! He would be firm but not dismissive.

"Good, that's settled." He smiled as he headed back to his car. "Only one more stop to make."

◆　◆　◆

Harry stopped at the McChesney family plot every time he walked in the cemetery. Today, prompted by his ruminations on birthdays and another year passing, he recalled the promises he'd made to his father on their very first visit together: how he'd wrestled with those and disappointed everyone, himself most of all, before finding his way. Even now, he was still searching for some of the answers to life's challenges, one in particular delivered by his uncle on another birthday, long ago.

He had rashly promised his father that he would somehow make up for their early loss, for the death of his brother. He was only seven years old then and had no idea how he would begin to do that. He thought he might start by learning to act more sensibly and rein in his reckless stunts so as not to drive his mother to greater distraction. Good luck with that. After finding out about Buddy, things only got worse. Some of his exploits were merely boyish adventures, albeit with a high-level disregard for danger; some bordered on hooliganism—swiping watermelons off the barges in the New Basin Canal, hot-wiring the kiddy train in Audubon Park late one night and running it off the tracks. Two episodes had more serious consequences, and both of them shocked his mother, Julia, badly enough to cause relapses of her nervous condition. One had resulted in hospitalization for Harry, and the other landed Julia in the sanitarium.

As soon as he had gotten his own bicycle, he began hitching rides on the rear fenders of trucks and getting towed across the Mississippi River bridge. When one of the trucks was sideswiped, Harry and his bike got caught in the squeeze of metal. He'd just missed getting killed, according to the policeman who brought him to the emergency room.

Every wild thing he did growing up increased the friction between him and his sister. She reacted with a mixture of rage—at his disregard for his own life and his mother's problems—and vociferous rejection of him as a brother. One time Penny's rage erupted into physical violence. That was the night the New Orleans police brought him home after he and Jack Pitre had sabotaged the St. Charles streetcars. He was in the tenth grade.

"Jesus, Harry! Dynamite on the streetcar tracks? You don't care who you kill, do you?"

"Relax, Sis. It was a dumb stunt, really dumb. I told Dad and Officer Conrad that, but those railroad torpedoes weren't supposed to knock those streetcars off the tracks, just make a lot of noise. The cars were too light; we didn't know there weren't enough people riding at night—"

"Enough, you bastard! You stupid idiot! Where did you even *come* from? Not this family. I *hate* you!"

Penny was still bigger than Harry back then, and she hit him with a book hard enough to knock him down. That seemed to sap most of her physical aggression, but she managed to spit on him as she burst into tears. She left home shortly after that incident. Harry knew that his behavior and another looming Christmas season were the reasons for her departure.

But his mother's condition was the one he'd felt the most anguish about that night. It was a terrible scene when Elmer told her what had happened. The same policeman who'd driven Harry home had to call an ambulance to take her to the St. Vincent de Paul's mental hospital. She underwent electroconvulsive therapy for severe depression before being able to return home. Harry didn't know what shock treatment was, but he felt he was completely responsible for her pain and suffering from that moment on.

As for Harry's other vow, the one about making his dad proud of him, he'd made a hash of that one, too, through most of high school. Still, his father never gave up on him. His uncle, on the other hand, made no effort to conceal his growing disenchantment with the remaining McChesney male. Finally, Harry decided to make some serious changes, shortly after the stakes were raised and the risks became monumental. It all started the day of the boxing match.

## Sixteen

Almost an hour after Sunday lunch, Harry was eager to get started. He and his friend laced up the gloves and begin sparring. He was trying to use the remaining daylight to his advantage, trying some dancing footwork to keep his neighbor, Jimmy Pellegrin, facing southwest in the sunny part of the backyard. Harry had recently turned seventeen. Jimmy was a year behind him at Fortier High, stood about five inches taller, but wasn't much heavier than Harry. Jimmy thought of himself as wiry. The kids at school called him "Stringbean" or simply "Bean."

In order to "try and put some beef on the kid," Mr. Pellegrin had bought his son two pairs of boxing gloves.

"Here, Jim, find some of your pals to go a few rounds wearing these. None of you fellas know a thing about boxing, but stick with it and you'll get a real workout. Grow you some muscles."

"Wow, Everlast gloves, same ones that the professionals use. But I thought you didn't want me and my friends fighting."

"I don't want you brawling bare-fisted on the playground or in the streets. That kinda stuff never proved anything. But I also don't like how the bigger kids pick on you. Besides, you won't be able to coldcock anybody with these pillows. You'll see. Give 'em a whirl."

Jimmy decided to make his boxing debut with someone he could keep at a safe distance if necessary. His pal next door, Harry McChesney, was pretty strong, but Jimmy knew from the basketball court that he had a two- to three-inch reach advantage over him.

Whiffing, flailing, and flagging quickly, they had both found themselves pretty exhausted after a couple of three-minute rounds. Harry's dad, Elmer, had done some amateur boxing down at the New Orleans Athletic Club in his youth and was happy to spend some time teaching both boys basic punching combinations and footwork. In addition, Elmer had some advice for his son on tactics and strategy and of course, on life.

"You've still got some growing to do. You're going to be bigger and faster than I ever was, but you're never going to tower over guys. Fortunately, I think you're blessed with plenty of brains from the McChesneys and from your grandma's people. In sports where one man squares off against another—tennis, boxing—you must learn to take control of as much of the arena as possible. There are no others to rely upon and no others to blame. You can whine, or you can learn accountability and self-discipline. Sometimes you have to find an unusual resource, an expedient—a Plan X—that will give you enough of an advantage to carry the day. Just remember, stay alert for the little opportunities; it's not cheating to look for an edge that the moment or the environment provides."

"Dad, right now I'm happy just to stay standing with my guard up for more than five minutes, but I follow what you're saying. Thanks for the boxing tips. Jimmy says he and his dad never talk except when he's going to punish him for something. I can talk to you anytime, and you don't just tell me things. You make me think a lot."

That Sunday, Harry was trying out a new application of his father's recent advice. His plan of attack was based on two observations. One: Jimmy was keeping him from scoring good blows simply by keeping him at arm's length—Jimmy's arm's length. Two: when Jimmy was boxing he didn't wear his glasses. He squinted at Harry the whole time they were squaring off. Jimmy was nearsighted, big time. Harry planned to maneuver him into the glare of the sun, dazzle him, and move inside for a quick strike.

Harry's fall-back distraction, should the dazzling sunlight ploy fail, was to have Jimmy's favorite music program playing on the radio while they were working out in the McChesneys' backyard. WJBW broadcast a jazz-and-pops program out of New York City every Sunday from one o'clock until three.

Jimmy knew all the big-band tunes and soulful ballads that year. The song that always stopped him in his tracks was Billie Holiday's "God Bless the Child." Harry was sure that WJBW would play it once or twice during the "Big Apple Hit Parade" while they were sparring together. Thus far, Harry was satisfied with the execution of his battle plan.

"OK, OK, we're a minute into round one, Harry, and you haven't laid a glove on me. Why are you pedaling backward toward that laundry pole? Think I'm going to get tangled up in the clotheslines? I ain't that tall."

"Footwork is everything, Bean. Stay on your toes, fella."

"Gee, that sun is bright. You look like a shadow, a darkie from over here. Big Joe Louis. Ha!"

Harry measured his openings and landed a couple of body blows. He couldn't believe it. The light was actually throwing Jimmy off, perhaps blinding him a bit.

**We interrupt this program for the following news bulletin. Go ahead, New York: the Japanese have just attacked Pearl Harbor, Hawaii, by air . . . President Roosevelt has just announced . . . the attack also was made on all naval and military activities on the principal island of Oahu.**

"What? What did he just say?"

Harry didn't hear or do another thing. He'd dropped his guard involuntarily while trying to make sense of the urgency in the announcer's words. Jimmy, who had heard nothing, saw his opportunity to strike a blow. Harry had maneuvered too close to the heavy steel, T-shaped laundry pole at the back end of the yard. When Jimmy's punch landed on his chin, his head snapped back and cracked into the thick metal upright. With a flash of light everything went dark.

◆　◆　◆

Jimmy approached the big Adirondack chair in Harry's backyard where they had been boxing. He and Mr. McChesney had moved Harry there after he went down. Jimmy was really worried about his pal; Harry had been out cold for too long. But Bean tried to make light of it now that he was beginning to talk back.

"Here, Joe Louis, hold this ice bag on the back of your thick skull. I can't believe you tried to knock down your mother's laundry pole! Don't you know it's set in cement?"

"Don't you know it's not fair to hit a man when he's dropped his guard and heading to a neutral corner? Ya bum! So what was the rest of the report on the radio about Japan while I was taking my little nap?"

"I didn't really hear the first part at all, and I didn't catch the rest because I was trying to get my gloves off and play nursemaid to you. Here comes your mother; let's ask."

"My Lord, Harry, I hope you two are finished mauling one another for today. We've all had enough excitement. You aren't bleeding, are you? No, don't show me; you know I can't bear the sight of blood . . . . Oh, that's better, just an ugly lump."

"Mrs. McChesney, what did the announcers say about the Japanese and all?"

"President Roosevelt said that the naval base on the big island in Hawaii was attacked today, just a short while ago. It was terrible: bombings and killing American men and women. Elmer says that we will be in the war for sure now, against both Japan and Germany. The radio said that more announcements from the White House are expected later today."

"Where is Dad?"

"He's talking to Uncle Harry on the telephone; he's been in there quite a while. After he helped Jimmy get out of his gloves and took a look at you, he went inside. Go see him and show him you're up and about and give him a hug. He told me you were tough as nails and would be fine, but he looked pretty shaken up about the attack. We all are."

"What do we do now? How can we join the fight?"

"Young man, hush up that kind of reckless talk! You've done enough fighting for one day. Besides, you just turned seventeen. Tomorrow morning you and your big goose egg are going to get up at the regular time and go to your first-period classroom."

It had just slipped out. He hadn't wanted to upset his mother any more today than she was already—the attack, him getting clobbered on the pole. But this war talk had been brewing for some time; even he knew that. Joining the fight seemed so natural to him. Maybe it was just another sign of what Penny called his "wild blood." It felt more like something his calm dad would do. Harry really wanted his father to know that he could be someone, a someone who would do something right for a change.

# *Seventeen*

About three months after the sneak attack on Pearl Harbor, they went out for a stroll in the neighborhood after dinner. Elmer thought his cigars tasted better in the fresh air, and Harry wanted his father's ear.

"Pa, we need to talk." Immediately, he had his father's undivided attention. "No, I'm not in trouble again—not yet, at least."

"I'm listening, son." Elmer's jaw muscles tightened reflexively.

"The country is gearing up for the war as fast as it can. I can't begin to understand how complex an operation that is, but I do know that the president said—"

"Jesus Christ, Harry, let's leave him out of this. I don't trust that progressive jackass and his cronies as far as I can throw them."

"Sorry. We're stuck with him for now—"

"OK, but just get to the point, please."

"Yes, sir. The country—our military—needs lots of good men to fight in this war. We're going to have to be in two parts of the world at the same time with all the might we can muster. There are thousands of able-bodied men signing up, but I don't think the volunteer forces will build up fast enough."

"You're not even eighteen, Harry. You couldn't volunteer now—"

"No. But as soon as I am, I plan to enlist and try to get in the branch of the service I want because I think a general draft will be called fairly soon. I don't want to take my chances in the draft."

Elmer was impressed with the seriousness of the argument. In that way it reminded him of the conversation he'd rehearsed before speaking with his father about the coffee business. He could now anticipate most of his son's concerns and how he might help the boy, but he let him continue after asking a leading question.

"So, what branch of the service are you aiming for?"

"The Army Air Corps. I want to fly. I've wanted to learn to fly airplanes ever since you took me to that barnstorming race over in Patterson, Louisiana."

"Ah, yes."

"I didn't sleep at all that night. Ma couldn't figure out why I was so excited about our visit to a Civil War battleground. We McChesney men have always had a few secrets between us, huh? I still remember you slapping the belt on your hand—"

"Yes, well . . . I prefer to think of those as manly confidences. I can assure you, Harry, the ladies keep theirs as well."

But Elmer knew that this was not one of their trivial deceptions, and Harry was not considering another fool's errand. Sooner or later, Julia would have to be told, and her troubles would begin again. Still, better to let him begin to define himself by charting a military course of his choosing. Any active role in the war was dangerous, seriously life-threatening. His boy was going to go fight, had to go sooner or later, and he was going to back him on this one, by God.

"I admire what you're proposing, son. I have to confess. I was a little embarrassed that I was never asked to fight in the Great War. Our army reserve unit was never called up; none of them were. But this time we're finally in it, all out, and we need to be."

"Agreed, we're not fighting somebody else's war this time. This one's for our country's freedom and for what's right."

"The Frenchies are overrun, and England's on their heels. Now we have the Japs on our left flank. All Americans need to be part of this fight. I haven't mentioned it to any of you, but I'm considering volunteering for the Civil Defense Corps. I can try to do my part along the riverfront, along the docks."

"You should, too. As for me, it will be a real bonus that while I'm doing my bit, I'll learn to fly planes. Of course, there's just one thing—that is, if you're with me on this, sir."

"Oh yes, your dear mother. I'll support your goals and try to help with Ma. And you'd better make peace with your sister too. Winning over Julia will have to be a family effort. Our main argument will be that you're going to have to serve, one way or another. Just don't expect an easy sale; in fact, I wouldn't expect any sale at all."

"But you're behind me. That means a lot to me, Pa."

They embraced, and for the first time, Elmer realized that Harry stood at least two inches taller than he. He wondered how and when that could have happened.

# Eighteen

Harry found himself more attentive to the news of the day and those everyday conversations between grown-ups—at Parisi's grocery, at the filling station, at the post office. They were all talking about the war: new gasoline ration stamps, basic household items that were getting hard to come by, the daughter who had moved to Michigan to work in the aircraft plant, the grandson who had perished at sea.

He had become more serious about his studies in his senior year at Fortier High and graduated near the top of his class. In order to pull his pathetic grades up he'd stopped goofing off on school nights, and he did it all without having to give up his favorite pursuits, daydreaming about his favorite girls and dating them on the weekends.

What finally did it for him, made him realize how out-of-touch and silly their little lives were, was just after his Fortier graduation when he accepted an invitation to join a couple of his pals for a week on the Mississippi Gulf Coast. Guy Hamilton's dad, a wealthy corporate lawyer, was footing the bill for the whole crew.

Harry couldn't help but be impressed with Mr. Hamilton's choice of hotels. The Edgewater Gulf billed itself as the Queen of the Gulf Coast. With over four hundred guest rooms, massive grounds, its own railroad station, and a soaring Moorish entry pavilion straight out of *One Thousand and One Arabian Nights*, it was the most impressive resort he had ever visited.

The entire hotel interior circulated refrigerated air so chilly that you had to sleep under a blanket in June. The Marine Room was ornately decorated with huge mirrors, vast chandeliers, and pink marble floors. Crisp, white table linens were laid with a different set of fine china and crystal at every seating. Jackets and ties were required for every meal after breakfast, and many of the guests from Chicago and the East Coast wore formal attire in the evenings. For the men from New Orleans and Memphis, white linen suits and two-toned shoes were de rigueur.

Despite the décolletage and fine food served up in the Marine Room that Saturday, the boys were having trouble sitting through the dessert course.

"Guy, that's the fourth time you've checked your watch since I ordered coffee. Would you fellas like the car keys so you can head to the dance? I know you wouldn't want to miss a minute of the action."

"Yes sir, that would be great. You know it's important to get a good table close to the dance floor."

"Mr. Hamilton, what your son really means to say is he's hoping to find a homely little Mississippi gal there tonight who will have pity on him. He has to get there early before some Long Beach Lothario claims her."

"Guy, you're driving, so no drinking whatsoever—not a drop. Harry, you and Nip are underage, so the same goes for you two. What you might get away with over in New Orleans has nothing to do with how 'y'all be' treated in Mississippi. The sheriffs and justices over here like nothing better than to eat a few smarty-pants from 'Loo-ze-anna' before breakfast. Got it?"

A trio of "yessirs!" preceded their run-walk to Mr. Hamilton's Cadillac. Guy was careful to keep to the speed limit on the short run along Highway 90 to the ballroom at the Broadwater Beach Hotel. Nip and Harry stretched out in the rear while Guy played at chauffer.

"Man, oh man! This Sixty Special Caddy is some fine automobile. Just look at the size of this backseat, Harry. Portia's couch of pleasure. Lordy, lordy, watch out ladies; here we come. By the way, who's playing on the pier tonight?"

"I think it's Louis Prima with his big band."

"Guy, you won't believe it, but we just passed a police car parked in that last bay and he's pulling out. Aw, man! He's turned on the flashers and coming up fast."

"Why? I'm barely creeping along this stupid highway. Goddammit! OK, John Law, I'm turning in at this filling station. Hold your horses."

A squat, bandy-legged old coot who looked like he'd swallowed a moderate-size sugar kettle adjusted his crotch, his cartridge belt, and his side arm—in that order—and rolled a toothpick back and forth in his mouth as he surveyed their vehicle and then sashayed up to the driver's window.

"This redneck looks more like a fat taxi driver than law enforcement," Guy whispered.

"Shut up, idiot. He's coming over."

"Evening, boys! Mighty nice car we got here, latest model. Loozeana plates, huh? And what's your name, son?"

"Guy, Guy Hamilton. Wha—"

"Mr. Guy, pleased to meetcha. I'm Roy Shiflett, deputy sheriff, Hancock County. Mr. Guy, since you're the driver, I'd be most obliged if you could show me your operator's license and your daddy's registration pay-pas."

"Yes, Sheriff, here they are. Can you please tell me what this is all about? We're trying to make it to the Broadwater for the big dance tonight and—"

"Zat so? Well now, ain't that nice! Who all's gonna be at your big dance, gennelmen? I ain't heard."

"Louis Prima and his big band—"

"Well, well."

"Yeah, he kept Sam Butera and a lotta the guys from the Dixieland Gang and went for the big swing—"

"Can it, Nip. I don't think the sheriff really cares too much about Prima's bio." Harry knew this guy was not just sniffing around.

"Sir, can you tell us why you stopped me, please? I'm certain I wasn't speeding."

"Speeding? That's rich. You big city fellas over for a big time here on the coast don't have a clue, do you? You see anything special about that car heading our way on the other side a the highway?"

Nip, ever the helpful passenger, piped up again, "You bet! Both his headlights are burned out; the man's driving with just his parking lights. Why don't you nab him, Sheriff?"

"I'm sure my lights are fine, sir; I always check them as I'm pulling out."

"Your lights are fine, are they, sonny boy? And what about that pickup coming our way back yonder?"

Guy had to crane around the sheriff's gut, but then he saw the olive drab truck, some kind of army vehicle, with funny little slits for headlights, nothing else showing any light. He got a tight feeling in his throat just as the fat man started to write in his ticket book. Suddenly, he didn't want to say any more.

"Hey, those guys have blinders on their—" A quick jab in the ribs from Harry silenced Nip in mid-blunder. It was clear to everyone else in the car that they were in trouble.

"You whiz kids ever hear that President Roozavelt declared war on our mortal enemies awhileago? You hear tell there's a shooting war on, perhaps? You fun-loving peckerwoods probably look over there and see milesa beach, pretty white sand where you go chase your gal friends and roast weenies and mushmallows after dark. Oh, and they's water out there, too. Fun, lotsa fun."

"Sir—"

"Shut up, I ain't finished. We got three major ports within fifty miles a here: N'awlins, Gulfport, and Pascagoula. They all vital to our fighting men and the war effort. The Innacoastal Waterway is just out there; deep sea shipping lanes futha out. So the Krauts and the Japs wanna sneak in with they subs and do a little damage if they can. They sit offshore and watch for the silhouettes of the big ships and convoys traveling at night. 'How come they can do that,' you say, 'it's pretty dark on shore, pretty-near blacked out?' Until fools like you come barreling along in your daddy's Caddy, high beams a-blazing, lighting up the heavens to help the enemy torpedo our merchant marine and battleships!"

"Sheriff, we had no idea; we—"

"Here's your citation. Since you from outta state, you hafta appear t'night before the Hancock justice a the peace. If'n I had my way, all y'all'd spend the weekend in prizzin and maybe do a little highway trash pickup before you got to go back home. You in violation of state and federal wartime blackout regalations.

You have anything more to say, tell it to the justice. He's waiting for you over at 101 Main Street in B'luxi. I'm staying out on the roadway to pull over more weekend idiots like yuselves. Do not even think about stopping by the dance, you hear? I'm gonna radio the J.P.'s office soon as you drive away and tell him to be expecting you, Mr. Guy Hamilton. If you ain't there in ten minutes, all y'all *will* spend the weekend in jail. Git!"

"Holy shit! We are screwed. I don't have much money on me. I hope we have enough between us."

"Guy, cut your driving lights now! Just the parking lights, oyster brain. Didn't you hear *anything* back there?"

"Sorry, Harry. Jeez—there. How's that? Dark as an Ethiopian in a coal mine. It's just a habit, you know: lights on for safety. Not anymore, not in this man's war, eh?"

Harry had lost his patience with his school chum. Guy didn't sound slick or even very smart any longer, just spoiled and whiny.

"Damned right, not anymore. Lots of things are going to change. Lots of things already changing, big things. The deputy spoke some truth; we've been leading sheltered, privileged lives."

"Aw, that old cracker was throwing his lard around. You heard what my dad said; they love to eat guys like us for snacks. I'll bet there ain't any subs out in the Gulf of Mexico."

"Don't you get it, man? Our parents have been coddling us, maybe hoping we'd forget about being a part of the war effort for a while. And we've been talking about doing our part, but we haven't been living any differently than when we all started high school. That's about to end. Yes, I'm going to summer school and will start Tulane in the fall if I can. But I'm going to enlist when I turn eighteen next October."

That got Nip's attention. Up until then all he'd wanted to do was to duck out on the fine; he had been busy hiding five-dollar bills in his shoe.

"*What* are you gonna do, Harry?"

"I want to learn to fly; I want to be a pilot in the Army Air Corps. I want a bird's-eye view of this war, not a worm's-eye view. Wings earn an officer's commission and good pay. Besides, I read where the government is going to institute an all-out draft soon instead of relying on enlistment. I want to get a say in what branch of the military I land in, not just assigned somewhere."

Guy had stopped listening to what Harry was talking about.

"Stop dreaming, my partners in crime. We're here."

# Nineteen

Gathering for Wednesday evening meals at Uncle Harry and Aunt May's home had been going on for as long as young Harry could remember. This was some sort of tradition that went way back to the McChesney clan's days in Scotland. Everyone present at those suppers knew that traditions and family honor were extremely important to Uncle Harry.

His uncle had always been kind and generous to him and to everyone on his side of the family. He was loving but stern. In recent years Harry's high-risk behavior and disregard for what his uncle termed "Julia's sensibilities" put a distance and distinct coolness between uncle and nephew.

The first Wednesday in October 1942 fell just before Harry's eighteenth birthday, so the meal should have been especially festive. However, Harry thought his uncle's behavior particularly reserved toward him that evening. He offered no toasts over supper and no cake for dessert. The almost-inevitable cigars and after-dinner cordials were dispensed with. Uncle Harry stood slowly after the last of the courses had been cleared away and bowed stiffly toward each of the ladies as he spoke. His manner was so extravagantly ceremonial, almost mock-serious, that Harry thought his uncle might have arranged some sort of surprise entertainment to follow.

"Dear May, Julia, Penny, you will excuse young Harry and me. We have some important business in the library. This could take some time. Good night to you all."

He said nothing to his brother, only nodded grimly. With that, Elmer looked down at his lap and never returned his son's questioning glance.

Harry had no choice but to silently follow his uncle into the depths of the library, where a solitary desk lamp cast a faint, reddish glow about the room. As he went to switch on a large floor lamp by the easy chairs around the fireplace, his uncle made a peremptory gesture, directing him to sit.

"Leave that alone. We're not here to read. We're not here to chat. I shall do most of the talking, and *you* will do the listening."

"Sir, have I done something wrong, something to offend you? Whatever it—"

"Hush, boy! *Listen.* This will be your only opportunity. Perhaps you can take something good and honorable away from our meeting. But let's clear the air regarding your question. Offend? Yes, you have a litany of offenses against our family's reputation that dates back far too long. I'll admit; you're not the first among us to have a wild streak. I am not so old that I've forgotten when I was an irresponsible pipsqueak, running with my fancy friends, disregarding my parents' concerns. Boyish derring-do and frivolity carried on into loutish behavior until my dear father, God rest his soul, put down his foot and made me aware of my responsibilities to our family and to others."

Harry shifted nervously in his seat. This was going to be a long evening. He wished he hadn't eaten so much; his stomach began to churn and rumble noisily.

"Sorry, sir. Touch of gas."

His comment seemed to soften his uncle's posture and expression somewhat; still, Uncle Harry wasn't even close to smiling.

"My dear Harry, let us not dwell on transgressions of the past—mine or yours. I must tell you, however, that I almost decided against our having this meeting. That is, until your father told me about your decision to enlist in the military and serve your country as an officer in the Air Corps. Now *that* is an honorable and rigorous road to which you aspire. It is certainly a worthy start. But there is much more you shall need to do if you are to assume the mantle of head the McChesney family someday. That is why we are here tonight."

Uncle Harry stayed in his formal-speech mode for the rest of the evening. He had no intention of letting his nephew off easily, getting chummy, even if he did love him dearly. He regarded the explanation of the Code and laying out young Harry's Three Challenges as the most important day of his life, and he was determined to imbue the ceremony with as much gravity as he could bring to bear. He remembered almost collapsing from stress the night his grandfather performed his introductory rights. Old Wallace McChesney was ferociously proud of his ancient moral heritage, and he'd never spoon-fed it to anyone.

Uncle Harry began with a brief account of the family's origins in Edinburgh, Scotland, eleven centuries ago and included a few phrases about the most prominent, revered McChesney men in more-recent centuries. Then he digressed a few hundred years.

"Beginning in 1326, Mortimer McChesney took it upon himself to set down in writing the precepts of conduct that his ancestors had passed down by word of mouth and hewed to religiously in their daily lives for the preceding five hundred years. The construct evolved from three universal tenets: steadfast faith in a Creator, ethical thoughts and practices, and compassionate outreach to others less fortunate than they. Mortimer's written account became known as the Code. Every man in our family over the age of eighteen is assigned a senior preceptor and is expected to learn and live by these dicta. Your father knows them well and honors them in all aspects of his life. With God's help, along with some time with me and two very old family documents, you will be schooled in every detail of what is expected of you going forward."

His uncle paused while the library clock struck the hour. He was pacing about as he spoke but now halted behind his desk and leaned forward so his face was illuminated from below by the only lamp in the room. The shadows and highlights gave his features a theatrical, diabolical accent.

"*That*, young man, is the easy part."

Harry was perspiring freely but did not dare remove his jacket or loosen his tie. He blinked away a drop of sweat from his eyelash and said nothing.

"Those of us who are in line to assume male leadership for each branch of the family have more stringent requirements to meet, more rigorous tasks to undertake before we can be considered wholly worthy of these responsibilities. These are known as the Three Challenges. Embarking on them typically takes a few years; completing them can take most of a lifetime. Only the family's judgment with the hindsight of history can ultimately decide how well a man succeeds in meeting his challenges. I have no direct issue to whom I can offer this immense opportunity. God and the fortunes of nature have left Brother Elmer and me with but one choice for this role. So, what say you, Henry Emerson McChesney?"

Harry's heart was racing. He had listened with his mouth agape; his throat was parched. He could not swallow much less speak, so he tried to cough to buy a few moments.

Finally, he let out a croak, "What *should* I say, sir?" He realized how feeble and dim-witted that question sounded and quickly added, "I mean no disrespect whatsoever by that question."

"Yes, yes, I understand. This isn't the Catholic catechism. Merely tell me that you wish to take up the Challenges, and then I can tell you what they are. The blood oath and the swearing in will come later."

The blood part so distracted Harry that he almost forgot what his response was supposed to be.

"I do, sir. That is, I wish to take up the Challenges." At the same time he thought about running out of the room and continuing running, right out of the city.

In brief, Harry the Elder set forth the following three challenges to Harry the Green:

1. He must choose and accomplish an extraordinarily difficult personal task. Uncle Harry reaffirmed his approval of the specific goal of becoming a commissioned pilot in the U.S. Army Air Corps to meet this challenge.
2. He must learn loving compassion and practice it often by reaching out to help others less fortunate with spiritual and material aid and comfort.
3. He must conquer whatever demons might stand in his path of realizing his first two goals. Some of his ancestors had perished in their struggles with their demons; successful men had found help from others, from those who could offer special protection.

Just when Harry thought his uncle was done speaking, he added a startling codicil to the Second Challenge.

"In years past every head of the family made do, in the best spirit of charity, to share whatever material resources they had—food, clothing, money—with others. In extremely hard times, when they struggled to scrape together enough for their own family's support and sustenance, others benefited much less, but whenever possible, McChesneys helped the truly needy. As you know, I have been particularly fortunate in the financial world, and in accordance with the Second Challenge, I resolved to reserve only a small portion of my wealth within the immediate family and distribute the remainder elsewhere."

"You've done more than your share, sir. The whole city knows that."

"Well, perhaps they will know even more someday. We have no children, and we plan to leave much of our fortune to various deserving agencies. However, there is much, much more than anyone knows of."

"What do you mean?"

"The day your father came to tell me of Buddy's birth, before anyone suspected he had terrible problems, I met with a good friend who heads one of the largest banks downtown. I set up and funded a special family trust. There is gold bullion resting in a secure vault in that bank in sufficient quantity to fund the charitable works of our family leaders for decades to come. It is sealed with a special key."

"Sealed?"

"Only the male family member who presents the key will ever have access to this account. The bank's chief trust officer holds documents to identify with certainty the bearer of the key and assure rightful ownership. The trustees also have documents describing the rights and duties of ownership of the treasure itself."

"What can the gold be used for?"

"No personal gains or aggrandizement whatsoever, only worthy causes for the betterment of others."

"Uncle, you've left out the most important piece."

"No, dear Harry. I'm not getting dodgy just yet, but you've struck upon the heart of it."

"Where is the key?"

"It is in a safe place: hidden, in fact."

"Hidden? You mean *I* have to find the treasure, sir?"

"Well, you have to find the key. The rest—the bank location, and so on—will all be revealed, most likely, but I'll say no more about that part."

"But, what if I fail? What if I never find the key?"

"Then, like all who came before us, you will be left to your own devices to carry out the terms of the Second Challenge as best you can. The gold will never see the light of day, never do the good it might otherwise do unless you or one of your male descendants can find it. That shame and disappointment will be yours to bear just as the benefice, goodwill, and gratitude of others will be magnified if you succeed. I believe this is a fair opportunity for you to make your special mark on the world, and I wish you well. Nevertheless, whatever the outcome, this is my codicil to the Second Challenge."

◆ ◆ ◆

The morning after his late-night sequester with Uncle Harry he awoke with a severe headache and a sense of dread mixed with excitement. He had expected nothing like this from his uncle. Before his eighteenth birthday he had thought that leaving home to join the army and become a pilot was going to be plenty difficult, demand his full attention. Now he was faced with tasks and challenges for a lifetime. But he couldn't conceive of shirking his family duty, not when confronted by the man who—next to his father—he respected and loved the most. Finally, there was the one irrefutable argument. Gazing at his bleary reflection in the bathroom mirror, Harry rephrased his uncle's "but one choice for this role" summation in starker terms.

"Buddy's not here to take this on. So, who else is there?"

He was sworn to secrecy, so he couldn't discuss any of his deepest concerns with either of the two women in his life who'd meant the most to him growing up, who'd always been there for him: his Maman and his devoted nanny, Bertha. And only later did he learn how his choice of so many rugged paths was the impetus for Bertha's solitary journey. Like Harry, because of Harry, Bertha had decided to undertake a mighty quest of her own.

# PART THREE

**Bertha's Quest**

# Twenty

I hates coming down here. Well, that ain't exactly true. I misses my family—what they is left—but I hates where I gots to get to, to find most of them. Kinda like missing a shoe. Crawling round under the bed or stooping round the back of that spidery closet hardly worth what you come up with, mostwise. This time, they's no choice.

Just fell to me to be on a mission, a spirit quest. Not that I checked it out with Reverend Green at the Tabernacle Baptist Assembly. Don't expects him to cotton to none of my dipping into the Old World beliefs. How he gone to advise me? No man of the church never had to try to cover all the bases. Anyways, I ain't left off with the Lamb of God. I still saying my prayers to Jesus and God Almighty and doing Sunday services when I's time. But this here's severe protection I in search of. Didn't trust no folks in New Orleans to steer me help; needed to go off the beaten track. Just wish it wadn't off in the marshes and will-o-the-wool haunts like Teche Country, where I's raised.

This the third bus I boarded since leaving the city terminal. Creeping through these small towns and transferring bad enough, but it a damned shame what they put us nigras through after we pays good money for a seat. After New Orleans, weren't no "Colored Only" waiting facilities neither—maybe we find a hard bench out back if we's lucky. Don't be no colored and go looking for no inside commode, even no privy out by the birches in Destrehan or Morgan City. Uh-uuh.

Knows to pack my own lunches, too. Sure ain't waiting by some alley window in the rain for a skinny little sassy white man to tell me they all out of the "Colored Only" menu. Leastwise, in New Orleans we have ourselves nearly as many good eating places as the white man. Hardly have to put up with none of that out-back flim-flam if you know how to get round in town. And we all learn that getting round early on, surely do.

These cane fields down along Highway 90 smelling something awful bout now. Hot and humid weather for this time in November, so we gots to have the coach windows open. All the workers be out in the rows with machetes and loading up the wagons with the cut stalks. All them husks and squished cane what fall off the wagons and rotting on the road, along with the sulfur and molasses fumes pouring out the refinery, don't know which stink worse. That sugar harvest is rough work, back-breaking as the rice crop. I knows bout both, and they's big part of why I left this sorry parish.

Joseph Albert kept his promise and married me honest and took me up to the big city. Said if he was going to keep working heavy labor, he was sure as hell going to get paid something for it. Stevedoring paid good and steady. Found us a good rent off of St. Claude. Would have started in on some children if my sweet man wadn't killed in that grain elevator.

Don't know what I would have done if old Mr. Harry and Mr. Elmer hadn't a both knowed Joseph from the docks. They good white folks to work for, just plain good folks. That goodness why I'm down here trying to find me a spirit woman to conjure up protection for young Mr. Harry before he run off and get into big trouble in the wars. Effen Mrs. Julia and Mr. Elmer lose another son—they last one—them poor peoples gonna just up and die theyselves. Then what I gonna do?

That Sister Ophelia what Nanaw, my auntie, sent me to, she call herself a sacrificing, fire-spitting, conjou woman. She said she could take the spells off Mr. Buddy, the most pitiful little wallydraigle that ever come into this world. Later I come to find out she just a root-digger. My grandmere, Hortense, say she the laughingstock of the countryside around Migues, the little bit a shade in the road where I was born. Hortense, she can barely parlay the anglais, but she tell Roulie to tell me that I's wasting my time *and* my money. She say Ophelia nothing but a low-life drunk who only took to her calling after her man threw her out the house. Ignorant thing couldn't conjure up a cold no more than she could take care a her man.

Well, hope the good Lord gots Little Buddy sitting and smiling at his right hand like the Bible say. Maybe He going to give him a chance to do good one time back here on earth before this work is done. Not that the little baby never intended no ill, just too sick to return all the love and stop the tears what got showered on him. I brought along a lock of hair I been saving from that dead infant as well as a sprig from Mr. Harry's fine head. Been collecting personal objects from most of the family members what might be used in the conjuring too: old button from Mr. Elmer's pajamas, watch fob from his brother, Mr. Harry, stuff like that. I wants the best spirit person in these parts to work some mighty powerful spell to ward off harm and hurt and evil from the one remaining son. No shoo-shoos this time around. Redemption, here we come.

◆　◆　◆

"New Iberia! Gateway to Evangeline country, home of 'Shadows on the Teche.' Any passengers continuing on to Lafayette or Crowley need to be back in your seats by 2:45 p.m.; that's twenty minutes from now. Thank you and have a nice visit."

No more backseats for me, Mr. Driver. A bit a walking going to feel good for this middle-aged nigra woman who ain't been back this way in four years. Now where exactly this coach drop me? Here come a kindly looking old soul.

"S'cuse me, mister. Can you point me over to the Avery Island road, number 329? Been too long since I been back thisaway, and y'all done moved the bus terminal on me."

"Two blocks over and left and there you are. But you got a long walk to the island."

"Only going a few blocks out of New Iberia today. My granny live on the Lapeyrouse property, and I'm staying the night with her."

"Thought all them Lapeyrouses moved on over to Jeanerette a few years back?"

"Mostly did, but Mr. Robert loved the land and had the money to keep working it, making it go. He and Mrs. Marie kept my granny on after the sharecropping work died out; she been there ever since."

"Well, you from these parts too, ain'tcha?"

"My momma's folks from down-road aways, at Migues; that's where I was born and raised. Can't rightly say I miss it. Tough times living out in that patch a dirt, for us anyways."

"I hear you. Maybe things will have a different look for you this time. *Bienvenue* and pass a good time with your *grandmere. Au revoir!*"

Burnt-up little raisin of a man tip his hat and smile and walk on. Folks still civil to other humans out here in the country—coonass, nigra, injun, some white folk too. Here we all mixed-up in the poor pot together with the nuns and the Jesuits looking on.

Mmm-mmh! Not much changed out this road from the look of things. Not much of that oil business or Cajun big shots musta made it over here from Morgan City and Lafayette quite yet. Rusty wagon wheels, mangy dogs, shot-out sign posts don't look too prosperous to me. Never could figure why Mr. Robert Lapeyrouse kept with cane and rice farming after him and his brothers lease that Little Bayou tract of marsh to Standard Oil.

Here they place now; damn sight better looking than the rest of the land I come on so far. See he gone over to soybeans, too. That man no fool; good Christian but a better farmer.

◆　◆　◆

"Roulie, that you, girl? Let me get a good look at you. You know'd I was making the trip over, didn't you?"

"Why, yes ma'am. Mrs. Marie told me last week. How you doing, Bertha? Hortense be mighty glad to see you. Well, don't know bout seeing you exactly. Her eyes gone all milky; doc says it's the cataract not the leprosy what doing it. Whatever, she gone to be happy you here."

"Gone to need your help with the *patois*, Roulie. Only way she and I can truly talk is through you. My Cajun French ain't got no better since I moved, that's for sure."

"You know I be glads to. I loves your granny like she mine, and we ain't even blood."

"Why, Bertha! I thought I heard voices. Come give me a hug. You want coffee? Roulie just made some gingerbread. I know you can smell it cooling. I did and was just coming down to get a corner piece. Come sit and have some. How was your trip? Long bus ride, huh? You were mighty mysterious with me on the telephone last week. What are you doing here in Iberia Parish?"

I loves that Mrs. Lapeyrouse, but that woman can ask a dozen questions before you blink. I forgets half of them before I can sit. No matter; she sweet as pie. Imagine eating together with a white woman in her own kitchen in New Orleans?

"Why thank you, ma'am; thank you kindly. You know I been neglectful of my grandmere since my husband killed. Back on my feet now, have been for a few years. Long past time to get back down this way. My granny Hortense, she my only kin from my daddy's side left round here. My brothers run off soon as Momma died. Didn't want nothing to do with no leper woman; told her she gone to have to go up to Carville, to the colony. If it wadn't for you and Mr. Robert, don't know what she would have done. You a blessing inside a miracle for her and me, and that's the God's truth."

"Bertha, hush, you've already thanked us past the point of embarrassment. We had that old cabin sitting empty on the property since we bought all the sharecroppers out in '29. I am so happy she is here with us. Robert looks in on Hortense every morning and evening. She raised him and all his wild brothers, you know; those Lapeyrouse men are forever in her debt. And Roulie here is just plain happy to spoil and fatten her with home cooking."

"I expects I better be getting out there to see her. If you can spare Roulie for a spell this evening, they some things I gots to talk over with my granny before too long. Thank you so much for your kindness, Mrs. Marie. I'll be back up to the house to see Mr. Robert when he get in, before y'all starts your supper."

"He had to go over to Crowley to pick up a new part for the harvester. Guess you noticed we've moved on to soybeans now. He'll be back before dark. You go get settled in and come get Roulie whenever you want. Welcome home, Bertha."

◆　◆　◆

"*Aloo, Grandmere? Grandmere, say moi, Bertha. Comment ça va, Grandmere? . . . Oui, oui, moi aussi, Cherie. J'ai fait trop* long bus trip—*voyage en coach moteur—de la Nouvelle Orléans. Tu etais la belle vision, le meilleur, pour les yeux et l'âme. Je t'aime très, très bo-coop.*"

And that is bout the most Cajun I done spoke in about ten years, bout the most I can speak, ground-up as it is. It do come back after some days a little better, but it ain't gone to serve me what I gots to say. Thank goodness little Roulie round.

Hortense look chubby, that's a fact, but that leprosy keep eating at her small parts. Hardly any fingers left, no toes at all. Used to be a pretty woman, too—I's seen old tintypes—before her face turned to cobblestone and her body all bent over. Still, feels almighty good to hug and kiss and hold on that woman, my living ancestor, my flesh and blood.

So dark in this cabin, can't see much of anything. Guess there don't be much need for daylight or candles if you mostly blind. Poor, dear thing. Still seem sharp in the head though. Thanks for that; gone to need her help to guide my way.

## *Twenty One*

**W**ell, well, finally getting moving on this conjuring project of mine. Bout thought I'd have to go home empty-handed; still don't have no clear idea what gonna lay down this road. Not sure what part of this be the devil's business and what part the good Lord might smile on. Fact is, I not too keen on finding out. But, here I sits in this rattly pickup with a man named Amos, who I don't know from Cain or Abel, heading to meet a Mambo, what they call a dyed-in-the-wool, pure-bred vodou priestess.

That first evening when I sat down with granny Hortense and come to tell her about Mr. Harry needing protection, seemed like Roulie wasn't doing me justice, not rendering my story across true to the Cajun side. Then I thinking maybe Hortense just not too interested in helping some little white boy she don't know, whose family not even from these parts. But my problem deeper than that. It finally come to light after I explained that Harry be the brother of the little one who died, and then I began complaining about how last time Nanaw sent me to an impostor, no-good conjuring woman when all I was trying to do is relieve some suffering off that poor baby, Buddy.

That when I learned these things can't be had like going

over to the corner store and picking up a pound of beans. Seems like the spiritual community round here wasn't accepting of me, so they threw no-count Ophelia my way. Hortense said way back, when I in such a hurry to leave out of here with my man, I never showed no interest in honoring the ancestors, walking the spiritual path, showing contrition, or accepting the moral authority of who she called *les mysteries*. These the spirits who also known as the low-ahs. It dawned on me that my granny talking about something more than some carnival, white magic sorcerizing. This the first time I ever hears her mention the word "vodou." I knows I in deep now, for sure.

So, Roulie, she letting me have it now from my granny. Stuck-up young Miss Bertha, she never made no nitiation rights, no sacrifices, and none of what granny call covenants with my own, personal low-ahs. Bertha skedaddled on out of here with the man gone to marry her and never looked back until she needed something later. Come then, folks down here decided Bertha didn't know what she needed and wouldn't know any better anyhow. Truly, I did not know no better until Hortense took pity on me and passed the word that Sister Ophelia just a hussy. Dropping the dime on her still didn't change how my family think of me. Bout now I feeling pretty foolish, and I sees this ain't going good for me or my quest. Right away I bends to my knees and begs forgiveness from my dear, sweet granny and asks if it too late to change my ways so I can help me and help this young man.

I could tell Hortense heart be softening toward me, but she don't promise nothing. She say she tired and want to talk to her low-ahs and sleep on all this. She tell me to leave the cabin and don't come back til I hears her snoring. No moon, no stars out over the soybeans to dream on, so I prays some on Jesus in the wilderness. Covering them bases.

Next morning, Hortense start right in on telling me what she dreamed and what she now need to do. Of course, I don't gets but a little of it, and she won't repeat herself later for Roulie. I pretty sure she gone to get word to some people to see bout seeing bout me. Again, she promise nothing. I all tore up not knowing but spends most of the day washing and combing and braiding up her hair and walking some round the place with the Lapeyrouses.

Before supper, Roulie come pow-wow with Hortense, and then they calls me in for the run-down. Word come back that I gots to have a Kanzo done over me before anything else go down. They explains this the vodou nitiation ceremony, closest thing to a baptism, except ain't no witnesses but your dead ancestors be called in and the priest pass fire and not water across your body. They looks at me then and waiting for me to say something or run out the door, but I swallows hard and nods my head, "Yes ma'am."

They tells me the priest a woman, a Mambo, who live some-where down the marsh on Avery Island. She the very-oldest thing ever because she always been on the island since folks' great-great grandparents remember. She one of the Nago people who got carried here with the first slave ships. She already known as a power person by the people she come across with, and she honored and protected ever since. Her place of living a deep, dark secret kept by three families on the island, but she do her ceremonies in a vodou temple, a peristyle, in a salt dome—a cave of salt—where they going to takes me. Before the Mambo agree to tie a wanga, cast a mighty spell for me, I gots to get swore in.

I trying to be accepting of the path before me, but I knows my eyes bugging out when I asks how I gone to find this spirit person and who I gone to ask for when I gets there. Hortense say that her true name only known by those who already serviteurs and it never spoken. But, if some occasion arise to refer to her out loud, people might whisper the word "Lete." My case, I just needs to keep quiet and do what I's told. Period. What I's told next is to fast from now until a man named Amos come from the island to fetch me tomorrow before sunset.

So, here I is riding in silence with Amos, who look bout a hundred years older than his raggedy truck, thankful that I ain't had to make no walking pilgrimage to meet my ancestors. Driving taking forever. I can't stands the quiet no longer. I takes a sip of water from a calabash Hortense give me for the trip and starts right in.

"Amos, you know I ain't never done any of this vodou before, so I hopes you won't get angry if I talks to you a little. Truth is, I feels alone and scared, but I wants to do what's right. I promised my granny."

He just hold his eyes on the road and don't say nothing, which I take as a sign to keep on.

"If I gone to take part with this priest woman, what language she understand, and how I gone to understand her? I hear tell she not from around here, and I can't speak much Cajun neither."

Not sure what Amos speak or if he even hear, but he finally turn and give me a little bit of a smile. He looking toward me, but he ain't looking at me. His eyes is alight with that far-off stare like I seen get on preachers at a revival.

"Lete gone to speak to you, that a fact. She might never open her lips, but you gone to hear what she have to say. She speak what-all language she need—Spanish, Bayougoula, Colapissa, Houmas, Cadien, what-alls."

"That some relief. You sounds like a good man who look like he been round thisaway for some time. You ever had the need to ask this woman for any power or protection? She ever help you directly?"

"She been helping for more years than I has on me, and I goes back from before the war between the North and South. When I's growing up, my mammy tell me Lete done a Rada ceremony when the first yellow fevers come up Bayou Teche. She put a Gad, a mighty protection, on this Catholic sister from Santo Domingo they called Félicité. That protection keep the fevers off the nun so she able to minister and save half the town of New Iberia and bury the other half. Catholic Church hear about it, and them Jesuits never give Lete or the vodou community no trouble never more, least not round here. City fathers put a statue up in the town square to honor Félicité, but don't nobody who know never say nothing about Lete."

That settle it for me. Yellow fever bout as powerful as bullets from what I knows. Maybe this woman is who I been looking for. Just don't knows if I up to the getting acquainted part.

## Twenty Two

Getting dark, the headlights is on. We pulls into this pitiful narrow track off a gravel road we been bumping on for a while. Can't sees nothing but some white clam shells in the tire ruts and palmettos and giant plantains and creeper vines slashing at the fenders and windows. We stops, and Amos cut the engine. He don't look my way or say no more. Two women wrapped in white gauzy dresses and headscarves comes out of nowhere. They taking me along when I remembers my offerings back in the truck.

"My chicken and my basket, I—"

"They will follow along; you keep quiet and remain with us, Bertha."

How they knows my name? Ain't thinking of asking. Cold bejeezus! We heading to a dock where a pirogue tied. Lord a mercy, I can't swim. They's moccasins and gators and gar fish waiting in that black water to swallow me up.

"We all getting in that tippy little thing?"

"This is not a joking time, Bertha. Just be quiet and trust us. We are your attendants for the Kanzo and will see no harm comes to you."

Somehow we all transported dry across the water and clambers out on a wood walk between the cypress knees that lead to a overgrowed hummock. How these women seeing they way? Some of these folks worship snakes, but them snakes don't respect me. Sheddup thinking, Bertha. Stay in the middle, girl, and stay close.

We crosses what I think a land bridge and hits on this thatch hut. Aways off, they's a piddly light coming from a parting of the swamp thickets. My ears playing tricks, or is they angels singing in the underbrush?

Inside the hut the women very careful washing my head and saying words over me. Then they dressing me in the same thing they wearing, only I gots a big green sash tied across my bosom and circled round my waist. They gives me a cup of milk with sugar to drink.

"We are going to leave you for some time but do not waste this time, Bertha. You are to reflect upon your zansyet yo, your ancestors. You come into this world standing upon their shoulders. They love you and will help guide you on a spiritual path and contribute to your well-being if you honor and tend to them. Name them and talk to them and ask them to join you in your Kanzo."

I trying hard to remember the first name of my daddy's great-grandfather, struggling to pay no mind to the shouts and drums and other sounds that coming somewhere yonder by the light after the chanting stop. My eyes closed cause I kinda praying, and as I opens up, they is my two helpers and three others squinched into my hut. How they get back in?

"Bertha, stand and follow me and Sister Martelle out of here. The others will follow us and ask for blessings on our path. There is no turning back now. Everything given you tonight is a sacred gift. Come, child."

We walking toward that slit of light and my heart flopping round like a dying perch. It hot and soupy for November, but I sweating and shaking with chills at the same time. I gots to scrunch low as Martelle part the vines and rosso weed. We is ducking into the salt cave. May God and my ancestors help me.

"Mind your step, Bertha, we are going down a steep way. There are a few candles set out but take great care. Try to even your breathing; otherwise, you will just become dizzy. Be brave and continue to think on your ancestors."

We sure bout in the first circle of the nether regions by now. Except there ain't no bubbling brimstone but more and more gray-white veins of rocky stuff; must be the salt showing up. I looking down on the trail at the chunks that been all ground down and bout run into Sister Martelle. As she stop, I gets my first look at the most wondrous spectacle I ever did see.

I now looking into a cathedral underground, filled with thirty or forty worshippers dressed in white outfits and head scarves. They flocked around in a half-circle and facing toward an altar that stand twice as tall as a house. The altar be draped in crimson cloth that shine and look fine, like silk. They is more than a hundred lit candles of all shapes and sizes along with different kinds of wild game and cooked food, tobacco pipes, whiskey, water jugs and mirrors, and so many other things I cannot tell them apart. Behind the candles, a beautiful painting of Mary, Mother of Jesus, be smiling down alongside another picture of some twin saints I most surely do not know. In front of the altar sit a big kettle holding a log fire that burning to beat the band. From the back it don't feel hot, and I still gots the shakes.

Hundred more red candles around the edges of the vault shine they light along the sparkling walls of salt but cannot shed light all the way up. The floor look to me at least wide as three boxcars be long. I can see fifty feet up, but there the darkness swallow everything. Then I hears a voice that I think coming from right in my ear.

"Let us welcome Bertha to our gathering and tell her something about us."

A tall man holding some kind of rattle and staff talking up front by the altar. His lips moving, but he don't sound far away. He inside my head. The shadows of the shapes on the salt walls be swaying with the flickring candles and the firelight. Sister Martelle, who is standing right close, start talking next, and I bout jumps out my skin.

"We are all descendants of the Nago people, the Nago Nachon. We are all blessed to have the Ogous as our personal lwas. We also revere and welcome into our lives Lemiye, the mother of all Ogous and the mother of the Nago Nachon, and Gram Batala, the rider of the white horse, the father of the Nago Nachon. Bertha, your grandmother, Hortense, is one of us, and tonight your Kanzo will begin your journey among us as well."

Then the other woman who first step out with me take my hand and lead me to the front, closer to the fire. Now I up front, I sees a little table with a rum bottle and a three-foot machete laying on top. The woman hear me catch my breath and continue where Martelle leave off.

"All of us here are serviteurs, those who practice the spiritual arts. Most are priests with special powers and many lwas. Those who consult us call us Houngan if a man or Mambo if a woman. There is one among us who is known in the world as Lete. Our Nago word for her you cannot know at this time, but it means The Source, or more exactly, The Mother Vine. She has been among us for as long as there has been a Nago Nachon.

"Your beloved grandmother performed your divination while you were together in her home. She determined that you were ready to join the serviteurs and most suitable for Hounsi Kanzo. She asked that Lete perform this and be your lifetime adviser. This is a singular honor. Hortense is favored among the Mambo, and thusly shall you be. Lete is the only Mambo who can perform all of the remaining steps in your Kanzo in one evening. Without her and her lwas' love and protection, mortals would die in such a dangerous undertaking. There are many rigorous steps. After the trial of fire, you will enter a swoon and not awaken until after your bapten, your vodou baptism ceremony. You will find yourself again in the djevo, the seclusion hut where we performed the Leve Tet and you were first mounted by your Lwa Met Tet. Don't look so surprised, some people are only vaguely aware of this visitation. Osanj, one of the Ogun, chose you and mounted very gently. He made your heart race and gave you the shivers."

That woman smile when she say that, like she know this spirit firsthand. Maybe she do. While she speaking, about a dozen priests starts walking, then dancing slow round a tall pole by the left side of the big altar. Everybody humming a hymn-like tune, some lowing like cattle, others chiming in with sweet, high-up sounds like a choir. Then the tall man begin shaking and stamping his rattle on the ground, and the pace pick up some—dancers and the choir.

My two escorts joins the choir, and I left up front with the big man who rattling over by the dancers. They's movement from round back of the altar, and a dark shadow pass across my face. I bout falls down—only some hands I can't see steady my shoulders and matter of fact, hold me up. Another priest lady making her way to the center of the altar, between me and the fire pot, only she ain't dressed like the others.

She like a high-society lady going to a fancy-dress ball. She have her a long, drapey gown of the same red silk as the altar. Her hair is jet black and twisted in a twirl and held up with gold wire and pearls. Her skin is light, like what they call high-yella, and her lips and cheeks are streaked with crimson. Her arms are bare and circled up top by gold snakes with ruby-red eyes. She barefoot and carrying a big flaming torch in her left hand and a silver machete in her right. Who this one be? Can't be no three-hundred-year-old Lete. This woman ain't a day over twenty-five, and she a beauty!

Well, well. She definitely the one in charge, whatever her name. Everybody stop everything and bow when she bow. She put down her torch and weapon and hold up a tobacco pipe and a handful of corn.

"Papa Legeba, we beseech you to open your doorway once again and let us visit with you and les mysteries. Open our minds and our hearts to your loved ones, as we do with our own. Help our new serviteur to learn her obligations along the Gran Chemin and comprehend the beauty of your creation."

Must be them flickring candles because I hears her speaking, but I don't sees her mouth move. She busy at the altar and don't pay me no mind, but I feeling like somebody drilling two holes in the top of my skull. Glad them invisible hands is still propping me up.

The dozen or so who been dancing, they runs behind the altar, and each get a drum and fill that dome with pounding thunder. Most of these drummers big, strong priests who playing with they hands, but they also two women who hitting little drums with curved sticks. They all attacking like they beating a war. The choir be whooping it up and hopping round the pole now.

The woman in red put down her gifts to Papa Legeba and take a swig of the rum. She take another one and spit it into the fire where it explode into flame. The drums going faster and the choir jumping. She walk over to me.

"Take this, Bertha, drink to your ancestors and your lwas. Toast to Papillon, the Ogun Feray; he is my Papa Ogou and will be yours after tonight. The planet Mars, the color red, the sacred blood, and the element fire will bond you together with him. They will be your refuge of power and dominion when the world closes in. They will be your platform of love and joy when others need you. Drink to Orisha Wago. All praise his name!"

The rum bout choke me, but I gets a teensy swallow down, hard. I ain't a drinker, and I ain't never drink straight from a bottle. Now I worried. Only thing I done had in my stomach since yesterday is some sugar-milk. This going to be some ceremony.

Some of the priests reading my mind because two of them now bringing me a tray full of sweet meats, hot yams, and rice. Lete back up at the altar and start fooling with a bottle and some contraption with forks sticking in a cork. She start that cork-and-forks machine spinning on top the bottle, and it ain't slowing down, and it ain't falling off, just going steady. Got to be spirit hands helping with this work.

One priest crushing leaves; one priest making a whip of palm fronds. Now two of them leans me back on a low part of the altar and opens my garments down past my waist. Nothing embarrassing me; seem natural as a baby.

The palm whipping start, but I ain't hurting. I just watching me from above, like in a dream. Ain't nobody around me, but I feels some hands touching me like my husband Joseph, soft and tender like. I hears a voice like his, but it talking in a strange tongue. Now the hands be working in my soft parts, down inside, just like Joseph know how to treat me. Getting all moist and breathing heavy, and I thrusting and grinding my hips and opening my legs to welcome my man only they's no man, just that voice and them joyful hands.

I don't feels no shame; it all wonderful. I even opens my eyes wide and moaning with pleasure. What passing before my eyes is down a little tunnel now, but still I sees. Lete dropping the flat side of the machete against my breasts, my belly, my womanhood. Slap, slap, slap. Every time she drop it, my pleasure go up a little more. I can't tell Joseph's caresses from them little smacks of the silver sword on my body. But Joseph never drive me wild like this, and the voice keep keeping on in my head. It telling me to open up and give myself to the spirits. I breathing so hard now I gasping. I writhing on the altar and things flying off, and I don't mind at all.

The sword gone and they's fire sticks rubbing over me. Flames ain't burning but just prickling, electric sparks jumping all over my skin. Eyes open, just the light, just the light. Mouth breathing in life, tasting the air rush in, rush out, in. Fire inside, in me, in me, in me, in me. Oh, please, oh . . . . Sparks everywhere: no me, no not me . . . . Oh!

# Twenty Three

"**O**y, Papa Legeba, hail to thee! Open your doorway tonight. Send all the great lwas to the aid of your serviteur, Mambo Parangou. We are blind and helpless without your kindness and blessings, your great powers. We are but dust without you.

"Welcome, Danbala Wedo, Sky Father. Welcome, Erzulie Freda, mistress of the Ogoun, Agwe, and Danbala. Welcome, Ogou Feray, ruler over war and battle, fierce master of the machete. Welcome, Ogou Sen Jak, protector from cannonballs and gunshots.

"Welcome, the Great Magician, Simbi Makaya to this Petro. Erzulie, give me vision to know the ancestors of these two children. Ogou Sen Jak, use my hands and breath to tie the wanga to protect the one who remains on earth from harm in battle and in war. Papa Ogou, give him strength to fight and courage to love. Bring him joy in his victories and compassion for his enemies throughout his life. Simbi Makaya, help us take the blood of this animal to seal the wanga.

"Take this hair I hold, one child's in my left hand and one in my right, to help me hear from their ancestors and know who among them will stand for the living.

"Wait? I . . . await. Yes. Welcome, Sacred Twins, welcome to our Petro, Holy Marassa. I did not prepare offerings; I am not worthy of your presence, Two-in-One. Blessings upon you.

"Yes, I feel it now, with your help. Of course, the hair is the same yet different. I understand; like you: two bodies, one soul. The Gede Lwa has sent the little one back to earth to honor the immense love of his living family. But his presence also clouds the life of his brother. Their names? Yes, the infant Elmer has returned as his brother, called Harry. Harry is honored and most blessed by the spirits but remains confused among the living. The special blessing of the Marassa will keep him forever young at heart and capricious and help confer both singularity and unity in his life. May he experience peace with his brother and close their shared circle of goodness and love—perhaps at death—perhaps before.

"The sun is coming soon. As I tie this wanga for this blessed brother, Harry McChesney, let us sing in honor of our lwas as we praise the arrival of the bright eye of the sky."

# Twenty Four

**H**ere we goes. Gone to be a long bus ride back. Fine. I accepting of that now, like some other things I accepting of since my Kanzo. Traveling give me time to reflect on what all done happened since I left out of Amos's truck.

When I finally wake up in the thatch hut, what they call the jay-vo, two nights done passed since I complete my ceremony. The two who first tended to me and washed my hair for the Leve Tet, Hounsi Martelle and Mambo Angelique, they watching over me steadfast as shepherd ladies. Better than shepherds. They gives me water and little tastes of sweet things now and then, keeps me clean and safe, and lets me sleep again. That nitiation take a lot out my body first off but put a lot of good things into my mind and spirit.

I don't know how Mambo Parangou, who I supposed to refer to as Lete, done it, but she placed in me the know-how to make a altar for my ancestors and one for my own special spirits, my low-ahs. She taught me songs of praise for my low-ahs in what Martelle say is a patois from the old time. Most important, she give me back a life with my granny who is my best living ancestor and who love me as much as I loves her.

Before I leaved the island, Lete also find time to tie the wanga for Mr. Harry—a whole nother ceremony that she do by her lonesome, except for the army of spirits she call in for the heavy lifting. Lete meet with me after, and this time she talking like regular folks, and such a sweet voice, too. Not that goblin-y sound she making in the cave. She say they was a surprise guest, guests be more like it, them twins that was in that painting on the big altar in the temple. Them low-ahs called the Marassa, and they be twin bodies but they share one soul. She say they come to celebrate at the Petro after she broke out them two locks of hair I give her because the hair also from two different bodies that share one soul. According to this highest and mighty of the Mambos, "Harry is his own living ancestor."

Well, Bertha ain't a Mambo and likely ain't never gone to be. I not wise enough to understand how that soul-sharing work or what exactly it mean in this world. I just getting the hang of talking to my own private spirits and such. The Marassa is way beyond my ken. Before she hand me the bag of magic she tie up for Mr. Harry, she remind me he a special case who got powerful magic all his own. Even so, the Marassa done put extra mojo in that talisman that will get him safe through the war and through a long life with many blessings. The last thing she say is don't try to explain the Marassa or any of what I been through to Mr. Harry or anybody who ain't on the path. He gone to find out how he and Buddy intertwined in the by-and-by.

If that good enough for my most-exalted, personal Mambo guardian, it plenty good enough for Hounsi Bertha. Me and Mr. Harry both gone to get a lot more good out of life than we ever think possible. Mine already begun.

# PART FOUR

## Leaving and Parting

# Twenty Five

**H**arry had taken more time at the cemetery than he'd planned. It had happened before. A piece of the day would just get away from him, side-slipping by before he knew it. This was not a happy development. As he slid onto the driver's seat he made a pre-birthday resolution to work harder to stay focused, stay mindful and productive. It was past five o'clock on Friday, August 26th, when he switched on the car radio.

The calm, clear weather was not reassuring, and the news on the radio was unsettled and unsettling. Unlike the dithering public officials in Metro New Orleans, local savants were coming on the media, urging specific actions to take ahead of the threatening storm named Katrina.

On the drive home he listened to an ancient, iconic meteorologist who had volunteered himself out of retirement to deliver a stark message, to try to impress upon the ignorant, the amnestic, and the usual assortment of cabbage heads in the radio audience just how serious the situation could become within hours.

**An Atlantic hurricane or tropical cyclone is a huge low pressure rotation that is driven by immense heat energy—a giant suction**

machine that pulls ever more moisture and heat and power into its core. The growing storm has a tremendous reach as it sucks the surrounding matter and energy into its deadly heart. Moisture and heat are drawn toward it and away from the coastal regions a thousand miles distant. Until the compressed violence of winds, storm surge, and torrential rains descends upon an unfortunate target, the calm before the storm is usually cloudless and fairly pleasant. Do not be fooled by this quiet period. It does not last for more than twenty-four hours, and the clock is already ticking. Use this time to secure your possessions and prepare to leave. Those in the coastal parishes should get out now.

◆ ◆ ◆

Arriving home, Harry called his oldest daughter about the change in birthday plans. Libby also quizzed him about the latest on the storm.

"I've lost track. What's this one called?"

"Katrina. It's still hundreds of miles from this part of the Gulf Coast but will regain strength now that it's back over water."

"So, what do the weather wizards say?"

"It's too early; the computer models predicting landfall are all over the map. We'll know more by noon tomorrow."

"Well, you'd better make a beeline here if New Orleans is anywhere near the bull's-eye."

"No problem, sweetie. We'll talk again tomorrow."

"Good night, Dad, I love you."

He wasn't hungry, so he mounted his two-toned Murray cruiser to tour the neighborhood. He never ignored hurricanes in the Gulf of Mexico. They were all a potential threat, but he was still uncertain what to make of this Katrina. He was curious to see what the neighbors were up to this Friday: who among them was making early preparations to evacuate and who was breaking out the steaks and cold drinks for just another summer evening in the Big Easy.

The drone of the fat bike tires along the pavement was soothing. Harry liked to ride bikes even more than walking, always had. He let his mind drift as he fell into a lazy pace. The streets and yards were unusually quiet, not much of any activity along his route. Many of the homes and driveways had been empty for weeks because of family vacations and the proliferation of second homes. Lately it seemed to Harry that banks were giving away home mortgages instead of toasters. He was glad to be done with mortgages.

He had bought his lot on Bellaire Drive from Latter Realty shortly after the old Lakewood Country Club closed its doors, almost as soon as the property got rezoned for residences. He built a fine, two-story brick home on the site in 1964 after he started work for Boeing at the NASA facility in Michoud. He was proud of his role as a project engineer for the Saturn booster rockets, and he was proud of his new home.

Harry never wanted the biggest or the most luxurious house on his new street. With guidance from his uncle years before he had developed a practical streak, but he appreciated style as well as good value. He chose New Orleans hard-tan brick for its link with local tradition as much as its durability. He found a young architect who could carry out an attractive adaptation of Southern Colonial with tall columns and a prominent gabled roof. When completed, he thought it splendidly modern with the warmth and the feel of a fine, old home. By now, the splendidly modern features and fixtures had devolved into decidedly old and funky but still reliable. Over the years he'd maintained the roof and kept the trim gleaming white and the traditional black-green shutters in good working condition. Until very recently, he saw to most of that himself—the McChesney way.

After he put his bike back in the garage, he showered, ate some leftovers, and waited for the ten o'clock evening news. He shouldn't have bothered. He'd learned long ago that the more government honchos and community bigwigs there were standing around a TV podium, the less there was that got decided and communicated.

He left his new Netflix mailer unopened and went early to bed. He would wait for the morning bulletin from the National Hurricane Center before deciding about closing up the place and leaving for his daughter's home in Shreveport. As he'd aged, he'd grown downright stubborn when faced with the prospect of any sort of leave-taking. He liked his routines and his familiar haunts. The stress of another departure began welling up within and flooded his dreams with partings of the past.

# Twenty Six

In the fall of 1942, Harry's deliberate leave-taking was just beginning. Dr. Archinaud had started his mother on some new medication, but it didn't prevent her withdrawing from all conversations about his impending military duty. And it wasn't just about Harry after a while; she began to cringe whenever the news of the world came on the radio.

Harry focused much of his remaining time on his sister, Penny. She had remained cool toward him but less openly resentful. He thought that she had begun to take notice of his more serious behavior, and she already knew he planned to enlist, that he would soon be going off to war. Most importantly, she had become engaged to marry a naval medical officer. His name was Walker Humphreys, and Harry really liked him. He was sincerely happy for his big sis but shocked by her announcement. How could she be so intent so suddenly upon one man when she hadn't been actively dating anyone a few months before?

Nevertheless, he was hoping that her latest declaration of independence from the family and new course in life would help relieve some tension, ease some of the burdens of the past between them. He needed to apologize to her for all of his stupid behavior. Then he wanted to learn more about what it was like for her growing up with a desperately sick little brother—to hear it from her. Buddy's life and death wounded the family survivors and cast them together on a dark ocean in one leaky raft. Her feelings about Buddy and her feelings about him were all part of that early history. He wanted to know more. He was eager to employ some of that compassion that Uncle Harry had talked about. He'd start the ball rolling by buying her lunch.

◆   ◆   ◆

"**O**ver here, Harry." Penny waved him over to her table along the wall. Saturday shoppers were packing the restaurant in the D.H. Holmes department store.

"Hey, Sis!" They hugged briefly, and Penny sat back down while Harry fiddled with his tie. "Thanks for coming. You've been so busy at the law office lately; I haven't had a chance to celebrate your engagement with you. I'm glad you could get away today."

"Please, Harry, sit down and relax. I'm glad I could be here too; I have been working hard."

"Yeah. Thanks. Good." A light sweat broke out under his sport coat. "Do you want a glass of wine with lunch?"

"No, my mind is already pretty muddled. Since Walker and I decided to tie the knot, it's been hard to concentrate on other things."

"Well, I've only met him a couple of times, as you know, but I think he is a fine guy—handsome as the devil too. I am really and truly very happy for you."

Penny blushed demurely but then changed the subject.

"You're looking sharp today. Is that a new jacket and tie?"

"Last year's jackets don't fit me anymore; tie belongs to Pa. I'm not crazy about bow ties, but I wanted the gumbo today. You know how I love to bring home leftovers on my clothes."

"Dad's tie is probably safe; more room on your shirt today, dear brother. Wave that waitress over to our table."

While they waited for their orders, Harry admired his sister. She was wearing a pale-blue linen suit with a gathered jacket and sharp shoulder padding. The color looked smashing against her rich auburn hair. The lines of the jacket accentuated her slender waist and pleasing frontal curves. Her face was slightly large but not noticeably out of proportion to her frame. Stylish finger waves swept up and back to reveal a high forehead and smallish ears. She wore a new Rita Hayworth red lipstick. Her only jewelry was an everyday wrist watch and a monogrammed gold pendant around her neck.

"Is that little bijou around your neck something new?"

"Engagement present. Uncle Harry and Aunt May gave it to me when I was over there for dinner last night. They are so nice to me, to both of us, really."

He thought briefly about the sterner side of his uncle and all the time they'd been spending together recently in his library. *If only she knew.*

"Harry is a peach alright."

"Yes, but he's much, much more than that to us. He and May *and* Maman have always been there for our family. Generous and uplifting in ways that money can't buy."

Was this his chance to start the conversation he'd come to have? *Better jump headfirst.*

"Harry and May lit up the room for you on some pretty dark days. And I was pretty much the opposite for you—my wild, inconsiderate behavior made your life miserable. In fact, made our whole family miserable."

Penny didn't flinch or turn away, so Harry pressed on and leaned in over the table.

"Look, Sis, I'm happy I could have you all to myself today. I wanted to congratulate you on your engagement, but what I really need to, *want to do* is apologize—*sincerely apologize*—to you for all of my stupidity over the years. I've hurt you and Ma and Pa, and I'm deeply sorry. They've heard my confession, but you need to hear it too. I can't change what's happened already, but I can promise to do a lot better in the future."

Harry felt like maybe he was getting through. Penny started nodding her head slowly as he spoke. He paused for a few moments while they just looked at each other. Then, to his immense joy and relief, she said, "Apologies accepted, but only if you accept mine in turn and listen to what I have to say on the subject."

Harry almost dropped his fork. "You bet."

"Harry, I know you and I have fought and butted heads almost nonstop while we were both under the same roof. You resented me for the babysitter, bossy-sister, tattletale role that I mostly relished. Recently, I've thought a lot," she paused, "even prayed some about why I resented you and your dopey behavior growing up. I think I finally understand why I took it all so personally. It was mainly about love and guilt and fear of losing you."

"I was hoping we might have this talk, what it was like for you. I want to understand it—understand you better."

Penny forged ahead and never batted an eye; she seemed as eager and ready for this conversation as Harry.

"Life and death swept over me like huge breaking waves. After Buddy was born, God never appeared good or caring or loving. Of course, He never appeared at all, ever—what did I know? He seemed hateful at worst, off-duty at best. Little Buddy was the victim of a terrible mistake or something unspeakably worse: evil. That was how Julia felt about it and still does, even though she won't talk about it anymore. Bertha, usually my rock in a rising flood, retreated to her magic spells and some conjuring woman to shield herself and the baby from the evil. God bless her for trying to help. But Mom felt cast adrift without hope for her little boy or her religion. I got infected with that sickness too. It was hard to escape. Only Dad kept the candle of love burning in the household by showering his devotion on that pitifully sick little infant, his Buddy."

"You were convinced that God was going to come snatch you, weren't you, while everybody else was fearing mainly for Buddy?"

"Half-terrified, half-hoping it would happen. You see, I became the Forgotten Child. Oh, every once in a while, Maman or Dad—even Mom—would make a fuss over me: my third birthday party, an Easter-egg hunt, something like that. Then, the next time Buddy had another blue spell or those horrible seizures, I'd be dropped like a wet kitten while everyone ran to his aid. Even on days when Buddy was not beset with the demons, Mom and Bertha were fussing at one another about putting his medicine away wrong, having too much or not enough clothes on his little body, on and on. Nothing was ever just quiet and peaceful. Dad would come home and not ever try to act as judge or jury like the others wanted. He would give me a few minutes of his time and then go walk the block with his son or stay in Buddy's room until dinner."

"So, you were the other McChesney kid God had abandoned, feeling as neglected on earth as you were in heaven, hoping to have some terrible illness and afraid at the same time that your wish might come true."

"My whole life felt porous, like a cold wind was always blowing through it. I began to wish Buddy would 'go away.' Those were the words I used when I talked about it to myself. I had heard the grown-ups talking, mostly in whispers, about death and dying, but I didn't really know what that meant: mortality, the finality. However I understood it, that was when the other intense feeling overtook me: unalloyed guilt."

"Yeah, I've been wrestling with a bunch of that ever since I found out I had a dead brother."

"Together, Mom and Dad and I were all wound up in this unwanted battle of emotions and allegiances that was only partly resolved with Buddy's death. They loved Buddy and were consumed by his suffering. They had little left for me or each other. They neglected me in spite of their love. They felt guilty about their neglect and about bringing an imperfect child into the world. A famous doctor told them that nothing they had done during the pregnancy caused Buddy's heart problem, but Mom, for sure, never forgave herself. Truly sad."

"Mmmf . . . ." Harry couldn't speak. Penny's narrative brought him into her life, into all this grief, as he'd never before been.

"I, however, was secretly thrilled to be the center of attention in the family with Buddy gone. Then, when I was seven years old, along came baby Harry. When it was too obvious to conceal Julia's condition any longer, she had Maman have a sit-down with me to break the news."

"Mom's never been good breaking the news or getting it."

"Your birth had everyone holding their breath. Julia started praying again and made Elmer a regular at Sunday services. Bertha started doing her happy dances but 'covering her bases,' as she called it. She broke out her little sacks of foul-smelling powders, twisted sticks, and bird feathers and hid them again all over the house. When the doctors pronounced you wholly healthy and you had a few months under your diaper, the celebration of Harry went into high gear.

"Your sister, however, started to withdraw into a familiar state of convoluted misery. I saw life as a kind of double jeopardy. I thought I had already paid for whatever sins God had thought it meet to visit on me and my family. Now I was going to pay a second time for having a second brother—one who was healthy but who was still going to be the center of attention and worry. A) You were a male and thus, could carry the family name forward—whoopee! B) You showed an early tendency to adventure and a blithe indifference to danger that had the entire family convinced that you were headed to an untimely end. All the old parental worries resurfaced, hand-in-hand with my reborn guilt about fearing/hoping for your premature exit. Love and resentment, all part and parcel of the same emotion."

"Wow, I get it. The Forgotten One has to reckon with me, the Second Chance."

"My fear for you and my guilt made me very angry at times. I said some hateful things, even struck you and spit on you. Please forgive me for all that. I love you very, very much, and I no longer wish you dead, not even a little bit." With that, she smiled for the first time that day.

Harry thought he was going to like living up to this part of his challenges.

## Twenty Seven

**W**hile Harry slept and dreamt of his sister, Katrina took a decidedly northwestward turn. By the time he arose to hazy skies, the storm had built to a Category Three intensity with steady winds of 115 miles per hour. Plaquemines and St. Charles Parish officials to the south and west of New Orleans ordered a mandatory evacuation at nine a.m. At ten a.m. on Saturday, August 27th, the National Hurricane Center in Miami placed Metro New Orleans on a hurricane watch status, the second-order level of risk. A watch meant that the likelihood of hurricane conditions were officially described as "favorable" in the area within the next twenty-four to thirty-six hours. Katrina was moving across the water at seven miles per hour with plenty of time for it to get bigger and nastier before making landfall.

Harry was going to go through his usual hurricane watch checklist, but he wasn't going to bust his balls doing it. He wasn't as energetic as he used to be, and he'd been through so many dry runs, false alarms, before. He put off calling Libby again; he didn't relish a six- or seven-hour drive to Shreveport on a jam-packed interstate.

*At least I got the old Ford filled with gas yesterday.*

His neighbors were not messing around. By noon, many of them had pulled out of their driveways, and others had made calls to local handymen and yard workers. Pickup trucks and crews were bringing in sheets of plywood to cover windows and moving outdoor furniture and other stuff into storage.

Harry puttered around but gradually made progress moving his own fly-away objects into the garage, getting some clothing and toilet articles into his travel bag, occasionally stopping to watch the incessant yapping from the cable news feeds. He wasn't feeling anxious about the storm, just going through his to-do lists and remembering the rest of his farewells before his days in the Army Air Corps.

*Now that was a time when the* whole world *was in upheaval, not just a couple of forlorn Southern states, patches of swamp and beach along the Gulf.*

# Twenty Eight

"Mr. Harry, why you want this big old bag to pack? You ain't gone to need much of them civilian duds in the army."

"Right you are, Bertha. Just leave me that little satchel."

"Well, your big day finally coming. No more chasing all them young girls. You gone to be buckling under in the army real soon."

"Buckling under? Soaring through the skies, learning to fly, Bertha. I'm headed to pilot training. I'll bet we don't do much marching where I'm going."

"Hmmph. I hearing all about them airplanes from your momma. She is *terrified* of what gone to happen to you even before you gets to the fighting. She say she never going up in one of them things and can't believe you actually choosing to put yourself in the sky where most anything can happen."

"Like I told her, there are lots of ways to serve my country, Bertha. All of them are dangerous in wartime. I am convinced this is the best choice for me."

"Well this probably a good a time as any to remind you how much I cares about you and wants you back safe and sound when all the fighting's done."

"Bertha, you are like my second mother—closer than that, really. I share things with you that I would never tell Ma. I know you work for us because you need to work, but you are still part of my family. I have always felt that way."

"You a handful, but you the best thing what happened to this family. And yes, you is like the son I never had with Joseph. Did a lot of thinking about that and wanted to do what any mother would want to do, keep some protection over the ones she love. You remember when I went down to see my granny in New Iberia right after you enlisted in the fall?"

"Sure do, but you never said much about your trip afterwards."

"That a life-changing trip for me Mr. Harry, change for the good. Someday, maybe, we'll talk more about it. But one of the reasons I done went was to get hold of protection for you, a young man determined to throw his self in harm's way."

"You know I have to go, Bertha, one way or another. I want to go and fight. That's not just me but millions of us."

"I knows; I knows. I accepting of that, but I wanted to try to do more for you than just prayer and a 'God bless, stay safe.' With the help and blessing of my sweet granny I found a very, very powerful person among my peoples who tied—I means to say—who made me a mighty talisman to ward off harm and death in the wars. This ain't some trinket what you picks up in the five-and-dime or down in the gypsy market by the river. This crafted specially for you by a woman priest who know these things from our ancestors on how to get the spirits' protection. You can't buy these blessings, Mr. Harry. The spirits must give them freely and tell the priest how to tie them together the best way for you. I been carrying it with me ever since I come back before Thanksgiving. Guess I been hoping this day don't never come. Here it is, January 1943, bout time I hands it over to you. Hold one second, let me fetch it out my purse."

"Bertha, I don't know how to thank you. I can tell from what you say that you thought a lot about this and went to a lot of trouble to get it for me."

"You might say that, but trouble ain't what it was. I told you: the whole time with my peoples be a true eye-opener for me. I only hopes as much good come to you from it as what I has received."

"What do I need to do with this little bag, Bertha? Do I wear it? Can it get wet?"

"Best to keeps it as close to you as you can all the time. Most folks wears it round they neck, some round they wrist. Sweat, nor water, nor tears, nor blood can harm it. Just got to stay tied up tight. Keep it with you, and it keep you safe."

"I will not forget your instructions. Most of all, I will never forget you. And don't you forget that I'm never too old to hug on you. Come here, Bertha. I won't get enough of your big love where I'm going."

"Ain't true, Mr. Harry. Remember, these Bertha's arms around you; they always be there."

# Twenty Nine

"**I** did my best, Dad; I really did. I can't help it if Ma is convinced that I'm not going to survive my first week as an aviation cadet. She's a bundle of nerves over my leaving, and there is no reasoning with her. I'm pretty sure she's still sitting in that chair in my bedroom, gazing down at the picture of all of us at Penny's wedding. At least she wasn't crying when it came time for us to head to the car."

Elmer knew the tears wouldn't let up for very long back home. Dr. Archinaud had warned him that the war was going to be a serious threat to Julia's fragile condition.

"You'll understand better someday, Harry. It's hard for parents to see their children leave the nest, hard and very scary these days when so many of our young ones who leave are going overseas to fight. I'm nearly as anxious about the war, but your Ma's got her old problems piled on too. I'll have to be strong for us both—keep hope and good thoughts alive for the two of us."

His dad turned the corner, and the U.S. Army recruiting office came into view at the end of Canal Street. Elmer agreed to say his final good-byes there, where enlistees were ordered to report for active duty, the starting point of a radically new life for his young son and so many others. Before parting, Harry needed to say a couple more things to his steadfast friend and loving father.

"Pa, getting into this war is about the most dangerous thing anybody, including me, might possibly do. We've talked about the country's reasons for going to war and my reasons for going, but there are two things that I've never talked about much. Uncle Harry has sworn me to silence outside of the men in our family, even discouraged me from talking to you before I finished my studies with him."

"Your uncle's not here; just speak your mind, son."

"OK, here goes. You know Uncle Harry has given me a huge set of things to do in my life, and this Air Corps job is just the beginning of all that. At first I was plain scared about all those challenges; he told me it was my last chance. But I'm beginning to see all that as my best chance, a way to find something outstanding in myself. I want you to know I feel good about what's ahead."

"Your uncle and I and every McChesney before us want only the best for you."

"This second thing, I don't know what to make of it, whether it's for better or worse. Every so often I have this thing—call it a feeling or an understanding or what Reverend Hunter told me is a divine presence—that fills me with a sense that I can accomplish whatever I want. Whenever I see a challenge in front of me, I feel some old frailty inside but also know I have to fight back, and even if I don't win all-out, I tell myself, 'You will overcome.'"

At that moment Elmer was the one looking overcome.

Harry continued, "Reverend Hunter said it was a blessing from God, this feeling. I'm not so sure you all would agree. I told him that lotsa times, that feeling had gotten me in Dutch with my folks, and Ma would ask, 'What the devil's gotten into you?' But he just smiled and patted me on the shoulder. I guess his message was that only God knows all of what makes me do the things I do, and I should be thankful that He is with me."

"Godspeed and safe returns, my dear boy." Elmer's throat was squeezing down, and he could say no more. They embraced tenderly at curbside. Long after Harry entered the building carrying his little satchel, his father sat in the car and pondered what he had just heard: distant echoes of inspiration whispered into the tiny ear of a frail infant over many nights, during many strolls together, years ago.

# *Thirty*

**H**arry's head flopped forward and woke him up abruptly. He jostled around in his seat in the crowded coach car as the train clattered across another set of switch points. They must be close to Beaumont by now. He had dozed off briefly after crossing the Sabine River Bridge at the Texas border. The orange glow of cigarettes and hum of low conversations penetrated the darkness. Not many others were sleeping either.

By the end of the preceding day he'd felt slightly numb, but he did not yet have any perspective on these things. Yesterday was but a brief passage, after all, through a tiny sidearm of the massive and repetitive processing machinery that would control his life for the next year of military training.

From the orderly hustle within the recruiting center the men were trucked over to the drafty bustle of the old Dryades Street Market where they swam through a sea of paperwork and physical examinations. The army docs and nurses were assembled at individual market tables where, previously, shoppers could roam about and examine the fresh meat, fish, and fowl for sale. Now naked men moved between stations for hours of prodding and poking by those at the tables. Harry could understand the need for close scrutiny of eyes, lungs, and hearts of the prospective air cadets, but no one thought it necessary to explain why they each had to bend over six times in one afternoon.

Before they left the meat market, Harry knew his training had begun. He'd learned Army Lesson Number One from the enlistees' unwritten book of conduct. The sergeant in charge asked who out of the forty-five in his group could type. About seven hands shot up before Harry had decided how to respond.

"You seven fall in here and follow me. You're going to load the luggage into the truck for the train depot."

Army Lesson Number One: "Don't volunteer for anything!"

◆  ◆  ◆

As Harry's truckload of men entered the Union Terminal on South Rampart, Jimmy Pellegrin and Jimmy's mother and father ran up to greet him. At first he thought that they were there to meet someone else. He was very moved and flattered to learn otherwise. Jimmy ducked into a sparring crouch and snuck in an affectionate right jab to his arm.

"We heard that you and your folks had already said your farewells, but we felt that someone from the neighborhood should come down to see you off. You'd do the same for me, pal."

Mrs. Pellegrin fidgeted with her gloves and nearly dropped something. Harry couldn't see what else she was holding.

"Jimmy," she broke in, "who knows where things will be when you turn eighteen? Nobody's planning to see you off anywhere, certainly not any time soon."

Mr. Pellegrin reached out and gave Harry a damp handshake.

"Young man, we wanted to tell you that all our prayers and

good wishes are with you. You're the first on our block to ship out, and we're all very proud of you."

Jimmy straightened up and stuck his hands in his pockets.

"Yeah, I can't believe you are going to pilot school. That's about the slickest thing ever. You're the only guy I know who's getting to do that."

Mrs. Pellegrin stepped closer, dodging a passing redcap with a loaded luggage dolly.

"We know how worried your parents are for you, and we wanted to do something to help ease their minds. Your sweet grandmother suggested it, actually. Well, here it is; we wanted you to wear this to protect yourself during your training and from now on."

She handed Harry a copper medallion about the size of a half-dollar hanging from a metal-link chain. On one side was a figure of a holy man; on the other side was a cross with the letters *C*, *S*, *P*, and *B* in the four angles formed by the cross.

"It's a St. Benedict medal. It protects the wearer from spiritual and physical dangers. It is one of those blessed by Archbishop Rummel during a special mass at St. Louis Cathedral for the men and women going into the service from New Orleans. Wear it in good health. Here, Jimmy, hold my gloves while I fix it around Harry's neck."

If Mrs. Pellegrin noticed Bertha's medicine bag already inside his shirt, she didn't say anything. By the time he boarded his train, Harry felt a reassuring warmth surrounding him, more than simply the press of the crowd. No other native son traveled to the San Antonio Aviation Cadet Center under heavier protection than he.

# Thirty One

It was almost five p.m. when Harry finished everything he could do that evening in the way of hurricane preparations. His biggest quandary was what to do with all that good seafood in his freezer. He was packing a big Igloo full of shrimp and lemon fish to bring to Libby's family. He had given about five pounds of wonderful red snapper filets to one of the workmen along the street who'd helped him move the big pots from the yard. Even after that, there was too much left to eat or give away. He wished he'd started on that part of the planning sooner. Harry hated to waste nature's bounty, and that's what was going to happen if the power went out for too long.

He stopped by the idiot box for a dose of the news. Governor Blanco and Mayor Nagin were among a gaggle of suits behind a podium at the New Orleans City Hall holding a joint press conference. Nagin was gabbing and dapping with his chief of police off to the side while one of the Jefferson Parish officials was sending out marching orders over the airwaves. Nagin looked distracted and was behaving without much decorum at a time when Harry thought all his focus should be on meeting the safety needs of the citizens.

When it was the mayor's turn at the mike, he waffled again when asked about the need for a mandatory evacuation of his city. In Harry's opinion the mayor was not a very polished or intelligent person. He certainly wasn't a community leader. Like his father before him, Harry didn't have much faith in government officials' abilities to provide for others in time of need. For years he had dedicated part of his time to helping others; he was proud of what he'd accomplished on his own.

Harry regarded any major storm as a threat to the future of this low-lying metropolitan area, a bowl surrounded by water and rapidly eroding marshlands. He never underestimated nature's destructive power but never thought Katrina posed any serious risk for his own survival. Confident he could evacuate safely, he was already thinking how soon he might return to help in the aftermath.

*The body and the Ford Crown Vic are both a bit creaky, but we'll get the job done.*

He fielded another call from his daughter; his son-in-law was on the line this time as well. They wanted to make sure he knew that the National Hurricane Center had raised the ante: as of ten p.m. New Orleans was on hurricane warning status. The storm was a little more than a day away from making landfall somewhere along the Louisiana-Mississippi Gulf Coast. He promised them that he would be on the road tomorrow just as soon as he'd closed up all the shutters and had a decent breakfast.

Sleeping in his own home, in a bed of his preference, was a privilege he valued highly. He was not looking forward to the jiggly box springs in his daughter's guest room. He stretched like a big cat and found his favorite groove in the mattress. He fell asleep quickly and dreamt again about the war: becoming a pilot, learning to fly.

# Thirty Two

"**K**eep it level, Cadet McChesney; you're losing altitude again in the S-turn. This is the last time I am going to tell you. Be aware of those crosswinds and make timely corrections."

This was not going well. Their group instructor, "Highway" Harrison, had returned only a couple of days ago to Bonham Primary Flight Training Center after three weeks personal emergency leave, and today he had Harry up with him for a severe grilling, a check flight. None of the cadets had met the little SOB before last Monday, but they knew about his reputation. A strutting martinet who was too short to qualify for military air service, he was one of the all-civilian team who ran the program at Bonham under contract with the Army Air Corps. Unlike most of the other instructors, he was a poor teacher and a stickler for only-by-the-book progress. The first thing that he'd told the men after his return was that he was aware of the high washout rate for groups assigned to him and he was proud of it. Class 44-A would find things no different. For him it was "my way or the highway, mister."

Rupert Brown, a tall, skinny, and easygoing Texan, was a veteran pilot who had been flying an airmail route between New Orleans and Houston before coming to Bonham. He and aviation pioneer Jimmy Williams grew up together and first partnered up by flying rum and guns between Texas and Mexico before the Great War. Brown stayed with Williams as a lead pilot when he started the Wendell-Williams Air Service, headquartered since 1930 at the big field at Patterson, Louisiana. He had flown everything from racers to multiengine jobs. Most importantly, he could teach kids, most of whom had never driven a car, to fly.

Harry and the other three cadets in his group were assigned Brown as their temporary instructor upon reporting to the center. Each had passed their supervised solo flights after only nine or ten hours of in-flight with him. Of their incoming class of 220 cadets, forty-three had already washed out of pilot training. Every primary flight class had only nine weeks to progress through the required ground instruction plus sixty hours of hands-on, in-flight skills. They all knew that the average class washout rate was between 40 and 50 percent.

Brown's kids had good breaks with the weather, and the old plywood PT-19s seemed easier to fly every minute they spent aloft. They were quickly mastering stalls, tailspins, snappy acrobatics, and forced landings. They looked forward to their first cross-country flights. Harry was not the most confident cadet in his group, but he believed that his chances of washing out were decreasing by the day. All of that changed with the return of Highway Harrison.

◆  ◆  ◆

**B**ertha had been right about the "buckling under in the army" part. Since his first day back in San Antonio, there had been a hell of a lot more marching and drilling and running than Harry thought pilots could ever use. Of course, the rigorous training got him in the best physical condition of his young life. Hazing by the upperclassmen in the first half of pre-flight training toughened him mentally as well, but he never enjoyed it much when it was his turn to harass and hector others. He didn't have a cruel or sadistic streak but began to understand how quickly it could surface in those placed in power over you.

His contact with women was practically nil. He hardly had any town leave in San Antonio, and with all the military men swarming there, the attractive gals were corralled and branded before he ever got a chance to look over the stock. He spent the few hours of personal time allowed the cadets each week writing letters home or studying.

One Saturday evening in his first month of primary, nearly all of the men from Harry's barracks went to scout an upcoming opponent in the trainees' baseball league. Tom Moak, a slow-talking Alabama boy, was the only other cadet who had stayed behind to study. Some of the guys from up north had dubbed him "Moaky," and Harry knew the nickname was not meant to be flattering. He could hear the derision in their voices when they imitated his Alabama drawl. Many of those who sniggered had reason to be jealous of Moak's flying skills. He wasn't one of Brown's Brownies, but he was damned good. In defiance of the smartasses, Harry made a point of calling him by his family name.

He had been stuck on a physics problem and was startled when Moak cleared his throat, standing right next to his bunk.

"Excuse me, Harry. Do you mind if I ask you a question?"

"Hey, Moak. You don't have to whisper; I'm not asleep. Have a seat over on Dinglehoffer's bunk. What's up?"

"Well, this may sound stupid—"

"Stow that, mister; you're not stupid. I know that, and you're one of the top cadets in the flying department."

"Hey, that's mighty kind. Well, it's about those training movies they been showing us."

"What about them? Most of them are pretty dull. Not much to puzzle on there. At least, I can't remember any—"

"No, sir, it's not about what they're trying to teach us. That's a cinch. No, it's the things themselves."

Now Harry was getting confused. "Maybe you'd better start from the beginning, Moak. You're losing me."

"The beginning, huh? Not really sure where that is. What I don't understand is how they get those people to talk and move around in that projector so that they can show it up on the screen."

Harry glanced around in the shadows of their quarters. He was looking for the practical jokers in hiding who had set him up and had enlisted Moak in their plot. Just before he started to laugh and spoil their gag, he noticed the guileless expression on the farm boy's face.

"It's all on the film that they run through the machine."

"I figured that much, Harry, but I want to know how it works. I've been embarrassed to ask anyone. I hear the guys laughing with each other when they call me 'Mo-key.' But you never did that; I figured you'd be a square shooter. Also, you're from a big city. I'll bet you've been to see plenty of movies. I grew up on a farm on the banks of the Black Warrior River. The closest town is Warrior, population 1,123—well, 1,122 since I left. Our county high school didn't get electricity until I was in the eleventh grade. We never had a movie projector."

"Ah-ha, well. Pretty interesting physics involved actually. Let me flip over to a fresh page. I think I can draw it out for you . . . ."

Harry knew he hadn't seen much of the world outside of the rather unique city in which he'd grown up, but he was shocked to encounter such a wide range of education and maturity among those he had believed to be elite enlistees. Age didn't seem to have much bearing on behavior. They were all young, but some were obviously so much better prepared to make their way than others. Parts of the country didn't much matter either. A guy from New York City had a lot more in common with a guy from New Orleans than with someone like Tom Moak. Everybody was struggling to adjust in some way or another, but Harry felt he had a leg up, unlike many. Under the press of events he remembered his uncle's challenge to learn compassion for others and reach out. His best efforts were when he could help the Moaks of the world without making them feel like jerks for asking.

For many reasons, however, friendships remained hard to come by. Most of the instructors encouraged competitive, self-centered behavior—what some called "the fighter-pilot mindset"—fostered by adolescent hormone levels and the selection/elimination process itself. Harry thought it a harsh way to try to impart self-reliance. He finally admitted that it was easier not being too attached or chummy with someone who might not be there the next day. Any day you might walk into your barracks and find a couple more beds empty and stripped: more washouts, mostly.

Most washed out because of unacceptable flying performance, but disobeying flight regulations was a sure ticket home. One of the hotshots in the class ahead of theirs was dismissed a few hours short of graduation when he returned to field with telephone wires hanging from his tailfin. Buzzing the locals without permission was strictly forbidden.

Jerome Haliday, whom he liked a lot and whose sister he'd hoped someday to meet, died in a training crash during Harry's second week in primary. Before Jerome's death he had not met anyone his own age who, suddenly, just wasn't walking around anymore. The inevitability of empty bunks and being conditioned to expect this as the new normal were the parts of training that truly disturbed him.

In spite of what he was being taught to feel or not feel, Harry was particularly fond of one of the men in his group. Greg Finley had spent three years at the University of Michigan where he was starting quarterback for the Wolverines and got the nickname "Rock." He was a big, muscular, square-jawed fellow who was not especially handsome although most women found him attractive in the same way people are attracted to the heroic proportions of monumental sculpture. Most men respected him as tough but intelligent, and he shared an ironic sense of humor and fine appreciation for pretty women with Harry. Rock was the first genuine friend he'd had in the service and the first one to call him "Mac."

Rock was a natural at flying and everything else. They studied for their ground training courses together and regularly scored among the highest in their class. Harry liked the fact that Rock never swaggered or bragged about his talents; he preferred to let his performance and competence speak for him. It was clear to everyone that he was going to be flying combat and was going to prove himself as solid as his nickname in no time.

◆　◆　◆

**H**ighway Harrison couldn't faze Rock, but he made Harry so nervous that he could not fly naturally and confidently for the man. On his first solo for Harrison, he had flubbed a couple of lazy-eights and a slow roll, both of which he had been doing effortlessly for Instructor Brown for over a week. Then came what Harry later recognized as the turning point, the day of their check flight together. He tightened up badly while trying to maintain altitude during simple turns. Harrison told him to bring it back down, "Just land the thing now." He came in high out of his final approach and dropped onto the runway from about twenty feet.

"McChesney, you've cracked the left landing gear. Ease this bird over to the hangar and bring me back a full report from the ground crew. Spend tomorrow back in the air doing those lazy-eights and rolls and report back here for another check ride on Friday. I also expect you to have mastered the snap roll by next week."

Harrison also ran him through more ground assignments, restricting his time in the air. Harry fell behind and grew more panicky about his chances every moment. Within ten days he had been scheduled for a civilian elimination ride. Rupert Brown's father passed away that week, and he wasn't around to rehearse with Harry and perhaps provide a shot of confidence for his former pupil. Harry failed the civilian e-ride and a few days later failed the military elimination ride with a stuck-up second lieutenant from Dallas. Harry's failure was now complete; he was devastated. He had exhausted his last opportunity to remain an aviation cadet.

"Mac, you busted out of here like lightning after they dumped us with Highway. I can't believe it's not completely obvious to these jokers that he's the bad apple and not those hundreds of guys he's washed out over the last year—especially not you. Nobody else even comes close to his failure rate."

Harry appreciated Rock's effort to blame Harrison for all of his misery, but he saw through it and could barely put words to his own regrettable performance.

"I screwed myself; I shoulda done better. The man is a jerk, but don't expect his civilian instructor buddies to complain. Besides, the army expects them to roast almost half of each class. I am fucked, but they're not going to get you, Rock."

"I had big plans for us in the next phase, in basic. Brownie was going to try to jigger it so that we could be at the same base and make those cross-country flights together—pick up some good-looking women in Los Angeles and San Francisco."

"Damn, I hope our paths do cross again. At least we saved that booze; I'm going to throw a farewell drunk this evening. The bigwigs are going to boot me out of here tomorrow. You know the drill: out of the air, off the base. I've put in for gunnery school, but I'm shitting bricks about what's happening next. If I can stay on as part of a flight crew, I'm going to do anything and everything to try to get back to flying."

"That's the spirit, pal. You got a raw deal, but you never know. This war is full of surprises for everybody. If I can ever do anything to help, you know you can count on me."

"Thanks, Rock, you're the best of the best. The worst was having to tell my family; I was so embarrassed and ashamed. I had been so confident about making it with this pilot and officer stuff. When I called my folks last night, my dad was great, as usual. My mom has been sick and didn't hear hardly a word I was saying. For once, I was grateful for that."

Mac hoped he could keep moving along through the system, staying busy, anything to stay in the air. He didn't know whether he could ever correct course, get back to flying, but he never, ever wanted to hear Uncle Harry's opinion of this washout.

# PART FIVE

## Contretemps

# Thirty Three

It was late-afternoon, Sunday, August 28th. Harry sat idling near Interstate 10, two blocks to the south of the traffic signal at Bonnabel Boulevard and Veterans' Highway. Unable to get his front fender onto the interstate, he had been snaking around, using familiar shortcuts through Old Metairie for the past three hours to find an uncontested artery north or west out of town.

The hurricane traffic on Interstate 10 heading west was in gridlock. Too many distressed drivers trying to access every on-ramp between the Mississippi River and the Lake Ponchartrain Causeway, trying to run right down on top of the angry souls already sandwiched into four lanes. Breakdowns littered and clogged the shoulders, along with the marginal creatures—the same ones who turn out for every grisly spectacle—who had set up lawn chairs to party and watch.

He'd first tried to inch onto I-10 from the ramp near his home at Metairie Cemetery and the Orleans Parish line. Interstate driving distance from there to the Clearview Parkway exit was less than two miles. Clearview was where the state police routed the snarl of westbound traffic into the additional lanes, into the other side of the divided roadway. All lanes of the eastbound interstate between Jefferson Parish and Baton Rouge were commandeered for the westward exodus from the low lands. The traffic engineers had dubbed their brainchild "contraflow." On most days the drive would take just over an hour. Today it could be days away, an impossible journey. This evacuation stuff might have been working fine for those who jumped in a car and left when authorities opened the system up Saturday afternoon. No longer. Now twenty thousand last-minute Charlies were sitting together in one big parking lot, getting hot.

Harry muttered, "Forget contraflow."

"**Constipation and no evacuation**," quipped talk radio host Joel Arpent, "The Mouth of the South."

The traffic was worse than the worst-case scenario he envisioned when he'd promised Libby that he would drive to her home in Shreveport. He decided against trying to call her again. His cell phone gave him a "no service" screen or a weird busy signal every time he tried to get through.

**Every Yat, Coonass, and Uptown Matron is trying to get a call into dey momma an em to tell de family where dey ain't going today.**

Again, the voice from the radio meshed with his stream of consciousness. It was all one babbling brook today. His reflection grimaced back at him from the driver's side mirror as he admitted to himself that he was now one of them, the "ain't going today" folks. He was merely trying to get *out* of the craziness and back to his house.

The back of his neck was in knots, and jolts of sciatica ran from buttock to calf. As he tried to stretch both his neck and his right leg, he caught flashes of action in his rearview mirror. Dense plumes of spiraling steam or smoke drifted upward from the clotted freeway. A large, red-and-white ice chest and some brown glass empties arced off the elevated segment of the I-10, launched by unseen hands into the face of whatever gods were out there impeding swift and safe exit from town.

No dodging the bullet this time. The National Hurricane Center narrowed the likely track again this morning; Katrina *was* coming. Category Four by the time she got up into the marsh—maybe even Cat Five—but coming close, probably just to the east of the city, close enough to cause some real misery. She had already killed seven people crossing over Florida on Thursday. A Jefferson Parish official searched for words to frame the rapidly building size and strength of this storm.

**For those of you who were unfortunate enough to be around these parts back in 1965 and 1969, I have some bad news. Katrina is now on the same path as Betsy and is bigger than Camille. For those of you who don't know what I'm talking about, lemme jest put it this way—this definitely ain't good, folks.**

The radiant heat from the concrete and the vehicle engines brewed the tropical moisture into a suffocating steam bath. On any other Sunday in August very few folks in south Louisiana would be cruising about in the swampy afternoon air. This day was exceptional in many respects. A mandatory evacuation had never been ordered before for the city of New Orleans. Mayor Nagin finally got off the fence and issued it at nine this morning.

Harry navigated the streets without the usual creature comforts of the New South. His old Ford was heating up badly. He'd shut off the a/c long ago. The whining noise up under the hood was pretty unmistakable: the bearings were beginning to go on his main radiator fan. He glanced over at the dozing driver of the overloaded SUV in the lane to his right.

*Poor bugger. Wife and kids probably kept him up all night. Well, Harry, life could indeed be worse. You could be stuck in their third seat, behind that fat one with the big hair.*

After a reluctant wave OK from the prisoners in the SUV, he crept over into their lane as he plotted his route home to Bellaire Drive.

Harry eased off Bonnabel from the right-turn lane about a half-block later, just as the fan bearings and the main belt froze up. Coasting to the curb of the side street, he took his overnight satchel from the backseat and locked his disabled vehicle.

*So much for all that wonderful seafood in the ice chest. Damn!*

It was going to be a soggy hike back to his home in the Lakewood South subdivision. His socks, fanny, and shirt were already sticky with sweat. Mental discipline and focus had helped him through many difficult times in his life. But today's events drained his faculties. He was vaguely aware that he was not making good choices, perhaps not making many choices.

"More like swept along," Harry commented to himself aloud. "At least I'm out of the traffic now. Get a grip. Think of something nice to take your mind off this."

No use. He couldn't seem to bring the cool and dark and quiet of his bedroom into his consciousness. Things had been a bit off-kilter all day. Maybe it was that positive ion effect that he'd read about that made people do and feel strange things before a big storm. He was more than a mile from his car when he remembered his best thermos jug full of ice water on the floor by the passenger's seat. He was not going back for it. Another more urgent water issue had arisen.

"About time to find a latrine, mister."

Harry had always thought himself fortunate. He regarded a cranky bladder, traveler's sciatica, and a slight quavering in his voice as pretty trivial physical nigglings, polite reminders that he was no longer young.

Out here on the pavement, senior citizen status offered no obvious benefits, and his sense of urgency had increased. He would settle for a ride to a restroom on an Elder Care shuttle if someone had been able to offer it. Nearing the backside of Dorignac's supermarket, he noticed two men climbing into a semi-trailer rig that was parked at the loading dock.

"Anybody working the store this afternoon, guys?"

"No, sir. Dey locked up de front about noon. Sheriff Harry Lee, he said, 'Mandatory e-vacuation!', and he even had some a his deputies come by to tell Mr. Joey to get his folks outta de store and on outta town. We emptied one a his freezers for him and are gonna try to drive dis rig to his Baton Rouge warehouse, keep all dat poultry and seafood from going bad. Nobody selling nuttin inside. De ones counting de money be coming out right behine us. I think de Pac-a-Sac down by Lake Avenue is still selling gas and stuff. You walking or what, mister?"

"Well, my car died a ways back. Never made it close to out of town. Right now, I'd sure like to find a bathroom and a bottle of water before I head back home."

"I hear dat about 'outta town.' Dat is sure a problem today. We gonna try to get out south across de Huey Long Bridge and take Highway 90 all de way to Lafayette before doubling back to Baton Rouge. Here, take a bottle of water. We got six cases in de cab. As for dat bat'room, well . . . ."

The driver glanced over at the back of the loading dock as he cranked the big rig and lit a cigar. He did not offer Harry a lift, and Harry was pretty sure he could make better time on foot. He was not so desperate as to wet down the timbers of the dock like a stray cat or one of the homeless.

"Good luck and thanks for the water. I think I can make it to the convenience store."

"Good luck to you, mister. Roads is tough today, but sooner or later we gonna be in de clear. It gonna get pretty rough an tough round here, so dey say. Pretty damned rough. Watch yourself. See ya round!"

Harry sprang forward, around the side parking lot of the food store and along the string of cars on Veterans' Highway, toward his rest stop. Some people eyed him suspiciously from their cars—in no mood to entertain a panhandler or hitchhiker. Others were so intent on the column of vehicles and brake lights ahead that he could have set himself afire and gone unnoticed.

The sky was getting darker with giant thunderheads towering in from the south-southeast. The bigger storm clouds were accompanied by gusty winds and turbulence. Lower level clouds had been scudding around since midmorning. Yesterday, the sky had been clear and the air eerily still and dry. None of this prelude had come as a surprise for Harry. He knew a lot about nasty weather. He was a veteran of named and unnamed storms that had battered his native city and a veteran of thirty bombing missions in brutal weather in World War II. Things were not looking good.

"We're already past quiet time. The giant is feeding," Harry thought aloud. "She's still over the horizon, but she's beginning to throw a shadow."

# Thirty Four

As he neared the Pac-a-Sac, he lost focus on the gradual change in conditions. He was wearier than he expected to be at this point in the afternoon. He felt vaguely distracted, not quite on his game today. Everything seemed a little blurry, a little deceptive, a little in doubt. Cars crowded around all of the gas pumps in front of the small quickie-serve store; others were in line, waiting.

"Great, probably the same way in the bathrooms. Better go get in the queue."

He entered the store and gave it the once-around: no inside restrooms. But he was sure there was a toilet to be had somewhere on the premises. He had spotted the weary merchant's advisory, a handwritten cardboard sign by the register: "Bathrooms for PAYING customers ONLY."

There was only one attendant. She was very young and stood tensely erect behind the front counter. Twenty-something was his best guess. She wore her hair in a short bob, and her shapely little ears were what people of his generation used to call pert. An olive complexion and flawlessly taut skin highlighted her angular chin line and high cheek bones. She was blessed with a mix of features that Harry would have found attractive had she not pierced her left nostril, hung shiny stones and wires on both ears, and dyed her hair with alternating streaks of black, emerald green, and fuchsia.

"She probably has one of those tongue beads too," he muttered while working toward her line of sight.

Her bright-green eyes flitted about. Multitasking was not her strong suit. She was either stressed out or dyslexic or both. Instead of lavishing her waning attention span on paying customers, she delivered a rapid monologue at three gothed-up young males who draped themselves on display stands and blocked part of the service counter. She botched change for two customers in a row and lost control of her turf. The male drapers were casually shoplifting every time she turned away from them to do something else.

"Oh, crud! Sorry, ma'am."

"Look honey, that's why they make cash registers that *show* you what the correct change is. You kids today can't add, you can't spell, and you can't write. But, Gawd help you if you don't even know your numbers. You should be able to just read them off the display there and not cheat me outta my gas money."

"Lady, I'm *truly* sorry. I was not trying to gyp you. I just misread the—hey, Ronald! Get outta the beer cooler. You know you're underage, and I gotta card everybody. Next, please."

Harry wasn't sure how to interject himself into her muddled world of retail and larceny, but he *really* needed to know if there was something called a men's room on the premises and how to get there. He wedged close enough to read "My name is ROBYN" on her Pac-a-Sac nametag. It was clearly time to move right to a first name basis.

"Robyn!" She glanced up from the register. "Excuse me, it's

Mac. I can see you're very busy. But can you please tell me where the 'Gents' is located?"

"OK, Mac." She maintained eye contact, smiled and frowned a little at the same time. *Like, I don't know this dude.* "First door around back to your right. It's unlocked."

"Hey, Ma-ac," one of the goths taunted in an infantile lilt as Harry pushed out the swinging door, "careful in there. Don't dribble on yourself, old man."

"Terribly funny little prick, hmmm." There was mercifully no line at the restroom door, and the only occupant vacated quickly.

"All yours, buddy."

While studying the graffiti, Harry decided that he'd pick up some Gatorade and sandwiches to take home with him. It had been a long time since breakfast. He felt a hungry headache coming on—something about his borderline diabetes.

The empty towel and soap dispensers were right below the large sign by the rusty lavatory: "All employees MUST wash hands thoroughly with SOAP & WATER before returning to work." He exited frowning.

"Everything OK, Mac?"

Glancing around, he could not quite tell where the voice was coming from. He even looked skyward. The clouds rotated in a slow, sickening dance. The gray and dark-gray regions had lost much of their distinguishing contours; most of the sky was tinged with an orange-greenish backlight. It seemed considerably darker than when he'd stepped into the bathroom. Objects on the ground had taken on a waxy cast. The air was vaguely translucent, as in a fog or mist.

Robyn was outside putting yellow plastic "Out of Service" bags on the nozzles of the last two gas pumps that had run dry.

The pump island was deserted. She had already placed some traffic cones in the access drives to dissuade desperate motorists.

"We're about out of everything, and I'm about to close up. Everybody's freaked over some hurricane coming this way, but my friends and I have decided to stick around and check it out. I'm outta here, just as soon as I can clear out those creeps inside."

"Before you close, can I come in and grab something to snack on before I head home? I haven't had anything since breakfast, and I'm feeling a little woozy."

She noticed a wobble in his voice; she couldn't afford to have anybody getting sick on her.

"Come on in. I'm about to close the register. Don't know about the sandwiches. They're pretty gross anyway, but you can probably find something in there."

"Thanks; right behind you. Hey, I think your friends in there are getting a bit out of hand."

"Not friends, just some serial lurkers who happen to know some of the same people I know and who think that gives them some special access to me. Hey, Goddammit, Ronald! I told you to stay outta the cooler. Jake, you're going to have to pay me for that beer Ronald stole and is drinking illegally on premises because I can't sell it to him. Larry, *where* do you think you're going with those cigarettes?"

Larry, the fat goth, continued to tuck two cartons of Marlboro Lights nonchalantly in his gangsta cargo pants. He grinned stupidly.

"Aaww, Robyn. Nobody's gonna miss 'em. Who knows what's gonna happen in this badass storm? I hear Katrina's a mean bitch, kinda like some girls we know."

"Very amusing, fat boy. I'm not feeling mean yet, but I can be if I think you're costing me my job. You're gonna pay me for the smokes right now, asshole, or put them back before you and your dipshit friends get outta my store."

Jake, the alpha goth who had taunted Harry, leaned down close to Robyn's face and gave the silver loop in the bottom of her left ear lobe a steady tug so that she had to stand on her tip toes, even closer to his mouth, to avoid serious pain.

He tried out his best imitation of a stage whisper and sneer, "You see, Robyn, little friend, we ain't going anywhere until you give us what's in that register. Me and my fellow dipshits need a little walking-around money to see us through the rest of the weekend. And don't think about doing a 9-1-1 on us or anything. Little Ronnie has been busy taking out the land line and disabling your cell phone. Besides, the cops have a lot on their plate today. They don't have time for bitches-in-distress calls."

"Let me go, turd face. Get out now! Ow!!"

Jake and skinny Ronnie had Robyn in their grasp and were moving her over to the cash register. As far as they were concerned, the old doofus who had come back in from his piss wasn't even there. Their backs were toward Harry as he moved down the aisle slowly from the back of the store. The fat one had gone outside with his contraband, somewhere out of sight.

## Thirty Five

**H**arry had left off browsing. The two remaining goths were oiled up on filched beers and seemed determined to rob this girl, maybe do worse. He had found a four-foot steel rod, a hunk of rebar, lying by the rear storage locker. Harry was not looking for a fight, but he never ran from one either. If there was going to be one, it couldn't be a fair fight. He was no match for these two barbarians at once. He quietly hefted the rod to assure himself that he could swing it effectively.

Robyn was still yelling at the top of her lungs. The two punks never heard the rod cutting through the air as Harry swung it with all his might into the back of their heads. He caught Jake squarely and instantly rendered him unconscious. Ronnie was dazed and staggered into Robyn. Harry moved closer and tried to swing again, but he was confined by the counters and displays. Before Ronnie could move, Harry grasped the rod horizontally with both hands and caught him under his chin, mid-neck, and dragged him backwards toward the door. Harry was breathing hard; Ronnie could only make a croupy little croak. His face was engorged with a purple hue.

"Quit struggling, stupid! You're going to break your windpipe. I'm going to let you go outside if you promise to find your fat friend out there and clear out. Answer me quickly, please, before you pass out."

Ronnie stopped grasping at the rebar and made bloodshot eye contact over his shoulder while nodding his head violently yes.

"Well, that's cooperative and sweet. On your way out, give Robyn back her cell phone and drag your sleeping friend here along with you. You may have trashed the phones here, but I have one. The sheriff is a personal friend of mine, and I'm going to call his private line as soon you and I stop dancing with each other. His men will be looking for three stooges who are stumbling around, dressed like Halloween. Better get home and get those bloody heads cleaned up, too"

Robyn shouted, "Stop, please. He can't breathe! We can't have two bodies lying around here." *I can't believe I was worried about having to call the medics for this old dude. Pretty amazing.*

"Sorry. Yep." He let Ronnie, who was now impersonating a sock doll, slump to the ground. "I didn't realize how long I was going on there. I agree; we want them out of here and on their way."

"God, thank you so much, mister. Mac? You OK?"

"Actually, my name is Harry. Mac is a nickname that I had back in the war, long time ago. Don't quite know why that just popped out earlier."

"War? Jeezum. We had a war in here for a while. I'd actually forgotten you were still here. I really can't thank you enough. Those creeps were getting pretty outrageous, and Jake—that one you leveled first—he is a really mean bastard. I don't know what he had in mind. He was starting to hurt me."

"I've never been in a brawl in a gas station before. I'd better sit down for a minute." The rebar easily weighed three or four pounds. He could have killed those stupid kids. His weapon clattered to the floor as he dropped onto the swivel chair behind the cash register. "Well, I think we're OK now. I guess the fat one saw what was going on and left early."

"Here, please take this. On me, the least I can do. You said you were feeling shaky earlier. I want you to take some things, some nourishment, and feel better before you try to go back home. How did you get here anyway?"

"On foot. My car broke down in the heat over by Bonnabel Boulevard. I was trying to find a clear road out of town ahead of the storm, trying to get up to Shreveport to stay with one of my daughters and her family. So much for waiting until the eleventh hour and trying to ride out on my ancient chariot. I had over 200,000 miles on that one. I knew I was pushing my luck."

"At least you got a lot of good out of that one. I'd give anything for a car. You also have some family to huddle up with. You're a good person, Mr. Mac. Sorry, I know your name is Harry, but my mom was always pretty strict with us and told me I couldn't call older people by their first names."

"Well, how about if we compromise and you can use part of my last name? You can call me Mac, but let's just drop the mister. I think I can live with that if you can."

"Yeah. No problem, as long as you call me Robyn—with a 'y'."

"Yes. I know how to spell it; you have it, strangely enough, right on your nametag. That's how I got your attention earlier. You were pretty busy trying to keep those kleptomaniacs at bay while you ran the store. The alarm bells sounded in my head as soon as I saw your predicament here."

"Well, again, thanks. Most people who stumble into Cheyenne territory these days just choose to duck and move on down the road. You did *way* more than worry about me."

"I got lucky. I don't know what I would have done without that steel persuader you keep in the back."

He unscrewed the top on his second Gatorade and finished a Hubig's fruit pie. His internist would not be happy with this high-glycemic diet.

"So, isn't your daughter going to worry about you? You're stuck in the city now; you can't evacuate."

"Whoa, what time is it? I think I'd better be moving on. I really do need to update my family. I don't have too far to go. I'll be fine back at my place. I guess. Let's hope and pray that this Katrina thing swerves like all the rest of them recently and gives us a pass on 'the Big One.'"

"My friends and I think we're gonna dodge another bullet. We'll drink some beer and tequila and rag on some boyfriends and probably fall asleep with the wind howling and the glass breaking. On Monday or Tuesday, we'll clean up the downed branches and debris and then part ways. They'll go back to their fancy university, and I'll head back to work at my crappy little job."

"Is that what you have to look forward to? A crappy little job?"

"This gig is to help out with my expenses while I am going to Delgado Community College part-time. I have six more credit-hours of math to finish, and then I can get into the UNO accelerated curriculum: business school or accounting. I haven't decided which. I want to do both, but I need to finish in three years. With loans it will be a ball-buster of debt when I get out. At least I should have a job path and some cash coming in by that time."

"Sounds like a practical approach, similar to what a lot in my generation did after their time in the service. But right now, you should get your cash drawer secured. I will wait around while you do that. Then we both need to head on down the road."

"OK. As long as you feel better, I am packing up this store as fast as the law allows."

"I'll make it, thanks. I really do need to get home and place some calls."

She promptly stood up and walked over to his chair, gave him a ferocious hug, and planted a big kiss on his forehead. He blushed crimson and turned away and coughed softly. He felt the cough, as gentle as it was, behind his eyeballs. Nearing exhaustion, he had over two miles to walk to get to the solitude of his bed. He estimated that he might get six to eight hours of rest before this hurricane made another landfall somewhere on the Louisiana coast.

"Stay well, young lady. I enjoyed meeting you, even under the circumstances. Good luck in the future."

"Good luck to you, Sir Mac, my sweet knight. I shall always remember your kindness. You are the best!"

Her voice rose and her shapely head tilted to the side as she delivered her parting remarks: sweetness and refinement. Metamorphosis of being? There was something familiar about her expression that he could not place.

Street lights sputtered on early in the cloudy gloom. A light rain fell through the lurid haze of the sodium vapor lamps. Traffic signals bobbed and swayed overhead, and all manner of unlikely items banged along the streets. He passed a boarded-up store front upon which the owner had spray-painted his Day-Glo crime deterrent with two-foot lettering: "I AM HERE. I HAVE A GUN." Harry dug in his satchel for a windbreaker and glanced at his watch; he hoped to beat the curfew. The thunder would usher him home.

# Thirty Six

He turned on some lights downstairs after punching in the key code for the burglar alarm. The house always smelled faintly of burned toast when he first entered after a long trip or absence

"Sure feels like I've been gone more than a few hours. What a day! Better call before I crawl into bed; I'll be out like a light."

Harry knew that many people who lived alone talked to themselves, and he wasn't really concerned that he was one of those who gave voice to his thoughts. With family or within earshot of strangers, he kept his thoughts to himself. Sometimes he muttered a few choice remarks and didn't care if others heard those or not. At home his sotto voce monologues felt natural and normal. Like so many other couples who were separated after decades of married life, he was, in fact, still talking to his late wife. Lorna had always been a sympathetic listener.

Before heading to the bedroom, he reached for the old red wall phone and dialed his daughter's number in Shreveport.

"Libby, hi, it's me."

"Dad, what's going on? Where are you calling from? You OK?"

"I'm really tired but otherwise fine."

"Tired, you did too much trying to get the house closed up?

How far have you gotten? It's nearly dark. You know how we feel about you driving at night."

"Well, I thought you'd notice from the caller ID. I'm back home. I tried to leave right after I did a few things and grabbed a late breakfast. I couldn't get on I-10 anywhere; the traffic is insane. I inched around for another three or four hours trying to find a back road out. I got stuck close to Veterans' Highway on Bonnabel, and then my car broke down from the heat, right behind the Jiffy Lube. I was lucky to get it parked on a side street."

Recounting his outing to his daughter was more like doing it again than just talking about it, a traumatic flashback. Sweaty palms, bounding heart, shallow little breaths, metallic taste in the mouth—like the flak fatigue he'd had during the war. He backed into a chair and sat down in the breakfast room.

"My God, don't tell me you had to walk home from there?"

"Well, I couldn't very well call Metry Cab. Things are crazy down here."

"Yes, we've been watching CNN and FOX. Thousands of people downtown trying to get into the Superdome. What is that idiot, Nagin, doing sending folks in there? The Dome will be a torture chamber once the power goes out. This ain't a Saints game!"

"Hey, we got the best politicians money can buy, you know: Morial, Jefferson, now this 'Ray Baby.' Not exactly looking after his peeps."

"Well, you're the only peeps I care about right now, Dad. This storm's a bad one. Get some rest; get some food; and hunker down tonight. When the winds die down and they start letting people back into the city late tomorrow, John and Caitlin will come get you. You know there's not going to be any electricity for days. I remember how miserable it was after Betsy."

"I certainly haven't forgotten. You and your sister were screaming little hot potatoes back then. We all were. One of the hottest
September I can remember after that hurricane in 1965, just
about one year after we moved in here on Bellaire."

"At least they have done a lot of work on the levees since then.
You ought to know. You had to put up with the pile drivers and
dump trucks for months."

"Yeah, our taxpayer dollars at work. Any time you get the
Corps of Engineers and the Sewerage and Water Board together
you have to wonder about the work. Look, I need to lie down
before the storm hits. I'll be OK. We all made it through Betsy
just fine in this sturdy house. I have already filled the bathtubs
with water. I have plenty of canned food and too much food still
in the freezer. I shall be fine."

"I don't like you there by yourself. You're a tough bird, but
you're our bird. We love you and want you safe."

"I'll call you as soon as I can tomorrow morning. I love you
lots; hug John and Caitlin for me. God bless."

"Good night, Dad, stay well. I love you dearly."

He hung up the phone and stiffly stood up from the chair
in the breakfast room. He wasn't hungry or dizzy anymore; he
didn't bother to open the refrigerator.

"I can eat again when I wake up or after something wakes
me up."

◆  ◆  ◆

In spite of its aching solitude, with rooms and memories he
preferred to leave as is, he loved his home and had no plans to
downsize, to leave it. In preparing to evacuate this morning, he

had closed all the shutters firmly with the sliding bolt hardware from the inside. The shutters would hold up against a steady, ninety-mile-per-hour wind and keep smaller flying objects from smashing windows.

For the duration of the hurricane threat, Harry had decided to move back into the downstairs bedroom that he and Lorna had shared for thirty-six years. He'd felt like a stranger coming back to an empty bed after her funeral. He slept that night in the guest bedroom upstairs. He'd slept there ever since and gradually moved his clothes and some keepsakes up there.

The master bedroom was the best place to weather the storm because of its protected location on the ground floor in a rear corner of the house. Two large magnolia trees, one on each corner of the front yard, could topple or break in a bad blow and damage either of the front bedrooms upstairs.

If Katrina stayed fifty or a hundred miles to the east of the city, New Orleans would be toward the safe quadrant of the storm. Rain-related flooding was inevitable in most low-lying areas. Harry wasn't concerned about that. Their home sat on a grade well above most of the subdivision and most of the city. Even in the drenching floods of May 1978, his yard never had standing water.

*The levees behind this house are unlikely to be topped by storm surge from the lake if Katrina stays around Category Three level. If she hits Category Four or Five, all bets are off.*

This was his last conscious thought as he fell asleep on top of the bed with his clothes and shoes still on. His storm-tossed dreams returned him to the early turbulence he'd hit years ago as a young trainee in the Army Air Corps.

# Thirty Seven

"Blindfolds on, men. Do not let me even *think* you are cheating and peeking out. You other geniuses with the stopwatches, ready, on my mark."

"Request permission to ask question, Sarge."

"What is it, Bolano?"

"Sir, what happens if the watch jams and we have to start over in timing the assembly?"

"Nothing is going to happen to the watches, Bolano. They are made by smart little elves at the Hamilton watch factory here in the good old U.S. of A. But, I can tell you what happens to the sad sack who should happen to jam his .50-cal during timed reassembly. He's going to be carrying that seventy-five pounds of mayhem the eight blocks down to the armament shop for repairs and then around on his shoulder for an extra four hours of sentinel duty tonight. Is that clear, Bolano—and the rest of you?"

"Yes, sir."

"OK, now ready on my mark, set, commence."

They had been sleeping with their .50-caliber machine guns since arrival at the Las Vegas Army Air Base. If the whole squad passed the timed blindfold tests, they would start tow target practice in the air tomorrow. So far the only thing they had been shooting were shotguns at skeet targets from the beds of moving pickups. Fun but not so much connected with their ultimate assignments.

Harry really missed piloting his own plane. He had thought about it a lot in the month since he'd washed out, but he still didn't see any way he was going to get back into that line of work anytime soon. He clung to the hope that he might yet find a way to train and fly the big birds, and he felt his chances were better the closer he stayed to the action. Grateful that the army had offered him another role to play as part of a flight crew, he was determined to be one of the best among the gunnery trainees, to earn his wings and earn the privilege of flying as part of the team, most likely in one of those long-range bombers, the B17s or B24s.

◆　◆　◆

"Looks like you smoked all those Jerries, Mac. I can see from here that your cluster is on-target. That's the fourth time this week that you've emptied the gun smack on your part of the sock."

Harry was the best gunny the pilot had ever flown into tow practice, and he liked the fact that this ex-air cadet appreciated what he could do as well. Lt. Jason liked to show his stuff, and he even let the kid fly their two-seater from the rear controls when they were up together.

"You have better eyes than I do, Jason. I hope you're right."

Harry was pretty sure he'd nailed it again and felt good. He was stowing his gun and unhooking his gunner's belt when the pilot asked over the intercom if he wanted to do some acrobatics before touching down. Harry signaled affirmative.

"Let me know when the gun is stowed."

"Stowed, now—"

Jason immediately pulled off a snap roll.

"How was that?"

When Harry's eyes caught up with the rest of his head, he yelled back, "Fine, now can I fasten my seat belt, you turkey? If you'd slow rolled or looped us, you'd have come home with one seat empty."

"That's what the parachutes are for, old buddy. Now, why don't you buckle in and take the stick for a while. Show me what you can do."

# PART SIX

**_Solo_**

# *Thirty Eight*

$A$ large object slammed against one of the upstairs shutters. From ground level it was hard to determine what side of the house had taken the hit. Winds battered the house with explosive force. Air molecules were traveling with the energy of bowling balls, smashing and twisting everything in their path. Irregular surges of groaning white noise from wind, rain, and flying debris made it impossible to relax. Intense cacophony bordered on the threshold of physical pain and grated on his nerves like a rock concert. Harry hated rock concerts.

"Great, this morning they are playing with real rocks, live ammo."

Harry stayed hunkered down in bed. He had awakened a few minutes before the sudden impact, but he knew it wasn't the first big hit. The enemy had too much in its arsenal. The winds were doing quite enough without airborne chunks of the neighborhood adding to the barrage on his home.

He estimated sustained winds to be well above hurricane force; gusts were probably registering close to ninety miles per hour. Angling close to a window, he peeked through the slats in the vibrating shutters. Electrical power was still on. A mercury vapor lamp up on the levee, one of those industrial security lights that he loathed, swung from its half-broken armature like a drunken trapeze artist, casting waggling green shadows into the room. His bedside clock read 3:20 a.m. Katrina was not yet in full throat.

In spite of the growing chaos outside, Harry slept again. When he next awoke, a feeble, predawn light was coming through the shutters. He hadn't bothered to close the drapes last night. He reached for a bedside lamp: no lights. The clock's luminescent hands had stopped at 5:15 a.m.

Intense, unremitting stress ultimately wears a man down. Irregular shocks and insults break him more quickly, and there was no pattern or regular rhythm to the violence of this storm. As he padded to the bathroom, all sides of the house were battered by giant hands. Then, just as suddenly, the vibrations ceased for a second or two, only to resume in random sequences: twisting, shaking, pulling, slapping. Katrina was at the door and all around the house. Harry's anxiety level was rising along with the storm's intensity.

*Definitely stronger out there. Hope this good place holds together.*

His thoughts poured out, hitting on all sorts of topics, not his usual linear, logical processing, more like a chicken pecking at scattered feed corn.

*Well, looks like I don't have to hurry and dress. I'm already dressed. Man, what hit me yesterday? What's coming today? Better get some food and water, need to take a look around, survey things from the inside when it gets light. Don't know when it'll be safe to go outside. Wonder if WWL is still broadcasting?*

He nodded gratefully as his portable radio crackled to life. Operating on emergency power, the WWL staff were hunkered down, sending out the news from somewhere in their building downtown. The first fragments of reporting caused more concern: the National Weather Service station at Biloxi airport ceased to function around six a.m., and Katrina had made another landfall near Buras, Louisiana, just after six. Harry did a rough mental triangulation and concluded that the storm was cleaving to the old Betsy track, but compared to Katrina, Betsy had been a dwarf. This one was lashing out with killer winds (enough to knock out an airport) over one hundred miles from the eye.

In the light of a candle Harry prepared a ham and onion omelet over the gas burner on the stove. The candle flame pulsed with the rapid oscillations of air pressure within the house. The walls and windows were moving like bellows.

While washing up the dishes around 8:15, he heard the announcer cough on the air like he'd just lit up a smoke—a bad, wet cough. He smiled in sympathy with the man's insouciance.

*Broadcasters have a little mute button that they can push to bleep that out; this guy obviously doesn't give a damn about protocol at this point.*

After clearing the mucous from his airways and without even a "sorry folks," he moved on to the next bulletin. Hurricane hunter aircraft had just entered the eyewall, located forty miles southeast of New Orleans. They reported constant winds of 135 miles per hour with higher gusts: a Category Four storm.

On Bellaire Drive the winds were topping 100 miles per hour. Cautious glances out the front windows revealed little whitecaps in the shallow standing water down at street level, thrashing tree limbs with hardly any leaves, and jumbles of debris everywhere. Suddenly, a wide section of wooden fencing spiraled out of the sky onto a house across the street. He quickly retreated from the windows.

More radio bulletins followed in quick succession. Mayor Nagin, speaking by satellite phone and trying to sound at the helm and on top of events, leaked a chilling tidbit of information from unnamed sources: "Water is coming through the levee in places."

Harry shouted at the radio, "*What* levee? *Which* places? Stupid son of a bitch, go back to your room."

Then the U.S. Coast Guard reported that storm surges had topped the levees on the Mississippi River-Gulf Outlet (MRGO) and along the Industrial Canal. Most of St. Bernard Parish and much of New Orleans East were experiencing rapid and massive flooding, estimated to be ten to fifteen feet deep.

"Category Four, levees topped, floods. Definitely not good, not good."

Harry wanted to stay busy, trying to quell rising apprehension. He decided to reconnoiter the interior. Buzzing thoughts thwarted his best intentions to calm down.

*Interior, hmmm. This storm gets much worse or we get big water, there may not be any difference between "in" and "out."*

Floods were nature's thundering barbarians. They were no respecters of boundaries. They destroyed the walls and berms and dikes and barriers men built in vain hopes of containment. No remorse, no quarter. Floods were born solely to overwhelm.

*This place could be overwhelmed, taken out. Never thought the wind could do it; never gave much thought to the water.*

The land lines were dead. His cellular phone battery was charged, but he could not get a voice signal out. He sent his daughter a text: *"Am awake and doing fine. Going to monitor the radio and keep safe. Still way too windy for any travel. Stay put. More later. Love, Dad."* The message went through.

The downstairs rooms hummed and vibrated with increasing ferocity. Harry's bones and that jelly stuff in his eyeballs resonated with the energy of the storm. But there was also another, deeper, low-frequency tremor that he could barely discern. He recalled a similar experience during a visit to Niagara Falls with Lorna before they were married.

"Harry, this is beautiful. I love the rainbows formed where the sunlight meets the mists, but there is something about the way the giant waters shake the earth that makes me nauseous. I'm glad we've seen it because I sure don't want to come back here on our honeymoon."

He was never sensitized to those earth-shaking signals. He'd never gotten seasick. During hundreds of hours in the air and thirty bombing missions in the war, he'd never experienced motion sickness. Terrified? Yes. Queasy? No. Until now.

*Something* really strange *going on in this storm. And me all wobbly, with fuzzy vision and churning stomach—what a way to have to face the day.*

He headed to the living room, his favorite part of the house, to try to regain a sense of balance. The focal point was an oversize fireplace with an elaborately carved wooden mantle. Not much use for a fireplace in New Orleans, but Lorna and the girls loved it as a family gathering spot.

In the gray morning light the room looked sepulchral and distorted. The sight lines were foreshortened and askew, like a fun house room where tall people are the same height as the short, fat ones. The folds in the drapes shimmered when Harry tried to focus on the shadowy parts, as if the whole room were illuminated by candelabra whose flames wobbled gently from the pulsing breath of clamoring voices. If one or two familiar voices had been audible within the moaning winds, they would have urged him to look about and choose among these touchstones of his life and family, snatch up a precious few and flee.

Two framed wedding photos standing on one end of the mantle top commanded his attention. The one to the left was a formal portrait of Lorna in her gown and veil, his angel in *peau de soir*. Short, dark curls surrounded a flawless face with full lips, rosy cheeks, and large, dazzling eyes. The camera had also captured her mischievous smirk, her youth and promise, palpable and beckoning. Harry longed to surround that tiny waist and hold her to him and hear her voice against his ear. He ached to tell her that, once again, they would be fine, ready for any challenge. Love was proof against danger—he once believed that romantic notion. Age and death had long ago parted that curtain.

Lorna was able to speak for a few moments before she died on the day of her massive stroke. Harry had seen men die during the war and since. He knew there was no sense in calling EMS. As he carried her to their bed from where she had fallen, her lips were cradled against his ear. She told him of the finality of this moment, "Afraid . . . love you," then only, "Miss you."

A sudden gust burst down the chimney and drove a bolus of soot and bird feathers into the room. Harry coughed and staggered into the guest bathroom to wash the grit and bird shit out of his eyes. He began pacing nervously and again, tried to calm himself with renewed vigilance. Upstairs was intact except for a broken window pane in the unused bedroom where the clutter slept.

*Nothing to do for this right now, not much water coming in.*

Securing the bedroom door shut, he checked the bathtubs to make sure the water hadn't drained out and headed back down to the kitchen. Like yesterday, events were pressing in, moving rapidly, and demanding a lot of energy. Perhaps the winds would begin to die down somewhat in the next hour or two. If things improved quickly, he might surely have time for another warm meal and a long nap before his family came to drive him out.

*Gotta find some mental separation from this damned Katrina. OK, as of this minute, the kitchen table is Base Operations. Com check? Still no dial tone on the wall phone. Wireless? No messages. Some Operations, some base. Pretty lonely.*

A little after ten a.m. a WWL reporter stationed at the Superdome reported that two holes had opened up in the roof. No other details were available. Harry didn't need many details to imagine the problems likely to arise inside the Dome, holes or no holes. He left the dismal news to take a bladder break.

◆　◆　◆

"**W**ell, hell! What have we here? Wonder where that is coming from?"

While he was in the bathroom, a small puddle of water had accumulated over the middle of the Mexican tile floor in the kitchen. He checked the ceiling and the plumbing under the sink—no drips, but the edges of the puddle kept extending outward. Upon closer inspection, the source became clear: water was bubbling up through the seams between the tiles. Outside there was a lot more water, nearly up over the driveway. A few hours ago there was only an inch or two standing down in the street. At this rate, it would rise high enough to force its way into the first floor of the house within thirty or forty minutes.

*Houston, I think we have a problem. If the canal levee here is failing, we'll need a boat or a miracle. A boat we ain't got. Need to relocate to the second floor. Whatever is causing the rising water in this area, it's happening pretty fast.*

In spite of the augmented threat he felt better, more animated. There was a job to do, a call to action. He always liked it that way. Over the next four hours Harry moved his radio, extra batteries, canned goods, a little ice chest with some cold and still-frozen things, a few plates and utensils, flashlights and a few hand tools, his bathroom supplies, and an extra pair of glasses to rooms upstairs. If necessary, from the second level he could get to the attic using the stairs off the back hall. The attic was floored over but never finished out after they had decided that two girls were going to round out the family just fine. There were dormer windows up there from which he could look east and step out onto the roof.

*No way in hell is that going to happen. No way.*

By Monday at one p.m. the winds had abated appreciably, but he was now wading through waist-deep water downstairs. The water, a rank mixture that included gasoline and sewage, seeped into the house through every seam and every corner. A weird assortment of flip-flops, household gadgets, boxes, and papers drifted out of cabinets and closets and mingled on the surface with an iridescent, oily sheen.

Around three o'clock, Harry was hungry, tired of moving furniture and paintings, and beginning to feel uncomfortable going back downstairs. The water was up to his armpits. Water? It was a foul, semi-opaque liquid that looked and smelled like diarrhea. Even though he knew his way around his home with his eyes closed, things had shifted around in the invading flood. He could no longer see the floor, only the walls and the rising water level inside and outside.

*Ah, yes. No longer any barrier between the "in" and the "out" down here. The barbarians are through the gates.*

Harry went downstairs for a final reconnoiter. He felt a churning anger in his stomach as he moved about. His home had been ransacked, trashed, violated, hit by a gang of lowlifes. The dining room was a crazy tumble of floating chairs and artificial fruit.

Bouncing along toward the stairs, his bladder began to nag him again. Reflexively, he turned to go use the guest bathroom but stopped and bellowed out his anger and frustration, a primal scream. Then he took a deep breath, exhaled a soft laugh, and let loose right in his pants, right where he stood. That moment of release brought temporary relief but with it an admission. Surrender of this part of the battlefield to the enemy was now complete.

*Time to get upstairs and get in the shower while there's a dribble of water pressure.*

With a last glance around Harry spotted the two wedding pictures on the mantle. As he half-scuttled, half-swam toward them, he ripped the front of his right leg open on something.

"Goddamned, motherfucking coffee table! Can't see crap down here anymore."

His scream echoed back at him within the narrow air space between the rising water surface and the living room ceiling. He rescued the framed pictures and headed up the stairs in searing pain, dripping blood and water along the upstairs hall and into the bathroom.

# Thirty Nine

The shower was warm and powerful. It was even more refreshing than the ones he remembered taking after flying. The compressed insanity and trauma of a bombing mission could never really be washed away, but the shouts and whoops of his crew members horsing around in the adjacent shower stalls helped recovery. Boisterous behavior celebrated the good ones, the safe returns in crippled aircraft through terrifying flak and confusion. However, subdued trips to the washing-up huts came around far too often—when someone in your squadron had bought it or if the whole group was still sweating out the mission, awaiting return of overdue crews. Still, the showers could refresh, rid you of the crust of heavy animal funk that had poured out of you during flight. The fliers knew it was a better life than most had in the service. For all of its unique insanity, showers and bunks and regular hot meals beat the mud-and-blood foxholes in the infantry any day.

He returned from this bittersweet reverie for another go at the old soap and rinse. He concentrated on his wound; debridement was painful and bloody. His physician brother-in-law had taught him some tricks with gauze and strips of tape to pull a wound together. He needed all of them. This one ran long and deep along the front of his leg, deep into the muscle and part of the shin bone. He rolled gauze tightly over his packing and strip-sutures. There was no disinfectant or antibiotic ointment.

He flopped on the bed with his right leg elevated, trying to remember if there were any plastic trash bags up here in his office. One would come in handy to dispose of his nasty shoes and clothing.

*Better check my pockets before I toss this stuff. Oh crap, my cell phone has been swimming in my trouser pocket* all *afternoon!*

Turbid brown water ran from the seams of his phone. Not a glimmer of life when he pushed the power button.

*Still have my little radio.*

One radio station in particular was meeting the challenge for Harry and millions of others. Sporadic cellular phone messages, mostly text, were coming into the staff at the WWL studios downtown. They were passing information along over the radio that they deemed urgent, reasonably reliable, downright important. Nothing could be vetted; everything was a judgment call. Occasionally, the veteran announcers felt compelled to offer disclaimers on the validity of their stories. The concerned, the frightened, the stranded, the suffering, the escapees—all the folks—glued to their receivers across three or four states automatically shook their heads and gave a little wave of their hand when they heard these journalistic caveats, as if to say, "Go ahead, son, we're with you; just tell us what you can." Within the course of several hours, as the immense scope of the disaster became apparent, these dedicated souls assumed a role beyond hard-working reporter, beyond providing a valuable emergency clearinghouse

188 | W.S. Culpepper

of information. They earned the mantle of the trusted uncle in every listener's family.

Harry's old Omega Seamaster said 11:30 p.m. when he sat down, propped his right leg up on his desktop, and dug into a candle-lit can of Hardy Beef 'n Vegetable, washing it down with one of the last of the almost-cold Heinekens.

> We are trying to keep everybody informed about the flooding and conditions around the metro area as reports come in. Again, we must emphasize that what we are giving you—in many cases, most cases—has not been confirmed by anyone in our news organization. Most of our people, like everyone else, are trying to stay safe. They will be out there for us before too long. We will continue to give you information from official city, state, and federal sources when we can. But honestly, folks, from what we've been able to tell since things really broke loose over the last twenty hours, some of our listeners have been giving us better reporting than anything we've gotten from the authorities. And we're definitely going to keep sending these stories along too.

> So, let's just recap what we've had phoned in over the last several hours: there are at least three levee breaches—major structural failures—at the London Avenue, 17th Street, and Industrial Canals. Flooding between seven and fifteen feet has been reported. One man and his family are calling for assistance from inside his attic in the Lower Ninth Ward. Carrie, are they still calling in? God help 'em! Let me tell you what we know for sure: 911 calls are not going through, folks. Also sorry to say: WWL cannot render any direct assistance or forward your requests. So, if you are in the unfortunate spot of still in your home and the water is rising, get to the roof if you can and wait for rescue. We believe that some first responders can now get out into the community.

Within the last couple of hours, we have had one or two callers who are certain that they have seen U.S. Coast Guard helicopters flying over and taking people off rooftops. Praise the Lord! Unfortunately, we have also received messages from nurses and doctors at the following hospitals: Touro, Charity, Methodist, Memorial, Tulane, and West Jeff. They are without power and are not, repeat, not accepting any patients. On the east bank only Ochsner Medical Center is fully operational.

Harry gave a shout-out from his solitary listening post: "God bless Jimmie Duckworth and all the rest of our U.S. Coast Guard. I knew he would have them out in the field before anybody else."

◆　◆　◆

It's 12:45 a.m., people, Tuesday morning, the 30th of August. We are now into the second day of this Katrina wind-and-flood disaster. The wind has died down, but something even more terrible has come with this storm. Just when we thought we'd dodged the bullet another time, the waters started rising, and they continue to rise. Levees have been topped and have failed. Reports from St. Bernard Parish and farther south are even worse: fifteen- to twenty-foot walls of water rushed like tidal waves into communities large and small. Details are spotty at this time.

We have had more than a dozen voice and text messages from grateful folks around New Orleans who have been rescued by the brave men and women of the U.S. Coast Guard and Louisiana Wildlife and Fisheries. That's the good news. But some of these people have been dropped off at the Morial Convention Center and were told that there would be buses arriving to take them to Baton Rouge and other shelters across the state. Some

**have been at the Convention Center since six last evening. The emergency staff at the Center is not allowing anyone inside. They deny knowing anything about the Center being used as a staging area or bus pickup site. Apparently, those stranded there have decided to take action on their own. We have heard from two different witnesses who say they are inside the Center with more than a hundred others looking for water, bathrooms, and a place to rest. We don't know where this is going and have not been able to get a response from anyone at NOPD or the mayor's office. Around ten p.m. the mayor's people sent out a text message that his next press conference will be at ten a.m. Tuesday, much later this morning. Perhaps Mr. Nagin is getting a little shut-eye; perhaps a little bird ought to fly over to the Hyatt and wake him up. His people are hurting all over town.**

The wind had sputtered out completely in the last few hours, and the house was eerily quiet. Harry checked down the stairs every thirty or forty-five minutes with his flashlight. The water level had not risen any more over the past five hours and was about one foot below the downstairs ceilings. That made the depth of the flooding ten feet at the house and about thirteen feet down at the street level. The radio had confirmed that water was still pouring in through the levees, but Harry knew there were many square miles of lower-lying parts of the city to fill in.

When he shined the light out in the back patio, he could just see the top of the tiered fountain, also ten feet high. A large raccoon clung to the copper supply pipe; his reflective yellow retinas blinked, on and off, at the light. On the last couple of trips to the stairs, fierce pains shot from his wounded leg each time he shifted weight to that side. His mind continued to surge long after he gingerly lay down in bed. His wound was going to throb and nag all night.

*Higher land here on the fringe of old Metairie Ridge, right up against the 17th Street Canal. Radio says the levee breach here is about a mile from me to the north. Unless the section gives way right behind me, I'll probably stay dry up on the second floor. Better crack some windows, going to be hot tomorrow without the wind. Too bad that stuff's so nasty; a swim would probably feel good in the morning. Wish I had a little bass boat in the back. Not sure where I'd go, maybe help out some other folks if they stayed around here. Do not want to end up at the Morial Convention Center.*

# *Forty*

"**S**gt. McChesney!" It was the second time today someone was calling for him on the track platform. The lieutenant's arm and head were leaning out the window of the train as he waved him into the car. "Come sit with us. Hurry, this one is filling up fast."

Harry had no idea who this officer was, just another uniform heading to Davis-Monthan Field along with him and a trainload of other men going to their crew assignments on the B24 bombers flying out of Tucson, Arizona. Inside the coach he saluted two officers who were seated together and stood up to greet him.

"Sgt. McChesney, please have a seat. I'm 2nd Lt. Tobias Harden, and this is 2nd Lt. Richard Frost. What an amazing coincidence, Sergeant. I was just daydreaming out the window, and I heard that Western Union kid paging a Sgt. Harry McChesney. I thought that there couldn't be two of you. You're a friend of Rock's, Greg Finley's, from Bonham, aren't you?" Without waiting for a reply, he nodded over at his seatmate and said, "Dick and I did our B24 training with Rock over at Tarrant Field near Ft. Worth, and he talked about you all the time. I can't believe it. You'll be happy to know that Rock will be joining us at Monthan while we get tuned up and sorted out. Boy, will he be glad to see you."

"That makes two of us for sure, sir."

"Hey, look, please call me Toby, and Lt. Frost here goes by Dick. We can save the titles and protocol for the top brass. We're all going to be flying these beasts together, and every man will be as important as the others."

Dick, the big man, spoke next, "We know a lot about you, Sergeant. Rock said your handle was Mac. He thinks very highly of you, says you got a raw deal back in primary. By the way, I hope that telegram you got wasn't serious. They don't send those out for little or nothing these days."

"Hey, thanks for asking. I guess it would rate a 'serious' designation, Dick, but not bad news. My big sis, Penny, has just given birth to a baby girl, Winifred Ann Humphreys. I'm a proud uncle."

"Hey, that's a sweet Southern name, I think. Congratulations."

"Dick wouldn't know a Southern name from Adam. He's from Bellingham, Washington—almost a Canadian—never been east of the Rockies before active duty."

"Hey, Mr. Philadelphia Main Line, what do you know? Your parents came over on the *Mayflower* or something, sent you to fancy schools, and you still think Washington is the nation's capital and not the finest state of the forty-eight."

Harry hadn't spent much time in the company of officers since signing up. The ones he had met were decent but seemed cliquish or stuffy about rank. If the crews of the new bomber group he was heading to had more guys like these two, things would be fine.

"I haven't been able to educate him at all, Mac. Dick thinks the District of Columbia is a Southern territory."

"Don't try to tell my father that D.C. is part of the South. He'd be insulted. He also thinks Roosevelt sold us out on Pearl Harbor and should be impeached."

"You folks in New Orleans have some strange political views, I gotta say."

"It's in the water down there, Toby. You should have heard his opinion of Hoover, but my dad at least knows his limits. He had to intercept a letter that my mother had written to the president to warn him that she was holding him personally responsible, as our commander-in-chief, for any harm that might come to me during the hostilities."

"Way to go, Mom. Gotta love it."

Dick stood up and reached for something in the overhead rack.

"Well, gentlemen, I just happen to have a flask of tolerable scotch in my satchel along with a cap that doubles as a shot glass. If you don't mind sharing my modest tumbler, we shall have a toast all around to our mothers, then to new uncles, and to sisters-cum-mothers after that."

"World without end, Amen."

"Cheers!"

# *Forty One*

"**R**ock, I can't believe you're here at Monthan. This is great. How the hell are you? Oops, excuse me; I didn't know this lady was with you. Hello, ma'am. I'm Harry McChesney, at your service."

"Mac, meet my girl, Ruth Higdon, the most wonderful woman in the world and the most intelligent. Most wonderful because she puts up with me, and the most intelligent because she knows instantly when I'm full of horse feathers and still puts up with me!"

"Hello, Mac. I feel as though I already know you. Rock didn't tell me about any other people he'd met in training but you. Good thing you're a guy, or I might be a little jealous."

"I don't think you'll have any real competition, Ruth. From what I can see, Rock's a lucky man to have you for a special friend. Just let me know if he gets out of line, and I'll slap him around."

"Hey, no need for that. Ruth and I are engaged. I want to make an honest woman out of her right away, but she wants to wait until my tour of duty is over and I get home safe."

"Rock, we've talked about this. Ann and I—she's Toby Harden's fiancée, Harry—feel the same way. That doesn't mean we love you any less."

"Well, you know how I feel, but I do agree that Tobias and I have our hands full with other things right now, getting in top form with these damned B24s. Mac, these things are beasts, I'm telling you. They seem reliable enough with massive power and armament out the wazoo, but my God are they brickbats to try to push around in the sky."

Harry wanted more than anything to try his hand at flying these multiengine jobs. Ever since he'd seen his first one up close, he was awed but dreamt of one day climbing into the driver's seat.

"I think you're exaggerating. If anybody can fly them, I'm sure you can, pal."

"I wouldn't call what I'm doing flying them, more like coaxing them into the air, keeping them away from trouble aloft, and praying them back down in one piece. Ruth already knows their nickname, 'Flying Coffins.' Sorry, honey, I promised not to say that in front of you."

"Enough of that flight-deck chatter. When are we going to get a chance to get together this week? I have two friends at the plant who are dying to meet Sgt. McChesney. If we don't start pretty soon on his social calendar, he may end up having to take both of them out at the same time."

"I could learn to live with that, Ruth. I'll take my cue from you on the dating arrangements anytime. Thanks."

"We're supposed to get our flight crew assignments in the morning and then go for our first training runs over the next couple of days. I can't tell you when our next time off base will be, sweets. They're getting more equipment, more B24s, in this week, so there should be enough for each crew to have one up every day. I'm thinking things will be pretty serious for the next couple of weeks, nonstop."

"Yep, Rock, and I know who one of the pilots is sure to be."

"If so, I hope you're my gunny, Mac. And I haven't forgotten my promise to you about getting you back on the flight deck, behind the controls. But whatever happens, it's great to be back together again."

"You have no idea how glad I am to be here, Rock."

## *Forty Two*

"**S**kipper, we have a re-plot on that heading since takeoff."

"Shoot, Roscoe, what are my new numbers? I was kinda happy with the assigned course although those clouds are spoiling our view up here."

Harry was officially part of B24 crew #1099, ten men who were learning to work together in the most complex weapons system that the army had ever put in the sky. Skipper, the pilot, was Tobias Harden, who had toasted mothers with him a month ago on their first train ride together. Dick Frost, the big fellow from Washington State, was flying as co-pilot. Rock, of course, was also chosen as a pilot, but with another crew. They were all flying now out of Pueblo Army Air Base in Colorado. At first Harry was disappointed he hadn't landed with Rock's crew, but he was getting to know his own and starting to feel like part of a team, officers and enlisted guys.

Navigator Roscoe "Ross" Merkle, one of two college graduates on board, was from New York City. He bled Dodger blue, having grown up in Flatbush, only four blocks from Ebbets Field. His Brooklyn accent reminded Harry of the hard-drinking men who worked in William B. Reily's coffee warehouses and lived in a part of New Orleans called the Irish Channel. Ross enjoyed a whiskey now and then, and also like the Irish, he had an endless supply of funny stories.

"We are restricted to present altitude, so we need to bear off to 209 degrees, that's two-zero-niner."

"Well, there are clouds over that way too, Ross. I've already had a workout turning this baby today, what's up?"

"Skipper, I don't know about your view, but this new heading is going to help your disposition for the rest of the morning. I've checked my numbers three times, and I'm sure the course they gave us at briefing is filled with problems."

"Like what?"

"About three miles dead ahead, hiding in those fluffy clouds is the first one. It's a snow-capped peak that is about three thousand feet higher than we are. If we make it through that one, call me back, and we can review my other concerns."

"Heading west to two-zero-niner."

Rock was right; the B24 was a monster. Longer than a boxcar at sixty-seven feet, nose to tail, with a wingspan of 110 feet, the new J-series was powered by four supercharged Pratt-Whitney engines with 1,200 horsepower each. With just the crew and a training load of fuel and ammunition, the plane lumbered off a runway passably well, but Skipper and Dick needed a lot of muscle to keep it steady in the prop wash while bunching up and flying practice formations. Harry took every opportunity to see what it took to fly the thing firsthand, standing on the flight deck just behind his pilot and co-pilot while on their training runs.

For the flight officers who had been training on earlier B24s, there were lots of modifications on the J-series that required more training. Bombardier Daniel Trimble from Pine Bluff, Arkansas, had a new version of the Norden bombsight and autopilot to get acquainted with. He had grown up hunting and could master anything with a sight in no time. Each member of the team had a background that made him especially suited to his responsibilities on board. Their growing confidence in one another's abilities fostered a camaraderie that began with the Skipper's egalitarian leadership and respect for his men. They would walk the wings for him if that's what it would take to get the job done and return safely.

The .50-caliber gun turret in the nose was manned by Philip Bertke from Roanoke, Virginia. He doubled as armorer for the team. The waist gunner, Seth Steiner, claimed to be the first Jewish plumber in Victoria, Texas, since the Spanish friars burned out the French and Hebrew traders. No one knew whether Seth was kidding or not. At age twenty-four he was the oldest of the crew and a serious, self-taught student of colonial Mexican history who always had his nose in some worm-eaten frontier diary. He doubled as the ship's assistant flight engineer.

Charles West was the chief fight engineer and a graduate of the School of Engineering at the University of Illinois. He also manned the twin machine guns in the top turret after takeoff. Growing up in Louisville, Kentucky, he should have been a Cubs or Cardinals fan, but baseball and flight decks made for crazy compatriots. Like the navigator, Ross, he was a die-hard Dodgers fan because he shared his hometown with Pee Wee Reese, who helped Brooklyn win the 1941 National League pennant. Westy and Ross hated the New York Yankees who had stolen the World Series from the Bums that year.

Radio operator John "Jay" Kemperman from Milwaukee and tail gunner Alexis "Lex" Pappanopoulis from Chicago rounded out the crew. Harry was assistant radio operator and manned the ball turret guns. Luckily, he wasn't stuck in there most of the time.

Just getting into the ball turret was a squeeze, even for a fellow of medium build like Harry. Many of their missions were to be flown between twenty thousand and thirty thousand feet, where temperatures averaged minus fifty degrees. Along with improved design features in the aircraft, the "Blue Bunny" heated flight suits had been replaced by a more reliable and streamlined outfit. Streamlined was a relative term. The men had written the following cheat sheet on the wall of their dressing quarters:

- Flannel long johns
- Wool shirt and pants
- Heated pants and jacket
- Socks and heated boot liners
- Fur-lined boots
- Nylon gloves
- Heated gloves
- Goggles and earphones
- Oxygen mask with microphone

When he added his flak suit and Mae West, he barely fit. He had to leave his parachute by the waist gunner's stand and hope it would be there if he needed it after he crawled out of the ball. Most men found that prospect as unattractive as the fetal position assumed facing the earth while suspended in the ball turret underneath the belly of the beast.

Being the "Fighting Fetus" was risky business, no doubt, but Harry concluded it was not much riskier than simply getting in the aircraft. Flak and enemy fighters were not threatening them over Colorado, but training losses of crews and equipment were

202 | W.S. Culpepper

heavy nonetheless. One team got lost in a thunderstorm, tried to find an alternate landing sight, and crashed at night, killing all aboard. The same week, a fuel leak started a fire on another aircraft, and only two men were able to parachute out of the bomb bay before the plane exploded. Later in the month, another entire crew was lost, flying into the same mountain range that Ross had avoided.

Each loss meant another set of empty bunks and personal belongings to pack up for shipment home to family. Sometimes these were the only identifiable remains that could be returned to the mourners. The unspoken understanding among all those who flew was that any liquor that the dead left behind was to be consumed in short order during the packing up. The alcohol might only dull the pain from loss of a close friend, but in each case those who needed it the most were never allowed to drink alone. A determined cohesiveness settled upon the remaining crews. Harry was certain he was serving in one of the best. Time was drawing near to receive their combat assignments.

# Forty Three

The upstairs bedroom was a steamy ninety degrees when Harry woke up among soggy sheets that clung like overcooked pasta. His leg wound was throbbing again, and he had kicked most of the covers off during a fitful eight hours. Clearing the sleep from his eyes, he glanced at his watch.

"Oh-eight-thirty hours, August 30th. This is the second night I've slept but felt worse the next day."

Remembering the threat of rising waters, Harry jerked up and over to the side of the bed facing the hallway and stairs. The moment his feet hit the floor, an intense pain gripped his right calf. A serous, yellow-brown stain had soaked through the bandages. An odor resembling ham left too long out of the refrigerator wafted up from his leg-and-gauze patch job.

"Smells rank."

Moving about required that he execute a bouncing limp to avoid weighting his right leg. He peeked over the banister; the watermark on the stairs hadn't risen or fallen since early morning hours. The night's sweaty undershorts were the next donation to his bag of storm trash.

It was still possible to summon a flood of fresh water from the shower head, and Harry gingerly unwrapped the foul dressings and tape from his leg. Dark-red blood oozed forth. Washing with soap and flushing the area was not as painful as bearing weight on that side. He hoped that he had done an adequate job. He had looked again last night for some antibiotic ointment but found none. The skin over the circumference of his leg below the knee felt boggy, denting like putty. His right leg was obviously fatter than the left. He'd learned enough about wounds in the war to be concerned about the swelling: infection could be spreading in the soft tissues.

The toilet still flushed without backing up on the second floor. The engineer in him couldn't help but wonder where the waste water was actually going. He also wondered if there was anyone else still in his neighborhood who might have cause to flush or shower today.

"Probably nobody left within a mile of here. You are the Lone Ranger, my boy. Tonto got the horses out while the trail was still dry."

It was almost noon by the time he got his leg re-dressed and ate some cheese and bread and an apple. He saved his last beer for dinner. He hobbled to all the windows in the upper levels of the house, searching in vain for any signs of activity in the immediate neighborhood and in the skies overhead. His plan of action for the day was to repeat his reconnoiter at least hourly from every vantage point and keep an eye on the flood waters. Meanwhile, he thought he should catch up on current affairs, courtesy of his friends at WWL.

**Our reporter just returned by canoe from the Superdome. The water on Poydras Street and around the pedestrian ramps is four to five feet deep. Over twenty thousand people have migrated to the building at this time, and conditions there are deteriorating**

rapidly. One person is confirmed dead, thought to be from complications of a diabetic condition and possibly a drug overdose. The temperature inside the building late this morning was over one hundred degrees. The stench from the overwhelmed toilet facilities is inescapable. Officials are doing their best to try to get food and some water out to everyone inside. They are considering locking the doors, not to keep people from leaving but to prevent any more from entering.

Judging from numerous citizens' reports, there is widespread looting in every sector of the city. The Walmart Superstore on Tchoupitoulas Street did not flood, and employees had set up an emergency distribution center off of their loading docks. They were offering people essentials like diapers, food, and water, but others out there destroyed the main entrances and decided that flat-screen TVs and stereos were essential for their survival.

Elsewhere, some of the looting is methodical, the work of teams of professional thieves moving from house to house. These criminals are very well organized with more boats and weapons than the city and state police have been able to muster at this hour. Somebody has been doing some planning, seems like mostly the bad guys.

Fires are burning in the Central Business District and probably elsewhere as well. We can see at least five large columns of smoke from the rooftop of our building just off the approach to the Crescent City Connection. Hundreds of people are milling around on the elevated levels of this roadway, part of the I-10/downtown expressway. We have also learned recently that hundreds, perhaps thousands more people are finding their way to the Morial Convention Center. As far as we know, there are no provisions at that site for anyone. One death has already occurred there, cause unknown, and gunfire is reported from inside the building. NOPD

**are not, repeat, not on the scene. We advise anyone who can hear us to avoid this location until further notice.**

**Mayor Nagin announced at his ten a.m. press conference that sandbags are being dropped by some Army Reserve helicopters into the breach of the 17th Street Canal levee. But, the small amount of material that they have been able to deliver today has simply disappeared into the waters rushing through the gap that is approximately two hundred feet wide and eroded to an unknown depth. We don't have details on conditions at the other levee breaches at this time. The mayor also said—**

He snapped the radio off; he'd heard enough. The reports were unremittingly disturbing. Like almost every native son who'd chosen to make a life in New Orleans, Harry loved the city as much as he loved to criticize and complain about it. He tried to distance himself from his emotions and his immediate predicament with a dispassionate analysis, but the words spilled out more like a eulogy. He delivered his grim assessment to the open window.

"Pretty soon the city and the lake are going to get to the same level. That is the only thing that will stop the inflow of water. Until construction crews can rebuild the levees and repair the pumping stations to start moving the water back out, the flooding will be with us—weeks, maybe months. Each stagnant day will be a false equilibrium. Under the waters, decay will accelerate with more death, disease, and destruction ahead than we've already had. Much of New Orleans will never be the same, might never recover."

For the first time it occurred to Harry that *he* might never recover, might not survive the ordeal. He rated that probability as fairly low, but he knew people almost always underestimated risk of serious threats, extraordinary events.

Before today, the calculus of his own death had never disturbed him. As a youth he was driven to foolish acts and was heedless of dangerous circumstances. He had dared death to take him as it had his brother. His uncle finally instilled in him a sense of purpose and held him to a higher standard of behavior. The McChesney Code and the Three Challenges were for a lifetime, but Harry never thought much about when his time might end except during the war. Yes, there were several times during the abject terror of the flak bombardments when he would have welcomed death, a relief from the agony of enveloping concussion and carnage.

Of course, death could come anytime, but before, during, and after the war, he had managed to be one of the lucky ones. He had buried and mourned many others, and he had come to accept death as just another part of life—a union of opposites. Still, his own good fortune kept him dancing with an understandable mixture of guilt and denial about mortality, others' and his own.

Occasionally, he might consider briefly his preferred mode of exit, and he always came back to something sudden. Almost every older person hoped for the same thing. And if he didn't make it through his present ordeal, heaven or whatever alternative might prove to be another good assignment. He was raised to believe in his soul's afterlife and was curious about what he might ultimately find when he quit his body.

As for the here and now, he had to admit that he had never been much of a philosopher, just happy to be a competent, hands-on guy. He'd always preferred the active over the contemplative side of life. Active, like his best efforts to meet the McChesney family challenges after he'd stopped being overwhelmed by their immensity. Active, to answer challenges that were calling again, just outside his window: his city and its people were deluged with misery. He wanted to be part of the solution, not relegated to another piece of the problem.

Life's journey, up to this unfamiliar point of stasis and reflection, had been satisfying. He valued that feeling far more than happiness—whatever that was. He'd embraced fully his uncle's challenge to reach out to others. He thought of hurricanes past when he was young and full of energy. He had helped people rebuild homes in the ravaged Lower Ninth Ward after the flood gates had failed during Betsy. He had spent almost a year of weekends with volunteers from his church to help the folks in Mississippi after Camille. There was always another task that beckoned, another person to help, another problem to solve. Good works trumped an uplifting sermon any day, laity over liturgy. But he'd achieved only partial success.

He regretted never finding the vast store of wealth that Uncle Harry had locked away. He could have done so much more with that at his disposal, but his uncle had refused to even discuss the matter after that first memorable night in his library. Harry had searched diligently for more than sixty years without success for the key that would provide access to the treasure. Ruefully admitting defeat, he often wondered why his uncle had been so cavalier with great wealth that could have benefited others. He concluded that Uncle Harry's main objective was helping his nephew, his successor, define himself and become a resourceful family leader by prodding him with an extra-difficult challenge. Harry was sorry the good man had overestimated him.

Sitting in his sweltering upstairs office, nursing a debilitating leg wound, he had to admit that his list of options and control over his own destiny were limited and shrinking by the day.

"Well, Dad, maybe there is no Plan X for me to discover this time. Uncle Harry, maybe I'm not up to any more challenges."

As soon as he'd spoken, his mind and body began to relax. As effortlessly as though it were a daily routine, he began to pray silently and meditate on his dead father and uncle and brother and the Holy Ghost and any other ghosts in his past who might render comfort if not aid to an old man in trouble.

# Forty Four

It was early Tuesday afternoon when Harry left off his meditation and prayers. Time to get with the daily regimen and reconnoiter round his refuge. Water levels inside and out had not changed after that first twenty-four hours of flooding. He decided that the flooding had already crested, at least in his part of the city. He would try to hold out in his home until help arrived. There was food and drinking water for perhaps a week but no more cell phone. Assuming his daughter received his last text message yesterday morning, he had to rely on his family's knowledge of his whereabouts and their ability to notify rescue parties. Even then, he would be listed as missing, unaccounted for, on a roster of names that was rapidly mounting into the thousands. Who knew when his home would be on anyone's list to be checked out?

If he sighted people or equipment in the area, he could try to make his presence known by using a smudge pot or some kind of signal from his rooftop during the day. He was agile and spry for an eighty-something gentleman before his leg injury, but he didn't relish a trip out his dormer window onto a pitched roof after the way he felt today. Swimming out in the bilge water was not a healthy option. He had no idea which direction would be the best to try to swim in. From his meager vantage point, flooding to a depth of ten or more feet extended for miles on all sides. He longed to leave the house to explore the situation but felt he couldn't risk exposing his wound to another massive dose of bacteria. No denying it now, his refuge had become his prison.

His sister, Penny, had suffered a more gradual loss of freedom in her senescence. Now eighty-eight years old, severe arthritis had her struggling with a walker. After three bad falls she still refused to leave her old split-level home for something safer, more user-friendly. Her son, Walker Jr., had snatched her out of town ahead of the storm last Friday. Harry was glad the rest of the family had dodged all this.

As the afternoon wore on, boredom layered on chronic fatigue from stress and infection. After a couple of hours reading the Bible, Harry's eyes began to close, but he hated the idea of sleeping again. He limped to his desk and stared at the papers and family photos before giving in.

◆　◆　◆

"**H**arry, come over here, please." Pattie, his current favorite and date for his sister's wedding, waved him over with her free hand while she advanced the film in her fancy camera. "Penny and Walker are sick of posing for pictures, but I still don't have one of you and them together."

"Hey, best man, come stand by your sister on the double; it's about time to greet the guests and drink some champagne."

Walker smiled and gave his new bride another kiss on the cheek. Decked out in his white-dress navy uniform, he was, quite simply, a stunningly handsome man. Trim, muscular, about six feet three inches, he held himself in a relaxed-but-erect manner that exuded self-confidence and goodwill. His wavy, brown hair framed an angular English nose and chin, hazel-brown eyes, and a neatly trimmed mustache. A slightly wicked little dimple dented his chin.

Penny stood proudly to Walker's right, the radiant bride. She was still holding her modest floral arrangement of small pink roses and trailing silk ribbons. Her dress of a satiny silk fell in beautiful folds from her tiny waist. However, it was her smile that captivated the attendants, including her brother. Harry was dressed in his white linen suit in honor of the occasion even though it was well after Labor Day in November of 1942.

"Sis, I don't think I've ever seen two more genuinely happy faces in my whole life. I am so glad I could be here, and I feel really honored that you asked me to be your best man, Walker."

"OK, happy people, look over this way. Last picture, I promise. I don't have to tell anybody to smile; I think that comes with the occasion. Nice, thank you!"

Harry really liked Penny's choice of husbands. Walker made him feel relaxed and welcome in his company. He always seemed to have a funny story to tell about his adventures as a medical student or resident-in-training. He treated Harry as an equal even though he and Penny were almost seven years his senior. He was also a physician and a lieutenant commander in the U.S. Navy. Harry's folks thought Walker walked on water, not just sailed over it.

The wedding and reception were at their Uncle Harry and Aunt May's home. It was a happy occasion indeed, on many levels. After Harry and Penny's lunch together a few weeks before the wedding, their relationship had entered a new and welcome phase. Partly because they wanted to wipe away the old misery between them and partly a spillover from how Penny felt about Walker, or so Harry thought. There were still many things about his sister that he didn't understand.

# Forty Five

Harry felt himself falling through space. He floundered and jerked himself around like a kitten dropped upside down from a basket. Harry was no kitten, and he wasn't falling either. He managed to wake himself up and stay in the swivel-tilt chair at his office desk.

As he massaged some blood back into his extremities, he looked again at the other wedding picture that he'd rescued from downstairs. He, Penny, and Walker Humphreys were standing in front of the baby grand in the petit salon at Uncle Harry's just before the reception. It must have been the trigger for the dream he'd just had. Who knew anymore? So many vivid images and recollections had bombarded him in the last couple of days. Might they begin to seem almost as real as what was happening while awake? He knew men under terrible conditions in war or during extreme isolation suffered delusions and hallucinations. When fully alert at least, he could still discern clearly between past and present, dream and reality. The importance of each was another question, however. Perhaps his dreams were taking on almost as much meaning and relevance as his waking thoughts and feelings?

Less hard to decipher from this end of time's tunnel was how he had misread his sister's character and conviction when she'd decided to marry Walker. As a gregarious youth who fancied himself a bon vivant, he'd had trouble understanding how his sister could jump from leading a reclusive life to settling down to married life without taking time to enjoy the company of at least a few attractive men. Oh, her loyal friends or family would drag her out of her shell for a while, like around her birthday or for some holiday fun. But back then she remained timid and introverted.

In retrospect, he understood how traumatized she'd remained from early childhood. She'd spoken to him movingly about the depth of her pain of rejection during Buddy's illness and how responsible, guilty, and at risk of a similar fate she felt at his death. It always came back to Buddy. He grasped much of what she told him at the time; then he experienced his own losses during the war. He became for a while like Penny, conditioned to expect impermanence, sensitized by mortality.

Finally he'd understood that her commitment to marriage was an act of great courage. Walker was a commissioned officer who was vital to the war operation. Moreover, as a navy medical officer, he was attached to the U.S. Marines who would be among the first waves of landings and bloody assaults in any battle. But the young couple touched each other with their passion and desire. Their emotions were strong enough to kindle in her a belief in shared love. That balance between emotions and belief was essential for her to accept the risks of a lifelong vow of fidelity. She was willing to risk repeating and reliving all life's early trauma at a time in history when wives and families were losing loved ones every day. Back then, the words "life" and "long" didn't seem like they belonged together.

Harry sighed and grimaced. Nature was not remotely considerate of the sensitive or protective of the cautious. Human nature could be just as inconsiderate and destructive. Years after Walker had returned safely from the war, after Penny had given him three healthy children, after she'd almost lost him again to complications from minor surgery, he took up with another woman, a physician whom he'd first met at a medical meeting in Chicago a week after their twenty-first wedding anniversary.

Little Penny under the bed knew that life offered only passing respite, never a bond of refuge. Penny of the wedding vows tried with all her fiber and spirit to believe otherwise. Those twin demons, rejection and loss, were only resting in their labyrinth. As though her latent uncertainty had called them forth, they arose and reached out and smote her and tore her flesh and devoured her heart and left her bones to wither on the weathered rocks of memory.

# Forty Six

Just before noon on Wednesday, August 31st, Harry studied the desolate waterscape while leaning against the frame of an open window. Scraggly, mostly denuded tree branches and top stories of houses and drifting debris broke the monotony of the hazy-glazy interface of sky and water. The only sounds he heard were his own breathing and a high-pitched ringing in his ears. A turtle sunned itself on the hood of his neighbor's semi-buoyant RV. No rescue craft plied the waters or the air above; not a bird or a voice called out. He knew it was close to one hundred degrees in the sun, but he felt tiny muscle quiverings along his spine that warned him of low-grade fever and chills. He'd had these since early morning.

The miracle of the tap water from the shower continued another day. He tried again to clear and cleanse his wound with the pressure of the water jets. Unfortunately, in the light of the office window the bugger didn't look too good. A thick, yellow coating of goop over the open part came mostly away with each treatment but reformed under each new bandage. He couldn't tell what was happening down in the exposed bone. The fleshy margins were exquisitely tender, with purple-red blotching extending out an inch or so into the surrounding skin. There were faint, red streaks in a cobweb pattern extending from the four-inch gash to above his knee. Those spider webs had not been there yesterday.

He was tiring more easily with each passing day. He made himself eat and drink, drink quite a lot. He was glad he'd filled both tubs for drinking water. He vowed to drink even more because of the heat.

"If I could walk out of here tomorrow, I'm not sure how far I would make it alone." He didn't pursue that line of speculation any farther; he held onto the hope of rescue, if not self-rescue. That was enough for now. He checked in with his adoptive family at WWL radio.

> Governor Blanco has spoken personally with President Bush and requested massive lists of relief supplies and FEMA personnel in addition to forty thousand federal troops. She did not specify how she had arrived at those figures or where any of the military would be drawn from.

> Marty Bahamonde, Regional Director for External Affairs for FEMA, said that evacuations of citizens in the metro area will begin today, starting with the worst of the sick and wounded at the Superdome. The Astrodome in Houston and other sites in Texas cities will be among the first centers to receive evacuees.

> Mayor Nagin has declared a state of martial law will be in force within the city beginning at seven p.m. this evening. As part of this new effort to control rampant looting, all NOPD officers will be directed to crime-control efforts, and police-related rescue operations will cease immediately.

He flipped the radio off and screamed at the little box.

"You fucking idiot! Taking police off search and rescue to keep the store fronts safe! There are hundreds, thousands of people like me out here—stinking and rotting away, praying for help!"

Harry decided he would be happy to entertain looters, anybody who might get him out of solitary confinement. He limped along the upstairs hall and went up the back stairs into the attic. He needed to visit another part of his enclosure for variety's sake and check outside from a new vantage point. Opening the windows on the upper level didn't offer any immediate relief from the heat. There was no air circulating up under the roof.

He gazed east over the section of lake now covering the interstate roadway. How many days ago had he tried to leave? He took off one of the dormer screens and leaned out to his right to see if the Southern Railroad trestle and tracks were above water, but the house immediately next door obstructed his view. Two disgustingly large flies buzzed inside before he could reset the screen. Harry's putrid wound inflamed his bloodstream and his imagination. He pictured countless bodies across the city beginning to fester and rise in the heat, floating feasts for carrion's minions. These two would regret having left the party.

The slate roof shingles expanded in the heat and made weird noises inside the attic. The space was nearly empty, and every sound had an echo. An ancient duffel bag from an ancient war, three pieces of battered luggage, and a few boxes of clothes were stacked under the rafters. He opened an old footlocker and took out a photo album that he recognized as dating back to his youth. Its bound pages were of soft, black construction paper, and he had written a remark or title in white ink under each of the mounted black-and-white pictures.

"This should be interesting, maybe a laugh or two in here somewhere."

He took it back downstairs to the office. A couple of apples, canned soups, and beans were the only remaining solid fare in his larder. He said his customary blessing before spooning up another meal. He swallowed two ibuprofen tablets and a multivitamin in lieu of anything meaningful for his bum leg.

He wanted to glance at the photo album before dark. He took it with him back to his bed and propped up some pillows for his leg. On the first page there was only a single picture of two scrawny young men with prominent Adam's apples and pointy elbows, dressed in shorts and undershirts. They were consciously posing, looking toward the camera and laughing while assuming a sparring stance, each of them laced into a pair of the largest boxing gloves ever manufactured. The title read, "Harry and the Bean, 1941." A few pages later he stopped at an eight-by-ten-inch glossy print of his bomber crew standing on the tarmac beneath a mammoth, olive-drab aircraft that sported some fancy nose art. He ran his right index finger lightly across each one of their faces, recalling their nicknames, and smiling at each as he dozed off again.

"You guys are *still* the best of the best. I love every one of you. God bless."

# Forty Seven

Lt. Harden, their pilot, gazed in admiration and said, "I don't think the ground crews have ever had to change the oil in those engines, boys." The big B24 had logged less than fifteen hours since leaving the factory. "Look how clear the cockpit windshield is."

"She's all ours, for sure, Skipper?"

"It's official, Lex; I had to sign a quadruplicate receipt for her."

Dick, ever the skeptic, piped up, "Hold on, how do we know this machine's a female? I grew up on a farm, and I don't see any quick way to sex this one."

Skipper and Lex rolled their eyes derisively at that remark. Looking for moral support, Dick shouted over toward the aircraft, "Hey, Mac, quit studying the instrument panel." Then, in a quick aside to his pilot, "Jeez, the guy's incorrigible, really wants to fly the thing, huh, Skip?" This time, more emphatically, "*Mac!* Come out of there and settle this debate, will ya."

Harry dropped out of the bomb bay and ambled over to his mates. Dick reprised the problem.

"Skipper's trying to go all nautical on us and assign the female gender to this noble craft. You're a man of some upbringing and culture, more like a noble savage actually, so weigh in, matey.

What say you?"

"Well, I've seen all sorts of names—genitalia too—painted on these babies. I say anything goes."

"'Anything Goes,' is that what you're proposing we call our new fighting home?"

"Dick, I always suspected you were a literal-minded philosopher. I like Cole Porter a lot, but I don't know about the rest of the guys. No, what I meant was that whatever gender and name we agree upon is right for our flying boat."

Skip tried to get on with it.

"We four are the decorating committee for the prom, girls. When I signed for this boxcar this morning, I told Ramirez, the painter, to come over here at 1000 hours and get his instructions. It's 0945; we need to come to a decision about nose art for our aircraft."

"I think we ought to go with something weird and wild to make the enemy think twice about taking us on. Don't you, Skipper?"

"Yeah, I like that, weird and wild! What do you have in mind, Mac?"

"I always liked the comic strip *Krazy Kat* when I was growing up."

The whimsical Kat tickled Lex's fancy, too.

"Oh, wow. With Ignatz, the brick-throwing mouse, and Offissa Pupp? That strip still runs in the Chicago papers. They are wild."

"I'm for that," Dick added, "lots of crews are going with big-breasted, big-assed women, but I'd prefer something like a comic-strip character. Tell those sons of bitches we're laughing at them."

"The artist that does the strip, George Herriman, grew up in New Orleans. Whenever people ask him whether Krazy Kat is male or female, he always answers, 'Neither, the Kat's a pixie, a little of both and neither at the same time.' So, there is your weird twist to go with the wild."

"Only in New Orleans, Mac. Sounds perfect, but what do we tell Ramirez to paint?"

"Well, for sure, we want the name, Krazy Kat, in big cartoon lettering. And below that, I imagined something like Krazy Kat finally getting fed up with Ignatz instead of in love with the mean little mouse, and turning the tables on the rodent. Krazy can be bending over and holding a big bomb ready to drop on Ignatz who is running like hell for cover—good advice for those we visit, too."

Lex and Dick were both laughing and shaking their heads in appreciation. Dick then spoke for them both, "About what we expected from the guy in the ball turret: totally whacko, totally great. We'll be proud to fly as a Krazy Kat."

"I take it that we're in agreement, girls? All in favor say aye."

"Aye!"

◆  ◆  ◆

Harry would have preferred to remain asleep. His jolt back to his present situation left him longing for the confidence and youth of his dreams.

*What the hell did I do with the flashlight? OK, here we go, lights. Almost midnight, almost September 1st, starting the fifth day of my captivity. Need to talk to my jailer about a better diet and some antibiotics.*

He didn't bother to take his temperature. He knew he had a fever and those total-body aches that felt like the flu or like someone had beaten him with clubs in his sleep.

*Getting weaker, sleeping more and more. Tomorrow . . . later today . . . Thursday . . . . Yeah, gotta try an escape if no one comes by noon. Come first light, I have to eat again. Need all the strength I can muster. Got to find help.*

Weak and uncomfortable, Harry rolled around, seeking a slightly cooler, drier patch of bedding. He tried to focus on a plan for the coming light but fell asleep again.

# PART SEVEN

## Krazy Kats

# Forty Eight

Hands on his hips and elbows akimbo, Ross surveyed the sweep of the harbor like a newly elected prime minister. The navigator was intrigued by his adopted native constituency as they carried out their daily affairs along the waterfront. Capverdiens were exceptionally tall and slender and extremely gregarious, launching into their indecipherable French dialect with any passing stranger.

Ross took in a deep breath of the damp sea breeze and then exclaimed, "Ah, welcome to the verdant Cape Verde peninsula, Mac. Other than the ninety-eight degrees and ninety-eight-percent humidity, this is a fine spit of a spot, is it not?"

"Sure feels good to stretch the land legs after twelve hours in the *Krazy Kat*. I'm glad God stuck this part of Africa way out in the ocean for us. Climate reminds me of back home in New Orleans."

"Called the tropics, I do believe. Feels like the inside of a greenhouse to me."

"Yeah, we've crossed the equator three times since we left Brazil. I was keeping pretty close tabs on things most of the time from the flight deck."

"Did you get any shut-eye on the way over or just moon about the whole flight behind Skipper and Dick?"

"Aw, ease up, Ross. You know I want to learn everything I can about the ship."

"And become the next co-pilot, too. Hey, I wish you luck, brother. I'll just stick to my charts."

"Did your precious charts show anything useful along this meridian, like Dakar's cultural attractions and drinking establishments? The only adult beverage they serve us enlisted men at Eknes air base is peanut beer. I'd sooner drink aviation fuel."

"Just contain your alcoholic cravings and enjoy the historic harbor sights a while longer. We're going to meet the whole crew at a spot down the quay for a French West African feast—complete with French wines and lagers—around sunset."

"You may think Dakar with its ocean view is swell, but I hear the base up in Marrakech is a lot nicer, including red-blooded American women to look after us at a three-star Red Cross Club. Just give me a few days with the Red Cross girls in sunny North Africa before we go freeze our asses off in East Anglia."

"Ask and ye shall receive, dear boy. No doubt the army is eager to reward you for your valorous seven days of service since we've left the States. Now, let's go find that exotic dining spot and make sure the drinks are safe to consume before the rest of the crew put themselves in harm's way."

"Lead the way, Lieutenant."

"I always do."

◆  ◆  ◆

Harry loved the food at the little dive in the port of Dakar. The seafood soup was dark and spicy, a lot like the Creole gumbo he'd grown up with in New Orleans. Some of the others hadn't adapted so well to the mix of abundant alcohol and peppery foods and were moaning in their bunks for several hours after returning to Eknes Field just before midnight.

The crews bivouacked in tents open to the night breezes with sides and doors rolled up. While commiserating with his ailing mates, he wondered about mosquitoes and malaria in these parts. They were issued one of the tents without any insect netting, but bugs didn't seem to be a problem as long as there was air stirring. He said a prayer to the trade wind gods and nodded off to the exotic sounds of jungle drums not far away.

◆　◆　◆

"**B**oss! Scuzemoi, boss."

Harry was not awake but was aware of a puzzling new turn his tropical dream was taking.

"Scuze*moi*, boss."

Now Harry *was* awake and looking up at a seven-foot giant whose eyes and teeth seemed to glow in the dark, in radiant-white contrast to the purplish-blue shimmer of his oiled and scantily clad body. The native was smiling broadly and slightly bent over Harry's cot underneath the tent cords. He wasn't armed or acting threatening but was jiggling something suspended on a leather braid from his left hand. There were larger amulets and gizmos dangling from around his neck and draped along his left arm, like a carnival huckster might offer kewpie dolls or a street thief his watch inventory. These wonders were clearly for sale.

*"Je m'apelle Natobó.* Me plenty *gran voo-doo medcín,* big doctor. Make plenty big power for you *en bataille, dans la guerre.* You buy one of my *gris-gris ce soir?"*

"Jesus, what time is it? How did you get in here?"

The eager vendor understood little but heard the word "Jesus," and was determined to make a sale in spite of his belief in the superiority of his local deities and ancestors over the lesser gods. He started to dig into a small pouch of crucifixes and Hindu phalluses.

Harry had to find a way to cast out this zealot. Then, Bertha whispered a reminder in his ear—at least, he thought it was her voice. He sat up and pulled up his undershirt.

"Here, Natobó, check these out, big man."

The intruder's eyelids suddenly peeled wide open, and Harry understood the term "eye-popping" for the first time. As Natobó drew back reflexively, he also stood up and almost took the side of the tent with him as he left. Whatever he saw draped around the neck of *l'américain* had impressed and repulsed him.

"Worked like a charm. Thanks, Bertha." And Harry slept peacefully the remainder of the night.

# *Forty Nine*

"**O**ther than the runways and the perimeter track, this sure doesn't look like the air bases we have back home. Security is not exactly bristling up at you either, Mac."

"I wouldn't fret overly much, Seth."

"It seems to me the odd cow hereabouts pulls most of the sentry duty. This is some wide-open operation, like a West Texas ranch."

"See those big oil drums huddled up over on the edge of that field? That's where we'll be sitting base defense duty tomorrow night with our .50-cals perched right on top of those cement-filled drums—or ones just like them in another damned patch of Brussels sprouts."

The *Krazy Kat's* four gunnery sergeants, Seth, Lex, Bertke, and Mac, were on the observation deck atop the control tower looking over their new home, Station 336, just outside of the little village of Metfield, Suffolk. It was one of 130 Royal Air Force and Army Air Corps bases crammed into East Anglia, a region on the eastern coast of England about the same size as the state of New Hampshire. The fighter pilots who had used the base first just called it Metfield. The fighter squadrons were transferred about a month ago to accommodate the pressing need for more heavy-bomber groups in the European Theater of Operations.

Only runways, aircraft parking—the hardstands—and the connecting perimeter track had priority over the locals' farmland. As on most other bases in these counties, the operations, support, and housing for three thousand staff at Metfield were dispersed widely across scrub land and densely wooded areas with most of the arable land still under cultivation. Washing up, mess halls, and latrines were a good hike from the men's barracks, all connected by slick, muddy roads. The villagers assured the men that those glorified cow paths would dry out eventually. One unverified account had them remaining dry "for an entire fortnight, once upon the summer last."

The flight crews and aircraft that were to make up the 491st Bombardment Group were touching down daily. This was a new heavy bombardment group in the Eighth Air Force that was being fashioned from whole cloth—new trainees and new airplanes. Lt. Col. Goldberg, Commanding Officer, was determined to whip his four squadrons into shape for combat duty in short order. He was a terse, gruff career man who expected excellence of his men. He also inspired devotion and loyalty. An intense schedule of indoctrination lectures, air raid drills, and calls to battle stations were just part of the getting-acquainted party he had instructed squadron C.O., Maj. Escar Watts, to arrange for the crews.

Watts greeted their first assembly with warm assurances that the weather in East Anglia had been pretty mild and dry for an English springtime. Since their arrival in late May 1944, soggy drizzle and penetrating cold were their constant companions. They had no idea what chilly and damp would feel like.

During the first eight hours of their indoctrination lectures, it became clear that a high standard existed to which they would necessarily be held accountable, known henceforth as "how we do it in the Eighth." Extreme precision in flying tight formations was required for success in bringing men and equipment home safely. Stragglers and crippled aircraft were preferred prey of the enemy fighters. Watts delivered a solemn fact of battle: not all of the men assembled that day would be around the next week. Everyone's job was to make sure as many as possible were. He spared them the brutal statistics, the losses that he knew other B24 groups had suffered. Not one man in the audience really wanted to know those stats just then.

◆　◆　◆

"Christ! Who was that guy, Dick? Second Goddamned idiot on the wrong heading since takeoff. I know we're not off course."

"Roger that, Skipper. This is nuts right now, and we haven't even finished forming up the squadron over the first radio beacon. Visibility sucks."

"Yeah. I'm going on the VHF and tell lead to look for some clear sky over the beacon at 21,000. We'll probably fight the contrails up there, but that's better than hide-and-seek down here. We're already ten minutes behind in forming up the group."

"Four squadrons in the drill today is part of the problem. And we're in the slot—low man out back. How the hell did that happen?"

"We're supposed to babysit some of the laggards back this way. Some guys need a helluva lot more work. Shit! There goes another dingbat off the left wing. Keep your eyes peeled while I raise lead."

Group command was pushing them hard. This was the sixth formation practice flight in five days. Each member of *Krazy Kat's* crew shared the pilot and co-pilot's anxiety—fear of failing to execute well and possibly harming others, compounded by the fear of getting knocked out of the sky by another plane.

Nobody in the 491st had any combat experience, but Harry thought the Krazy Kats worked together with great precision compared to the other crews that shared their Nissen hut. Still, there were two perfectionists among the ten who took the slightest glitch way too hard. He worried that one or both of them were heading for troubles ahead if they didn't go easier on themselves.

Westy, the flight engineer, had not noticed that his pilot forgot to adjust cowling flaps after takeoff yesterday and had been jumpy ever since. He was supposed to be the third set of eyes and ears for the team during the hundreds of check-offs required for run-up and takeoff. He felt he had let everyone down even though the problem was quickly corrected while climbing to the first beacon.

Ross, the navigator, was struggling to become proficient with the G-box, the newest navigational aid, a form of Loran that had been fitted on a few of the planes since coming to England. It seemed to be accurate only about forty percent of the time, and he took that personally.

Nerves were raw. Too many harrowing near-misses plagued the group again today. Everyone knew that assembly and formations were still in the poor-to-sloppy category. They had to get better fast. *Krazy Kat's* ground crew chief had been watching the planes come in and caught up with Skipper at the hardstand.

"Nice landing, Lt. Harden, how did it go up there today?"

"FUBAR again, Sarge, thanks for asking. Sunday drivers all over the assembly, and life in the backseat was dreary, wallowing around with the old ladies, trying to keep them off my balls back in the slot. I can't wait to review it all with Operations."

"Well, life's a real bowl of cherries down here too, as you probably know. Whoever decided to make the ground crews up by taking some guys from other BGs and throwing them in with our guys who trained together Stateside was a real genius. Everybody's either a know-it-all or a prima donna, too many chiefs and not enough indians. On top of the full-time whining, there's real work to be done, and not a damned one of those mechanical bomb hoists have arrived to help relieve the situation. The loadings are pure grunt work. I don't think you could call us a well-oiled team."

"Guess it's all going to take more time than any of us thought."

"Yeah, but I hear that our first mission is right around the corner. The quartermaster has orders to find 450 flak helmets by tomorrow afternoon."

"I'd keep that to myself, Nolan."

"Cat's out the bag, Skipper. You're one of the last ones in today, only reason you haven't already heard."

# PART EIGHT

## First Mission

# *Fifty*

Here he comes. Sgt. Fritz is CQ today, that little turnip-nosed fellow with a cold—sneezed twice already coming up the path outside our hut. Don't waste any time rousting me, Fritzy. I've been awake since the motor pool guys started cranking the trucks, probably an hour ago. Never heard them before. Some of the others in here stopped snoring about the same time. I know Seth's already awake with his cap on. I can see the glow from his cigarette—always smokes with his cap on—last thing at night and first thing in the morning before he gets out of bed.

"Wake up call for Lt. Harden and Lt. Carpenter's men. Yep, that means you, Kemperman. You too, Bertke, rise and shine. Give your dick a rest, Fairfax. Everybody sitting up and smiling?"

Who gave him a happy pill?

"OK, fellas, listen up. Official time is 0332 hours. Full English breakfast with real eggs today starts at 0400 hours. Crew briefing is at 0500 hours and engine start-up at 0645 hours. Everybody look sharp, and good luck up there today. Get moving."

Our big day. Where the hell is my other pair of socks? Damned if I'm going to fly my first mission in skuzzy socks.

"Hey, Westy, you almost ready? These movie stars are going to primp all morning, and I want to get in the front of the line to see if I remember what a real egg looks like. Fritzy better not be kidding us. I will not eat the green, powdered ones today."

"Coming, pal. Bring your flashlight; mine's dead. I don't want to wait around for a ride in the truck."

◆  ◆  ◆

How are we going to take off in this soup? The flashlights bobbing along in the fog look like a scene in the Walt Disney movie that Penny and I went to a while back . . . *Fantasia.* "Ave Maria" might not be appropriate for this bunch. You never know though. Lots of men may be feeling more religious today.

"Looks like most of the crews have the same idea, Sgt. West."

"Pretty quiet bunch today. Not the usual chatter. Can't blame 'em. Gotta tell you, Mac, I have a knot in my stomach. Been awake, tossing around on those springs all night."

"Know what you mean. I've never heard the trucks in the morning before. It's not just you, Westy. Remember, we're all doing exactly what we've trained like hell to do. And we couldn't ask for any better than Skipper and Dick in the drivers' seats."

"I just don't know if I measure up. Things are still happening really fast when I'm on the flight deck with them. I'd better not fuck up again today."

"I think we're all singing that refrain."

"We'll be dodging whatever the enemy sends up as well as our own guys today. I hope I'm good enough."

Westy is saying what everybody feels. We're scared. I usually rely on him for advice, so I don't know what I can tell him. We've talked about a lot of things, personal stuff. For sure, I can't bullshit this guy. He knows I don't have two seconds more duty time than he does.

◆ ◆ ◆

Ick, the mess hall grease cloud is heavier than usual today. Our chat hasn't helped my appetite. Better try to eat something. No telling when, or if, we'll be back here. Now I'm doing it!

"OK, Santini, you thieving magpie, how many dozen eggs have you kept for yourself? My friend and I want eggs Sardou. Double up on the artichokes, creamed spinach, and Hollandaise, and I'd better not find any lumps in the Hollandaise."

"Sorry, Mac, we're all out of artichoke bottoms this week. How about the eggs Benedict instead?"

"Santini was a line cook at Galatoire's, one of the best Creole restaurants in New Orleans, before he aspired to the quartermaster corps. He actually knows how to make those dishes."

"Swell, Mac. I'm already queasy, and you're talking creamed spinach. Santini, just give me one fried, over medium, on a piece of that cardboard you call toast."

"Don't let this shock you, Sergeant, but they're all the same: overdone. Just take some if you want."

Westy's hands are shaking. He can barely raise his coffee without spilling. Man, this is serious. I'd better keep an eye on him. Skipper already has enough on his mind today.

"Go easy on the coffee, Westy. You know what a pain bleeding the lizard is after we're all suited up. Speaking of which, I'm heading over to the brick meditation rooms and then to shave my face before I wrap that oxygen mask on. Call me prissy, but I can't stand the itchy feeling of rubber and ice on whiskers at twenty thousand feet. See you at the briefing."

Whoa, there's a line around the corner for the three little commodes this morning. Nothing like an appointment with the

Krauts to loosen up the old bowels. And no seated performances once we're airborne.

◆  ◆  ◆

"Ten-*hut!*"

"At ease, men; be seated. I'll be brief. Intelligence has a lot to cover. Your target today is the largest V-1 rocket base on the coast; its code name is 'No-ball.' This is your first combat mission, and many of you will learn a great deal of good about yourselves today. I think you'll find out a lot about balls and no balls. I have complete confidence that our officers and enlisted men, flight crews and ground support personnel are capable and dedicated to the success of this and future missions. Regardless of your role, each man is vital. We value each member of our team, and the team is the source of our strength.

"By the same token, we have key areas where we still need improvement. I am certain that most of you are aware of the highlights and the disappointments of our group's very first mission of two days prior. We can and shall continue to improve, as you shall show starting with today's outing. Good luck and good hunting. Cpt. Lacross will carry on from here."

"Thank you, Col. Merrell . . . ."

◆  ◆  ◆

So, all we do is follow the little red spool of yarn to St. Gabriel and back. Yeah, and back. I'll bet the tourists at that pretty little Normandy resort never imagined Hitler would build a nasty V-1 rocket site smack on their beach.

Col. Merrell came across loud and clear about needing improvement. Other than possibly West, I'm not worried about our crew. Unless another aircraft runs us over in the clouds, I know Skipper, Dick, and Ross will get us into formation and onto the bomb run.

Just hope the radar jockeys in the Pathfinder plane are on their game today. Weather guys said coastal fog and low clouds, so we'll probably be counting on their instruments for the drop. Maybe the blind squirrels will find some nuts today.

"Hey, Mac, you studying for the bar exam in there? Time's getting short; give another gunny a shot at the pot."

"Just keeping it warm for you, Parker. Out in half a minute."

Intel said they didn't expect much in the way of enemy aircraft along the French coast. Just the same, I'm happy our fighter escorts, our Little Friends, will be along for the ride. As for German fighters, my catechism lesson for the week is, "Don't shoot at me, and I won't shoot at you."

◆　◆　◆

"Lex, is that a lucky rabbit's foot or what's left of your yingyang after Marrakech?"

"You're the one taking the magic pills four times a day, Jay. I'll take my good luck charm over whatever you got. Here are Seth and Mac. Let's ask them what they're carrying."

"'Lo boys, how's the suiting up going? You get that DDT powder from the doc, Sgt. Kemperman? I heard there were large crabs seen leaving your long johns after our last flight."

"Very funny, Seth. But tell us, what does a Jewish plumber from Tex-ass carry along on his missions for good luck?"

"Well, my mother was Irish, so I have a shamrock taped to the inside of my yarmulke that I wear underneath my leather helmet. Solid way to stack the odds, but have you guys noticed what Mac has underneath his grimy undershirt?"

"Never been inside his undershirt. OK, Mac, show us whatcha got."

"Potent medicine. I'm afraid I can't reveal my protectors. They might get offended and hurt some of you. Wouldn't want that."

"Aw, c'mon. Let's see . . . wow! What the blazes are those things? They *do* look different."

"Yeah, talk about covering the odds. You get that little leather bag from the witch doctor that paid us a visit in Dakar, Mac?"

"Never mind where I got it from. Think of it as a hand-me-down from my ancestors. They went through a lot to get it to me. I wouldn't make fun of it either. Some of my dead relatives are pretty touchy folks."

"Relax, nobody's insulting anybody's family. What's that other gizmo, that little coin on the chain?"

"St. Benedict medal, blessed by the archbishop himself. My next-door neighbors gave it to me when I left home for training."

"I know that one. They did the same thing for the Catholic servicemen in Milwaukee, but my folks missed out on getting me one."

"So what *are* you taking along, Jay? I was kidding you earlier about the pills. You should have something that means something special to you. We're all riding together."

"I don't even have a St. Christopher or a scapular, Lex. I—"

"Here, Jay, take St. Benedict. I'm only about one-quarter Catholic on my granny's side. I know the family that gave this to me wouldn't mind it going to a full-time mackerel-snapper like you. Seriously, take it, with Archbishop Rummel's blessing."

◆　◆　◆

"I'm telling you, Sgt. West, I do not like how those 500-pound bomb clusters loaded in any of my planes today. They were balky going in, and they may hang up coming out."

"I will report this to the Skipper—"

"I already have. Hello, men. All suited up and ready to dance, are we? I was just telling your flight engineer here—"

"We heard. Our waist gunner may have to walk over and kick some of our load out on the Germans before we come home."

"Like I said earlier, Mac, just one more thing on my mind today."

"Not yours to worry about, Westy. Seth here is in the waist. He and Jay will be the ones dangling out in space over the bomb bay if we have to deal with hang-ups. You can crank me up from the ball, and I'll give them a hand if need be."

Damn, I love the guy, but West is beginning to get on my nerves. Saw Bertke and Lex rolling their eyes at his last comment, too. Time to load this baby up and get going before we all get the shakes.

"Good morning, men. Skies are brightening up in the east. Should be a clear trip over the Channel until we hit the French coast."

"Good day to fly, Skipper."

"Westy, unlock all the access doors, please, and let's get our checklist started."

◆　◆　◆

Man, that's sweet music. Nolan and his ground crew know their way around these huge engines. Some of these planes sound like sick outboard motors warming up.

"Run-up complete on engine number three [check!], four [check!], two [check!], one [check!]."

"All mixture controls on auto rich [check!]."

"All engine head temps nominal at 160 [check!]".

"All superchargers in; manifold pressures four nine, forty-nine inches [check!]."

"All engines back to niner zero zero, 900 RPM for idle [check!]."

"Generators on at my mark: four [check!], three [check!], two [check!], and one [check!]."

"Reset engine RPMs to 900 [check!]."

"All cowling flaps to one-third [check!]."

"Landing gear lever is down [check!]."

"Kick-out pressure is nominal at eight five zero, 850 [check!]."

Good, Westy. I think you just need to stay busy and stop all that thinking.

"Green flare! All right, men; let's go get in line."

◆  ◆  ◆

Oh, Lord, our plane is so heavy, and thy runway is so short. Please lift us over the trees and Farmer MacGregor's barn. No fallen sparrows today, dear God. Amen.

"...70...80...90..."

No stopping, no turning back now.

"...95...100...105...110..."

Stall speed. We are carrying a shitload today. Why is this taking so long? Shut up, Mac, and watch the undercarriage. Runway lights still white. Jesus, *come on!*

"...115..."

Bird getting lighter, landing gear extending. Good. Red lights flashing by—almost out of highway. Not good.

". . . 120 . . . 125 . . ."

Easing off the ground. Yes! Am I the only one in this plane helping Skipper pull that wheel back, coaxing this beast into the morning sky? Over the trees . . . *and the barn*. Go, Kat, go!

". . . 145 . . ."

"Wheels up! Thanks, Dick. Flaps steady at ten degrees until we hit 170, then zero-up, set some trim adjustment, and get ready for the beacon derby. Looks like we are going to have some clouds to get through before 12,000 feet. Good job, Westy."

"Thanks, Skipper. The engines were singing today."

"Yeah, *Krazy Kat* practically flew itself."

Like hell it did. We have an ace pilot for this riverboat, and that's that.

◆ ◆ ◆

"We're over the beacon now. I have all twelve of my aircraft assembled at 14,000 feet. Repeat? . . . . Copy. You get with Lt. Ames and agree on your new configuration. Thank God we are the only group flying this mission. Couldn't have been a worse start. Roger. Will await your arrival here. Tighten it up, Lieutenant. We should have been on our next heading seventeen minutes ago. Roger and out."

"Listen up, men, I've been on the horn with Lt. Fairchild who is now the new squadron leader for today. We've lost one a/c in a high-speed stall and seven others turned back with mechanical problems. Ames and Fairchild are putting the remainders together to bunch up with us. I estimate new departure at 0910 hours. And I have one reminder for all my loquacious friends, no more intercom chatter after we leave Selsey Bill for the Channel."

Sunlight breaking through over Selsey Bill. Brilliant reflections off of the water in this estuary, like an etching with dark patches of marsh grass and boggy ground. What a view! I hope the boys up front have a chance to enjoy it for a second now that we have the stragglers located. Maybe someday we'll all be flying something resembling a combat formation. Maybe someday I'll be flying.

Must be a half million men in those ships massing along the south coast. Something very, very big is afoot. Hitler has to know the invasion is coming, can't hide all that equipment.

Ho, here come our Little Friends, P47s and two squadrons of Mustangs, almost as many fighters as we have bombers on this run. Come on, fellas, the more the merrier.

"Battle stations, men."

"Hey, Mac, it's Lex. Before you crawl in the ball, tell me what you did with that extra flak helmet. I gotta take a leak bad. Seth's gonna help me out of the tail, but he's an insect or something— never pisses and never knows where you hide your latrine."

"My donation's already frozen solid, sitting right behind the walk-around bottles in the right waist. I left some room for you."

"What a pal; someday I'll return the favor."

"Get off the Goddamned intercom!"

◆　◆　◆

No flak and no enemy fighters. I'm not sure we were ever over the target. Well, maybe the Pathfinders came through for us. Somebody shot a few rockets at us from down there, or else those were the V-1s, headed for England. I know we've released our bomb load already. This bird soars like a glider right after we salvo until Skipper gets it trimmed up again.

God, what a good pilot we have! Took command of that abortion of a group assembly today like he'd been flying combat all his life. Got to find a way to get him to teach me some basics on this equipment. Got to measure up.

We should be leaving the French coast any minute. One of our escort squadrons turned back already. *All right!* Heading back home. Can't wait to get out of this stinking gun turret and have a drink with my mates. And, man, am I thirsty. I'll bet I've lost five pounds, been sweating like a pig. My outfit is soaked. Can't even smile, snot frozen in my mask. I'll be swimming in sweat or fixed in a block of ice if we really get into it with the Germans on the next mission. Next mission, that sounds pretty good. One almost down and only twenty-nine to go. Wonder if I'll remember this one when we get to the other end? Maj. Watts said that all flight crews remember their first.

# PART NINE

## Crucible

# Fifty One

After debriefings and chow, the crews had four hours before the pub in the village closed. The little establishment was not crowded, no other uniforms in sight. Lt. Harden and the Krazy Kats had distinguished themselves on their first mission. Maybe the others felt there wasn't much to celebrate. The mood was even more somber because of the confirmed loss of an aircraft and crew.

Harden tried to lift their spirits but acknowledge reality with a toast, "Drink up, raise your glasses to the crew of the *Krazy Kat*. The deputy CO let it be known that our squadron's performance was the only bright spot in the day. Sorry to say, the rest was pretty miserable. The worst, of course, was losing the only combat veteran our group had."

"Shit, I didn't even know we had one. Who was it, Skip?"

"Lt. Cliff Townsend came to the 491st to be a lead pilot. He had completed twenty-six missions before today. During assembly his co-pilot radioed in that they were in a high-speed stall after maneuvering to avoid another aircraft. Townsend never got out of the stall, and none of the crew could parachute out. He crashed near Sizewell, killing everyone."

Neither Mac nor anyone else at the table knew the man or any of his unlucky crew members. But the enormity of the dismal tale stopped conversation at the table for a long time.

*Poor bastard, only four missions short of heading home, transferred over to a rookie group to add some experience and leadership and lost it without ever engaging the enemy. Dead crew who probably thought they were wrapped in the arms of Jesus on their first mission, flying with a seasoned veteran who knew every trick in the book. First fucking mission. This war has more wrinkles than any of us could have imagined, and dying's not the worst. When it comes to playing sick jokes in the haunted house, fate's twists take the prize. Fate is one low-sick motherfucker.*

Harden sensed where this was going and decided to invest in a pot of whiskey. He had been keeping a special eye on Sgt. West since Mac confirmed his worries about their flight engineer. This evening West looked particularly withdrawn and agitated. He poured his crew another round before sharing the rest of the sorry details he'd learned earlier.

"I might as well get the rest out, what I know about today and then some. The Pathfinder crew totally missed the target. We blew up an abandoned amusement park. Not a bomb hit the target, no balls at all!"

"Son of a bitch!" Dick, the gentle giant who rarely uttered a profanity, spoke for the group. "Ross, when are they going to turn you loose with that new G-box of yours? Why are we following the Three Blind Mice around over enemy territory?"

Suddenly, Sgt. West made a sweeping gesture with his right arm and knocked his shot glass across the table and into the stone hearth. The sound of the shattering glass caused the other patrons to turn around just as the young Yank stood up and shouted,

"Ten more empty bunks tonight!" He clenched his trembling hands into fists and hunched his shoulders up toward his ears as he stared at the fire. His face glistened with sweat, and his eyes were bloodshot. He pivoted suddenly and bolted past the publican's wife and out the door.

The crew exchanged knowing looks and head nods. They all remained silent and seated. The other patrons politely resumed their conversations as the barman moved to clean up the breakage.

"Mac, will you bring Westy's cap back to him? He's a good man. I will speak with him again in the morning. I want us all to try to keep him in our crew. For now, however, it's probably best that he doesn't hear the rest of what I have to say tonight."

"Not sure I want to hear either, Skip—"

"Can it, Lex. As far as the group's very first mission on Tuesday, there is still no word on Lt. Lewis and his crew who were shot down. They are listed as MIA, but the boys who saw the flak hits didn't see any parachutes. Also, the 854th Squadron, the only ones on that mission who flew the planned route to Bretigny Field—they weren't even in the right neighborhood."

The guys groaned and muttered curses. Skip continued before any of them could smash another glass into the fire.

"But, they hit another target. They nailed it, not a bomb wasted, so Ops wasn't too upset they knocked out another enemy airbase."

The mood immediately shifted, and the men began cheering and thumping the table. After Westy's funk fit, they all wanted something to cheer about. Skip wasn't finished, however, and called them back to order.

"Now huddle up here. Last call for my booze, gentlemen, and I don't want to raise my voice. You all saw the activity in the Channel today. Something big is coming, coming soon. The

491st will be called in for tactical support. We have to do better with our assemblies. We're going to be in division formations with over a thousand planes—maximum effort. We have to do better with our drops. We don't want to take out any more of our own in the air or on the ground."

"You're preaching to the converted, Skipper. We're totally with you."

"I know it, and I'm glad. Drink up, and let's get to bed."

# Fifty Two

The first briefing on D-day, June 6th, 1944, was guarded by MPs. Col. Goldenberg led off with a brief comment on the monumental importance of the day and the key support role he hoped his 491st would play in clearing the way for the ground and paratrooper advances. Almost any aircraft that could fly with a full crew was to be pressed into service along with those from thirty-one other heavy bomber groups of B24s and B17s.

Assembly was somehow conducted without any further loss of men or equipment from Metfield. However, dense clouds prevented any bombing in advance of Allied troops in the target areas around Coutances. All were under strict orders to release bombs only when visual confirmation of each target was certain. The mission was a huge disappointment.

After debriefings and lunch, the frustrated men headed back to barracks to sleep. Before they could stretch out, the CQs came through again. *Krazy Kat's* men and about half of the other crews were mustered out for a second briefing and another go at the objectives around Coutances.

Their squadron began forming around the first beacon at precisely the scheduled time and altitude when the base reached them on the Operations channel.

"Listen up, men. Control has just scrubbed the mission. This is the second time we've dressed for the dance today, and I'm not too keen on sitting this one out. We have been given the option to try to link up with the 93rd and the 489th and get another mission under our belt. They have targets farther to the east in Normandy where the weather may be lifting. We'll get home after dark, but they said they'd keep the porch light on for anyone who wants to fly."

"Let's do it."

"Jay, check the codes and frequencies we need and patch me through to our new wing commander. Let's go get in the show."

◆　◆　◆

Unfortunately, the miscues and mishaps continued for the 491st through the next several missions. The ground crews' misgivings about the bomb clusters proved well-founded. On June 7th a large number of bombs hung up in the racks. Some released through closed bomb bay doors on the way home and hit populated areas northwest of London and around Portland Harbor.

Disasters rocked Metfield again on June 8th. A gunner from Lt. Snow's crew walked into a turning propeller before boarding. He died instantly. Lt. Tharp's *Lucky Penny* lost an engine on take-off, dragged a wing on the field, and crashed, tumbling into five other aircraft. Two of the 1,000-pound bombs aboard exploded during the crash along with all the fuel. Forensic teams found sufficient remains to place in only six caskets. None of it was identifiable.

Everyone was "feeling snake-bit," as Danny, the bombardier from Pine Bluff, described it. Harry and Danny were back at the pub with Rock and his bombardier, Weclav, trying to forget the past several days. Bad weather had grounded the June 9th mission, and not a soul had complained about not getting to fly.

Rock summed up their misery, "We keep shooting ourselves in the foot before we even engage the enemy, and it just goes downhill from there. It seems to me that the worst problem we continue to have is getting assembled. These pilots are way better than what they're showing so far."

"Well, in the old country when my grandfather had some of his sheep herd fat for the slaughterhouse, they brought the Judas goat from the village to lead the way. Our boys could use a Judas goat to lead the assembly. We don't want to go to slaughter, but we don't want to kill ourselves just getting sorted out neither."

"By God, you old Polack! I think you have put your finger right on the fix for our lost sheep."

"Polish goats don't fly, Rock. English neither."

"Yes, but we can find ourselves an old goat of a B24, maybe even paint it up bright so it really stands out, and have it lead the assemblies. Build the formation around this colorful clunker, and then have it head back to base for the next run."

"Might work."

"Damned right it will, and what if I'm wrong? The army's out a few gallons of international-orange paint? Big deal. Better than losing more of our men bunching up. I am going to see the major tonight if I can or first thing in the morning. And I'm going to do something I've never done. I'm going to volunteer to fly the first run in the Judas goat."

# Fifty Three

"Thanks for coming along, Mac. I was almost as nervous about talking to the captain about my transfer as I have been on the last few missions. I feel terrible about bailing out on our team, but I know I'm just not helping anymore."

"I think everyone will respect your decision, Westy."

"Yeah, but not staying with you and the rest of the guys is still tearing me up. Look at you. You washed out of pilot training but didn't quit on the Air Corps and haven't given up on trying to fly. You and I have talked a lot about how you've handled things. Now, here I am turning tail. I just couldn't tough it out."

In addition to pub crawling, Harry and Westy had discovered bicycles, another release from the stress of the missions and the war. They rode the country lanes at every opportunity. Sometimes they would pedal as far and as fast as they could until exhaustion hit. When the weather broke especially warm and dry, they would pack beer and salami and ride to a distant hillside to shoot the breeze and gaze at a few hundred clouds.

"I've had my share of troubles, and there are some special reasons why I just can't give up on my goal of flying. I told you a while back, it was part of a solemn oath I made. Your situation is different. I'm glad you're able to make the change, but selfishly, I will miss your company a great deal."

They were pedaling slowly, dodging puddles and slipping on the mud road back to barracks. The late afternoon was almost pleasant, midway into June in the Suffolk countryside. With double-daylight time the sun remained well up in the sky at six p.m. and felt lukewarm after the clouds had moved off.

Harry was not just being kind. He was feeling pretty miserable about Charles West's opt out. Their exchanges were a meaningful departure from the typical bluster and boyish banter that passed for conversation among other airmen they knew. In his company Harry wasn't reticent to talk about his feelings or personal concerns. Westy reminded Harry of his father, another genuinely caring person. But Westy was no stoic, and this war had means to bring any man low. The stress of his present posting had nearly crushed all the good from a good soul.

Harry had learned during his short time in this war that there were many ways to destroy a man, and most of the victims had little say in the matter. Death was the ultimate negation of a man's potential and was heedless of any distinctions between worthies and villains. The war's remorseless grinding down and grinding up of young men was close at hand, among his squadron mates, and distant, among the evil and the innocent upon whom his bombs fell. Those who he helped to kill with bombs and bullets in the zone of combat were lumped together as the enemy, and he could separate himself from any regrets about collateral damage and death of ordinary citizens in the wrong neighborhood. But when adversity befell a brother-in-arms, he suffered from a sorrow that was like the pain amputees felt in their phantom limbs, a burning in the mind from a thing removed. Parting from a psychologically battered friend who was also a respected role model was an unexpected and especially painful episode. Harry's education in the rough schools of loss and destruction was just beginning.

"I feel the same way, Mac. You're one of the few men I've met since I joined up who knows about Dolph Camilli's slugging in the homestretch of the Dodger's pennant race and also appreciates what Wilfred Owen and Sassoon were saying about the savagery of the last war."

"Yeah, but I never would have read them if you hadn't leant me your modern poetry anthology."

"No, you would have found them along the way, with or without me. Your education's just beginning."

"You read my mind. That's what I was thinking."

# Fifty Four

The group's next mission was to bomb Ploermel Bridge on June 12th. At the pilots' briefing, a new weapon in quelling the chaos over the buncher beacon was unveiled. The officers were told to look for a bright-yellow-and-red aircraft around which they were to assemble at designated altitude. Once formation was achieved, the mission leader would assume his duties and join up with the other two BGs comprising the combat wing. The assembly craft would then waggle off and return to base. Up until this morning most of the pilots knew nothing about the new scheme, and no amount of briefing could prepare the men for what they saw in the sky when the *Little Gramper* made his debut.

"Jay-zus, would you look at that! It looks like a flying banana that's broken out with big red measles. *Little Gramper,* we can see you from twenty miles out, probably pick you up over the horizon if we needed to."

"Just come on in, fellas, no dawdling. Gather up around Gramps. We're here in the old rocking chair, waiting on you."

"*Little Gramper,* this is Lt. Crosby, 844th Squadron of the 489th BG. We'll be forming on your high right for this run. I just gotta ask, who and what the hell are you?"

"Lt. Greg Finley, 854th Squadron of the proud, fighting 491st BG, and this old heap here is the greatest thing since the telegraph, Lt. Crosby. The *Little Gramper* is the point around which our guys are massing so smoothly today. I don't know if your people have ever had any problems in that department, but I suspect you might be seeing a version of this advanced weapon at your field real soon."

"You're a bit light on armament, aren't you, Finley? Easy target for the ack-ack too."

"This D-series has donated lots of spare parts. Besides, he's stripped-down for just one job, to get my guys in a tight formation to meet you and the Krauts. Then I go home and leave the rest to you."

"Love the tomato-red polka dots, Lieutenant. Lotsa luck with your mission."

"So far, so good, Crosby, same to you!"

At completion, the mission crews, Rock, and their group command were more than happy with this outing. They had finally achieved a perfect assembly and perfect drop without loss of planes or personnel.

◆ ◆ ◆

"The old Wolverine quarterback scored big, Rock; you made us all look great today. The entire base is celebrating. I've got a feeling that the *Little Gramper* is the long-term cure for the flying flu that had settled on us."

"You know, Mac, we really owe it all to my bombardier, Weclav. You were there when he told the story about the Judas goat. I just translated that old Polish tradition into a shape that the Eighth

Air Force could understand. But you're right; once everybody starts believing in themselves, training and skills will start to take over. I think the *Little Gramper* is our silver bullet."

The two friends were walking to the pub to meet the rest of their crews for a celebratory round. Unlike the last time they were at the little watering hole, the lounge and bar were chockablock with fliers that evening. Officers and enlisted men joined there to welcome a surge of confidence returning to their ranks. The publican, Clancy Brewster, was already in flagrant violation of the premises law that forbade consumption out in the village streets. He was trying with little success to hustle happy customers around back, out of sight of the local constabulary.

"Hey, Clancy, where's the party? You giving away free inventory?"

"Ay, Lieutenant! Hello Sgt. McChesney! Glad to see ya again. Just do us a favor before I lose me license and me livelihood. Step around back to the Dutch door and give Maggie or Burt you orders. You'll find a nice little gathering spot in the garden for a summer evening. Got to get these men off the street. This ain't no festival day or whatnot. Pardon me, gents."

As they walked into the back garden, men of every rank began to converge on Lt. Finley and offer congratulations. Along with the news of a highly successful mission, word had spread around the base about the identity of the *Little Gramper's* godfather and first pilot. Mac left Rock to his host of admirers to find them some refreshments.

The garden was lovely that evening. Mrs. Brewster's climbing roses crept over the walls and half-timbering of the building, and others wove through old whitewashed trellises scattered along the slate paths. The heady aromas from a profusion of blooms and her well-tended spice garden were an even match for the tobacco smoke that hovered over the men.

While he waited for the drinks, Mac was admiring the fine figure of a young woman who was chatting with Reverend Jenkins, one of the few locals present that evening. He thought she demonstrated excellent judgment in staying out of groping distance, away from the uniformed members of this little garden gathering. Just as he was served and thinking of offering his protection to the solitary maiden, she and the good reverend exited through the side gate. He realized that this was the first time he had thought about any woman since he'd arrived in the U.K.

"Ah, blood's beginning to stir again through some vital organs. Things might be looking up around here."

"What's that, Mac? Talking to yourself? You haven't had that much to drink, have you?"

"Hey, Skip, where are the rest of our guys? Let me go and give the conquering hero his well-deserved highball. Then I'll join you. Rock's going to be hours telling his version of today's success to that crowd, and he won't need me to stand him for any more drinks."

"Good, I have some very exciting news for everyone and was hoping you would be along soon. We are all over by that big chestnut tree in front of the hedgerow."

Walking back toward his crew, Mac glanced down at the big slate flagstones that formed the garden paths. The familiar smell of thyme had been haunting him since he stepped into this attractive outdoor space, but he couldn't locate its source. This was a spice that he strongly associated with Bertha's cooking, particularly the savory stews and roux-based sauces she made for special occasions or Sunday dinners. A wave of homesickness and longing to see his family and his loyal friend Bertha overwhelmed him. Just then, he noticed a strange but not unpleasant sensation. A penetrating warmth began to spread into his chest from the spot where the talisman hung below his neck. He thought his body was playing tricks on him because the evening air was fresh and cool. About this time something prompted him to look more closely at the space between the stones of the walk. Instead of sod grass or weeds, tiny leaves and flowers of the thyme plant mounded between and around the slabs of slate. English husbandry had discovered long ago that the spice was delicate enough to add grace to many a hearty meal yet rugged enough to stand up to a bit of foot traffic. At that moment the pungent aroma acted as a catalyst for an emotional connection between his family and a larger one whose home and hearth were threatened here. His vague regard for the English villagers who welcomed him and thousands of other Yanks onto their farms and into their homes swelled to warm affection.

"Quit daydreaming, Mac; c'mon over here. We have some new orders, and Skipper won't tell us what's up until we're all aboard."

"Sorry, fellas. I was thinking about home, home cooking, thyme, and kinship."

"OK, attention, men, this is actually quite an honor for us. I hadn't been expecting anything, much less anything directly from Col. Goldenberg. Here's the quick version. We are being reassigned to the 93rd BG at Hardwick, Norfolk."

"Gen. Timberlake's outfit? Ted's Traveling Circus? That group is the oldest and one of the best."

"*The* best—"

"Hold on, let me finish. This is big, a big honor and a big responsibility for us. We're not only going to the 93rd but to the 329th Squadron. This is an elite group, all members of which have been chosen to perfect the experimental G&H-band navigation system for blind bombings, when targets are totally socked in. As such, we will serve as a squadron of lead crews for all the groups of the Second Air Division. Crews of the 329th will fly lead during the most challenging weather conditions for all the B24 missions in the Eighth Air Force."

That quieted the bunch. This was more information than many of the men could quickly process. They were going from marching somewhere in the band to leading the formation and holding the baton—conducting the music—at the same time.

Some replacement crews were expected at Metfield within the week. Reassignment would take place simultaneously with the new arrivals. Skipper then excused himself and took his officers with him. They had further consultations with the major. The moment they left the party, a dozen questions bubbled up.

"Anybody else joining us from the 491st?"

"We gonna still be flying in *Krazy Kat?*"

"What the hell is a G&H-box?"

"What the hell do we know about flying lead?"

"Wonder what it's like, out there in front all by ourselves?"

"Who's buying the next round for this lead crew?"

# Fifty Five

"Mac, I hear you're going to be out of a job."

"Out of a turret, Rock, and into the right waist-gunner spot—frying pan to fire. Just another hired gun who'll work wherever he's told. Yep, the 93rd has already gotten rid of their ball turrets. What bothers me is that with all of the new responsibilities and gizmos to learn Skip and Dick will never have time for me up front."

"Hey, look, stay positive. An opportunity to be in a lead squadron and fly with Timberlake's unit, that's a real honor for starters."

"You'd be there too if you weren't such a rising star in the 491st, a victim of your own success. You and Skip are two of the best pilots in the group. Goldy is not going to let both of you go just when he is getting the attention of the entire Second Division with his assembly aircraft regimen. You'll probably be the flying ambassador to help put that into service across East Anglia."

"Well, get this. High command has already burst our balloon. Turns out that your man Timberlake and his 93rd have been using a painted-up assembly aircraft for almost a year now. Instead of *Little Gramper* they call theirs *Ball of Fire*."

"Jesus, Rock!"

"That's the word; I swear. Heard it last night from the colonel himself. Why those geniuses at General Headquarters never shared that info with other BGs before now, I'll never know."

"That's a shocker. At least the word will spread now, help some other lost sheep."

"Yeah, and I'll be happy to go back to flying missions. We only have six tucked away while some of the crews that started with us at Metfield already have nine."

"We're on lucky seven."

"Look, old friend, here's what I really came by to say: keep your eyes open for that chance you've been looking for. I had a long talk with Skipper Harden when I heard you guys were moving on, reminded him of how good a pilot you already are."

"Thanks a million; I owe you one—I hope. You've always been the best of the best *and* full of surprises. I never thought I'd have much chance to see you after I washed out at Bonham. Then, all of a sudden, you turned up in Pueblo, and we barnstormed all the way to the U.K. together."

"And we'll cross paths again, too."

"Well, meanwhile, take good care. We have to be over at Hardwick tomorrow afternoon."

"Will do, Mac. Have fun in the Circus."

◆ ◆ ◆

They were the only crew from the 491st on their shuttle run into Hardwick from the southeast, only nine air miles from their old base. They could have taken a truck, but that wasn't the way they did it in the Eighth. Less than five miles out now, they had just passed over the hamlet of Bungay, and the pilot was giving them the local landmarks for homeward bound crews.

"Norwich, the biggest city in the county, is over there to our northeast about eight miles. Has about four thousand local blokes and about four dozen pubs. That's where we catch the trains into London."

"*When* we get leave, *if* we ever get leave," Dick complained into the intercom.

Skipper reminded him why they were taking this ride.

"I doubt there will be any leave for the next several weeks while we're getting trained in the new nav system. All the flight officers will be on training flights about twelve hours each day. Our enlisted men will either be in ground school or farmed out to other crews that need replacements."

When Harry heard that, his heart sank. Sentenced to the mind-numbing repetition of ground school or stuck with unfamiliar shipmates, he would never get his chance to fly again. He pulled off his earphones and just stared out the waist gunner's window. He'd heard enough.

"Lt. Harden," the pilot interrupted, "we're onto our final approach, and today we'll be using the main, north-south runway. That little settlement is Topcroft, and the slate roof with the round bell tower to our left is St. Margaret, the parish church. Coming back from the continent, when you see that tower, you'll know you're almost home safe."

"Too bad the army didn't harvest those trees at the end of the runway. That's quite a hurdle to hop over when we're fully loaded on the way out."

◆　◆　◆

Hardwick was an older base, a bigger operation than Metfield. It had three hulking hangars and over fifty hardstands around the perimeter track. Command, briefing, and other administrative buildings were clustered fairly close to the runways. The barracks and mess halls and sanitary facilities were scattered over the remainder of the property in the usual fashion. Officers and enlisted men had their own clubs but alas, no bar for the noncoms. Hardwick even had its own Aero Club operated by the American Red Cross where a rotating bevy of gals from back home dispensed coffee, doughnuts, gum, and small talk with grateful men of the 93rd. Most of the shorter off-base excursions were into Hemphill or Norwich as the only pub in Topcroft was a sorry affair and the only eligible women had taken vows of perpetual service to St. Margaret.

On their second day at Hardwick, Harry was nosing around the Aero Club when he thought he recognized a familiar figure in the lounge. The officer was facing sideways to Harry and speaking quietly to a staff sergeant. He was razor thin and would have had barely a profile except for an outlandish shelf-butt and a beaked nose. His brown hair was trimmed close in typical army buzz cut, and this only served to accentuate his huge ears. If Harry was correct, from full-front view those ears stuck out prominently from the sides of his triangular face that ended in a pointy chin, a configuration that gave precise definition to the expression "jug ears." His friendly smile, dancing eyes, and ebullient humor distracted from all this angularity so that most of his friends noticed it only in photographs or when strangers would point him out in a group and ask, "What about that weird-looking guy?" When the man reared back and bellowed a deep laugh—an improbable sound from such a reed—Harry didn't wait for his old friend to turn toward him.

He called out, "Jack Pitre, you laugh harder at your own jokes than anyone I've ever met!"

Jack also recognized a familiar voice and immediately turned around and marched over to embrace his high-school chum.

"Mother MacReady, look what flew in with the June bugs! Harry, my good man, you're the last person I thought I'd see in this part of the world."

"What?"

"I thought the army was keeping you as their secret weapon against the subs off the Gulf Coast. Actually, I thought you were still in jail over in Gulfport after breaking blackout. Actually—"

"Bullshit, Jack, I know my dad told your dad that I was in East Anglia with the Eighth, just down the pike in Metfield."

"Of course, but I never knew the 491st was going to let loose of a valuable piece of killing machine like yourself, share you with the 93rd. What a sight you are! Lost a few pounds on this good army chow, huh? Not exactly oyster po-boys and red beans and rice every week, eh?"

"You should talk! You're skinnier than ever except for that load in your pants that passes for an ass. Hey, let's take a walk so we don't disturb these scholars poring over last month's issue of *Yank* magazine."

Harry's old running mate was now a bombardier and a commissioned officer who had been with the 93rd since they'd returned to England after the Ploesti Raid. Rank, of course, meant nothing between these two, and Jack did his best to make his pal feel welcome. Jack was in the 330th and impressed that Harry was flying as a lead crew among the 329th, a whole squadron of lead crews.

"My advice, old boy, is to beg your pilot to find a reason for you to get up on the training runs with the officers. Otherwise, you're going to be in for a lot of ground school—rehashing a lot of crap you can recite in your sleep. Maj. Atlee, your CO, is a decent chap and will pretty much let his pilots take anybody along for an outing."

"That is the *best* thing I've heard since arriving; that's *great* advice. Maj. Atlee, I'll remember that name. Jack, you have just atoned for a lifetime of sins, my good friend."

Jack shot him a puzzled, sideways glance but said nothing while his suddenly elated sidekick rattled on.

"And what is it with this 'old boy' and 'chap' patter? You going Limey on me, Jack?"

"I dunno; the lingo sort of grows on you, mate. Speaking of lingo, are you familiar with that wretched beef extract they call Bovril?"

"Heard about it, never tasted it. I know the Brits are almost as crazy about the stuff as their beloved Brussels sprouts."

"Yeah, and it's advertised everywhere, kinda like Burma-Shave back home. You should see this forty-foot sign they have in Piccadilly Circus down in London."

"I hope to see that one day, along with a lot of other goodies in the big city."

Harry gave his friend an energetic nudge and what he hoped would pass for a world-wise wink, thus interrupting his lead-in to yet another joke.

"Yeah, sure. Well, anyway, there are these two airmen, buddies from back home in Alabama, and they're riding back on the train from their first leave in London. They must have missed the Bovril sign in Piccadilly, but they start noticing them on the route back to base. It's a very foggy, misty night, and as they pull into the next station, the first thing they see is another sign with just one word, Bovril. Fred turns to Red and exclaims, 'Miserable-bad night out!' And Red says, 'Yeah, really bad fog. This guy's jest circling; we've been through Bovril twice already!'"

And with that, Jack broke out a hearty stage laugh, slapped Harry on the shoulder, and left him at the door of his Nissen hut. Harry's hutmates wondered what the new guy was up to, this hyped-up transfer from the 491st who sang, whistled, and tap-danced around barracks all evening.

In the weeks that followed, Mac was able to escape the thrice-served curriculum offered up in ground school by flying with his pilot and other officers training in G-H navigation. Skipper convinced their squadron CO that it would be valuable for Sgts. Kemperman and McChesney, as radio operator and assistant, to learn some of the functions of the new onboard transponder in the event that something happened to the navigator. This argument was more convincing since they hadn't yet found a permanent replacement for their former engineer, Lt. West, who might have served in that role.

Jay did spend a fair amount of time learning the system with the others, but Skipper had another assignment in store for Mac. Toward the end of their first practice mission, he called for his gunner to report to the flight deck. However, he was napping up against the bulkhead, out of some of the noise and draft. Mac was so excited about the chance to go on the training missions that he hadn't slept in two nights. He had finally passed out after they were airborne.

"Where the hell is Mac? We're usually tripping over the guy up here. Dick, flip on the AFC and move into my seat. I gotta go take a leak, and I'm going to find our former air cadet."

Dick smiled, knowing what Skipper had in mind. When roused out of his slumber, Mac raced across the bomb bay catwalk and forward through the radio/navigation compartment, but hesitated at the rear of the flight deck awaiting specific orders from his command pilot. Skipper took his time, however, with the communal helmet. Dick continued to gaze at the horizon and pretended not to notice Mac. The pedals, levers, instruments, and screens in the cockpit looked more intimidating than the last time the sergeant had been up this way.

"Go ahead, Mac, take the co-pilot's seat. I want you to get comfortable flying this boat. Rock said you were every bit as good a pilot as he was back at Bonham, and that's damned good enough for me. Redundancy of function is the key to safety and survival. We can limp home most of the time if we lose two engines, but we can't fly if both Dick and I are banged up badly or dead. I want my crew to get home with or without me. If necessary, I want you to be able to get us there."

And thus began the resurrection of Air Cadet Harry McChesney. He was certainly not the only enlisted man to ever fly a B24 in the Eighth Air Force, perhaps not even the first in the 93rd BG. But there was no one more thrilled by the confidence that his chief demonstrated in him and no one better trained on the job. Skipper gave out the same positive signals that Harry had responded to so well under Rupert Brown, his first instructor. Only this wasn't a plywood, forgiving, nearly crash-proof, single-engine trainer, and the course for gunners to become emergency-grade pilots was not recognized or permitted anywhere in army regulations. Nobody in the crew thought it was in the least bit undeserved or illogical, even if it was technically a violation of the rules. Maximum damage to the enemy and safe return were the priorities of each mission.

Harry never missed a training flight over the next three weeks. Like combat, his time in the cockpit was vibrant, new, and variably terrifying, but he progressed quickly under favorable weather conditions, with undamaged aircraft and patient instruction. Meeting Uncle Harry's first challenge began to seem like a real possibility. On July 2nd he flew the landing approach over the field and made the final flap adjustments while Dick flared the big bird and stuck the landing. Harry applied the brakes and was amazed at how much runway it took to stop the thing.

Lt. Harden and crew were scheduled for their first lead mission with the 93rd on Independence Day 1944. Their target was the Luftwaffe airfield, Beaumont Sur Oise, about twenty miles north-northwest of Paris. There were rail and oil depot targets assigned to other groups in the mission. Each was led by a different plane from the 329th squadron. Five hundred B24s from the 93rd plus seven other BGs hit their primaries through dense cloud cover with the aid of the G-H navigation systems.

Even though the German ground batteries could not see the initial waves of the assault, their radar detection and aiming techniques had become more refined and deadly. A total of twelve bombers were shot down; five crews died instantly when their aircraft exploded from flak hits. Harry's squadron was distant from the slaughter, and they lost none from their group that day. The 93rd had one aircraft drop out, but the pilot was able to land with his crew on the liberated French coast with the help of fighter escorts. It was challenging enough to fly the big bombers in clear skies. Harry couldn't imagine getting a cripple home safely.

Back in his spot as waist gunner, Mac flew three more missions in quick succession with his crew against German positions in

France. The G-H system was proving very effective in combat situations, but it was limited to targets within three hundred miles of the ground-based transponders, still situated in England. Plans were afoot to set up two new systems on the continent to provide reach for blind bombing of targets in the heart of Germany.

◆   ◆   ◆

One sunny Saturday afternoon, about midway into the month of July, Harry and Jack Pitre were walking back toward barracks along the edge of a small wooded stream. A huge explosion interrupted Jack's latest joke. The noise rolled over them from a distance of several miles and continued to reverberate through the surrounding hills and woods. As they looked in the general direction of the sound, a dense, black cloud of smoke mushroomed upward and eventually towered 1,200 feet over the horizon.

The two men stayed alert for any more explosions as they jogged back toward the control tower. If this was the start of an aerial attack, it was going to be huge. What else could it be? They knew that this explosion was much bigger than anything that might be explained by one plane crashing, even a fully loaded one. The base grapevine later explained the cause of the disaster, another outsized portion of misery visited upon the ill-starred 491st, Harry's old group at Metfield.

The official narrative stated that at least 1,200 tons of high-explosive bombs and other ordnance, nearly the entire bomb dump, exploded at approximately 1415 hours (cause or causes unknown). Five ground crewmen were missing and presumed dead. Five aircraft were destroyed, and six others were severely damaged and dismembered. Instruments on every aircraft on the field were damaged by the blast. The explosion left a crater over sixty feet in diameter and thirty feet deep. All buildings within a mile of the bomb dump sustained moderate to severe structural damage.

The Eighth Air Force brass were soon on the scene, including Gen. Doolittle and Maj. Gen. Kepner. Their findings were filed in confidential reports, but word leaked out. The 491st had never gotten their hydraulic bomb lifts, and the ground crews were still working overtime to get all the planes repaired, maintained, refueled, and rearmed for every mission. Short cuts were taken in the interest of time and energy and at the expense of safety. Just before the explosion, a group of men were unloading unfused bombs at the dump in the customary manner, by dropping the rear tailgate of the transport vehicle, driving in reverse, and then hitting the brakes sharply to stop the truck while the bombs kept going out the back. This initial cache of bombs exploded and set off the entire stockpile within seconds. The axel of the truck was found over one mile away in a field. Witnesses within three miles of the base were knocked flat to the ground. Windows were shattered in the little town of Bungay five miles away.

One of the *Krazy Kat's* original ground crew, a conscientious mechanic, was among the vaporized. Harry remembered the expression on the man's face—only five weeks ago—when he'd learned that he had to change a propeller that a tail gunner had walked into after engine start-up. The mechanic was deeply saddened that the gunner had met his death from such a careless oversight and vowed that none of his flight crews would ever suffer because of anything he could prevent.

The 491st flew no missions that day. They would fly very few more from Metfield. Within two weeks the entire staff and any aircraft that could be repaired were removed to another air base to replace a bomber group with even worse misfortune, combat losses so bad that it no longer existed.

Such was the accelerating destruction of the men and machines in the heavy bombardment groups as they pressed the European air war effort to the maximum. Harry felt relieved, for a time at least, to have moved on from the prodigious woes of the 491st. He had no desire to be among the crews that deviated from their return flight paths to sightsee over the gaping crater that smoldered for a week after the accident.

# *Fifty Six*

Shortly after the Metfield disaster, the 329th learned that the G-H ground equipment was going to be moved to France and that another unit was going to Belgium. There was time for one more mission before they were to stand down from combat during the move. Harry was in his gunnery position in the right waist on their last blind-bombing run into France.

"Oxygen check: Lex?"

"Good."

"Seth?"

"Roger."

"Mac?"

"Blinking green."

And so on, from aft to nose, as each crew member responded to the bombardier's query about their oxygen supply. At altitudes above 10,000 feet everyone was required to connect to their mask and supply hoses at their respective duty stations. Low oxygen levels in the blood, known as hypoxemia, could cause rapid impairment and result in death within minutes. The condition was insidious and befuddled the victim without causing considerable alarm or distress. As a preventative measure, the bombardier was required to run through the oxygen system check every three to five minutes under at-risk conditions except during the bombing run. Each hose had a sensor light that blinked green with each inhalation when oxygen was flowing properly. Any failure to respond appropriately to each query required immediate investigation by someone nearby.

If an emergency arose and a man had to disconnect from his regular oxygen supply, he switched to a walk-around bottle, a small cylinder of oxygen that could be clipped to his belt. Vigorous activity could deplete this portable supply within a few minutes. Time was of the essence.

Time wasn't terribly critical after bombs away over LeGraude. Flack was thin and haphazard, and enemy fighters rarely came that far west since the Allied advance. However, some of their 100-pound bombs had not released. Kemperman from the radio room told Skipper to leave the bomb bay doors open because he could see that some were hung up. They decided that they would wait until they were over the Channel to try to free them from the shackles.

"Jay, Mac here, I'll kick them out. I've got a walk-around already on my belt, and I'm closest."

"OK, pal, watch your step. You won't be able to wear your parachute and squeeze out on that little catwalk. It's a tad drafty out there. Hang on tight."

"You forget, Seth and I live by open windows; it's always windy back here. We love it that way."

Skip suggested, "Seth, go with Mac and hang on to him."

Mac turned to his partner in the left waist and waved him off. "Stay where you are, Seth. I'm taking your bottle along in case I need more than one."

"Just look my way if you need another hand. I have more bottles, and I'll watch from in here."

"That'll work, Seth. Ross, tell me when we're over the drink. I can't see through the clouds below us."

"You can head that way now. We only have a few minutes over the water anyway."

"Roger. Signing off and going portable."

"Hey, remember, that's live ammo, and the spinners may have been turning some in the breeze whistling through that bay. Don't kick too much ass, Mac."

"Don't worry, I'll be gentle."

Harry got his first blast from the turbulence in the bomb bay as he neared the forward bulkhead in the waist area. This was not going to be an easy undertaking, and the 150-mile-per-hour wind was cold. Noise from the wind and engines obliterated everything but his running internal monologue. He was off the intercom, and his own thoughts were his only company as he put his first foot on the passage between the racks. The twelve-inch-wide metal grating was a tricky foothold over the open bomb bay, four miles above the English Channel.

*Hmm, six of them, all on the right side. Good, I can deal with all of them at the same time. I'll never know how these wire loops got so tangled up in just a few minutes. Whoa, that was a big gust—nearly took my goggles off. Better get my arm through this rack. Got to kick this bottom one off first and work my way up. I don't have any leverage on these things once they break free. Damn, those snap rings are tight . . . . There goes one.*

Mac had been working vigorously for almost four minutes. His visual fields had started to constrict. Tunnel vision was one of the earliest signs of oxygen deprivation. He was concentrating so hard on the task at hand that he did not notice anything untoward. He also appeared to be functioning normally from Seth's limited perspective as he freed up the second bomb. His judgment and motor coordination were already impaired, but he felt alert and confident. He completely forgot about his spare oxygen bottle. The third and fourth bombs were farthest above him on the first rack to his right, and he leaned against the upright while balancing on one foot to grapple with them with both hands, dangling most of his body over the open bay.

*Three gone, now we're talking. Gee, new problem. Got to take a glove off for just a sec to get the kink out the wire around number four. Can't seem to make the old hands work right. Mmm, fingers purple, cold as a witch's tit out here. Dark purple. Have I seen that before, been that before . . . always that way . . . . What? Pa?*

Harry worked with a maniacal fixity of purpose and did not bother to look around to see where his father was. His voice was serene, so soothing, and Harry wanted him to continue, continue reading the story he had started once before.

*Behold! Human beings living in an underground den, which has a mouth open towards the light and reaching all along the den; here they have been from their childhood, and have their legs and necks chained so that they cannot move, and can only see before them, being prevented by the chains from turning round their heads. Above and behind them a fire is blazing at a distance, and between the fire and the prisoners is a raised way; and you will see, if you look, a low wall built along the way, like the screens which marionette players have in front of them, over which they show the puppets.*

"Mac!"

"Pa?"

"Mac, look at me! It's Seth."

Harry staggered against his friend as they side-stepped off the catwalk and into the waist. Harry swung his weight back in the other direction—back to the bombs—and almost pulled both of them headlong into thin air.

"God, *no*, Mac, come this way. Come with me right away. Jesus Christ! You are *so fucking purple* . . . . OK, sit down. Breathe, man, breathe deep, *now!*"

Seth had decided not to wait any longer. Mac was over ten minutes into his acrobatics with the bombs and had not looked his way to flash an OK or anything. His buddy was still breathing as he plugged him into the main oxygen supply and set the mask to the flush setting. Mac flopped down under the right waist window and leaned against his parachute. Seth yelled for help over the intercom. He had never seen anyone that color who was still alive.

Many anxious minutes passed. Skipper, Lex, and Seth monitored Mac's progress back to a foggy-headed but recognizable state. No one paid any attention when he asked if he could talk to his father. Even though he could tell his crew members who and where he was, Harry had no recollection of what day it was or what their squadron's call sign was. He candidly told Skipper that he not only didn't know but also didn't give a rat's ass.

"Well, that sorta sounds like our boy, don't it, Skip?" Lex was looking for reassurance from his commanding officer, but the only reassuring sign that Skipper saw was his gunner's improving skin color.

"He isn't out of the woods yet. Mac needs medical attention. I should never have let him go out there by himself. Lex, you keep an eye on him. Seth, you and I are going to get that last bomb out of the rack, and then I'm dropping flares and coming straight in when we near the field. Let's move it."

Harry puzzled over many things during the next four days in the base hospital. The flight surgeon who discharged him back to full duties explained to him how he had almost died from lack of oxygen while working to free the bombs. He told Harry that hearing a parent's voice and experiencing transcendental feelings of spiritual union with his dead brother were hallucinations or aberrant perceptions caused by the effects of oxygen starvation on the brain. The doctor was surprised that Harry had remembered them so vividly, but he had read of similar cases reported when patients were successfully revived from near-death experiences. He confirmed that Harry's version of his father's story was the beginning of the "Allegory of the Cave" from Plato's *Republic*. He certainly couldn't explain his patient's intense residual attachment to the chimerical events or his insistence that he'd never heard of nor read the story of the cave. His last hospital chart entries affirmed that Sgt. McChesney had suffered no irreversible cognitive or sensorimotor deficits and that his residual psychological disturbances were likely transient but labile, capable of sudden reversion to normal or to more severe aberration. "At present," the doctor wrote, "these problems are no worse than those exhibited by any of the other airmen on the base."

Harry never understood and remained unsettled by the whole situation. And things got even more disturbing before his mind began to clear. While coming around in the hospital, he had several episodes that started with a recurrence of his constricted field of vision. In the tunnel that remained, he saw a crude doll fashioned of scaly twigs and twine that he knew was his brother. The naked stick-child was struggling, falling ever-deeper toward the bottom of a dark, icy lake. Harry was watching the scene but couldn't see much of himself, only his own arms and hands.

He knew he was a giant kneeling at the shore who could easily reach into the bottom of the lake. But every time he stretched to rescue the tiny figure, it vanished and reappeared in another part of the water. The vision always ended when Harry withdrew his empty hands in frustration and noted the same bluish-purple cast as when he'd last worked in the bomb bay. Only instead of regarding his cyanotic skin with the indifference of an oxygen-starved gunnery sergeant, he was seized with waves of nausea and terror. He was alone during each of these spells, and he didn't report them to anyone. Even months later, he could hardly find words for them, just feelings of dread.

On his second hospital day Buddy and the icy lake disappeared completely, about the time he again became aware of an inner warmth that originated somewhere between his throat and his solar plexus. He attributed that feeling to Bertha's talisman although the little bag never changed temperature. This sensation was sometimes a message of comfort and healing, but at other times it was an alarm bell ringing, like when his father tried to warn him of grave danger in the bomb bay. Having it was like carrying around a little friend who couldn't speak your language but liked to talk a lot anyway. Harry decided that he would try to listen and learn as best he could under the circumstances. The circumstances were about to get a lot worse.

# Fifty Seven

It was Guy Fawkes Day, first week of November 1944, and there was already a foot of snow on the ground with temperatures remaining below freezing across East Anglia. Army weather services predicted the coldest winter for Britain in fifty years, and the men of the 93rd were taking this prediction seriously. They had begun laying-by extra coal to feed to their tortoise, their name for the single pot-bellied stove that provided the only source of warmth in the uninsulated metal huts. They poached the coal from the main base stockpile at every unguarded opportunity and stashed the plunder under every bed and in every locker. As the winter wore on, it became more precious than special food and gifts from home, and huge hunks appeared in the pots of high-stakes poker games between barracks.

The weather did not stop the combat missions or training flights although ice formation on the aircraft increased the hazards of each outing. Harry continued to train in the co-pilot's seat while the G-H transponders were moved closer to Germany. By the end of October the forward navigational bases were fully operational, and the 329th was back in the lead squadron business. The next big assault that called for blind bombing was directed at one of the most deadly locations in Germany, the refining and armament facilities of the Ruhr Valley.

The antiaircraft defenses in what the Allied air forces termed "Happy Valley" were massive, with over 3,500 flak emplacements of 88-mm and 105-mm cannons. Heavily defended targets there employed an astounding 300 to 500 weapons each. The Germans were relying on their ground defenses more with each passing month and saving their depleted fighter squadrons to attack crippled bombers that couldn't stay within the protection of the regular formations and escorts. The average loss of aircraft on a B24 combat sortie was 1 to 2 percent. In the Ruhr Valley losses regularly exceeded 20 percent of aircraft, and the crew casualty rate was about as high. The men flying Ruhr missions were not exaggerating when they described themselves as "ducks in a shooting gallery," especially during their fifteen minutes of agony and death on the straight-and-level bombing runs to target.

The Eighth Air Force had ordered a sustained, all-out attack on the remaining German industry in the Ruhr Valley. Harry's 329th Squadron was leading the way. Through the ports in the waist Harry could see the precise geometry of the explosions in the sky ahead and their sickening effects on the first wave of bombers flying through the killing zone.

With over ten minutes to go until reaching their drop point, Harry could smell the cordite. The shock waves of the 105-mm exploding shells now mixed with the prop wash to make control of each aircraft extremely difficult. Sudden maneuvers to avoid other disabled planes were impossible. The only conversation within the ship was between bombardier and pilot. The rest of the men were all praying to GodinHeavenJesusLordChristOur-SaviorAmightyGodHolyMaryMotherofGodHolyGhostAmen.

As the lead wing plunged into the cauldron of fire and shredding metal, the lower-left and trailing formations took the worst of it. Twenty-six aircraft in the trailing formation alone sustained crucial hits. They burst into flame and exploded within seconds or slowly dropped out. Soon it was Harry's turn to enter the shooting gallery.

The black carpet of smoke changed to yellow flash before concussion, then to immediate, bright-orange noise. Explosions rocked Harry's plane from every direction. One extremely close burst threw him over into the left waist and was followed instantly by a second and third. There was a new window slashed into the skin of the fuselage about where his head had been a few seconds ago. The explosions dazed him slightly and left him deaf in the right ear. Shrapnel repeatedly ripped through the ship. The large piece that had almost taken off his head had severed some of the control cables for the right elevator. Skipper was struggling to hold formation as they approached release point.

Before bombs away, two ships off their right wing were hit. The closest held steady as the outboard starboard engine began smoking. The next-adjacent aircraft was destroyed. A flak burst had cut the left wing into two pieces, and the plane pitched downward, slicing the tail off another aircraft before it exploded. The struck plane went into a flat spin. No parachutes escaped from either bomber. That one sequence of fire-noise-death took place in less than fifteen seconds. Harry stopped looking out the waist windows. There weren't any enemy fighters stupid enough to be this close to the slaughter. There was nothing to shoot at, and he had seen enough for a while. Skipper managed to keep his lead position in the wing through the rally point and dropped out only after crossing into liberated France where they arranged for a fighter escort back home.

The next mission was only a few days later to another refinery in the Ruhr. They were the lead ship for the entire Eighth Air Force on that drop with not a single aircraft in action in front of them, only the terrible density of the barrage into which they headed and somehow passed through safely. However, the toll exacted for this visit to the valley was worse than the previous: 176 aircraft lost with over ninety men in a single squadron killed or MIA, 800 casualties overall.

Upon return to Hardwick, they learned they were scheduled to fly again the next morning. The target: Castrop refinery, Ruhr Valley. Harry slept that evening, perhaps because he no longer cared. He was ready to die in the next mission. He hoped it would come early in the sequence of events, early enough to spare him most of the random exploding terror of the run to target. He awoke with a terrible headache and cramps in his jaw muscles. He had been grinding his teeth in his sleep. When the CQ came through for wake-up, he was drenched in perspiration even though it was only forty-five degrees inside the Nissen hut.

After two trips to the Ruhr, he was nearly deaf in both ears, and voices sounded hollow and distant, echoing like noises within a giant sewer pipe. That morning he didn't feel awash in fear as he had in the worst of the flak. But he was aching and tense as he arose, shivering the way exhausted torture victims described the reverberating agony between kicks to the gut or shocks to the genitals.

They flew the second sortie of four that day into Castrop. The refinery and storage tanks were already ablaze. Acrid black smoke drifted up through the cloud cover that spread below 12,000 feet. The under-lit clouds were a diffuse dirty-orange with bright-orange clusters indicating the biggest fires. Ten thousand feet above that fiery cloud-lake the flak thickets blossomed, showers of colorful bouquets and sharp metal thorns. Another blood bath ensued with the enemy dealing out in kind nearly as much as it got.

The entire sky around their ship filled with flames as the next barrage exploded. The top turret cover burst off, and the smell of 100-octane fuel began to fill the radio operator's compartment as well as the bomb bay. Jay picked up the nearest fire extinguisher and yelled for Skipper to shut down the inboard fuel tanks and switch to the outer supplies. They left the bomb bay doors open after the drop point while Seth and Mac joined with more extinguishers from the rear to keep a small fire from spreading. They got it extinguished, but Richard Hardy, their replacement engineer, had not come down from the top turret to help assess the damage.

Skip called again over the intercom, "Hardy, we've probably taken the worst of it for now. Come down, and let's get a full report started . . . . Hardy, can you hear me? Check in, Sgt. Hardy . . . . Dick, get damage reports from everybody while we're heading to the rally point. All the instruments look good, but I want a detailed visual inspection as well. Mac, see what's up with Sgt. Hardy."

"I'm already up here helping Jay. There's not much left of the top turret. The wind is screaming over the hole where the Plexiglas used to be. I'm working from below, and I can't get up in the turret with him. I've got Hardy's belt off, but he and his parachute are kind of wedged in the seat. Jay, give me a hand. We need to help him out right away; I don't think he's getting any oxygen. He's not moving or responding to me."

"There's not enough room for two people in this damned access, Mac. Try to lift him up a little by the waist, and I'll pull him down to me. On three, you lift, and I'll pull. We've gotta get him hooked up to an oh-two supply. Ready, one . . . two . . . three! Ah, JesuspleasenoJesuspleasenoplease."

Jay said no more. They had managed to move their engineer into the space behind the flight deck. As Harry came down, Sgt. Kemperman was vomiting into his oxygen mask. Neither of them could apply one to Sgt. Hardy.

"Skip, Hardy's dead. Better come when you can; I'm looking after Jay."

"I'm coming. What's wrong with Jay?"

Harry was helping Jay with auxiliary oxygen while he cleaned up inside his mask. When Lt. Harden first looked over at Sgt. Hardy, he was going to ask why he had taken off his flak helmet. This was asking for trouble; they were still under fire although not like before. Then it registered. Hardy's head was blown off in the explosion that had taken away the rest of the gun turret. His body was drained of blood by the blast of air moving over it. They later learned that the Ruhr had left one more indelible mark from this terrible passage. The ground crew could never completely wash off the dried brown stain along the top of the fuselage.

◆  ◆  ◆

Right after debriefing, their squadron CO, Maj. Atlee, pulled Harry aside. Atlee gave him a long looking over; the major seemed hesitant to speak.

"Sgt. McChesney, I think you know that your old group, the 491st, has had a rough go of it, what with the bomb dump going off at Metfield and then moving over to North Pickenham. They seem to have caught a bit of a break in their losses since the move, but I'm afraid that they've reported another downed plane today. The pilot was Lt. Greg Finley, and I understand that he was a close friend of yours."

Atlee did not wait for Harry to respond. He could see by the man's distant gaze and unchanging expression that the events of the day, of the week, of the war had stunned him almost beyond reply.

"Fighter escorts reported that two engines in their aircraft were aflame over Belfort, in northeast France, when all ten men parachuted successfully. Regrettably, they were still over German-occupied territory. Damned rotten luck. This was their twenty-eighth mission. However, there is some cause for optimism. There are many resistance units active in the area. Nothing else is known at this time. I'm sorry to give you the news. I know you have lost your engineer today as well. This can't be easy for you. Go get some food and try to sleep, young man. Your crew won't be called out tomorrow."

But they were called out the day after and completed six more missions in seven days. By the end of that week Harry was reacting inappropriately, slogging through his duties. He was withdrawn at times, giddy at times, but his actions and feelings never seemed to catch up with whatever was at hand. His barracks mates stopped kidding with him and tried to ease him through his bout with the flak demons. There was really nothing they could do but hope they all got some leave before too much longer. More than one needed to find a quiet spot in the middle of the stream again.

◆　◆　◆

A poker game had started after dinner with Lex, Seth, Jay, and four men from Lt. McKenzie's crew around the pot. One of them, Anthony Mosca, was also a waist gunner from New Orleans. He had just received a Red Cross package from home that contained a rum cake from Solari's, a famous delicatessen and catering company in the French Quarter. Anthony was proud of his present and told all the men that he wanted to wait until he finished his last mission to share it with everyone.

McKenzie's men had the most missions of the four crews in their hut, and they were close friends with Harry and the rest of Harden's men, who were not too far behind them in the count. Both crews had surpassed twenty-five missions, the old magic number required for completion of active duty. Earlier in the year this almost impossible target had been revised upward to thirty for lead crews, thirty-five for others.

Harry had a sickening feeling in his stomach the moment Anthony made his promise to divvy up his treasure. For weeks he had been flinching at anything referring to future events, especially involving others. Comments like these tugged at tender spots in his psyche, scabs that never quite healed before the next trauma, open sores left behind when men whom he'd known were ripped away from the group on a daily basis.

He was in his usual spot, on his bunk next to the poker circle, lying passively with his head on his pillow and basking in the friendly patter and teasing and boasting that was as integral to the gathering as the betting and dealing. Like an exhausted retriever after a day in the duck marsh, he wasn't expected to do much more than soak up the warmth and soothing sounds of the fire from the family hearth and rest up for another outing early the next morning. He already knew they were listed for the next mission, and he wasn't sure how much resting was going to help. It just felt better to be around the family for now. Alone was not an option.

Harry's malaise was exacerbated that evening well before Sgt. Mosca laid out his plans to celebrate his last mission. The posting for tomorrow had Lt. Harden's crew assigned again to aircraft 817-P. This much-battered bomber was only now returned to service after its last run to the Ruhr Valley when it had sustained 156 flack hits and lost a top turret along with its flight engineer. This was the last B24 in the 93rd that Harry wanted to climb back into. He fell asleep long before the poker game concluded.

The CQ came through the following morning and called out McKenzie's team but no one else. Harry was content to roll back over and didn't even turn out for late breakfast. Upon return, Seth and Lex woke him up to tell him that he'd missed real bacon, pancakes, and orange juice, a special treat from Gen. Timberlake for the enlisted men.

Harry greeted their news with a yawn. "Off my chow. Food doesn't do it for me anymore. Sleep's all I want."

"Yeah," Lex observed, "you signed off during the poker game. Seth was the big winner last night. He cleaned out Anthony, who got real insulted when no one wanted his rum cake in the pot."

Seth was trying to size up his good friend, who still hadn't bothered to crawl out of the sack. When Mac looked at him, Seth shook his head and offered up a weak smile. Right at that moment the walls of the hut thundered, and the door burst open from the outside. A fully loaded B24 had failed to clear the trees at the end of the main runway and crashed with a massive explosion.

The aircraft involved in today's mission were just getting going; the first three struggled against wing icing to gain altitude in near-zero visibility. The fourth ship hadn't made it. After the next in line narrowly avoided the same fate, the mission was scrubbed. Harry and his crewmates awaited the return of McKenzie's men to the hut to ask them who had gone down. About an hour later Cpt. Jessup from Operations came by with the news. He asked the men to start putting the McKenzie crewmen's personal effects in order. Forensics was still looking for body parts; there weren't going to be any individual burials.

The morning dragged on. Their remaining barracks mates gathered as word got out about the identity of the lost crew. When Seth, Lex, Jay, Bertke, and Harry learned that McKenzie's crew crashed in 817-P, they asked the others to let the five of them honor the men who had died in their place. They alone would undertake the solemn task of putting each man's things together for their loved ones back home. Harry tried to write something to include in the box going to Anthony Mosca's mother and father. Lex sorted through the gunner's stuff and brought his rum cake over to the table where Harry stared at a blank page. The scent of the sugar and the liquor brought back Anthony's happy remarks about when and how he would savor the gift from home. Harry bent over with the dry heaves and fell to the floor, half-moaning, half-weeping. Lex snatched up the carefully wrapped cake, ran out the door, and smashed it against the snow-covered trunk of the nearest tree. A brown glop of cake remained frozen on that tree until spring thaw, a dark blot against the white background—a period, certainly not the exclamation point that Anthony had hoped for.

# Fifty Eight

They had completed twenty-six missions. Gen. Kepner had issued a written citation of merit for their work on the G-H Pathfinder navigation equipment. They had never aborted or failed to complete a mission. And since their arrival in the ETO back in May, Lt. Harden and his crew had never been on leave to London. The drought finally ended the Friday in December following the loss of McKenzie's crew.

Skip was deeply concerned that their three-day break came several weeks too late to help Mac. He didn't want to lose another good man, one of the most dedicated of the lot. He had filed a written request that Sgt. McChesney receive extended rest and recovery in one of the flak houses, but so far, nothing had come of it. The advice of the base medical officer was to bring him along and hope for the best. Mac had told the doc he felt safe being with his family; he wanted to follow along, try to join in. But the more closely Skip observed him, the more he worried about him. The enlisted men who would be lodging with Mac in London promised to do what they could. They all had stress relief and long-deferred plans of their own to attend to.

By truck to Norwich, they piled out at the rail station and joined hundreds of other servicemen heading to Liverpool Station, Bishopsgate, London. For the three to five hours of travel down to the city in the jam-packed compartments, Skip and Dick decided to pull rank and commandeered three seats, two for themselves with Mac immediately facing.

Mac had developed several nervous tics: blinks, grimaces, head twitches, and one big shudder every so often that was difficult to ignore, especially if he were eating or drinking something at the time and made a mess of it. He rarely spoke unless asked a direct question and then only in a hollow, almost automatic way that deflected further conversation, a marked departure from the engaging young man that everyone loved. He no longer feigned sociability or involvement with his friends. His face and eyes were as expressionless as a prisoner in a cave. That opaque surface masked the confusion and turmoil within.

Ross shouted across the crowded compartment at Dick, "Just our luck, leaving on a Friday. London will be jumping on the weekend, but we'll play hell finding a hotel room."

"Word is we need to go to the Rainbow Corner Red Cross Club, near Piccadilly Circus down in the West End. The angels who work there can find something for us."

"I heard that some of those Good Samaritans are pretty good looking. You know Rusty, the crazy bombardier from Roland's crew? Anyway, he found a willing local lovely—swears he didn't have to pay her. Who knows? They shacked up in some hotel that was only half-standing, hit by one of Hitler's buzz bombs just a couple of days before. He said it was nuts with women running in and out of his room for two nights, no sleep at all. Ha, nice problem to have."

"I don't think you'll have to settle for a fleabag like that unless you're determined to get your lodgings through one of the Black-out Queens around Piccadilly."

"Everybody told him he was safe, that it was a great place to stay. I guess they believed that the rockets would never strike the same place twice. I think that's a crock. Don't know how the Germans do it, but that's not how our side works—keep hitting 'em and damn the torpedoes!"

Ross was getting louder as the train rolled closer to London. He had had several drinks at the Officers' Club before leaving the base, more since then from his hip flask. He was among the five or six airmen standing in the compartment, and his shouting only added to the hubbub.

Mac wasn't listening to what was being said. He was just trying to find a soothing rhythm somewhere between the buzz of excited comments and the rattle and clack of the railcar. But when Ross shouted "Damn the torpedoes!" he flinched one of his big ones and caught the lieutenant sitting next to him in the ribs with his elbow.

"Hey, Sergeant, watch your manners."

Skip quickly leaned over from the opposite seat and spoke to smooth the good man's ruffled feathers. Fortunately, nearly everyone was in a happy mood in anticipation of their time in London, and everyone knew what battle fatigue looked like.

After the second louie yelled at him, Mac tried hard to tune in, sort through all the turmoil and cigars.

*Smoke, choking me. Too many talking, too fast, too far away. Echoes. "What's the latest rate down at Piccadilly?" "Who's playing at the Windmill?" "What's a Bovril?" "What's a farthing?" Shapes, sparks, flashing wheels on passing trains, flashing by. How much farther?*

Skip's attention drifted back to his gunner across the aisle. Mac's lips were moving.

"Did you say something, Mac? Can't hear you, sitting over there."

Mac made eye contact, and Skip thought his troubled friend had heard what he had just said. Dick was also watching for signs that Mac was still at home inside his head, but he didn't see much in the way of porch lights or a fire going. Dick looked over at Skip before he tried his own conversational gambit.

"So, Mac, after we get ourselves a place to drop our bags, what will be your first stop? What do you want to see in the big city?"

*Dick. Skip. Good men, good to me. Loud in here. Echoes. Loud crowd. Ears still bad. Flak! Say something. London.*

"London."

"Yeah, in London, what's on your list?"

Dick glanced over at Skip to make sure he'd noticed a single ping from their target of interest. He pressed on.

"I want to go eat at Mulatta's on Half-Moon Street and partake of some of their warm beer, maybe more than one warm beer. Then I'm going to see if there's a hot band playing at the Rainbow Corner. That place is more than just a dinky way station for homesick Yanks, you know. They say it's loaded with women. I'm going to find some sweet English lass and show her all my best moves: swing, Lindy hop, jitterbug. Then I'm going to take her to Covent Garden and dance her legs off some more. I'd love to have you come along."

Mac nodded his head and said, "Thanks," followed by a quick grin or another one of his enigmatic twitches.

Dick was exhausted but happy that he'd elicited such a lengthy dialogue. Maybe a night light was on after all. He smiled over at Skip and lit a cigar.

◆　◆　◆

When the crew gathered at Liverpool Station, Ross tried to call the Red Cross Club about hotel rooms but somehow managed to bugger up the big pennies or the coin slot was already jammed or their navigator was already too drunk to admit that he was already too drunk. Everyone decided it was a lovely afternoon for a go at the Underground trains, and they headed for Oxford Circus on the Red Line.

Ross, tipsy but still the best among them at dead reckoning, led on above ground to Piccadilly Circus from Oxford Street. The streets, shops, and restaurants of the West End were filled with every imaginable sort of folk. Yellow-red-black-gray-blue-brown-white-blotchy skinned people conversed in a Babel of tongues while sporting uniforms of every Allied nation or draped in exotic religious garb or native costume. The boys began to appreciate a new meaning for the ubiquitous term "circus" in this ancient city. And there were attractive young women at every turn.

The urban energy and hedonistic bent of the crowd were infectious and curiously uplifting. Harry, rather than becoming more disoriented and confused by the profusion of colorful strollers and foreign voices, began to relax a bit and take in the kaleidoscopic scene. For the first time in weeks he noticed a faint return of soothing warmth in his chest. Events became more digestible. With real threats at a distance for the moment, the phantasms also withdrew and gave him some space. He took a few deep breaths and smiled at a Gurkha major passing by with a woman on each arm. His smile stayed in place as rubbernecking became the sport of the moment. His gaze wandered above street level, and he spotted the Bovril sign towering over Piccadilly.

"Ha!"

His spontaneous syllable immediately caught the attention of his mates. They looked nervously at one another, not sure what the outburst meant—good omen or ill? Lex had a hunch and spoke first.

"What, what's the joke, Mac?"

"Bovril! One of John's stories, very funny. Can't remember."

"Aw, yeah! You told me that one. Your skinny little pal from home . . . ."

And Lex began his best recollection of the two Alabama airmen who circled through Bovril one foggy night. The punch line brought them to that end of Shaftsbury Avenue brimming with American servicemen who were all converging on the stone façade of Rainbow Corner.

The five-story Red Cross center was impressive. Its ground-level display windows were bracketed with red-and-white stripes of American bunting, and large U.S. military service emblems were proudly displayed on the blackout drapes. Inside the tall-columned rooms the bustle was slightly intimidating to the uninitiated, but newcomers soon found many helpful young ladies, the hostesses, to rely upon. Nine grateful flight crew members from the 93rd were no exceptions. The four officers snagged the last two rooms in a posh spot in Mayfair, the Howard Hotel, but the enlisted men were relegated to a small hostel out in Camden just off Argyle Square, the Argyle Arms.

Bertke was itching to get a move on and had already gone back to the information desk for directions to their lodgings. For grins, Lex took Mac over to the big board where people posted their whereabouts for others to see. They decided no one really cared if they were in London although Seth later scolded them for not thinking about friends from the 491st who might want to see them. Mac didn't say anything but tried not to think of Rock and all the other Metfield MIAs. His tour with the 491st seemed like in another lifetime. Bertke came back from the info desk looking a bit baffled.

"The damnedest thing, fellas. I got directions to our 'billet,' as the lovely lady calls it. I got 'tube stops'—what we know as the subway way to get there—and I got walking directions. But the English don't think in terms of blocks when giving land-marks and distance. She kept telling me, 'Head straightaway for round about seven minutes and blah-blah-blah and take your first right over the bridge and blah-blah-blah and'—here's the best part—she ends with a smile and says, 'You *cawn't* miss it!' I told her that she clearly did not know my bunch if she was so sure we couldn't miss it.

"Anyway, here's what I suggest. If I have the minutes of walk-ing toted up right, it ain't that far, under two miles to the east of here. We should walk there, so when they roll the sidewalks up later and the subways stop running, we know how to stag-ger home. We can take the Underground back this way after we register. We should be back in the action down here in less than an hour."

Without further ado, the five men headed back up Regent Street, across Oxford Street, and continued along Portland Place. They had a tricky little time when they reached what they were sure was Euston Road but only saw signs for Marylebone Road. Lex kept pronouncing it "Mary Lee Bone" and swore the road was named in honor of a famous prostitute from the time of King Henry VIII. Seth and Jay kept reminding Bertke, "You *cawn't* miss it, luv." Harry kept feeling better and laughing more.

As they took their proper heading east into Euston Road, they noted that the neighborhood had more industrial buildings but more importantly, more concentrated damage from bombs and rockets. A couple of sites were still smoldering and attended by members of the Home Guard. Bertke was puzzled by some of the local infrastructure.

"What are those big tanks, Jay? There sure are a lot of them along this stretch."

"They look like storage for either petroleum or natural gas—what the Brits call 'coal gas'—methane. They look like the ones we have in Milwaukee. You have anything like them in Chicago, Lex?"

"Yep. If you get close, you can see they're in two sections; top rides up and down on the bottom when more or less gas is in the tanks."

"So, that's probably what the rockets and bombs were trying to knock out, eh?"

"Dunno, man, but if one of those babies blows, you sure as hell don't want to be anywhere near. My guess is that big crater over to the left is where one used to be."

"Impressive. Hey, see that big clock tower up on the left? If my Red Cross princess got it right, that ain't no church. It's called St. Pancras Chambers; it's a fancy-ass railway station, close to King's Cross station and the Underground. And it's our landmark for home this weekend. Argyle Street, where we'll find our hotel, is just opposite the steeple, to the right off Euston. I'd say we're ten minutes from the Argyle Arms. How's that for navigating, boys?"

Bertke earned a rousing chorus of "Jolly Good Fellow." Their spirits stayed buoyant upon finding that they had lucked into a lovely spot in the Camden neighborhood, thus far unscarred by the aerial bombardments. Argyle Street was a prim and trim residential row of four-story town homes with masonry fronts and brightly painted doors. At the end of the second block where the street curved to the left, they found their hostel. A jovial Mrs. Braxton welcomed the men and showed them to two large rooms overlooking the quiet street.

# Fifty Nine

Bertke was still in a hurry. Jay, Seth, and Lex decided to take a one-hour snooze before setting off. Mac shared the room with Phil Bertke and set off with him. They jumped the Victoria Underground line back to the West End and into the first lounge bar along Great Windmill Street.

"Mac, they have a Limey version of the boilermaker; it's called a gin and Guinness. I think we should celebrate our first evening in London by having one. Whaddya say?"

"Better not. You go ahead. I'm going to eat something first."

"Pacing yourself, huh? Whatever suits you, my friend, it's early. I'm just glad you're here. Tell the man what you want. I'm going to reconnoiter a table."

They never did get a table. Bertke wandered toward the front door with his boilermaker to people-watch. Mac had wedged himself into a space at the main bar and was eating a bowl of pretty decent corned beef and cabbage, thinking about the last time he had enjoyed that meal. He and his dad were at Parasol's bar in New Orleans on St. Patrick's Day in 1943, a few days before he had reported to the Army Recruiting Office. The owner refused to let them pay for their food and drinks when he learned their last name. One-sixteenth Irish was good enough for him that day.

"Well, Sergeant, that's either great food or you're homesick and daydreaming about your girl back home."

"Sorry, hello. Little bit of both I guess. Well, not quite— homesick, yes, girl back home, none."

Harry thought surely he must have been daydreaming not to have noticed the attractive young woman who moved into the space that had opened up next to him. Everyone else in the room had and understandably so.

She leaned in, gave him a conspiratorial sidelong look, raised one eyebrow, and whispered, "Most people would take this opportunity to introduce themselves, or should I just leave you to your dreams of home?"

He was not himself, but he wasn't brain-dead either. The platinum blonde with Mediterranean blue eyes wore an exquisitely tailored black-and-cream houndstooth suit over a heavy silk blouse that framed a huge emerald-cut gem on silver links, resting comfortably in her cleavage. Her curly hair was cut short; her ringlets were tousled, a bit mussed, like she had left her bedroom in a rush. She fished for a cigarette in her crocodile handbag but only came up with an ivory-and-silver cigarette holder, looking up in time to catch Harry vigorously shaking his head side to side. She smiled wickedly, and her eyes danced as she followed his head waggle.

"No! Don't leave. My name is Harry McChesney; pleased to meet you, Miss—"

"Mavis, Mavis Sinclair. Howdy do, may I call you Harry, or do you prefer Sgt. McChesney?"

"Well, I really do have to apologize. I have not been myself lately, not at all . . . ."

*Jesus, Harry, don't lose it; you can do this. This woman is trying to talk to you. Heaven just dropped her right in front of you, practically in your lap. Shake out the cobwebs.*

"Fascinating, Sgt. Harry."

"Please, just call me Harry or Mac; that's what the guys in my crew call me."

"Very well, I prefer Harry. In fact, I'm just wild about Harrys—up until now. You're not going to disappoint me, are you?"

"Gosh no, I wouldn't want to do that, Miss . . . er. Say, that's a lovely amethyst. My aunt May has one, same cut, but it looks nicer on you."

"Let's not tell your auntie. I shan't. And you may call me Mavis. Now that we're properly introduced, do you think you can find a cigarette to put in this empty holder I've been waving about?"

"I am a jerk; please forgive me. What kind do you smoke? I'll get you a pack from the barman."

"Player's Navy Cut will do fine, thank you. You don't smoke, do you? And you've never been in here before, or you'd know that Player's is the only brand they sell."

Harry waved over the barman and purchased the cigarettes. He was too busy with the English money to notice a nod of recognition between Mavis and the man behind the counter.

"Right again, Mavis, first time ever in London, actually. And, no thanks, I don't smoke but don't mind if you do, of course. May I ask a question?"

Someone offered Mavis his bar stool. She sat down facing Harry and didn't acknowledge the other gentleman. In addition to her screen-star beauty and expensive couture, Mavis exuded self-confidence and expressed herself with a directness bordering on the peremptory. In an age dominated by men in authority, she was clearly used to giving, not taking orders. She walked into any room with every feminine, intellectual, and social advantage, the power to enthrall men and establish immediate intimacy with whomever she chose, if she so chose. Right now, she made it clear to everyone around her that she had chosen Harry that evening. She was now sitting close enough so that one of her knees was touching his thigh. She handed him a slim silver lighter and rested her hand over his as he lit her cigarette.

"I was hoping you might ask me a question, perhaps more than one, in fact."

"OK, I'm starting to catch on. Sorry again. Would you like to join me in a drink? Question number two, have you ever lived in America? You don't have an English accent."

"Oh, Harry! This is beginning to sound like a much more interesting evening. Yes, please, I'd love an Irish whisky and soda. I'm part Scottish, part Irish, probably like the McChesneys. I come here for the corned beef and cabbage too. My mother is English, and my father is American—both Catholics. So when we moved to St. Louis where my father started a freight transport company, I, of course, got closeted away with the nuns of the Sacred Heart Academy."

"Yeah, I know; we have one of those in New Orleans, too. My grandmother, Elvige, almost went there, but her parents had other ideas."

"Lucky grandmother, I'm sure you're the better for it too. She could have turned into a warped old crone like me. Well, almost. I escaped the nuns' clutches by outwitting them and graduating early. I promised my father that I would resume my studies after he let me work in his firm for three years. I made myself indispensable in sales and marketing. When he went to work for President Roosevelt, I moved to London to take over our company's European operations. We transitioned over to supporting the Allied supply chain well before America entered the conflict."

"I suppose your father is someone famous, someone I should recognize, but I have to plead ignorance of governmental affairs and captains of industry. Maybe you're famous as well. My dad works for a coffee company in New Orleans. He's highly respected in his field, but I wouldn't call him famous."

*I am having a conversation. This feels so good, like driving down the highway in an open convertible and singing at the top of my lungs.*

"Harry, I don't care a pig's whisker if you've never heard of the Sinclairs of St. Louis. And I would have given anything to have grown up in New Orleans and not the Midwest, but I didn't come over here to explore your genealogy. I want to have another drink and go out dancing with you. I've grown up learning to trust my judgment: you're a good person. I can tell you've had some hard times lately. So have I. Perhaps our best plan for the evening is to enjoy whatever respite the gods of war have granted. However, I must confess. You're the first person in a very long time that I have had to lead this far through the carpe diem argument."

"That's because you've bonked me on my already senseless head. Don't be offended; I think the angels have smiled on me, Mavis. I swear that you are the best-looking woman I've ever laid eyes on. And yes, I have had some rough weeks lately, lost a lot of good friends. But that all happened before right now. Right now, I am so very happy to have landed here with you. I will try to show you a good time. If I disappoint, you have my permission to dump me overboard at any time."

"I'll drink to that. Let's finish up here and see who's over at the Apollo Ballroom. It's just up Shaftsbury. After that, who knows?"

She tossed her head around as she spoke, a wild and wonderful sprite of the evening. Before finishing her whisky, she leaned in, stared deeply into his eyes, and took his hand.

"I'm not dumping you, Harry. I'll be here, and I'll be holding on tight. If things get weird out in the crowds, let me know, and I'll hold on tighter."

She released his hand and went to the powder room. Harry ran over to Bertke to tell him of his good fortune, but he needn't have bothered. Phil had been watching the action in the room and knew that Mac had won the lottery.

"I only wish she had a sister, Mac. Have a great time, my friend. I don't expect to see you later; just be careful out there."

◆ ◆ ◆

The Apollo was nearly packed. The crowd of bodies on the dance floor moved as one thousand-legged creature, sweeping generally clockwise while some of the legs and heads and other wild articulations swooped, dipped, and swayed, coiled and intertwined as though the creature struggled to control its diverse parts and was destined to fall flat on at least a few of its many happy faces.

There was a preponderance of women over available men, all eager to dance every dance. Established protocol did not permit Harry to ignore their determined tapping to break in, but Mavis always came back to join him between tunes and was never far away. He experienced a surge of well-being in her company unrelated to the mild buzz from the West End's watered-down hooch. Terrific music and high spirits filled the room to the exclusion of recent memories. The shadows and lights flashing across the walls and ceiling were no longer threatening, and the ringing in his ears was one more pleasant reason to hold her close while they spoke or sang to one another.

"Harry, I'm getting quite warm and thirsty. This is fun, but let's escape the press of bodies for a bit. Besides, I'm tired of sharing you with all of these other women. We'll walk over to the Royal Opera House in Covent Garden and nip in at the Cross Keys on the way. They're not but about fifteen minutes from here, and the night is lovely, not bitter cold like last week."

"Mavis, you don't have to twist my arm to have me all for your very own. I'm just not sure I'm ready for the opera; I was really enjoying 'In the Mood.'"

"Ah, no, no Puccini for us tonight. They've taken out all the theater seating and made the place into an ornate dance hall. For the duration the Opera is another ballroom, quite lovely, but it swings like the Apollo."

"I'll get our coats."

The streets were jammed with black taxis and the occasional military or governmental staff car, all creeping along in the dark. The sidewalks were slow-going as well. The soot-covered buildings reflected none of the meager visible light and made the blackout truly inky, almost opaque. Harry loved it when Mavis hugged his arm and pressed ever closer as they moved past another couple or dodged a raucous gob of celebrants. Since she knew her way around between Knightsbridge and the City blindfolded, they made good time even though Harry didn't have a clue about which direction they were headed. He didn't care either. They were happy to be with each other, and each sensed a promise of more to come.

As they passed a small park, he diverted them out of the flow and onto a gravel path. He reached round her waist and kissed her neck, cheeks, and lips. She met his embrace and drew him closer at the hips as she entered his mouth with her tongue and moaned. Harry was ready to melt right there.

"God, I've wanted to do that ever since you spoke to me this afternoon. I was slighting you when I said that you were the most beautiful woman I've ever met. You're intelligent, sexy, and probably everything a guy could ask for. I wish we had endless time to get to know each other—forever. What was that movie with Gene Lockhart? *Escape to Forever?*"

"No, I think it was called *You Can't Escape Forever,* and therein lies the tale. Oh, Harry, take a look sometime; you're pretty special yourself. You make me feel great too, but forever? Nothing is forever. Surely you must know that. Not now, not—"

"Ooof! I am so lame, babbling away like a mooncalf." He caressed her cheek and whispered, "Seriously though, you're speaking from personal experience, aren't you? You've lost someone in the war, someone close."

Her tears answered his question. "Just kiss me and hold me. I don't want to talk about that. You are all I want, all I care about now."

So, they lingered in the park and longed for more of one another, but Mavis didn't want to rush their lovemaking. After a while she gently swayed in his arms and began humming "In the Mood" to suggest they rejoin the crowds and the music before those diversions stopped for the evening. She said she wanted another drink. She'd already told herself there would be plenty of time to savor sweet intimacy, just the two of them, before a leave-taking.

The Cross Keys was a venerable pub with decent whisky, and the Royal Opera at Covent Garden had a bigger dance floor and fewer extra women than the Apollo. Harry and Mavis found an outer boundary on the floor out of the main flow where they existed only for each other, every dance. Lost in the darkness and the music, they entranced one another and barely spoke a word. They explored with fingertips and hips, lips and tongue and breath. They discovered secret little zones on wrists, ears, eyelids, thighs where gentle pressure or a whisper brought special pleasure to the other and thus, to them both. The orchestra played for almost two hours before taking a break.

More than a minute after the music stopped and the lights came up, Harry and Mavis surfaced from their plunge into a private ocean. They blinked and looked about like love's hatchlings washed up on a crowded beach, then grinned like idiots at one another, grabbed their coats, and headed for a pub on Drury Lane to pass the interval between sets.

That was when the coastal radar picked up the buzz bombs coming in over the Channel. At first all they heard were the air raid sirens. The search lights flashed on and started sweeping the skies. Then they heard distant artillery firing. The frequency of the salvos increased and got closer.

Harry started perspiring and stopped talking. Mavis knew that was trouble. She had lived through the doodlebugs before, usually didn't even stop whatever she was doing at the office or at home. But this time was different. This airman needed some close looking after, or his demons were going to return and devour him completely.

"There's a deep shelter at Holborn Underground. I'll lead the way. I'm on familiar ground; my office is practically around the corner. I have tickets to the side tunnels in Holborn where we can be comfortable—as comfortable as possible. You'll see. Don't worry, just keep moving."

Just then a monstrous, blatting roar like a dozen motorcycles at full throttle approached from somewhere overhead. They glanced up and tried to walk briskly at the same time. Harry stumbled on a gap in the flagstone sidewalk and went down.

"Ah, jeez!"

"You all right, darling?"

He tried to joke, but the sight of the huge bomb attached to a stovepipe spitting fire and noise put a quaver in his voice. The searchlights were tracking it as the antiaircraft batteries down by the Thames opened up. Mavis could barely hear his reply amidst the racket.

"Gad, look at that! We tried to bomb one of their launch sites a few months back. Now they're after me—got it, by God! Good shooting, men! Owe you one!"

They ducked reflexively and scooted along even though the aerial explosion was over a mile away. Others converged as they doubled their pace toward the entry to Holborn Underground. Once through the gates and on the stairs down, things were amazingly orderly and the pace more deliberate. Mavis helped light the way with a blackout flashlight. They could hear the roar from several more buzz bombs as they descended.

There were a few families stretched out on pallets and blankets along the passenger platforms, and the odors wafting up told Harry that many of them had been there for quite some time.

"This area was hit hard during the '40–'41 Blitz, but it's not as residential as many other London boroughs. So, these side tunnels are pretty empty, only a few displaced families. The ones sleeping out on the platforms can't stand the smaller space of these side enclosures."

Mavis showed the warden two admission tickets for the tunnel to their right and walked with Harry toward the far end where they could have some privacy. Over one hundred cots with pillows, sheets, and clean blankets lined one wall.

"I can't think of a finer spot to wait out the all-clear than here with you. I was starting to lose it up there on the street. I know you saw that. You were brave and tender and sweet and looked after me—just like you said you would. *And* you called me darling. Thank you."

They embraced standing up. "My pleasure, sweet knight, why don't you slip off your shoes and coat and get comfortable? I happen to have a small flask of Bushmills that I've been saving for just such an emergency. When you get more accustomed to the public accommodations, we can slip out of most everything and nip under the covers. They never turn the lights on down here, and there's no checkout time in the morning."

"That's about as close to forever as I think I'm going to get in this life."

She bit him playfully on the neck. "Kiss me, stupid. They *will* sound the all-clear *sometime* tonight."

Harry's hands trembled as he undid his shoes and buttons, as much from anticipatory pleasure as from tonight's brush with the flak devils. Mavis guided him through her buttons and zippers, over her taut nipples and moist labia. She found him firm and eager and showed him what she wanted and how to pace himself to her needs. She guided him on journeys that tasted of the sea, that rocked him like the sea, that wet him in her warm currents, and fed him from her vast stores and treasures. She assumed all forms and was all vessels from which he drank and filled with pleasure and drank again. On this transit of a dark, subterranean sea void of zodiac, sun, or moon she was his figurehead, his water nymph, and his pole star—protector, playmate, and heavenly guide.

# Sixty

**H**arry flinched, but Mavis was already awake. The all-clear klaxon had sounded and was still echoing through the tunnels. She had moved to an adjacent cot. Harry was sprawled diagonally across his narrow berth with nary a scrap of rumpled English blanket covering his nether parts.

"Darling, you'd best cover up. The warden will be around soon with his torch to see to the slug-a-beds."

"Come here. I want you by my side. I don't care if he burns me out."

"Not that kind of torch, silly."

She lay down next to him and kissed him but would not partake of his obvious joy in her presence. She tossed the blanket over his erection and prescribed an early breakfast for her love-struck swain.

"This cot is passable for emergency trysting, my love, but I have a more tempting bower to offer you after we get some nourishment. Come back to my digs, and I'll fix us a decent English breakfast. Then let's see what develops after that."

"Just whistle. This puppy will follow you home."

"I hope you're housebroken. I don't often do this part. I'm never bashful around men, but I don't share my private space with them either. For some reason I feel OK breaking my own rules with you. You are different. Do all women trust you so unreservedly?"

"I don't know how to answer that. I have never known a woman as I have you."

"Oh, God, forgive me, for I have deflowered another one. You're a good actor, Sir Harry Lothario, a fine performer too. Well, we'll sort my sins out later. The trains will be running again soon." She nodded at his member, still at half-staff under the covers. "Get things buttoned up for now, and we'll take the Piccadilly line back west to my place in Knightsbridge, behind Cadogan Square."

"Is that you or the train whistle I hear?" She smacked his butt. "Yes, ma'am, coming!"

◆ ◆ ◆

They could hear the sirens and see the smoke and flames as they came up to street level on Brompton Road. Rockets had struck close by, and things were not under control as yet. Temporary barricades directed them over to Cadogan Square and around to Milner Street so that they came at Lennox Gardens from the south, past the old church on Milner and Moore. They traversed some of the most expensive residential real estate in the West End.

"Nice neighborhood for a working girl. Looks like there's more trouble up ahead, on—"

Mavis, more agitated now than he'd seen her all night, finished his sentence.

"On the right, yes. Oh-oh." She trotted ahead and then stopped abruptly. "Well, well, I think my #35 used to be up there in that burning rubble, Harry."

Two or three of the stately town homes in the lower third of the east crescent were destroyed from a direct rocket hit. A ruptured gas main belched a column of flame fifteen feet into the air in the midst of the ruins. The area was dense with fire equipment and personnel. Anyone sleeping in those homes last evening was still under the pile or already in the city morgue. One older resident a few doors down was clearly suffering from the traumatic events. He was outside, walking about in his ascot and dressing gown to survey the damage, but had neglected to put on any shoes or slippers.

"Oh dear, oh dear! Miss Sinclair, can it be you? I thought surely you had perished along with Lord and Lady Fairleigh and those poor souls on the other side. Pardon, in such a state, I can't recall their names. But thank goodness you've escaped!"

The old gent noticed Harry but failed to put them together or how she might have been elsewhere during the neighborhood disaster.

"Good morning, Sergeant. Terrible thing, terrible thing. Damn these bloody Jerries—pardon, ma'am. We've been living with their bombs and now their rockets for too long, too long . . . ."

Trailing off his invective, the distracted survivor left them alone again as he walked toward the solace of the open church doors, a barefoot pilgrim amidst the ruins. Mavis moved to call after him, but Harry pulled her to him.

"Mavis, thank God we were together where we were last night. But what now, what can I do to help?"

"Well, breakfast at my place is out. Oh, that's awful and not funny. That's what the war has done for human decency, mine anyway. There are newly dead people here. You must think me horrid. Forgive me, but I was so looking forward to more time together."

"Nothing to forgive. If you've offended anyone's memory, they can't hear you anymore. Let's try to think of what to do for the living, for you."

"Fate has smiled on me twice tonight. I've met you and escaped certain death. I have lost only possessions that can be replaced if necessary. Appearances notwithstanding, what remains before you is not a homeless waif. I am a wealthy child of a wealthy family, Harry. Let's head back to the City. We'll find our breakfast, and then I've got some work to do at my office."

*"Work?!"*

"Listen, I need to get through on a transatlantic connection and speak to my father about the townhouse and other arrangements for me. That could take most of the day. After our repast I will put you on the Underground back to your hotel. Get some rest, and we'll meet again tonight at the little spot on Great Windmill where I had the great good fortune to find you yesterday."

"No. I'm not leaving you by yourself. You're—"

"Harry, please, you're my knight errant in love and war, but I need to move quickly and efficiently. I don't want to be distracted by your lovely, considerate presence. Saturday is a difficult enough day to try to accomplish anything on either side of the Atlantic, but I've got to do it. I shall meet you at six o'clock sharp, or as you military blokes say, 1800 hours."

◆ ◆ ◆

The Singing Lyre was roaring when Harry shouldered his way in just before their designated hour. He had missed his Underground transfer stop coming in and was upset with himself. He knew Mavis would never have been so distracted. After having lost her home and possessions, even when they were making love the previous evening, she had seemed in complete command of her world. Well, he could live with that; he felt supremely happy under her command, more so than under any other in this war. After helping to bring him back to himself, she had led him through a maze of danger during the rocket attack and preserved his sanity. He longed to see her and hold her again.

Mavis was definitely not in the room yet. She would have stood out like a flashing beacon. Besides, unless she had been shopping this afternoon, he was pretty sure he knew what she'd be wearing. He worked his way to the bar and did his best to catch the eye of the barman at his end and stake out a notch for them both. As he surveyed the crowd, another barman tapped him gently on the shoulder.

"Pardon, guv', ain't you the sergeant who was in here with Miss Sinclair last evening?" Harry nodded, obviously puzzled. "Hold on, I've got something for you."

The man went over to the register and fetched an envelope. Harry's hands trembled as he opened it. He had already read the return address on the top corner: "Sinclair Shipping, Ltd."

*Dearest Harry,*

*I shall not be there tonight with you. By the time you get this I shall have already left London for my uncle's place in Berkshire. My father has arranged for a jump seat out of the UK tomorrow morning on an RAF flight from Greenham Common. When my parents learned of my most recent brush with death, they became nearly irrational, wailing and pleading with me to come home immediately. Part of their anxiety has to do with my having had two previous near-catastrophes in London and the balance having to do with loving parents' worries that are magnified by distance and my status as an only child. My reasoning with them otherwise was to no avail. I have decided to honor their request and return to the States for the duration of the war in Europe, something that my father thinks is close to winding down. His conjecture offers little consolation for the abrupt end to our relationship, however. It also did not help bolster my side of the argument to stay. In their hearts there is only one argument: I am their only child, and they want me home. The war has made them—like a lot of others—older than their years, and I feel I must do this for them.*

*That's my painful news. Please try to forgive my shameful way of getting it to you. The beautiful part is my memory of our time together. Prior to our meeting, I had not given myself so wholeheartedly to anyone since I'd lost my fiancé, an RAF fighter pilot, two years ago. After that I'd never sought another commitment, only escape from my own losses in the company of other men, using them for a quick laugh or sexual release. As I told you early on and repeated later with all my heart, you are different from those other men. You are giving and caring and bright, someone a worthy woman will gladly bind herself to when the time is right because you are bound to honor and appreciate her in return.*

*I hope that we can meet again after the war. If you choose to make that possible, I have included my parents' home address at the bottom of this letter. Perhaps you might still think me a worthy woman, but I know enough about the twists and turns of life in the last three years not to expect your call. I can have no demands on you. But might I hope? Please do not equate my precipitous action, my acquiescence to family, as any measure of my feelings for you. Whatever happens, I will always treasure what we had*

*and what might have been. Stay well and stay true to your heart.*
*You will always be my Good Knight, my Sir Harry.*

*I love you,*

*Mavis*

All the barmen were swamped with other customers, but the one who delivered Mavis's letter returned after about ten minutes when Harry continued, without moving, to stare blankly at the letter. He heard nothing of his surroundings, trying hard to see through the pages, through the words into an immediate future without their author. That future felt lonely, drab, and sickly. Then he reminded himself of her closing invitation to meet again; this separation might not be another final verdict from the war. But equanimity and reason only went so far with a wounded heart. He decided on some short-term relief for his injury right about the time the barkeep, his fateful messenger, was coming to offer the same nostrum.

"What'll it be, sir? The first one is on the house."

When Harry had finished his third scotch, he was feeling less sorry for himself but reflexively gazed about the room whenever he heard a woman's laugh or caught a gesture at the corner of his vision that told him surely she had changed her mind and was coming back. The Singing Lyre was not going to provide a bed of forgetfulness, and he decided to look elsewhere. He'd heard about a funny and sexy "Revuedeville" at the Windmill Theater down the street. "Live nude statues" and other entertainment were on offer, twenty-four hours of every day. The Windmill sounded like a better distraction than more whisky at present.

## Sixty One

The women were lovely and almost nude and only batted eye-lashes upon assuming their graceful poses. The vaudeville acts were loud and lively and suitably corny, but Harry was not inclined to stay for more than one performance. He returned to feeling sorry for himself upon reflecting how poorly the women up on stage compared to his goddess of the previous evening. Leaving the Windmill, he unknowingly followed the same path on which Mavis had led him the previous night. When he recognized the park where they had first embraced, his heart sank. Perhaps only brutal measures could temporarily fill the emptiness that Mavis had left behind. He set about to test his theory at the Cross Keys pub, another bad turn on a journey that had yet to offer much escape from lost romance.

After last call Harry was just short of falling-down drunk and found it convenient to shore himself up in the company of some stout ANZACs and their dates, all of whom seemed to have an endless capacity for drink and hilarity. Back out on the streets, they were trying to teach him the words to some ribald Aussie toasting song about a wallaby and a wanker as they drifted along pleasantly with arms linked or draped about the women. No one in the bibulous troupe cared a whit about what direction they marched or for how long.

In fact they had been circling the Seven Dials column in Covent Garden for the past dozen minutes or so when a couple of the ladies begged for a sit-down. The men of the Australian and New Zealand infantries refused to quit their campaign and swept the squealing laggards up in their arms and headed down Monmouth Street and on to another stanza. The air raid sirens interrupted their songfest. The troops were not willing to halt, but the women scurried for shelter about the time the first salvos erupted from the ack-ack batteries. Someone spotted an Underground entrance, and Harry ran after them.

The platforms and the side passages were brimming with long-termers who suffered from chronic congestion and unhappiness. They turned surly and mean with the onslaught of new arrivals. Those who had been living there made it clear that they did not welcome any of the drunken jostling or the stepping-on of hands and bedding and meager belongings. They had no homes. They had no foreign army pay to lavish on frivolity.

Only a few blocks away from the relative tranquility and hospitality that reigned at Holborn, Leicester Square station was a bitter kingdom underground. The atmosphere grew openly hostile and more than one scuffle broke out. Harry began to feel claustrophobic and experienced a familiar total-body shudder that hinted at a return of his combat willies. However, he was just numb enough to ignore them and just sensible enough to know that the deep shelter was preferable to being trapped aboveground in a hail of rockets.

Even so, when some of his ANZAC escort decided to leave, regardless of what was going on upstairs, he decided that he'd better try to wheedle some sort of directions home from one of the locals. That proved harder than he imagined. The resident campers shooed him away or were more direct about where he could go as far as they were concerned. Finally, one of the weary wardens happened past, a uniformed man, a kindred spirit of sorts, no doubt.

"Pardon, sir, but I'm looking for some directions back to the Argyle Arms. Can you help me?"

"Never heard of it. What street, what borough are we talking about?" The man didn't wait for an answer and turned to move away from yet another drunk. Harry blocked his only open space.

"Ah, all I can remember at this time is some big station that looked like a church but wasn't. My hotel is close to there."

"Look, Sergeant, there are thousands of places that call themselves hotels and such that serve our visiting military."

Even though they were sandwiched against others on the platform, no one within earshot stepped forth to help the Yank airman. But after a long silence a tiny elderly woman who had been eavesdropping on their failure to communicate tugged at the warden's elbow.

"He means St. Pancras Chambers, I'll wager!"

"Yes, yes ma'am! St. Pancras, with the big clock tower. Very close to my street."

"Ay, Sergeant, then you need to get back to Camden Town or King's Cross. But not now. The all-clear's not sounded; I don't advise being out and about just now."

"Can't wait, I have to be back at my base by noon tomorrow, have to leave with my crew. Gotta take my chances on the streets."

"Well, if you're determined, walk on the diagonal across the intersection at the top of the stairwell and head north for about half an hour on Charing Cross Road. The name of the road will change, but just follow your nose. You'll cross Oxford Street and many smaller ones. The next big east-west roadway you'll get to—if you dodge the doodlebugs—will be Euston. Head to your right and watch for your St. Pancras tower on the left after a bit. You can't miss it!"

Harry had absorbed about half the details of the good man's directions. He was still quite buzzed. He had to make it happen somehow.

"The fresh air will do me some good. Thank you for your assistance, Mr.—?"

"Jamison." They shook hands, and Harry saluted him for good measure. "Good luck on finding that fresh air, sir."

◆　◆　◆

**N**early four in the morning, the streets looked abandoned compared to a few hours earlier. Searchlights and sirens mixed with orange haze and spatters of bright flames over the low skyline. Occasional blattings from more buzz bombs jolted Harry's nerves. He mainly heard the sound of his own footsteps as he tried to strike a confident trail north. He thought he was still heading in the proper direction, but even the big streets curved this way and that through ancient neighborhoods. The rare pedestrian wore a foreign military uniform; no one looked like they could help with a mid-course correction.

*More servicemen, half-stewed like me, trying to find a berth away from the rocket barrage. Ain't easy.*

More warehouses and electrical switching sheds appeared as he walked along. He had crossed Oxford Street a long, long time ago, it seemed. About three blocks ahead, he thought he might be approaching another big intersection. He felt a little surge of confidence just before the rockets came again with a fury. Harry had walked himself into a primary strike zone.

The terrible sound was close and everywhere overhead. He began to run and realized that there were two terrible sounds: the rocket engines and the explosions, separated by a hideous, empty interval when a bomb stopped flying and fell to earth. Only it wasn't merely earth. It was buildings, bricks, pipes, windows, beams, and people. The earth rocked, and the buildings crashed down. Choking dust and smoke made it difficult to breathe or see. Nowhere around or between the buildings offered protection. He reached the big cross street, turned to the right, and kept running.

*This better be Euston Road. Shit! Not even a mailbox or trash bin to hide in, under. Probably a waste of time. Keep moving. To what? The next explosion, maybe my last one. Damn! That was close. Too much like flak. Flak! Fucking ground flak, these rockets. Bracketing me just like over Happy Valley. This fucking road, just like our bomb runs—straight and level.*

He jerked around to his left. He thought he heard machine gun fire and dove to the ground. From his exposed position he tensed for the bite of rounds into flesh. Then he located the racket—a man running with a pushcart down a cobblestone side street. The steel-rimmed wheels were bounding along the stones and striking like rapid-fire shots. He got up, much shaken, and again made himself lope along in what he prayed was the right direction.

The next rocket hit a structure deep in the same block, but the explosion was ten times larger than any so far. The shock wave threw him into the building across the street; a piece of flying debris grazed his head and knocked him out. Within minutes another close hit woke him up. He rolled over and propped himself against the side of the building. He didn't remember going down. He could no longer open his left eye. Clotted blood and matted dust and filth from the street kept it stuck shut. He touched his head where it hurt and noticed that the wet stuff was fresh blood on his hand and shirt front.

*Up! Keep moving. Ducks in the fucking gallery. Nothing for me to shoot at, just bastards shooting at me. Ground flak! Aaaah!*

The vision in his only working eye was blurry. He couldn't pick out anything other than large forms and light and dark at a distance. The situation was direr than he knew. He was less than a block from a cluster of methane storage tanks. A hit on any one of them would instantly take out the remaining tanks and the surrounding city within a quarter-mile radius.

When another rocket hit three blocks away, Harry reflexively dived to the gutter and hugged the grating of a street drain. He was falling back into the morass of terror and confusion that he had been able to climb out of for a blessed while this weekend. His life and his mind were in extreme jeopardy where he now lay, trying to press himself into the sewer. It was only a matter of minutes.

*Not good. Not good. Get up! Get up! Please, God, please, someone help me!*

Another rocket hit close by. He gripped the grating tighter and threw up. When he stopped heaving, he heard another rocket motor shut off, the prelude to another explosion. But he also heard something else—young voices, kids' voices?—calling his name, his full name. Only the Army Air Corps knew his full name.

"Henry Emerson McChesney, look up and rise up. You must come with us; there is grave danger here. Come now, come away *now*!"

He still didn't move. Head trauma and fear made the world a nauseous, spinning nightmare. He stayed prone against the pavement. Then he felt a pressure around his chest, a good squeeze like a big hug from Bertha and strong enough to break his terrified grip on the iron grating and lift him up to standing. He had lost a lot of blood. He briefly passed out, but something, someone held him steady and upright while his consciousness returned. He blinked repeatedly to try to clear the hazy vision in his right eye.

Two kids, maybe teenagers, dressed in weird priest frocks or colored togas, like strange costumes out of Biblical times, stood before him on the sidewalk. They wore funny sandals and each held a small box under one arm. Smiling like traveling salesman, they glided over, one to each side. With their free arms, they clasped him firmly under his arms and moved him at terrific speed down the road. He should have been running, but he knew he wasn't. These two had picked him up so that his feet were dangling a few inches above the pavement. But they were shorter than he was, and worse, he couldn't see their feet or legs moving. He could almost get his mind to accept that they were flying over the street. He was now pretty certain that he was either crazy as a loon or dead.

Within moments they approached a large building that Harry thought might have been St. Pancras station. He wanted to ask how that was possible, but his question was interrupted by a massive explosion from the direction where he'd latched onto the street drain only minutes ago. He passed out again.

When he regained consciousness, he was lying on a table in a room that smelled dank, like a leaky basement. A yellowish, pre-dawn light came through a series of small casement windows high up along one wall. The rocket attack had ceased. He could now open and see clearly through both of his eyes. His flying priests were attending to him. They had removed his filthy uniform jacket and blood-soaked shirt and cleaned him up. The boxes that they carried were full of vials and jars with liquids and ointments, some of which they had applied to his head wound and some they now gave him to swallow. When they both stood before him, he saw that they were identical twins. They were still smiling. Harry felt safe and clear-headed and was overwhelmed with gratitude in their presence. He wept silently. It was several minutes before he could speak.

"Thank you for finding me. Thank you for saving me. I would have died outside earlier if not for you; I know that much. I have so many questions, and I don't know where to begin. Perhaps, if you tell me about yourselves—wait, but no! You called me by my name. Please tell me who sent you and how you found me?"

Two youthful voices responded, but neither priest moved their lips. They were still smiling.

"Your questions are not surprising, Harry McChesney. We are many things to many peoples and faiths of the earth. To some we are spirits or lwas. Some call us saints. We have many names. You may call us Marassa. We embody many qualities of the universe and have many powers, mostly tied to our unique relationship with one another. We inhabit two bodies and share one soul. Our duality is also our unity. We dwell in heaven and on earth. We represent the diversity and unity of all existence. We invoke special blessings on children and family. We have a special bond with you and your brother."

"My brother? But he is dead, long dead. Is there some mistake?"

"You and your brother, Elmer Wilson McChesney, Jr., have led two lives but share one soul. That soul has returned to your family in you. You cried for help through this most dangerous passage. Your brother's love called to us to protect you. We were able to find you because of a gift given you by a powerful priestess." They each laid a hand on his talisman, and it glowed with intense heat. He smelled his flesh and hair singe, but he felt no pain. "She tied that for you."

When they lifted their hands, Harry saw that the little bag was as clean and dry as the day Bertha had placed it around his neck. The skin immediately underneath had a bronze tinge, like an old burn that had healed without leaving a thick scar.

"How can I ever thank you properly?"

"No need, we have already found your offering to the Marassa. You carried it in the side pocket of your outer garment." They each held aloft two foil packets and pointed to his military jacket lying in the corner. "Doublemint, our favorite!"

Harry abruptly sat up in disbelief. "Chewing gum?" He fell back and laughed in spite of his headache.

The Twins laughed too, and this time their mouths were moving. "We are your protectors throughout the present strife and for a long and productive life. We will guide you at the end as well. We minister to all twins and have a special kinship with you, Harry/Elmer McChesney. We have cleansed your wounds with healing unguents and placed a balm upon your tongue. You will rest here until the sun rises and then go in good health to your friends nearby. Remember the Marassa and remember your ancestors in your prayers, for you are your own living ancestor."

Harry was completely bewildered but not anxious. In that moment of fellowship he trusted in the Twins and closed his eyes and slept. He knew they would not be there when he awoke but believed that they would stand by him. Before he lost consciousness for the last time that morning, he heard their young voices singing together,

> We are invincible;
> We are immortal;
> We are the Twins;
> We are Marassa.

◆ ◆ ◆

Harry woke, collected his foul pile of blood-caked clothing, and left through a heavy wooden door. A small portico sheltered a side alley of the stone building. He walked toward the street, feeling steady and refreshed as if he'd slept in that basement all weekend. Squinting in the early morning light, he saw that he was standing in front of St. Pancras Parish Church on the Euston Road sidewalk. He spotted the big clock tower a few blocks down and quickly walked to his hotel. He hadn't thought of how he might appear to others but realized that the simplest account was also honest if incomplete: he was among the lucky ones who'd escaped last night's attack with only a bad whack on the noggin. He decided to omit many of the events of the past two days in speaking to his mates.

Trying to explain the marvelous and the magical could only lead to more difficulties. Besides, he had yet to sort them out with himself. In the bright light of morning he wondered, What was all that about him and Buddy? Could he begin to accept his brother as a good thing in his life after all the misery he'd brought? Could he count on the Twins' protection or on his talisman, maybe hope for help from another disappearing woman? Were his demons banished or still lurking? How could he possibly hope to win another fierce battle? Were the power of suggestion, the romantic language about demons that Uncle Harry had used to frame his Third Challenge, and his own urgency to succeed in his quest overwhelming his remaining good sense? Other than a bad blow to the head, did anything last night actually happen, or was he simply losing his mind?

Back at the Argyle Arms, the others hardly mentioned his banged-up condition. The big buzz amongst his crew was not about the buzz bombs last night but another miraculous sighting. Harry thought at first the Twins might have been in more places than one, busy saving others around town.

But no, as Lex put it, "We thought we had really overdone the bad hooch and were seeing ghosts. Jay and Seth spotted them, or rather, heard them first. Just before closing, who should stroll in like regulars at this dive down by the river? None other than Weclav, the big Polack navigator, and three other members of Rock's crew. God Almighty, what a splendid sight! We cleared the floor with all our hugging and dancing about and shouting out their names."

Seth continued, "They were the first to make it back to England. All but four of the crew got into the hands of the French underground after they'd bailed out over German-occupied France."

Harry was afraid to ask but interrupted anyway, "What about Rock?"

"The big man is fine; he was in another village close by, getting fattened up, living with a prosperous family and their beautiful daughter while the Resistance hatched a plan to get him and the others out piecemeal. They were all stashed with different families but kept in touch through the Frenchies. Rock should be back with his group sometime this week."

Harry tried to listen closely to the rest of their tale, but some of the happy details were lost on him. Another wave of gratitude and well-being flowed from his heart and filled his limbs with strength and vitality.

Waking to his qualms about the future this morning, he had begun to feel stretched again, like a high-voltage line vibrating in the wind. Now the image of a massive, ancient oak tree flashed across his consciousness—a live oak, like the spreading, venerable trees of his hometown. He began to feel more solid and rooted and substantial, like someone who could withstand a mighty blow, a mighty storm. Someone who could take on the rest of this war, whatever the battles. Rock had made it with the help of some new friends, and with the help of Bertha, Buddy, and some amazing recent acquaintances, he was going to make it too.

# PART TEN

## Discovery

## Sixty Two

Stuck in a strange house, trapped in a giant toilet bowl was not where Robyn expected to find herself five days after she left the Pac-a-Sac on the eve of Hurricane Katrina. She felt hot and itchy, smelled like crap—along with the rest of the waterlogged world—and was desperate to find help. Thirsty *and* desperate. Why else, she kept asking herself, would she trust her life to some dim memories of high-school physics? Relative density? Buoyancy?

She wrapped another layer of duct tape over the top of the five-gallon plastic water jug. She had finished the last of the water early this morning and needed more. The frequent sips she'd allowed herself were never enough to slake a chronic thirst. She had been rationing herself to about a half gallon each day since Tara and Blair swam away and left her. No more denying the obvious or hoping for rescue, she was going to have to get in that stinking water to search for water.

They hadn't planned on drinking the bottled stuff anyway. Party refreshments were beer and tequila. For brushing teeth, treating hangovers, and other emergencies, they did like everyone else. They filled the bath tubs with water before Katrina, but all of the drains leaked. By the time the hurricane hit most of the tub water was gone.

Blair's parents were gone long before that. The Mortensons had no intention of staying around for a hurricane party after hearing the most recent warnings on the storm. Mr. Mortenson had called the girls all kinds of names after they'd refused his final offer to get in the car and head to Little Rock where he had three rooms reserved for the week. So what if she and Tara were going to have to ride in the back and share a room with two high-strung Weimaraners?

*Oh, to be in lovely Little Rock today, even Memphis, even Dallas . . . yep, even Dallas. I hope this stupid excuse for water wings works. The nuns always said, "Prayer and duct tape."*

She had never learned to swim. Blair-the-Fair and Tara were pals on the swim team at Mt. Carmel High. Robyn didn't have their glam looks or their family money to flaunt. Still, she'd liked hanging out with the most popular, preppy girls in her school. She knew that they cozied up to her because she was smart and could help them with written assignments, even lend them her notes to study for tests. Funny how that had worked out. They were admitted to Loyola University with swim team scholarships, and she scrimped to attend Delgado Community College, part time.

It wasn't like they were still fakey close either. She wouldn't have been invited to this disaster of a Katrina party had the oh-so-elite "B&T team" (their own lame nickname for themselves) not stumbled across her when they stopped by the Pac-a-Sac last Saturday for ice and beer.

It was an awkward situation; she hadn't seen either of them in almost two years. Robyn was the only clerk at the store, so they couldn't pretend that she didn't exist. She ended up accepting their half-hearted invitation. Almost as soon as they'd left the store, she was ashamed at how she'd instantly regressed under that beam of insincere affection, how she'd gushed and giggled about their surprise reunion, and kicked herself for chirpily volunteering to supply the booze. Her New Orleans Catholic upbringing offered a convenient way out of the dilemma. She acknowledged her transgressions against herself, feigned contrition, granted herself absolution, and decided to go anyway—her unspoken indulgence. As it turned out, the heavens were all out of indulgences. God decided to exact a heavy penance instead.

They met at Blair's, Blair's parents' home actually, since none of them had places of their own. Blair and Tara were almost fun company until the shooting started—ice-cold tequila shots. Loyola girls could never hold their liquor. By ten p.m. those two were looped and freaking out about every little thump and bump outside. Tara in particular was getting on her nerves. A bit later when the wind really howled and things slammed ferociously into the house, she had everyone crawling up the walls. Right after the big pine tree fell into the front corner of the house, Robyn poured the rest of the liquor and beer down the drain. She huddled with them in the powder room under the stairs until the water started rising the next morning and drove them to the second floor. They grabbed some peanut butter, Eggos, and the half-empty jug off the Kentwood cooler in the kitchen and hauled them up for breakfast. Her fickle friends ditched her a few hours later.

Slimy water was above the axels of Tara's SUV when they decided to make a run for it. Robyn was leery of trying to go anywhere and getting stuck in rising water. Tara and Blair argued that they could probably still drive to the interstate over by Lake

344 | W.S. Culpepper

Avenue and then head out of town past the airport. Yeah maybe, like yesterday, before the shit-storm. It didn't matter anyway; the car would not start.

As they stood yapping over the next good idea, the water continued rising. It was soon up to their waists, close to the vehicle's headlights. Robyn wanted to return to the safety of the second floor. The two dipsticks were determined to wade or swim their way out of Lakewood South to somewhere else. They had no plan. Robyn's plan was to grab a hammer or a hatchet from the Mortensons' garage to use to hack her way onto the roof if the flood got Biblical, otherwise try to salvage more things to eat from the kitchen and wait out the situation upstairs. She found a serial-killer hatchet and made three trips with food before the water got too deep downstairs. She hadn't had time to think about Tara and Blair and their swim outing. When they'd left, she'd hoped they would get lucky and find a skiff in someone's side yard and come back for her. Later she just hoped they'd come back.

All that drama had happened four days ago. Right now she'd welcome a little ruckus—*way* too quiet now. No cell phone, no internet, no TV, and no radio. The water pressure had quit shortly after they'd lost electrical power on the first night. She knew diddly about the situation around her other than what she could see from the windows: water, deep water, all the way to the horizon. The Eggos and all the previously frozen foods were gone; the peanut butter was almost gone. Neither her stupid friends nor any other humans had appeared on that steamy horizon.

She was now on a mission to find another place to wait for help, somewhere with running water, food, and other people. And she wasn't so sure she wanted to run into people unless they were driving a boat and wearing Good Guy badges. No telling what kind of creeps and creatures were lurking in these flood waters.

To get from where she was now to someplace better required a personal flotation device. Her Kentwood water jug was—*please God let this work*—her ticket to ride. The hatchet was her ticket in.

The flood was not quite up to the second floors of most of the homes. Tying her hatchet around her waist, she slid off the little terrace outside the master bedroom while hugging the water jug. Her heart pounded in her throat as her head went under the foul scum before popping back up. She blew gunk out her nose and shouted, "My God, it's working. This sucks, but it's working—and no leaks!"

Her eyes burned, but she could see and breathe. She kicked and floated out to where she thought the street ought to be and looked for houses where she could get up on a porch roof and climb through a second-story window. The view from water level was very disorienting. She kept getting turned around. She swam through dead birds and globs of floating stuff she couldn't identify.

What was down *in* the water was even worse. While maneuvering around, she screamed every time her legs brushed against something strange, every time she bumped into firm or squishy things below the surface. She got tangled up in a vine or some slimy rope for a few seconds and absolutely freaked. She wanted out fast after that. The next big house to her right would have to work, at least for starters.

Breaking in the windows was harder than she imagined. Most of the smaller ones had burglar bars. Some of the bigger ones were covered in plywood and wouldn't budge.

She hadn't decided how she was going to announce herself to any stranded homeowners or fellow exiles of the floods. By the time she had bashed and slashed her way into the first house, she understood that a formal announcement would not be required unless the owners were stone deaf. Any dead ones weren't going to mind, but she knew they were out there. She feared she might stumble on a corpse before she smelled it after paddling around in *l'eau de merde.*

Two forced entries only served to increase her frustration. All the food was rotting out of reach in submerged refrigerators or pantries. She yelled at her angry reflection after slamming shut another disgusting bathroom cabinet.

"Never going to make it as a food burglar. Why would I think that people built kitchens or snack bars on their second floor? The only thing I can score is allergy medicine, deodorant, and hair-removal creams."

Robyn indulged herself by using several clean toilets and never flushing. Why bother? Where would it go now but into her private swimming pool? She also checked the taps in every house. One home closest to the levee, inexplicably, still had brisk water flow. She stuck her head under a faucet and drank. Later she could come back here and take a shower and wash out her stinking clothes. She hated the floral wallpaper and colored bed linens in every room, but she would make an exception under the circumstances. Still no food.

*Last chance today to try to pick a winner or else return to this place with running water. No sense in going back to Blair's. Nobody's coming to rescue me there. Those party girls are either dead or swilling beer in Baton Rouge with LSU frat boys. Maybe eating oyster po-boys.* "Robyn? Robyn who?" *Hope they choke!*

The next home she floated by on Bellaire Drive immediately caught her attention. All the windows on the second story were open, as if to catch some breeze. She could grab hold of the lower part of the window frame, hack out the screen, and lift herself inside in nothing flat.

*What if people are in there? Why else would the windows be open? Even a doofus wouldn't evacuate because of a hurricane and leave the windows open. Maybe they were out of town already, decided not to come back, just said, "Fuck it; we have insurance!" Probably not. Who leaves town in August with their windows wide open? So, who would still be here and why would I want to tie in with such losers? Because they might have lots of hot pizza and cold beer, that's why. Can't hurt to find out. Easiest break-in all day. Here we go!*

Robyn paddled around to the back and found a rear-entry overhang that provided easy access to the upstairs center-hall window. She questioned the screen before she made the first hit.

"Yo, anybody home? Yo . . . ." *No, you smelly tadpole. Told you so. Here we go: in-side.*

The first room to her right was an office where there were canned goods and clean plates and fresh fruit.

"Jackpot! A freaking cafeteria!" *These folks must have gotten rescued right after they washed the dishes. Well, thank you, Mr. and Mrs. Good Housekeeping, thanks a lot.*

She grabbed the can opener and studied the labels while eating one twelve-ounce Bush's "Country Style Lima Beans" with "real onions and bacon" and most of one "Family Size" can of Campbell's "Hearty Beef and Vegetables [Ready to Eat!]." Profound thirst returned as she finished her high-sodium hobo's feast.

*Where is the bathroom? OK, yes, plenty of water still in the tub. Well, sister, you have found your new home. Probably has running water too. Yep. Whoa, what is that stench? Me? No, but what is that sack of crud? Someone was hurt. God-awful pile of bandages.*

Dipping a thirty-two-ounce Mardi Gras go-cup into the tub, she ambled around upstairs. Her short career as an abandoned-home invader had given her a false sense of isolation. The door of the room to her right was stuck shut. Slurping water as she rounded the corner into the bedroom to her left, she was looking into the cup and not where she was going. She lowered the cup and belched softly and casually looked around.

"Aaagh, disgusting!"

Her cup hit the floor and splashed water up her crotch. This caused her to scream again. A naked body lay on top of the sheets, on its side and facing toward the wall, a guy for sure—she could see a scrotum and hairy butt from where she stood. No reason to go any closer.

"Oh my God, it's moving. He's alive!"

"Mmmgh, whozat?"

"Hello, mister, hello! I came looking for help. My name is Robyn. Do you need help? Oh, shit!"

As Harry started to roll over, she turned away and ran back out into the hall. She raised her voice and continued talking from there—short, clear, non-threatening—hoping the man wouldn't just start shooting at her through the wall. People shot looters and burglars—that much she knew—even before the fucking hurricane.

*How the hell did I get into such a stupid situation? Because I'm a hungry, thirsty idiot, that's how.*

## Sixty Three

**H**arry was weak and groggy and didn't really know what was going on at first other than there was somebody upstairs—a girl or young woman by the voice.

"Who's there?" His voice was hoarse and shaky. Robyn pictured him reaching for his twelve-gauge. "You with Search and Rescue, Coast Guard?"

"No, *no sir*. Afraid not, I'm looking for help myself. I'm all alone, *just me*. Please don't shoot. I didn't mean to surprise you." He sounded harmless, but she stayed on the other side of the wall, backed away down the hall a bit more, just in case.

Harry's head was clearing: *definitely a young woman. Why would I shoot a young woman?* Then he remembered: *looters. Hmm, so what?*

"I don't have a gun, no weapons. What's your name?"

"Robyn, Robyn Garner."

"Robyn? I know a Robyn. Not Robyn with a 'y'?"

"Yeah, how—?"

"Can't be! Robyn from the Pac-a-Sac?"

"Harry? Mr. Mac? Oh, Jesus, I'm dreaming!" She almost rushed right into his bedroom, then remembered he was buck naked.

"Hold one second while I get decent. Haven't had any company for a while, you know!" *I'll be damned!*

◆　◆　◆

It didn't take them long to get reacquainted. Robyn gave Harry a quick rundown on her pissant friends and how she'd ended up in his bedroom. She certainly owed him that much of an explanation even though he didn't seem at all upset, more like grateful to be talking to someone, anyone other than himself.

He was and was not the same brave and good and strong old dude who'd run those creeps out of her store before the storm, ages ago. He was weak and pale and short of breath just from pulling on a pair of shorts so she could sit and visit with him in the bedroom. Her eyes confirmed what her nose suspected; he was the injured party, suffering with an ugly, swollen leg.

Harry felt groggy but extremely happy to see another friendly face, someone with whom he was acquainted if only through another set of difficulties. They began to talk about his days alone since the storm, but he didn't mention his leg wound.

After a pause in the conversation, Robyn winced in sympathy and pointed. "How did you get that?"

"When the water started getting pretty deep, when I had no business still mucking around where I couldn't see what I was doing. Walked right into my own glass-top coffee table downstairs."

"Looks pretty bad. What have you been doing for it?"

"Trying to keep it clean. I have soap and running water but no antiseptic or antibiotics. Guess I haven't been doing such a good job, or the bugs are those bad ones I read about last year that eat you right up no matter what." He smiled to try to alleviate her obvious concern. Others first, Harry's perennial point of reference.

"Can you walk on it? How much does it hurt?"

"You're beginning to sound like my physician. Are you sure you're not a doc in your spare time?"

"Doc? I wish! Well, maybe not, I'm not the bravest person around blood and stuff, but you're cleverly changing the topic."

"Not on purpose, and I do appreciate your concern. I'm very glad to see you, that's all. I'm glad you're here, safe and in one piece."

"Me too, really. Isn't it weird how Katrina keeps throwing us together?" She smiled sweetly and wrinkled her forehead slightly and tilted her head, spontaneous body language that spoke to her sincerity.

At that moment Harry completely lost his train of thought. He was transported simultaneously to two other situations, recollections from other times, one recent and one only recent because of his febrile dreams and memories of wartime.

*The store, when she thanked me and called me her good knight or something. The same facial expression and the same words: couldn't place it all then, forgot about it. Mavis! The storm, being sick and by myself has brought it all back. She looks so much like Mavis when she tips her head and looks you in the eye and smiles. My God!*

Robyn quickly saw his focus change from here and now to who knew where. His lips trembled as he raised a hand to his forehead and bowed his head. Harry's face flushed, and he shed a couple of tears behind his hand.

"Is it hurting badly? Can I help you get to the bathroom? I'll even try to help you clean it if you need me to."

"No, no! I got completely distracted by the way you smiled . . . . Someone from very long ago. Forgive me; I am a silly old man who hasn't seen anyone in days. I don't even know how to act anymore." He reached for a handkerchief on his nightstand and blew his nose.

Robyn nodded her head and spoke without hesitation, making the emotional connection that he'd obliquely alluded to. "I remind you of someone?" She waited for him to explain.

"Yes, your expression, lovely smile—a wonderful woman I knew in London during the war. She helped me through a very difficult time."

"Uh-huh."

"Not the way things usually happen. I mean, I'm typically the one who does the caring for, the looking after, the fixing. But back then I was pretty messed up, a kind of battle fatigue. She was terrific. We were only together one night, and then the war had other plans for both of us. Sorry for getting so distracted. What were we talking about before I drifted off into another world?"

"Please, don't apologize, and I don't think your mind is as far off-target as you believe. If most of your life has been like the time that you helped me out of a jam, you *are* a Mr. Fixit. What did I call you before, my noble knight? Thank God for good souls like you. Right now, you look like you could use a hand yourself. That's what your survival brain is telling you no matter who you think I look like. And we have a connection too—this Katrina war."

"War, huh? I guess so."

"Let's start by getting that wound cleaned up and talk about what's next."

Sitting on the stool while Robyn worked the shower jets and used a washcloth to get at some of the pus, Harry clearly saw the severity of his wound, as though through her eyes. He sensed she was trying to be as brave as possible without losing her last meal down the drain. The wound cavity was more eaten away and looked like bad hamburger—not healing in. The swelling in his lower leg involved both front and back and extended down onto the top of his foot. The skin was shiny and pale everywhere down there and his toes were a bluish-white. The red spider webs extended all the way up his thigh and his groin was swollen with a lump that made it hard to sit down. The spoiled-ham smell no longer washed off. Fifteen minutes of her scrubbing and rewrapping had exhausted him.

"Mr. Mac—"

"Please, Robyn, just call me Harry."

"OK, Harry, this is some serious shit, my non-professional opinion of course." *Boy, am I* not *a doctor. Almost lost it in there.*

"You OK?"

"Yes! Quit worrying about me; it's you who's the patient, remember?"

"Yes, non-doctor, sorry."

"Are you strong enough to sit here while I change the sheets on your bed?"

"Yep."

"Good, then I'm going to put you to bed and get you something to eat before I head back to the last house I busted into before yours. Somebody there left a big container of cipro tablets behind. I know that's a pretty strong antibiotic. I took it for a bad case of turista south of the border once. My mom used it for something else; I forget what she had. You really need to be in a hospital, but I don't know how to get you there by myself. You say your kids know where you are, so maybe help is already on the way. Meanwhile, the best thing I can offer, other than my sunny disposition, is to try some antibiotics."

"You would do that for me?"

"Small payback for how you helped me—end of discussion. I'm going to get busy. I'm also hoping you have a plastic bag or something I can seal those pills in while I go for a swim."

"Bottom-right desk drawer in my office down the hall. Should be some small zip-locks I use for photos and stuff."

"Your office? Oh, you mean the cafeteria?" She smiled that sweet, half-teasing smile again. "Gotcha, I know where that is."

# Sixty Four

Harry was shaking with chills and fever when Robyn got back with the medicine. She had tried to bring back a bottle of peroxide and some other first-aid stuff but had dropped them in the water—not enough hands to stay afloat and keep control. Control was never her strong suit, just like that day when Mac had helped her out, when those assholes had tried to mug her. Brute force was called for then. She wasn't sure what today called for, but maybe she could do better this time. She vowed to try her damnedest, for Harry and for herself.

He kept his food and three of the cipro tablets down and fell asleep again. After three immersions in the filthy flood, Robyn was dying to take a shower and get into some clean, dry clothes. Harry had told her to look in the boxes in the attic; he thought she was about the same size as his late wife. She assured him that almost anything would work while her things dried.

The second box in the stack was marked, "Lorna—for Goodwill." She told herself that she was shopping at a thrift store, not rifling through some dead woman's clothes, about to wear them in front of her sick husband.

*Yeah, Rob, that works. Now that's all you'll think about unless you can bring yourself to tell him how weird you feel wearing her clothes. Don't just let it hang out there and wonder what he's thinking, OK?*

*Here are some fairly blah old shorts and a top that will fit. Hope my bra dries fast. Maybe hang my wet stuff up here; it's hot as shit. Hmm, old footlocker like I took to camp. Harry must have been up here poking around. Wow, army medals and an old leather jacket, cool. Wonder what the "8" stands for? "Lead Crew Certificate of Commendation." Gonna bring some of these papers down, ask about them.*

◆ ◆ ◆

After a long shower and a nap, Robyn felt better than she had in days. She was grateful that Harry had slept as long as he had and woke without fever or chills. He ate an apple and peanut butter she'd brought him and downed another slug of pills. Even though he managed a smile, she had no idea how he was really feeling—like a limp biscuit most likely.

"Before I ask you about some things I found in the attic, please tell me if you're OK—or not—with me wearing your wife's old things."

"I already told you to use whatever you need. Lorna would be happy that they went to someone as nice as you. I feel the same way."

Now it was Robyn's turn to tear up and get red in the face. Her parents didn't have one generous or charitable bone in either body. They had never said anything nice about each other or their kids, much less somebody else's.

Harry saw her distress and wanted to help, as usual. "There are some clean hankies in the top drawer of that chest over by the closet. We have a long time until dark—what is it you wanted to ask me about?"

"Thanks, because I really don't want to talk about the two selfish lushes who happened to give birth to me and my brother—parents in name only. Let me run and get some things I brought from upstairs. It's about your time in the army or whatever, when they called you Mac. See, I remembered."

Harry was impressed. Why would any young person remember obscure facts about him? Yes indeed, he was truly grateful that Providence had sent her to his home. He was glad he could keep the antibiotics down because she had gone to such lengths to get them for him. If only he'd had them four or five days ago. He was getting weaker by the day now. If things didn't change quickly, he was going to die, and he wanted a friend by his side if and when the time came.

"So, I can pick you out in this one—the handsome boy with the killer smile. Down here, right? Yep, but what's going on here?" This time she pointed to the nose of the big bomber. "Did everybody have cartoon characters painted on their planes? Did they allow that during wartime?"

He smiled as she handed him his crew photo in front of the *Krazy Kat,* taken when the whole gag with Ignatz and Krazy was still fresh and brash, like the young airmen.

Harry had looked at another copy of this same picture in his old album a few days ago when it first unleashed a flood of vivid details and names and places. He jumped right back into those memories as though the picture were taken last week.

"That was right before we left Harrington, Kansas, with Rock and Benbow and the others, flew the southern route to the European Theater of Operations. We were part of the newest Heavy

Bombardment Group in the Eighth Air Force, the 491st, based at Metfield in East Anglia. And that was no ordinary airplane, Robyn. The *Krazy Kat* was a beast of a bomber, a B24, the most advanced aircraft of its time—"

"You flew in that thing to bomb the Germans? I know it must have been dangerous as hell. I would have been scared shitless, were you? Were you wounded? How many men did you kill? Did you lose a lot of friends?"

"The sad, short answer to most all of those questions is yes. Perhaps I should back up a bit first . . . ."

They talked for hours. Harry began with a brief rundown of his dashed ambitions as a pilot and made a vague reference to a solemn promise he'd made his family about the undertaking. His delivery quickened; he gestured animatedly as he spoke about his great good fortune in joining up with the Krazy Kats as a gunnery sergeant and how he'd finally pestered and wheedled his way behind the controls of a B24 under the patient tutelage of his talented pilot. He chuckled as he recalled some of the pranks and lighter episodes: the endless harangues around the card games, John Pique stories, Ted's Traveling Circus, poaching coal from the base stockpile to stay warm. Like the ancient masters of oral tradition, he wove humor into the fabric of his war ballad to give his audience some emotional relief from the weight of its dark and somber elements, all the relentless carnage and waste: the early and late Metfield disasters, the gruesome deaths of friends and hut mates, the terrors of flak and aerial battle, the incredible odds stacked against successful completion of thirty combat missions.

The swamp air had cooled down to tolerable when Harry called a halt to the oral history lesson around midnight. He fell asleep almost immediately but dreamt again of combat missions, of the war. Robyn had found the stories exciting and disturbing. She sat up for several more hours reading wartime letters from Harry's parents. His mother came across as a constant handwringer, a first-class worrywart. Harry had explained to her how his older brother had died in infancy, that his mom was never the same afterwards. But still. His father's letters made her weep, partly in mourning for the parent she was denied but mostly in sympathy with his words of encouragement and love, an extended lifeline from home.

Around two a.m. she came across one envelope that was separate from the other bundles. In it was a note that began, "Dearest Harry"—she stopped reading. He told her to read whatever she found, but her feminine instincts sensed something different here. Perhaps she was affected by an ink smudge at the bottom of the first page or the emotional flourishes of the script. Whatever, this one gave off a different energy entirely. It belonged only between them, a private part of their wartime and not for her eyes. She slipped it into the envelope marked "Sinclair Shipping, Ltd." and placed it back in the footlocker before going to bed.

# Sixty Five

**R**obyn found a thermometer and measured Harry's morning temperature before they started in on his wound care.

"One-oh-one-point-five degrees, let's hope that's lower than before. At least no shaking chills overnight, right?"

"Nope, I'm practically cured." He attempted a bound from bed to show how well he felt—not. "Whoa!"

Robyn grabbed him under the shoulder. "Steady boy, you're not quite ready for the Labor Day 10K. Coming up next week, you know? Only this year there is going to be a special category: pirogue."

"Ha-ha, your bedside humor is improving."

"Why don't we try walking to my wound clinic instead of jogging?"

"OK, I'm not used to hitting the showers after such a short workout, but I don't get invitations to shower with pretty women every day either."

"Getting frisky, huh? I'll have to prescribe something for that."

She wanted to prescribe something more for his leg after unwrapping the dressings. It was worse, no denying it, especially the toes. The middle ones were purplish and cold. Neither of them said much during his treatment; the silence was painful.

Finally, Harry asked, "Did I exhaust your patience with my prattle about the war last night? I haven't spoken about most of that to anyone other than my wife, not even with my own kids. I think I got carried away. For some reason it's one of the main things I've been dreaming about, ever since Katrina and again last night. You got it right; they *are* both like wars for me. Bloody disasters, my life's bookends, huh?"

"Your stories are fascinating to me, the girl who thought history was bunk—before yesterday. I just wish I had a voice recorder. Why don't we get you comfortable in bed with that foot elevated? You can tell me more after we get some food and your antibiotics."

"Hit the sack at 10:45? It's still the shank of the morning."

But Harry was happy to head back to bed; the spontaneously sociable self was already exhausted. His illness was tearing down his body and his expectations. When Robyn went more than a few paces away, melancholy crept back like cockroaches from behind the baseboards. He wanted to see his children and grandkids again but didn't think the odds were very good on that score. Their attempts to reach him had gotten lost in the chaos.

◆　◆　◆

"You didn't tell me you had a radio. I've been listening to WWL while I was eating and getting your breakfast together. Hope it's to your liking, the breakfast that is. The world according to radio remains shrouded in darkness and ignorance."

"Tell me what you know. I can take it."

"President Bush was giving some news conference with his head of FEMA and giving him a big attaboy. I think his exact words were, 'Good job, Brownie.'"

"What planet is he living on?"

"Exactly! And Congress is giving themselves a big pat on the back for staying up late last night to vote ten billion dollars for relief and rescue of Katrina victims."

"Yeah, when in doubt, throw money at it, but what about the local action? What's happening in the big puddle outside?"

"The only thing I heard was that the NOPD is still on shoot-the-looter alert and not out rescuing anyone. Plus, some brigadier general sent a thousand National Guard troops to storm the Morial Convention Center where the law of the jungle has reigned—bad scene. And that's the way it is, folks, Friday, September 2nd."

"So, nothing good happening out our way. Have you been keeping an eye out the windows in case someone happens by in a boat?"

"Roger, sorry to report: no sightings today."

They paused and exchanged looks. Both tried on their most invincible posture and determined facial expression, weak attempts to bolster the other. Almost immediately, they shrugged and raised their eyebrows and smiled, putting the lie to any false bravado, as if to say, "What can we possibly do?" Harry tried to think of another Plan X; nothing came. He hoped Robyn had one, for her at least.

"Can we look at some more of these photos and stuff? I can follow along and keep a lookout for the cavalry at the same time. It's so quiet out there; we could hear a canoe coming two miles off."

"Sure, but today's the day; I can feel it."

"Right. Who's this cutie in the diaper sitting on the Hog?"

"My niece, Winifred Humphreys. She's my sister's first child, about eighteen months at the time. And that's no Harley, lady;

that's my faithful Indian. Got that motorcycle in California, right after I finished up my combat tour and returned to the ZOI, Zone of the Interior—the army's name for the good old U. S. of A."

"You mean they didn't just set you free, discharge you after all that battle in Europe? Wasn't that enough?"

"We finished our thirty missions—by the skin of our teeth—in January 1945. The Germans hadn't surrendered yet, and there was still a severe shortage of experienced bomber pilots. Most of the surviving pilots from the ETO were brought back to the States to start training in the new B29 bombers for the air assault on Japan. An unlucky few were sent straight to the Pacific to fly their old boxcars, the B24s, against the Japanese. I considered myself very lucky. I was assigned to Keesler AFB over in Biloxi as a gunnery instructor, sixty miles from home. I took little Winnie's picture while I was on leave at my parents' home in New Orleans."

"Well, at least that was way better than being shot at, the flak and all . . . ."

"More comfortable for sure, but not much safer. We lost almost as many men and aircraft in training accidents in the ZOI during the war as in combat. The army never publicized those horrible statistics after the war. Anyway, I was finally discharged after about fourteen months of active duty, about a week after Japan surrendered."

"Whoa! How about this? Who in the world is *that* weird looking dude? And is that your mom standing between him and you?"

"That's my crazy high-school buddy, Jack Pitre. He and I got in more trouble growing up, but we also served together in the 93rd over in England—great and funny guy. This was right after I was discharged and returned home."

"Your mom's smiling big."

"Jack was always cracking jokes, but she *did* smile a lot that day. It was the very first time I was able to convince her that I wasn't going to die in the war. No, I'm serious!"

"Well, from what you've told me about the dangers, she had a point, always worrying."

"Yes and no, it was way more complicated . . . . I don't think we have time to go into all that. Anyway, we had a very emotional reunion, Mom and me and my pa and my sister Penny. My mother thanked me for coming home alive, for keeping my promise to the family. Said she was going to start trusting in her family more and stop going to church so damned much. She had us all in stitches, something I had never experienced before in our house. And she made me feel like I'd had a lot to do with us feeling better, especially with her feeling better. Jack had swung by to take me out for a drink after dinner when this picture was taken."

Harry also remembered that day as the first time since Buddy's funeral that his mother had agreed to visit his grave. He drove her to the cemetery the next Sunday with a bouquet of forget-me-nots, and they placed them at the family plot. From that day forward she slowly began to pare her rancor away from the sorrowful loss of her son, became accepting of God's will, and started to move from the shadows of depression. She had finally begun her journey back to a deserving place within the family.

"How about this one? You and this handsome black woman, all dressed up and looking spiffy in your uniform and she with her nice dress and hat with a veil. You look like you're going to church."

"We were, to *her* church. That's Bertha, the woman who'd worked for my family since around the time my sister was born.

She helped take care of Buddy, my dead brother, all through his sickness. And she was more than my nursemaid too; she was family to me. Bertha may have had more to do with my making it through the war and being here today than any other person on the planet, but that is another long, long story.

"The week before this picture was taken, my church had held a memorial service for all of the military personnel from the parish who had lost their lives and to offer thanks for the survivors who had returned. I was one of those who were to stand and be recognized, and I invited Bertha to the service. My mother found out the day before we were to go and said that no Negroes had ever worshipped in the First Presbyterian Church since its founding and tomorrow wasn't going to be any different. My father overruled her and said that it was about time they did and that anything I wanted to do was OK by him. Ma had started to do a lot better with some parts of her life, but she never gave up her racial bias. She didn't put up a fight but threatened to boycott. Bertha said she 'didn't want no ruckus in the family' and asked me if she could stay home. That's just the way things were in those days. I bit my tongue with my mother but told Bertha that the only way she could decline my invitation was if I could accompany her to her church the following week.

"The Reverend Green greeted Bertha and me at the door of the Tabernacle Baptist Assembly and introduced me to a Negro officer who had served with the famous Tuskegee Airmen, a member of the 332nd Fighter Group in Europe, one of our fierce bomber escort groups, our Little Friends. We all had fried chicken and potato salad in the shade of the parking lot after services. It was a fine Sunday. I returned to the Assembly many years later to be a pallbearer for Bertha's funeral."

"Too much, she sounds like a good person who was devoted to you."

"More than I could possibly explain, she had her loving arms around me as long as she lived—maybe longer."

"I'm glad you were there for her farewell."

"I suppose. At my age, attending funerals for dear friends and family is one of the few regular events in life. I've said good-bye to too many; I don't look forward to that part of churchgoing, never have."

Robyn didn't know whether she should press on. Harry looked tired although it was only a little after noon. The temperature inside the house wasn't too bad, but she didn't have a fever either. Perhaps sharing this much of himself was too much effort. Something told her to continue, that it was important for both of them.

She wanted to ask next about the mystery woman, the "someone from very long ago" whose memory came flooding back to Harry yesterday. Could this possibly be the same woman who had written the tear-stained letter? She hesitated long enough for Harry to wonder why she seemed discomfited. Then she gazed at him and smiled to relieve the momentary tension. Again his mind flashed back to Mavis.

"Do you want to know about Mavis?"

"Is that her name, the special someone?" Harry nodded; he was OK with where this was going. "I . . . I guess so. If you're uncomfortable talking about this, we can forget it." But her tone of voice clearly said otherwise.

So Harry told Robyn of the woman who helped to heal his psychic wounds during a chaotic weekend in London. He told her enough, but of course, never spoke of their most tender moments. Robyn could read the emotion in his face and hear the love in his voice. She could easily fill in the blanks of how their night together had gone. He told her how they had planned to meet the following evening and how Mavis's parents had intervened in her life to bring her home.

"She wrote me a beautiful letter, as beautiful as she was in every way. I never blamed her for bending to her parents' will and returning home. She told me how strongly she felt about me—loved me—and asked me to find her after I returned Stateside. Her family lived in St. Louis, and her dad was a big shot in President Roosevelt's war effort. They had companies all over, and Mavis was a key executive in the family business.

"Back in the ZOI, I tried writing her. She had included her parents' address in her letter. Maybe they forwarded my letters somewhere—probably not. Months went by, and I heard nothing. After I was discharged, I was accepted to the School of Engineering at Washington University in St. Louis. I went to her home where I got a chilly reception from her mother. She denied ever hearing Mavis speak of me. I knew she was lying. She announced that Mavis was living in Manhattan and engaged to a young man of considerable promise. I didn't linger long enough to find out what that meant. The mom wasn't giving out any current addresses and hustled this ex-flyboy off the premises. It was very clear she thought that I wasn't Sinclair material . . . ." His voice trailed off.

Robyn brushed back a tear, but this didn't sound like Harry. She couldn't picture him quitting the field so easily.

"You never heard another word?"

"I don't think her parents ever gave her any inkling that I had written or paid a visit, at least not until after Mavis was safely married. I got a late-night, long-distance call in the spring of my freshman year. I think her mom must have had too much sherry one evening and spilled the beans about me. Mavis was beside herself, crying and banging something on a desk while she tried to speak to me. I could hear some muffled shouting in the background. She swore to me she hadn't known I'd still cared. She shrieked, 'I'm lost! Oh God, Harry, I'm lost! They've beaten me.' I thought she was trying to say, *'I've* lost.' But whatever it was, we were lost to each other. Divorce was not an option for a woman in her position, and her parents were going to do everything possible to keep us apart."

"Did you try to see her, meet with her?"

"She wanted to, said that she was coming that night, but I decided it would be terrible for both of us. After thirty minutes or so of her crying and begging my forgiveness and raging at her parents, my heart was breaking, and I told her I had to hang up. I told her I would call her back in the morning.

"When I called the next day, her husband answered and told me that she was under a doctor's care. Of course, the doctor had given strict orders to keep her heavily sedated. We spoke briefly one other time a few months later. By then Mavis was resigned to her situation. She still blamed herself entirely for having lost faith in my feelings for her. I tried to remind her how fine our brief moments together had been and that she was the one who had convinced me to live for the day, back in our day. I told her I'd forgiven her, which I truly had. But I also told her that I was ready to move on with my life. I was never a very good liar, but she took me at my word.

"I never heard from her again. It was another year before I started dating again, and shortly after that I met Lorna, my future wife. After we got engaged, then happily married, I didn't think about Mavis again until the war started creeping into my dreams a few nights ago."

Harry was looking somewhat relieved to have finished the story of his lady fair. Robyn knew it was time to change the subject. She reached for the document that had caught her eye when she first looked in the footlocker.

"This looks important. I now know what a lead crew is, but please tell me about this Certificate of Commendation."

"Ah, January 13th! Remember that I told you we barely finished our thirty? Everybody got hyper-superstitious as their magic number approached: thirty missions for lead crews like ours, thirty-five for the others. Why anybody agreed to fly their last mission on the thirteenth of the month with thirteen crewmen onboard that day I'll never know."

"Did you have a choice?"

"Of course not, but the *coup de grâce* was when they told us at the briefing that this one was a cinch, 'Just a milk run, men.' Danny Trimble, our bombardier from Pine Bluff, was an honest-to-god sharpshooter regardless of visibility. He and Ross, our navigator, helped perfect the special equipment the Eighth Air Force used to bomb when the targets were obscured by clouds. 'Blind bombing,' they called it. He was obsessed with doing this target right, an important bridge in Germany that was located smack between two churches. We knew they had the usual antiaircraft batteries to defend it—nothing huge, but the enemy batteries had sharpshooters of their own. Danny was adamant about nailing that bridge without disturbing one tile on those churches. He didn't want the hand of the Lord to smite us for any collateral damage on our last run. So, his religious concerns distracted us from all of the lucky thirteens on the mission . . . ."

And thus began the tale within the tale, the one never mentioned in the official Certificate of Commendation for their final mission.

# Sixty Six

Not a word passed over the intercom since they'd crossed into Germany. The regular crew was moody and tense because of the occasion, and with two photographic specialists and another navigator making his last training run with the G-H equipment, there was no room to spit in the duty stations forward of the waist.

Ross was the first to pick up the clearing skies ahead and broke the silence. "Danny, Skip, would you look at that. The weather gods are smiling on us; the eggheads back at Pinetree got it wrong again."

"Not a cloud, not a stray stork between us and the target. If everybody flies their formation right today, we should nail that sucker."

"Two minutes to IP, men, and not shit for flak so far. Let's take this one in and out and home. May God bless us all."

"Amen!"

◆ ◆ ◆

Right after bombs away, Skip cheered his sharpshooter. "Perfect drop, Danny, the strike photos ought to be tight as a gnat's ass. I'm taking over and heading to our rally point."

They heard the bursts hit the aircraft as soon as they saw the bright flashes. The flak batteries were well hidden in the trees along the river. They always went for the lead aircraft, but waited until after their drop this time. Something new, Harry thought, even after thirty missions.

Ross shouted, "Skip, I think I'm hit!" Ross's right arm was grazed at the elbow. He had no feeling in most of his forearm, but he didn't see much blood coming through his flight outfit. Ross repeated his injury report—still no response from the flight deck. He told Lt. Wainwright, the trainee, to take over while he took a closer look.

"Hey, Mac, come forward right now! Skip and Dick are hurt bad!"

Two shells had exploded directly below the flight deck. Hunks of shrapnel came straight up through the bottom of the aircraft. The right side of the co-pilot's jaw was broken and the wound carried upward along his face. He was slumped forward, unconscious and bleeding profusely. Another fragment of steel had smashed Toby Harden's right tibia. The pilot could no longer control the rudder pedals. Skip looked up as Ross staggered onto the flight deck with one arm dangling. He activated the switch on the auto pilot just before passing out.

Ross yelled again into the intercom, "Jay, Danny, get some walk-around bottles and come give us a hand, pronto! We've got casualties on the flight deck."

Jay and Danny moved Dick to the waist and were administering first aid. Harry sat down in a puddle of blood in Dick's seat and flipped off the AFC.

"Ross, call Seth up here to look after Skip. I want you to help me navigate back to base; I don't know Wainwright at all. Donovan, give me a damage report. All the instruments read OK, but that's not good enough."

Skip began to come around and moaned softly into his mask. He regained focus and glanced at a familiar face to his right. Releasing the wheel, he saluted his new co-pilot.

"Second officer McChesney, nice to see you."

The supernumeraries were taking all of this conversation in over their headsets. Gratified to hear the pilot's voice again, they had no idea what was going on. When Bertke up in the nose told them that one of the waist gunners was now flying the aircraft, they knew he was making sick jokes at their expense.

Skip was pale and starting to shiver. Seth looked over at Mac, nodded OK, and spoke to his chief, "Sir, we need to get you looked at and into a casualty bag to stay warm. You've lost some blood and need a tourniquet on that leg, maybe some morphine."

"Hell, Seth, you must be worried, calling me 'sir.' Help me out of this seat and onto the deck here. You can check me out, bandage me up, put me in the heated mummy bag, but no morphine. I want to be awake—if I can—to talk to Mac. No dope, understand?"

"Mac, Donovan here. Other than hits to our crew, we've sustained no more than a few holes in the skin of the ship, but Dick is pretty bad. We're throwing shit out to lighten this baby up and get more airspeed. He needs to get to base ASAP."

"Ross, give me the optimal airspeed, altitude, and headings as I need them. Jay, you alert the squadron that we've got wounded. We're dropping down out of formation as soon as we're out of enemy territory. Have Albright move up into lead, and rustle up some escorts for us down on the deck just in case."

◆ ◆ ◆

Over the Channel at 10,000 feet, the adrenalin began to fade from Harry's system enough to permit nervous thoughts and memories to crowd in and dent his concentration. A tense fatigue set in, and his confidence sagged. In spite of immense effort to remain awake, his commanding officer was slipping in and out of consciousness. Harry thought back to the time he had dropped the PT-19 trainer onto the runway from twenty feet with Highway Harrison. The same maneuver in a B24 would do more than fracture the landing gear. They would probably tumble for a half mile down the runway before bursting into flames.

"Mac, have Jay get the base on the emergency sideband frequency." Skip had roused himself. "Tell them we've got casualties, and we're coming straight in. To hell with the approach pattern. You'll be the first home anyway. Mac, we're gonna come in hot, redline the son of a bitch. Drop your flares, crank the flaps out full, hold your glide path at five degrees, and land the bugger. You're a good pilot, Mac; you've landed us before. And don't forget, this is just a milk run."

Skip smiled wanly and slipped off again. As the big bird gained speed in the power glide, the control wheel began to vibrate. Harry made a final adjustment of the propeller pitch and followed his engineer through the landing checklist. Donovan also handled the landing gear while helping him maintain proper ground speed and descent rate. The more eyes the better right now. The lights of the runway were coming up faster than he'd ever seen them. The wheel was now shaking violently with a mind of its own. Each time Harry took one hand off to wipe sweat from his eyes, he would have to re-correct the glide path. He could feel his heart pounding in the back of his throat; he was close to blacking out.

*Yep, I am going to kill us all. Hold this thing steady. Steady, baby. Steady. Jesus, we're going to hit! Throttles back full, nose up!*

"Brakes, Mac, brakes! We're down; you did it! We're down. Hold the fucker in line. Whooo-hoo! Yahoo-hooey!" And his engineer stomped the deck so hard that he roused the Skip. As Mac turned off the runway and stopped on the taxi strip, flashing lights from three ambulances raced toward them.

# Sixty Seven

"My God, Harry, you're terrific. Terrific? You're a war hero; you saved the whole crew. I mean you got them back safely; did everyone survive?"

"Richard Frost, our co-pilot, was seriously wounded and needed a lot of plastic surgery to build his face back up. But he lived and returned to the States to the family cranberry business. He passed away two years ago last June. Our Skipper, Toby Harden, still has some German steel in his leg and gets to *skip* the weapons screening machines when he flies to our Eighth Air Force reunions. He's still going strong. Roscoe, our navigator, never played tennis again but had a great career as a Wall Street lawyer—"

"But what happened after you landed the plane? What did all the generals say about a gunnery sergeant flying men home from the mission?"

"They never knew a thing. Such an outlandish event was very much against regulations. How was I supposed to have learned to fly the thing in the first place? Only my commanding officer could have been responsible for such a breach, which, of course, he was. Instead of a severe reprimand or maybe a court-martial, he was awarded the DFC, the Distinguished Flying Cross, for valor and extraordinary achievement in action. The regular crew, those of us not in ambulances, got together before our debriefings and agreed on the story of how Skip managed to land the plane with a shattered leg. The visiting firemen, the three officers who flew but were not part of our crew, didn't need any convincing. They truly believed this was what happened in spite of all of Donovan's shouting and stomping. They were the ones who really sold the story to the brass. We did have to do some fast talking to explain how we got Skip zipped up into the casualty bag so fast after the landing, but we finessed that somehow. We tipped the wounded to our account long before the medals were passed out. Their stories were never questioned."

"But the guys you flew with all knew."

"Yeah, our little secret from the military. Besides, the wounded deserved their medals; Skip should have had his DFC long before that. All of the rest of us got the Certificate of Commendation for nailing the bridge without breaking any stained glass in the churches."

"You're the one who deserved the DFC or whatever for extraordinary valor under fire, Sgt. McChesney."

"Toby gave me his medal at a very private ceremony, just our crew members in attendance of course, during our first reunion back in 1950. It's up there in my footlocker. At least, I hope it still is. Means a lot to me—mostly for the confidence my commander had in me to train me to fly the aircraft and for the teamwork that helped me get the thing on the ground that wonderful-terrible day."

"You are amazing; I am awestruck. I have *never* met anyone like you."

"I am just an ordinary man, Robyn. One of thousands who did what we had to do back then."

Harry had never shared the real story of his last mission or much at all of his combat experiences with his parents, wife, or uncle. He easily could have. Many a man home from the war made sure that loved ones knew all about their heroism and bravery. In Harry's case, of course, there was the added satisfaction of how magnificently he had overcome adversity and met and surpassed his uncle's first challenge: to master the rigors of flight. Deeply gratifying, yet the whole grand achievement wasn't something he wanted to call attention to. It was more like a second skin or another extraordinary organ of the body that only certain people had. It was there; it was God's gift; you valued it; you didn't abuse it or neglect it. But you also didn't take it out or peel it back and show it off.

He considered the most intense episodes of combat, that flashing kaleidoscope of grief/danger/joy, bound up in a sacrament of solidarity and reserved for those with whom he'd served. Their brotherhood was like a perfect communion; their triumph and agony and sacrifice were the outer forms of an inner, spiritual grace. Their blood was in there too, always and forever precious blood—for many the final offering.

On the other hand, sharing his stories with Robyn seemed natural and inevitable. In lieu of resurgent health or worldly treasure, these memories were his only form of thanks and repayment to someone trying to save him; they were his last and best offerings.

# Sixty Eight

Harry said he wasn't hungry, but she made him eat another apple for late lunch along with his antibiotics.

"Loaded with vitamin C, good for wound healing, so I'm told. That's the last one, however."

He didn't resist or try to make any jokes, just turned on his left side after swallowing the pills. Robyn didn't bother him to check another temperature. His forehead was dry and hot—hotter than this morning. The miasma of the sickroom suddenly overwhelmed her. She paced anxiously around the upstairs and made circuits through the attic while her thoughts raced.

*Enough already, I've exhausted him. He's talked out; now he's turning away so I won't have to see him in pain—see him die. God, help me do something for this good man! This is not some stupid movie we're in. The studly guy in the tight jeans isn't coming to save us. Harry is the real hero here: he saved a planeload of men, and he saved me and who knows who else in his life. Shit, why can't I think of something?*

She stopped and was standing at the back hall window, the one she'd now climbed in and out of several times, looking off into the sky. There was a new wrinkle in her field of gaze that had made her stop, but she didn't notice it for a while.

*The levee, the top of the levee is poking up; the water level has dropped some. I might be able to get somewhere, find some help from up there. At least I wouldn't have to paddle around with my nose just above the stinking waterline; I could look around, get around. Oh, thank you, Jesus!*

She crossed herself and genuflected at the window, at the altar of the levee. Somewhere, the nuns were smiling.

"Harry . . . ." No answer. "Harry!"

He murmured but didn't open his eyes at first, "Mmm?"

"I'm sorry. I know you need to rest, but I need to leave for a little while."

*No, don't go!* Panicky thoughts urged him to sit up and act alert, but a huge hand was pressing him into the bed, holding him down. He could only turn his head and look, try to read the truth in her eyes. "Why? What is it?"

"I don't know whether or why I just noticed it, but part of the earth levee is exposed above the water this afternoon. Before, all I could see out the back window was part of the concrete floodwall. The flood waters have dropped some; I'm sure of it. I can see a brown waterline on the concrete where the level was yesterday. I plan to swim over there and see how far I can get, look for help. We've *got* to get you out of here, Harry, and I can't do it alone; neither can you."

Harry just closed his eyes and tried hard to think, think of something to say that would help nudge her in the right direction. The big hand was pressing on his brain and keeping the thoughts down, like his body.

Finally the idea surfaced. "Railroad . . . Southern Railroad."

"What about the railroad? How does that help us?"

"The tracks run east-west just north—no! Sorry, just south of here, they cross the levee about five blocks to the *south*. The roadbed and the tracks are a little higher than the levee. You might be able to get along them to someplace that isn't flooded, east toward the city or west into Jefferson Parish. Might be worth a try."

"Oh, Harry, I need to try. I don't want to lose you. If rescue teams have already been through this area and they missed us, they might not be back for a long time. Your family could be trying to get word to the authorities, but so are thousands of others. You need to be under a real doctor's care—today."

"Yes, go for it, but for Christ's sake, be careful. It's important that you look after yourself at this point. Don't get injured for this old man. Whatever happens, remember, Robyn, you've been terrific to me, like I would have expected one of my daughters to be: brave and kind and resourceful. If for some reason you can't come back, I'll understand."

"I'm not leaving you behind for the enemy, Harry. I'll be back; I *swear*. I don't want to wait until tomorrow. There are a few more hours of daylight left this evening, and I'm going to use them."

"I'll miss you. I'm incredibly tired, sleeping too much, but I don't like being alone today. Our talk about Bertha has given me an idea though. Before you leave, please run up to the attic and bring me the little green Luzianne Coffee can from my footlocker. It's in there someplace. You'll know it when you see it; there's something in it that I want."

*What?* Up until now he had been making perfect sense, but he was burning up with fever. The antibiotics weren't doing shit to help his infection, and she wanted to get going. But she made another trip to the attic. She located the ancient can and brought it to his bedside. He was already dozing off again, or worse.

"Harry . . . Harry, here it is, right? 'Luzianne' on the top . . . ."

She noticed a coarse tremor as he reached for the can. He

twisted off the top and pulled out a small leather pouch that was gathered and sewn shut at one end. The leather looked very old and stiff and part of the seam had started to unravel.

*What the fuck?*

"Don't look at me like I'm crazy. I probably am. Bertha got this for me just before I went off to war. I think it protected me, kept me alive—helped anyway. I wore it for almost thirty years until the string or whatever it was that passed through here and around my neck rotted and broke. I tossed it in this empty can, my dad's coffee, after that. I wish I'd been wearing it during the storm. Maybe it's not too late; maybe it will help friends and family find me. It has before."

*What do I say to this? Nothing. Gotta go.*

"Whatever, Harry, we'll talk about it later. There's plenty of water and pills right here on your nightstand. I'll be back as soon as I can."

They kissed and hugged. He felt like a hot, frail twig, and she was afraid she might snap him. His illness had wasted him away dramatically in just a few days. Her tears welled up as she swam for the top of the levee.

◆　◆　◆

The steep, muddy slope offered little purchase as she tried to slither up the slick embankment to the narrow junction of exposed land and vertical flood wall. Thin, waterlogged turf tore away, and her old Reeboks just slid in the clay beneath. She fell face-first into the water a couple of times before being able to claw some handholds and pull onto the mushy path that looked so welcoming from afar. Anger and fear replaced her tears.

*Swallowed more toilet water just now than I have all week. Which way did he say to go? North? South? Right? Left? Calm down, Rob, and think. South. OK, left. Yep, that little hump down there must be the railroad tracks crossing the levee.*

Her hands were caked with rotten-smelling clay, but she managed to hold onto her precious Kentwood jug. In spite of her promise to Harry to take care, she was walking as quickly as she could with her eyes on the tracks in the distance. Sudden, plashy sounds right at her feet called attention to ripples at the edge of the water where three large snakes swam away from the warm mud. They had been sunning themselves seconds before. Trying to stop suddenly, she slipped onto her butt and slid down the slope a bit before stopping. From this perspective she could see at least four more clumps of snakes along the path just ahead.

"Oh, God, I can't do this! I am scared to death of snakes. Why is this happening?"

Robyn banged the bottom of the empty jug against the concrete wall for emphasis. The closest pile of snakes uncoiled and slithered into the water. Something about the vibrations from the jug or the wall alarmed the reptiles. She began drumming her way along and clearing the path, trying not to piss them off too much but happy with the results. It was slow going, another thirty minutes before she reached the railroad right-of-way.

*Now which way? Double tracks to the left, but only one set crosses the canal to the right. That dinky trestle over the water looks old as shit, maybe damaged. Toward the city: high and wide. Left!*

She left her jug at the semaphore signal by the track switches. There was rooftop flooding on her right, south of the tracks, that looked about as bad as what she'd left back in Harry's neighborhood. After about a quarter of a mile, she passed Metairie

Cemetery on her right. The tops of the largest marble mausoleums were visible above the waterline. Floating coffins bunched up against the crosses and religious figures atop the burial vaults like skiffs tied up for a party below. The place was vast, but Robyn wondered if there was going to be enough room in all these cities of the dead to accommodate the new toll from Katrina. She finally made it to the train overpass at I-10. To the north was nothing but the tops of some light standards outlining the shoulders of the highway and more water. About two thirds of a mile south, the roadbed rose up out of the flood where it passed over Metairie Road. There were two amphibious vehicles, some sort of military rigs, parked on the downslope facing her but no emergency flashers, no people anywhere.

"Hey, anybody over there? I need help! H.E.L.P. Help!"

She continued east, past Greenwood Cemetery and more submerged stone temples. In the distance stood the First Baptist Church—wind-damaged but isolated above the waterline, perched on a manmade expanse of landfill and blacktop, a New World Mt. Ararat. More train tracks joined the elevated roadbed from downtown, heading east. Robyn yelled for help, casting a voice across the waters every minute or two. Her cries skittered and sank like rocks beneath the flattened waterscape. Not one echo returned her call.

She continued to scan the rooflines for movement while remembering to watch for snakes underfoot—again, slow going. Passing over Canal Boulevard on another rail overpass, she spotted a hand-lettered sign advertising the "Sunken Gardens Nursery."

*Katrina's little ironies. Bet the owners aren't laughing. What a bitch!*

The tracks cut across a large expanse of Olmstead's magnificent City Park. Crowns of two-hundred-year-old oak trees were visible above the flood. She went another half hour or so but stopped at what she thought was Bayou St. John. Everything looked like the bayou or Lake Ponchartrain, both having reclaimed their old, luxuriant boundaries. The elevated I-610 corridor ran to her left, littered with abandoned cars and debris. No emergency vehicles, no people. Ahead, the top floors of the LSU School of Dentistry looked like a badly carved jack-o-lantern with teeth, eyes, and mouthparts scattered randomly, wherever Katrina had chosen to smash out some of its windows. Several miles away, above where Robyn guessed the Mississippi River ran, two orange Coast Guard helicopters cut the silence as they sped southward.

*Somebody's on the job, too far from me to help. Nothing but more water in this direction. Only an hour or so of light left. Time to head back and try the other direction. Maybe, just maybe, things are better across that canal. Maybe.*

She stopped searching so diligently and concentrated on trotting briskly back from where she'd come.

# Sixty Nine

Harry's spirit sank when he'd heard Robyn splash into the nasty water and start kicking for the levee. He wedged himself up against some pillows and reached for the solace of his lucky talisman. How many times had it provided warmth, warning, escape from peril?

He held it to his chest, hoping for the soothing sensation—like Bertha's warm embrace—that, by itself, was often all he needed to get through a tough passage. Nothing.

*Don't know what I was expecting after all this time. Charm's over. Luck's run out. Old Bertha's long dead. Harry on the way.*

With a calm and final acceptance of his fate, his thoughts turned back to Robyn as he unconsciously began to knead and roll the little sack of leather through his fingers, like a supplicant with his prayer beads. Eyes closed, he was trying to visualize where her path might have led, trying to help her on her way.

The ripe stitching that had kept the sack closed snugly all through the years began to unravel further with Harry's handling. A few coarse grains of something—small crystals—trickled out the opening and through his fingers, followed by a mother-of-pearl button.

*Oh, oh. Hmm, old thing's falling apart, just like me. Losing its buttons! How the hell did that get in there?*

He examined the crystals more closely, straining to focus without his reading glasses. Then he remembered the incredible story Bertha had told him after he'd made it home safely from the war, the story of *her* journey home and the ceremony in the salt dome. He put one of the crystals in his mouth; he was pretty sure he knew what it was.

"Salt, Avery Island salt."

Once again he began to feel a wave of love—warmth and goodness—rise up from his heart and chest. His mind seemed sharper, filling with clarity. There was still life in this wonderful gift from his dear friend. He remembered her asking for a lock of his hair. Looking at the button, he guessed she must have asked for little things, personal objects, from others in the family as well.

*God only knows what else is in this thing—*

Suddenly, his eyes and mouth shot wide open as he sucked in a deep breath—*aaah!!*—like someone shocked by a live wire or slapped in the face, even bigger: a lightning strike. In a stupendous flash, his search was over. Without yet seeing it or feeling it through the leather, he knew now where Uncle Harry's key was. He had no idea what it would look like when he found it, but he knew where to look.

*Uncle Harry, you old rascal, Bertha told you what she was up to, and you gave her the key, knowing how the vodou priests did their mojo, made their charms. You knew that it would be with me, right under my nose, as long as I lived.*

Now he really needed his reading glasses. Of course, they were nowhere to be seen.

*Left them in the office.*

He carefully placed his talisman in the inverted lid of the coffee can and set it aside before making a supreme effort to walk. He struggled to sitting but almost passed out when he tried to stand and bear weight.

*Going to do this if I have to crawl.*

And crawl he did. While in his office, another thought came— at least his mind was still in the game. He put his glasses on, stuck a notepad between his teeth, and clutched a rollerball pen as he dragged himself back to bed. He would need everything before it was over.

Harry was breathing heavily, and the room spun about crazily as he pulled himself up onto the mattress. Another red-out and run of heart palpitations finally passed. He stayed focused on the matters at hand. He wished there was better light to see what he was doing.

*This will just have to do.*

The upturned coffee can lid easily held all the contents of the talisman: rock salt, the button *(Pa's)*, two locks of hair *(two?)*, a tiny mirror fragment *(Penny's?)*, a silver cross *(Maman's)*, a corner of embroidered hanky *(Ma's?)*, and a small gold ornament or charm. Harry didn't know what it was called, but he knew it was his uncle's, knew it was the key to the treasure. He had looked upon the design, seen the same figure hundreds of times in his life, beginning when he was seven years old.

*It always comes back to Buddy, always about Buddy.*

Examining the little ornament in the shape of a cross with a loop on top, perhaps taken from the end of a pocket-watch chain, he also understood where the second lock of hair had come from.

*Buddy.*

Eight numbers were engraved on the back side of the key but nothing else.

*No problem. I know which bank holds the trust account.*

And with that he took up his pen and paper and began to write with a shaky hand but clarity of mind and purpose. When he finished, he leaned back against his pillows, completely spent. A cool breeze—cool, refreshing breeze!!—wafted along the upstairs hall, through his door, and across his bed. His body felt light and airy like the breeze, like it was expanding to fill the entire room, perhaps the whole house.

# Seventy

Time was short. Heading back west now, Robyn needed to hurry, but the uneven gravel and rail ties made running a tricky proposition. Nothing was easy; nothing was assured. Success was like the shimmering mirage off the creosote-blackened crossties that made the tracks vibrate and squiggle in the distance, mocking what she'd hoped would be a straight-and-narrow course, moving away ever farther as she approached.

Ten minutes of jogging was all she was capable of in the heat. Robyn chastised herself for being so unfit, another thing to work on if she ever made it out of this mess. Her to-do list was running off the page. Someday she might even make a dent in that list now that she had a hero for a role model. That thought inspired a smile, and she resumed jogging—more slowly this time—after a few minutes.

The bright orange ball of the sun was low in the sky and directly in her face as she passed by her trusty water jug. The prospect of crossing the narrow railroad bridge, just an extension of the roadbed on some pilings and barely above the waterline, did not seem nearly as daunting now that she knew what lay in the other direction. She decided to take the jug along for flotation, just in case. West into Old Metairie was her only chance now; she was desperate. The Apostles' Creed, the Lord's Prayer, the Hail Marys spilled out, followed by endless loops of the Holy Rosary, just like on the old radio program her granny used to listen to every afternoon.

*Pray for us sinners, now and at the hour of our death. Amen . . . . Granny and Papa Joe, their graves are ten feet underwater over in Gentilly right now. Granny never learned to swim either; she's who I got my fear of water from . . . . Holy Mother of God!*

Her prayers and meditations had gotten her safely across the long trestle, across the parish line, and several blocks into the neighborhood behind Metairie Road. She dropped the jug and gazed around, stupefied.

*Blocks and blocks of dry streets and houses and fire hydrants and fresh anthills and cars—gotta be some people back in here too.*

Just then she saw a Jefferson Parish Sheriff's cruiser, emergency flashers going bonkers, cross the railroad grade at Metairie Road. She cut over to the street alongside the tracks, to level— *dry!*—land and sprinted after it. That one quickly disappeared, but there were two more patrol cars parked right in front of a bar down by the crossing. The owner had set up a propane cooktop out of his rear service entrance and was feeding anyone who happened by. The chalkboard read "Jambalaya: $1/safe water & hot beer: free." Some kids were kicking around a volleyball, playing a game—*playing!*—a combination of soccer and baseball. The juxtaposition of these wholesome, almost-familiar activities against the struggle that she and Harry had waged, against the waste and devastation extending for miles in the other direction, jarred her head like a mallet blow. She had stumbled upon a lost world, the abrupt discovery of which rendered her speechless and slack-jawed. The burly owner-cook noticed her standing in the middle of the street: another filthy, dazed refugee from the storm who needed some cheering up. He swigged from his longneck and broke her trance with a loud belch.

"Whoa, excuse me, miss. It's the hot beer. We're all outta ice, but the shrimp and sausage are good, best jambalaya in Jefferson. You look like you could use some. We take IOUs too. Come on over!"

Robyn blinked and rubbed her eyes, still not trusting her perceptions. Then she moved quickly toward the only new voice she'd heard in days.

"Please, mister, I need help, big time. Are there J.P. cops in your place? There's somebody who is dying, needs rescuing fast."

The man put down his big spoon and wiped his hands. This chic was shaking and clearly not steady on her feet.

"Come sit down here and let me get you some water—"

"I DON'T WANT ANY FUCKING WATER, MAN! I NEED HELP; I NEED A COP OR SOMEBODY—NOW!!"

"OK, OK, look, there are guys and gals in there who have been working overtime to help folks, who know what to do. Let me get—"

But he didn't have to go get one of them. A female officer heard Robyn's roar and walked out, still chewing her food. She swallowed hard and asked, "What's wrong and how can we help, ma'am?"

*God, oh, God, thank you!* And as hard as she tried to talk and make sense, all Robyn could do for the next several minutes was to grab on to this woman and sob.

# Seventy One

**D**azzling afternoon light, shimmering from the ripples on the water, making it hard to see. It's important to see, see what's out there, traveling fast over the water. I can feel the breeze, a cool breeze, rippling the water and flowing over me. So refreshing, so different from this morning.

"The breeze is what we sent you first, Harry. To cool the suffering from your fever, to restore your spirit. Your soul followed it out the window before we could join you in your home. Too bad for us, we usually time things better."

"Yes, Harry Emerson McChesney, we were hoping you still liked Doublemint."

"We *love* Doublemint. Ah well, here we are together again."

"Together again with my Flying Priests."

"Marassa."

"I remember, the Twins. Where are we going? Where are you taking me now? Back to the church?"

"No, you are taking us. Your soul is taking us; we are your companions."

"My soul? Am I dead, already dead? I didn't feel a thing. I thought . . . ."

"Your body is withering under the sheets back in your bedroom. Hot, moist, tender leg wound: the microbes are winning."

"Soon your body will rejoin the earth under the waters over which we soar."

"Look, isn't that Robyn? She is in a boat with others, with men. She has done it! Good girl, brave girl! She is bringing help. I am *so* proud to know her."

"She feels the same way about you. She is very attached to you."

"Yes, she is strong and will prosper, with me or without me. I love her like a daughter. At least we have said our good-byes."

"She thinks of you as family, the best she has known."

"My family—no farewells there, a large sadness."

"You are fortunate to have a loving family, one who cherishes your generosity, your bravery, and your tenderness. You have answered every call and finally, every challenge."

"You will always live in such a family, as long as there is memory. You felt compelled to fulfill all of your brother's desires, earlier denied, in addition to what you yearned for. You tried to be both brothers before you even found yourself. Frustration and rage drove you to wildness. Your uncle helped you rise to manhood and laid out your quest. Your father's loving example taught you to balance your urges with humility and restraint."

"My father, is that he? Coming down South Johnson Street with his newspaper and jaunty stride? Yes, I can smell his hair tonic and the coffee. He's bringing home his personal blend of coffee, one that his company never sold in stores. The light is so bright; I've lost sight of him. No, there he is, holding me on his lap, reading to me, singing sweet and slow. He gave me so much, taught me so much."

"The desire to always do more for others burns strong in you, another gift from your father and your uncle."

"And from Bertha, a faithful *serviteur* who came to the altar and received many blessings from her ancestors. At her behest the mighty Mambo Parangou tied your wanga, your talisman of protection, and bound us together with you."

"You have not squandered life's blessings."

"Bertha's faith in you was well-founded, and she spared your parents further loss. Her love was indeed powerful."

"There is still so much to do, so much I could learn. How many lifetimes should it take?"

"You can wander over these waters for but a short time to look upon what you need to see. If you cannot decide your path, you will enter a period of trial and darkness wherein universal forces take over. Souls still attached to living in the earthly realm will ultimately return there."

"But enlightened souls can leave this sparkling earthly realm of promise, excitement, and desire. The realm that also harbors despair, disappointment, and suffering."

"Your soul can merge with God, become one with the Ultimate Principle."

"You can choose this final union or you can return to the cycle of rebirth and death. We can only show you what is on the face of the waters, not where to go."

"Why me?"

"As the old saying goes, 'If you have to ask . . . .'"

"I am not worthy."

"We are not here to judge."

"What waters are those? The light looks different, pink and yellow, early morning light. I remember; it's that estuary on the English Channel along the coast of East Anglia, Selsey Bill—how beautiful! Ah, but the ships are there too, thousands of ships and millions of men, the staging areas along the coast for D-Day. So many brave men die to turn the tide against evil and oppression: on sea, land, and in the air."

"The problem of evil; it is ever thus. Free will and the ebb and flow of the tally sheet. Sometimes evil triumphs for centuries, but this time with great sacrifice and years of suffering, freedom and the rule of just laws prevail and flourish. This is part of your generation's patrimony, your legacy to the century."

"Take pride in your list of good works. It is long and venerable: success on an arduous quest, answering the family call for help, and minding daily chores of the humble householder. But the earthly temples we build are frail, in need of constant repair. Your soul has been in service to the world for countless lives."

"Is it time to pass your banner and sword to another? To come away from the fight?"

"I am a simple man who relishes these tasks. Imperfections and suffering are part of our existence; they cannot be eliminated. Accepting that, I am drawn to ease them. I can endure the darkness and the demons, but I am not ready to touch the face of God, to become one with Him.

"So, just as you said, I have taken us to here. I have led myself to this truth about myself: I am not worthy because I am not ready to let go. I know what my path will be. My body will die today, and my soul will return to another life on earth. It is good and meet that I should again labor in the earthly temple."

"As you wish, dear friend, we travel similar paths; we shall meet again."

"And, please, next time, don't forget the Doublemint."

# Epilogue

Robyn was uncomfortable agreeing to meet anyone in a cemetery, especially *this* cemetery. A long blast from the air horn of a passing freight up on the Southern Railroad tracks echoed off the tombs with a fading moan and brought it all back.

The creepy memories and major regrets of last year hadn't let up: trapped in the Katrina flood, racing around trying to find help for poor Harry only to come up short. What a bad choice to turn left at the tracks instead of heading over that shaky railroad trestle. She could have gotten help right away on the other side of the canal. But how could she have known that part of Metairie was spared? And the medics swore they couldn't have done anything for his infected leg, even if they'd arrived two days earlier—still, they might have saved *him*. She couldn't stop kicking herself.

Harry had taken time to write her a beautiful and inspiring note before he died. She'd cried for weeks every time she read it. There were lots of reasons to cry, all day and every day after Katrina, and most of them hadn't gone away yet. All those things that she had logged into her self-improvement list, the ones she was going to do for herself with Harry as inspiration and then, after the funeral, in his memory? They were pretty much on hold since the storm. The stinking refrigerators and the flood waters were gone, but the city remained an emotional and economic disaster zone.

She'd gotten a couple of temp jobs, with FEMA no less, trying to help people get sorted out with assistance applications and trailers and stuff. Her last gig was going to run out soon, and it had barely paid for groceries. Even if there had been an afford-able place to rent, she had no rent money. She was back living at home with her alcoholic mother. The Pac-a-Sac was hit hard by looters after the storm and remained boarded up. Sometimes she found herself longing for the drudgery of that cheesy outlet. At least she was enrolled at Delgado back then and had a plan and a timeline and what she thought was a glimmer of light at the end of a bleak tunnel.

Harry's letter had something to do with why she was back at the McChesney family plot at Metairie Cemetery this afternoon. She just wasn't sure what for. In a postscript he'd asked her to please deliver an important family memento he'd enclosed along with a second note he'd written that final day. She had to get them to his nephew, Walker Humphreys, the one they called Junior. That seemed to her a pretty silly name for somebody who had to be at least fifty or sixty years old by now, but that was New Orleans for you.

She'd handed over the note and the little gold doojiggy to him at Harry's funeral and hadn't heard any more about it until this week when Mr. H. called and asked her to meet him at Harry's gravesite today at two p.m. She thought maybe he was going to bring some flowers for Harry and at least tell her thanks for bringing him something that his sweet uncle had left him from his deathbed. He hadn't said much of anything the first time they'd met; he'd treated her like some communicable disease. But when he called Tuesday, he was civil, almost friendly-like, called her "*Miz* Garner." So hip, this Mr. H.

◆ ◆ ◆

"Hello, Miz Garner, I'm Walker Humphreys."

"Robyn. Please, call me Robyn."

"Good, and please call me Walker. I'm so glad you could meet me here today."

He *did* bring some flowers; she was already feeling better about this guy. Mellow voice from a not-too-stuffy-acting, nice-looking uptown sort, some of the same features as the young Harry from those war pictures. What was with the briefcase though? Not exactly her first choice of accessories for the cemetery.

"OK, Walker, I guess. It's just not how I was raised—the first-name thing."

"Well, I understand and appreciate that, and I hope you'll accept my sincere apologies. I was very rude when we first met, and that's *not* how I was raised. I'm sorry."

"No worries."

"I was terribly upset over my uncle's death, and I hadn't known how much he thought of you. I hadn't read his letter."

"Me, he mentioned me?"

"Quite positively and specifically. He told me how you tried to save him, and more—"

"Aw, *Jeez!*" Robyn's face flushed; her chest felt like a big balloon was swelling in there, about to pop. She started to turn away, but Walker moved again to face her, speaking quickly, "He knew he was dying when you left for help."

"I was *so* trying to help."

"You did more than help, and he loved you for that. You see, it was his request that we meet here today."

"Oh God, I need to take some deep breaths."

"Well, please do, and I'm getting a little ahead of myself anyway. Before I explain, let me change out the flowers in the vase. I brought his favorites, forget-me-nots. Hard to get them at the florists anymore, sort of old school they tell me."

"They're lovely, I think, just like Harry."

"Yes, he was a wonderful person, certainly a loving uncle to me and full of goodness toward others."

That did it. Robyn had promised herself she wasn't going to cry today, not like she had at the funeral, but all of her affection for him came pouring out at that moment.

"I'm sorry; I swore I wasn't going to do that."

"Please, I understand, take as long as you wish." He offered her a hanky, just like Harry once had, and she bawled for another five minutes. After more deep breathing and a walk about, she returned to where Walker stood.

"Better?" he inquired. "Look, it's getting warm this afternoon. Why don't I show you what Harry wanted me to show you here, and then we'll go find some shade over on his favorite bench by the lagoon to talk about the rest."

"The rest? I don't understand."

"I can sympathize with that. The whole thing was pretty mysterious to me for a while. My uncle left me a very brief note, almost cryptic, you might say. It took me some time to piece things together and put this part of his affairs in order. But never mind all that, I can spell it out in pretty good order for you now—all I know of it, this McChesney stuff."

"McChesney stuff?"

"Yes, traditions and codes of conduct and all. My mother, his sister Penny, wasn't in on much and never spoke of it to me. Apparently this was all on the men's side, and in Harry's case between him and *his* Uncle Harry, but that's sort of where it ended—with them."

"I remember him mentioning his uncle and some promises he made."

"You may know more than I. I never got to join the club; guess I wasn't a direct-enough descendent. All I know about is what Harry—*my* Uncle Harry—wrote about in his last letter and referred to as 'the treasure.'"

"Now you've lost me."

"OK, according to Harry, one of the foremost obligations of the men in the McChesney family was charity: helping worthy causes, personal and civic. You see the inscription on the right-hand side of the monument back there, 'Serve and love them, in My name'? That is part of the credo, the marching orders if you will, for the family, and all the men in the family are buried over on the right."

"Under their orders for eternity—including all the Harrys."

"Precisely. The *old* Uncle Harry, my great-uncle, was quite prosperous, died without children of his own, and left all of his fortune to various charities about town—or so we thought. The old fellow must have been quite a romantic and a bit eccentric . . . ."

And Walker proceeded to tell her all about the set-aside trust with a treasure in gold and the hidden key.

"Harry didn't know what kind of key he was looking for or which bank held the trust. He did know it was a small fortune in gold bullion, one that has since grown to quite a huge fortune."

"How do you know? Did he find his treasure?"

"He looked most of his adult life and thought he'd failed completely although he continued to do his best to help others."

"I can vouch for that."

"Harry found the key on that last day, just before he died. He told me in his note that when he finally found it, he knew exactly what it was because he'd seen it, or a rendering of it at least, throughout his life. Well, here it is."

Walker handed Robyn the object from within Harry's talisman.

"Sure, that's the little gizmo he asked me to give you. He must have found it after I left for help, or he would have shown it to me."

"Yes, it's called an ankh, an ancient Egyptian symbol of immortality, everlasting life."

"One helluva good-luck charm."

"Or maybe a symbol for a treasure so vast that it was supposed to have a long life of its own. Who knows what the old boy intended?"

"But how did he know it was the key and where the treasure was stashed?"

"Old Uncle Harry had originally set up the fortune for young Harry's brother. One of the lines in my uncle's note read, 'It was always about Buddy.'"

"His dead brother. OK, so I guess he's buried over there, too?"

"Yes, a very small coffin. Right under the inscription—"

"Of course!"

There it was, way down on the lower right of the monument's face, a small ankh carved into the stone.

"But what's with the initials, 'W.N.B.'?"

"I always thought they stood for the name of the monument

company or were the initials of the proud craftsman who'd carved the stone. That's what Harry told me long ago. However, once you know that the ankh is the key to a fortune stashed in a New Orleans bank, it's obvious: Whitney National Bank. That's where I've been for several months, working with their trust officers to carry out Harry's final instructions."

"Unbelievable!"

"Almost, except I can tell you that I've seen the figures, and the money is all very real, vast sums. Now, why don't we take that walk I suggested?"

◆　◆　◆

"I don't think I've ever seen this part of the cemetery. Very cool."

"I've walked here with Harry several times during his later years. It's nice to think maybe he's with us today." Walker rested his briefcase alongside the bench where they sat and continued, "Harry instructed me to convert the treasure from a trust into a philanthropic foundation, a type of tax-exempt, charitable organization. The suits down at the bank thought that was a sound idea and figured out all the best ways to make it happen. I have all the final papers and brought them today, along with the contracts. All that remains now is for us to appoint the remainder of the board members."

"Wow, you're going to have no problem getting people to be on the board of such a worthwhile—"

"Yes, I hope you're right; I hope *we're* right. I did say 'us,' you know."

"OK—*wait a minute, 'us'?* You didn't mean, 'us' like *you and me,* did you?"

"Yes, I most certainly did."

"No way!"

"According to all the legal minds at the bank, I must be chairman of the board of the newly minted foundation. None of the board members or the chairman are permitted compensation. However, there is one salaried executive position, director of operations, with compensation well into six figures. On behalf of my uncle, I'm pleased to offer that position to you with *one* important prerequisite. In order to qualify for the position, you must first complete a bachelor's degree in business administration and be accepted into a master's program that specializes in management and finance."

Robyn grimaced and looked away. "No offense, but I might as well jump over the moon while I'm at it, too. I think I could ace the academic requirements, but the finances are flat out of reach. I can't even afford rent right now."

"Perhaps being the first grant recipient from the Harry McChesney Scholarship Fund might improve your reach. The award covers full academic and living expenses for any accredited four-year baccalaureate program in the U.S. or Canada."

"For me?" This man was looking her straight in the eyes, and she was feeling suddenly giddy. "You're seriously *serious*, aren't you, Mr. H.?"

"Perfectly and precisely," now he smiled, "and in the interim while completing your studies, you will assist me as intern to the chairman to help get the McChesney Family Foundation operational."

Robyn's eyes started to roll about ever so slightly. The opportunity, the responsibilities—all coming at her so fast.

"We will ramp up slowly, I assure you. The foundation won't

be able to take on too much until our director of operations is on board. It's all in the contracts."

"In the briefcase." She couldn't wait to read the documents, the roadmaps for her future.

"Yes. Harry thought a great deal of you, Robyn. I'm sure you and I will come to know much more about each other in the future, and I am looking forward to our association—providing, of course, you accept the offer."

"Accept? Oh, yes, yes, yes! Oh, I only hope I measure up. I really want to prove I'm worthy of all this."

"'Prove . . . worthy,' that sounds like something Uncle Harry would say, like a hero in one of those old stories."

# *Acknowledgments*

This work would never have been possible without my uncle George's boundless generosity, patience, and encouragement. George McLean is the inspiration for my tale and preeminent among my primary sources, particularly for the courageous feats, day-to-day privations, and improbable adventures of the men who fought with the U.S. Eighth Air Force during World War II. Over the past four years my uncle has unselfishly given me countless hours of his time, speaking with great good humor and modesty about his service in the Army Air Corps, growing up in New Orleans between two world wars, and witnessing what has been termed "the Great Deluge" following Hurricane Katrina. He has shared his library of reference books, personal memoirs, and mementos as well as unpublished recollections, poems, and artwork by close friends who also served in the Big Eighth, flying Liberator bombers back in the day. I am pleased to note that his most precious gift predates our collaboration on this current project. Since my earliest childhood, he has embraced me with unwavering friendship and unconditional love and thus, has been the best uncle any nephew could ever ask for, "the best of the best," as my story's hero, Harry, is fond of saying.

Marjorie and Richard Roniger had to swim out of the flood that engulfed the New Orleans home in which they sought shelter during Hurricane Katrina. They had first told me their harrowing tale of immersion and escape when we reunited a few months after the storm. Nightmares about their experience plagued their sleep for more than a year. After finally putting these traumatic flashbacks behind them, a long-time friend called about a year ago to ask if they would be willing to sit down and recount all their painful memories about these events, relive everything, for a book he wanted to write. They agreed without hesitation, testament to a loyal friendship and our mutual love and respect. With the help of a good bottle of Bordeaux, we waded through a memorable evening that provided me with incredibly rich material for the Katrina flood scenes.

Sallie Ann Glassman, a practicing vodou priestess in New Orleans, generously shared her faith and personal knowledge of the lwa pantheon, ancestor invocations, wanga and kanzo ceremonies, and other details of spirit worship that appear in this story. She promised no harm would come to those who purchase this novel.

My wife, Martha, and daughter, Jennifer, have read countless revisions and offered much useful feedback to help hone the manuscript. They have afforded me all the support a home-based scribbler could possibly ask for, including protecting and respecting my space and time for such matters.

Judy Nicholson has been a tireless and perceptive reader of early versions of the manuscript. She provided many important, no-nonsense suggestions on characters, dialogue, and narrative that I used to improve the final product. She was responsible for the well-deserved banishment from these pages of endearing but distracting characters. Aside from the author and editor, no individual has spent more time slogging through these pages than Judy.

Robert Hurst is another early reader who offered excellent critical advice in addition to his expertise on the influences of birth order on personality development.

Finally, I am deeply grateful to Peggy Payne, my faithful and talented editor. She is responsible for helping me to make this work the best that I am capable of.

*W. S. Culpepper, 14 July 2012*